GRYPHON RIDER ACADEMY

4

WILD FLIGHT

Flutterbye Trail Press
797 Sam Bass Road #2541
Round Rock, TX 78681

First edition

Editing by Red Loop Editing
Cover Design by Black Bird Book Covers
Chapter Art by Etheric Tales
Map by Reva Design
Printed Interior Design by Enchanting Covers
Published by Flutterbye Trail Press

ISBN: 978-1-954582-16-3 (E-book)
ISBN: 978-1-954582-39-2 (Paperback)
ISBN: 978-1-954582-35-4 (Hardback)

Feedback: Encounter a problem with this book? Let us know at
elisehennessyauthor@gmail.com

BOOKS BY ELISE HENNESSY

Books in the Altare World

GRYPHON RIDER ACADEMY
Second Chance
Chosen
Storm Front
Wild Flight
Gryphon Rider Academy Omnibus 1: Books 1-4

ROYAL SPY INSTITUTE
The Crown Heist
Five & Chance

Also by Elise Hennessy

BLOOD LEGACY SERIES
Dream Walker
The Winter Key
Queen's Return
Court of Illusions

Shadow Dance
Rule the Night
Dhampir's Wish
Blood Curse
Blood Legacy: The Complete Series

MAP

You can find a full-sized version of this map at: www. elisehennessy.com / maps

GRYPHON RIDER ACADEMY 4

WILD FLIGHT

ELISE HENNESSY

CHAPTER 1
A NEW LIFE

Once the celebrations for Altare's victory on the Storm Front were over, I was exhausted. I'd spent over a week hyperaware of the public's attention on me as the newest Hero of Altare. I had to stay primped and polished, never showing an ounce of discomfort from the weight of so many expectant pairs of eyes.

Others would love being at the forefront of everyone's focus. I, on the other hand, was too afraid my stutter would come through every time I was handed a voice amplification device.

Each time I was asked to speak to a crowd, I was more than aware that there were many dreams being built up of following in my footsteps, so I tiptoed around the worst experiences and focused on the positive. I spoke to them, those girls with stars glimmering in their eyes, of how I'd saved the life of my gryphon, Arimus, by becoming his Linked rider, and how together we'd intercepted and killed the Kingmaker to protect the court of King Cortes.

A feat that should've been impossible, especially for the first female gryphon rider and her blind gryphon. No one needed to know how involved the gods were, or the gifts they'd left behind in the form of ten jewel-like eggs; the new start of the eldrafn race, held securely back at Fortress Aerie.

That was my destination once it was finally time to go. It was with relief that I packed everything I owned and left Kaiamear. My gryphon and I flew away from the capital with a sense that this was it. We could rest and rebuild and finally fade from the public's eye.

We returned to the eastern mountain range that marked the edge of Altare, surrounded by the gryphons of Wild Flight, making the trip in record time with favorable winds and an endless blue sky balanced above us. It was beautiful weather for flying, and I loosened my hold on Ari's reins to spread my arms and feel the wind flow over my riding leathers and flap my hair like a braided red-orange flag. The gryphons called and cried to one another, rolling and dipping in playful loops. We were all going *home*.

My human family and friends peeled off to settle in Fortress Aerie, but Ari and I kept flying. The wild ones lived in the fields northeast of the fortress, which marked the end of human civilization.

I helped Ari follow his heart amongst the wild ones as they marked where the fortress was and chose to settle a short flight away to roost. Through our extra-strong Link, I felt Ari's love and yearning for Sunset nearly as strong as if the emotions where my own. He used my eyesight to admire her red and maroon feathers in the light of her namesake as she waited for me to free him from the burden of the saddle and bags tied to his proud form.

Ari swung his beak toward me, a question lingering on his side of our Link. I knew what it was without him needing to speak it to me mentally. *Will you be all right if I go for a while?*

My best friend, the gryphon who shared a bond with me as deep as our souls, hesitated on the verge of offering his heart to his beautiful female. This would be the night they forged their mating Link, as long as I did not interfere.

I hugged him around the neck, our foreheads pressing together, emotion and images flowing between us. It was how gryphons communicated between each other, and over the years, I'd grown more comfortable with how honest and deep it made our conversations.

Without a word, I expressed to Ari that I wanted him to go and start the family he desired with the female who'd become a Skymother to be his equal. Who'd joined his father's flock and convinced him to give humans a chance, to fly the might of Wild Flight to our rescue when we needed them most.

He deserved a mate who saw no issue with his blindness, who understood the kind of raw agony that came with losing a rider. I'd be all right without him for a while. I could sort out the loose threads left waiting to be stitched closed before we could start our new life.

In turn, he gave me a feeling of gratitude, plus the reassurance he knew I needed: he wouldn't forget about me. I was still his rider, his second chance, and his *Sivvy*, the silly nickname he pictured with the sweet squeak of Puzzlebox's enthusiasm.

Then he was gone, pressing to Sunset's side and prowling further afield for some privacy. I gazed down at the battered saddlebags that'd somehow survived on his back through an entire war, alone for what felt like the first time in many months.

Deep fatigue slumped my shoulders the moment Ari shielded his side of our Link. It wasn't just from the flight eastward or the pomp and celebration I'd just endured, but many stressful days and tense, sleepless nights catching up with me all at once. The idea of walking back to Fortress Aerie just to sleep in a more comfortable place was out of the question.

I unfolded my old bedroll, setting up on a flat patch of ground cushioned by a carpet of grass. I was just pulling off my riding boots and flexing my toes with a hiss of relief when a dark shape passed overhead along with a drift of wind.

Ironfeather trotted over, his beak parted with a happy twitter. *"See, I knew she was out here!"*

I heard his mental voice clearly even though he wasn't my Linked partner or speaking directly to me. The dark gray gryphon gave me an affectionate nuzzle before nudging me to my feet.

His rider wasn't far behind him, still finger-combing his overlong auburn hair back into place. "You didn't return to the fortress?" asked Acton Weslecker.

My heart rate ticked up to see him. He was from my training flight, formerly off-limits for any romance while we were in the Gryphon Rider Academy together. He was *Weslecker*, a partner in surviving the unique challenges at the school.

But we were knighted now and placed in separate roles, which made him *Acton*, hopefully my husband-to-be if his family approved. There'd be no more chances for whispers of fraternization to follow us even if we walked hand in hand through the mess hall in front of everyone.

That wasn't why it felt like my breath caught, though. We were alone together for the first time in, well…

"Were you going to sleep out here?" Ironfeather asked. He trampled my bedroll and then curled up on top of it like an overgrown cat.

Mostly alone, I amended mentally. "Ari's going to be spending some time with Wild Flight. I figured I could make the walk back to the fortress tomorrow," I said with a shrug.

"We could fly you there?" Acton offered, taking my hands and leaning forward. We kissed for a long moment, until Ironfeather croaked a complaint. Acton had grown and maintained some facial hair around his mouth, which scratched my lips lightly as he laughed.

"It's too late to fly back," Ironfeather whined rather than

protest the fact his rider and I were kissing in front of him. Keeping affection private was more of a human thing.

I smiled up at Acton. "Guess you're stuck out here with me."

He cupped my cheek in his palm. "You say this like I'd rather be anywhere else."

He squeezed my hand, then went over to Ironfeather to relieve him of his saddle and bags, placing them out next to mine. He must've had some idea that he was going to spend the night outside, as his bags were mostly empty save for a bedroll and a couple sealed rations.

The thing about Acton was that he sounded like the kind of highbrow noble who'd turn his nose up to a night out in nature. A few years in the Academy and in the military had shaved off the worst of his tendencies—like how he used to brag about his family's holdings in a casual conversation, as if every time we spoke was a chance for one-upmanship—but it hadn't shaken loose the accent he'd picked up as the fourth son of a duke.

I'd really taken to this quirk of his, though. Just like I enjoyed counting the flecks of color in his eyes and committing his every little expression to memory.

I waited a moment for a snarky comment from Ari. *Oh, yeah.* I needed to get more used to having my mind space to myself. It saved my gryphon from experiencing my every infatuated thought.

"Shoo," I said playfully, chasing Ironfeather off my bedroll as Acton placed his next to mine. We laid out together as the stars started winking into being across the night sky, and the gryphon quickly resettled on his back between us, completely oblivious to the way I was starting to reach across to stroke his rider's arm. I had the feeling Ironfeather would keep our hands from wandering tonight.

I burrowed into the warmth of my bedroll instead as the

air turned nippy. "Do you see that constellation?" I asked, pointing out the curve of a hunting horn as it took form.

He leaned up slightly. "What is it supposed to be?"

I made an exaggerated gasp. "You don't recognize Cria's Horn?" Something told me there wasn't much time for stargazing in a noble's education. I leaned over Ironfeather and used my finger to trace the loop and bell of stars that made the constellation.

"That's supposed to be a horn?" Acton asked doubtfully.

"I see it!" Ironfeather exclaimed.

I rubbed the soft fur on his belly, earning a happy chirp. "At least one of you does," I said.

"Show me more," Acton invited. He made hums of acknowledgment and agreement as I pointed out all the shapes in the stars that I knew. At some point, my sleepy voice broke off to silence, and my pointing arm dropped for a cushioned landing on Ironfeather's fur.

I woke with my fingers tangled in Acton's.

I TIED up loose threads one at a time while Ari honeymooned with Wild Flight, catching rides with Ironfeather when I needed to go somewhere outside the untamed land the gryphons called home. They claimed a territory very close to Fortress Aerie so the gryphon riders could visit them without a problem.

I gathered up a few of the king's officials after the wild ones showed me to the sheer rocky face of half a mountain a couple miles out from the fortress. Good hunting lay beyond, in the hill-filled plains that led up steadily into craggy mountain peaks, marked by the placid sound of a flowing river nearby.

"We'll build the new roost here," I told the king's officials as I shaded my eyes from the glare of the sun and eyed how far up the natural wall reached.

Fortress Aerie was built into a similar mountain face, though it was larger and more difficult to reach on foot due to some terraforming done by Tulari mages in ages past. This location had fields' worth of space to build a new structure to shelter our gryphon friends. It just needed to be broader than it was tall.

Workmen and supplies started arriving on the wings of Final Flight, and plans were drafted to bring the rough sketches and ideas that I'd created with my brilliant friend, Ellie, to life. They marked off the locations where they'd build a stable and a set of temporary housing so humans could start coexisting with the wild gryphons.

Our alliance with the gryphons was labeled by the military as Wild Flight. It was a grand experiment, a movement for peace and mutual benefit between human and beast. If it worked out, it would change the entire system of how gryphon riders were selected and trained for the better.

CHAPTER 2

LOOSE THREADS

Before my father was promoted to Commandant, I never had business in the Commandant's quarters. I had my first peek inside them on Acton's arm when we went there together, following an invitation to come to dinner. Acton had met my father, mother, and sister on separate occasions, but now he was a suitor under the combined scrutiny of my parents.

Space was at a premium within the fortress, but Father was a Marshall now and in charge of all operations inside of it. Because of that, my parents had a modest receiving room that Mother let us into. Father sat in an upholstered chair, bent to the task of cleaning his cavalry saber unsheathed on an old but well-maintained coffee table.

"Good evening, you two," Father said, gesturing to the empty seat set up across from his. "I just wanted a few words with the young man before we eat."

Acton swallowed audibly and patted the hand I had resting on his arm. I mouthed *good luck* and followed Mother into the next room. She muffled a laugh delicately behind a hand. "He's wanted to give Acton a little scare ever since he learned who he is to you," she told me quietly.

I rolled my eyes. "They've been to war together. Was it really necessary to pull out the sword?"

They had another extra room, with a large table big enough to host meetings, or have a private dinner. It was already set for four people, with a couple covered dishes set up at the other end. I recognized the fortress kitchen's efficiency in the dents here and there on the metal. Anything that wasn't actively falling apart was put in use, even for the Commandant's family.

Mother and I settled across from one another. Mirth danced in her eyes as she answered, "Completely necessary. Now, when you meet with his family, there are quite a few etiquette rules you need to be familiar with…"

Acton wasn't the only one sweating by the time we actually had dinner and our talk transitioned to easier topics like what would become of the Gryphon Rider Academy. I was going to eat my words, as I'd asked Acton earlier, "Why are you so nervous? My parents love you."

They did, too. Father's lighthearted, teasing side came out when he spoke to Acton, the kind of thing he usually reserved for family time. And Mother, well, she made no secret that she was happy I wasn't about to become a spinster. She'd felt it was a legitimate concern, with how I preferred the company of gryphons to other people most days. I was afraid she'd be asking for grandkids shortly.

Mother equipped me with as much advice as she could before Acton and I set off to Kaiamear to buy a dress fine enough for me to meet a duke and duchess. I knew I'd agreed to make this trip and that it was necessary for Acton's parents to see me like my parents had seen him, but I was beyond nervous. I had a reputation most strangers now knew. Would his parents judge me for being an ordinary person when I appeared at their estate?

I groomed meticulously for the event, spending hours in a salon having my hair tamed, trimmed, and styled semipermanently into waves by having it soaked in a specialized potion. It was apparently *the* style nowadays.

Once I was ready, we traveled to his parents' estate. I had to accept the help of a maid, as she'd been assigned to me and more stubborn than a mule about delivering her assistance and removing Acton from the room.

Together we applied the last layer of polish before I was to meet with the Wesleckers. I donned my new gown, which was a deep sapphire blue that brought out the color in my eyes. I'd bought modest earrings in a similar shade and decorated my bare arms in gloves that reached up to my elbows. They covered my calluses with a barrier of soft fabric. The maid painted my face efficiently with a layer of cosmetics.

Only once she approved of her handiwork did she let Acton back into the room. It was worth it to see his face when I turned, the shock that became a wide smile of glee at seeing me so far removed from my usual self. He stood behind me and looped his arms around my waist as we looked into a full-length mirror together. The maid lingered in the room to police our modesty, though she hid a smile behind her fingertips.

"You're finer than any noblewoman I've met," Acton murmured in my ear.

"You think so?" I asked. My heart was still as flighty as a hummingbird.

Still, I marveled at how different I looked. Primped, polished, and painted for such an important meeting and first impression. Even King Cortes hadn't seen me made over with such high effort.

An impish smile crossed his face. "Why are you so nervous? My parents are going to love you," he said in a teasing tone.

I smacked his arm, ruining the illusion that I was anything other than a tomboy pretending to be refined. Acton laughed and squeezed me tighter. "But I still love you more, no matter what you look like," he added, pressing a kiss to my cheek.

Under the layer of cosmetics I wore, I flushed. "I love you too," I said.

"Promise me you'll let me take you to a few functions with you dressed like this," he said. The approval in his gaze was obvious, even if I was also admiring the cut of his shoulders in his formal uniform, his medals polished and gleaming on his chest.

"Only a few," I hedged.

He offered his arm and walked me through the maze that made up his parents' estate, to a private dining room. I held my breath when a pair of servants opened the doors and Acton's steps slowed so we entered at a stately pace.

Several people were within, but I recognized the servants from their uniforms. His parents were standing together and observed our entrance with barely restrained enthusiasm, especially his mother.

Maybe this won't be so bad, I thought.

Duke Weslecker was a fair-haired man wearing the signs of a good, easy life with the extra weight he carried in his belly and arms. His wife was a slim bird of a woman and had the same distinctive red-brown hair Acton did. They exchanged a meaningful glance and came forward to meet us.

Duchess Weslecker seized Acton's face and kissed either cheek. "Hello, my darling boy," she said.

"Mother, Father, this is Sivana Walker," he said more formally.

She turned my way, and I received a similar greeting, learning that she was doling out air kisses. "We've been waiting so long to meet you," she enthused.

"Yes, ma'am," I answered, conditioned by years of military training to default to agreement. I kicked myself mentally. "It is a pleasure to meet you."

Of Acton's father, I received a handshake and an invitation to sit down. He was a man of few words, I learned, as he settled and looked over at his wife. "To think the Hero of Altare herself came in on our boy's elbow," she said, fluttering her lashes with a dreamy sigh. "Oh, you must tell me how you two met."

Acton had been placed across from me at the table. He pursed his lips. "I must've written of her often enough while we were at the Gryphon Rider Academy," he said.

"Yes, but I want to hear it from Sivana," she said.

Servants came forward to supply us with water, wine, and the first course of our meal, a hearty-smelling soup. I left my bowl untouched as I turned toward Duchess Weslecker's expectant face. "Well, we were assigned to the same training flight. Acton was Linked to Ironfeather, a gryphon I'd cared for when he was a baby."

A smile crinkled the lines around her eyes. That genuine look had to mean I was doing a good job, right? Acton jumped in. "He was absolutely beside himself to see her again. That was our first meeting, and the first time I realized Sivana was something special."

The duchess sipped her wine. "Of course, of course," she answered.

"We couldn't date at first. The military saw that kind of thing as fraternization, but Acton supported me in different ways. He taught me to use a cavalry saber and protected me when I needed it most." I flashed him a grateful look across the table. In return, he lifted his spoon, starting in on the soup, which reminded me to do the same.

"It was an honor," Acton replied. His father released a grunt that sounded like approval.

I had the impression from our dinner that Duchess Weslecker existed on wine and gossip, as she filled the air when I wasn't directly answering a question and barely took two bites of her meal. She spoke at length of her many traveling adventures, estates, and woes of not being able to visit said estates when eldrafn were threatening the coastal villages under the Weslecker dukedom.

I kept my mouth shut and listened attentively, nodding at the right times as I tried to eat the steak I'd been presented with ladylike precision rather than gobbling it down. It was the best food I'd had in months, and it *wasn't* fish, which, in my mind, made it perfect.

She seized my arm toward the end of the meal, her nails manicured to be longer and sharper than expected. "Oh, when you have a venue selected, do write," she practically purred. "I can't wait to see you wed to my dear Acton."

Acton, who'd sat quietly with his father through the whole meal, shot me a confident smile. *You see?* his look seemed to say.

"Yes, ma'am. Of course," I answered. After she said that, I wasn't sure why I'd been dreading this meeting so much. His parents were high nobility but still people, just like I was a person behind my titles.

All we needed now was for Acton to propose, which he hadn't done yet. I figured he was waiting until after this dinner, or perhaps past the next, less pleasant event we had to attend.

BEFORE WE COULD SETTLE into our new lives and roles at Fortress Aerie, Acton and I traded our fine clothes for funeral black. We joined a small group of nobility and important government officials at the Church of Mercy for a private burial.

Few tears were shed, the affair more strained than somber. After all, Isaac had been disowned and executed under the order of King Cortes, who'd called for an open casket with all the ruthless logic of a betrayed royal. I didn't miss that he avoided looking that way, though, his eyes bloodshot while his body remained straight-backed and his speech polished.

I stood at the back of the group between Acton and a hooded Mercy, dry-eyed Odalis released from her duties to pay her final respects to her deceased brother. We mingled in awkward whispers with Mateo standing nearby. The newly elevated crown prince had an angry resting face and a shake of his head whenever someone wanted to talk to him.

"He's not my brother, not after what he's done. I'm only here out of duty," I caught him mutter bitterly to Acton, his best friend.

I still exchanged a few quick questions with Odalis, making sure she was still safe and happy as a Mercy. She couldn't tell me much. The followers of the Gatekeeper had many secrets, and it seemed she now carried many of them on her slim shoulders.

The biggest shock of the day was that King Cortes had truly gone through with Isaac's execution. Instead of delivering a speech to a dearly departed son, he reminded us of the many crimes Isaac had committed, including conspiring with our enemies and inciting war. He then invited us to see that the man in question was dead, standing beside the casket as we processed.

"Are you all right, Your Majesty?" I whispered when it was my turn.

The king's look of contempt was quite familiar. It said, *what do you think?* without him having to utter a word. "I thought you would be celebrating, Chosen. Gloating over his demise," he answered aloud.

I finally let myself look down and take in Isaac's face. I felt a twist of sad satisfaction at seeing his still features no longer full of cunning ambition. "To be relieved is different than celebrating death, Your Majesty," I said.

"A good answer, as always," he replied woodenly.

Before Isaac had chosen to sacrifice Altare's blood and

treasure, he'd schemed to use me and my story to sway the populace to his side should his bid for the throne come to civil war. His help was a sword with two edges, as with one side of his mouth, he'd promised to help me and Ari and uplift us as a sign of change, while at the same time, he'd convinced one of my rivals to try taking my life in broad daylight.

Nothing he'd done to "help" me had been without consequences.

"Goodbye, Isaac," I said quietly.

I laid a flower in his casket, thinking the one place he couldn't retaliate against me was from the grave. I was free of him at last.

The gods do love their irony.

CHAPTER 3

NEW BEGINNINGS

5 MONTHS LATER

I WOUND around the piles of timbers and stone blocks stacked outside the foundation of Wild Flight's roost, calling in a singsong voice, "Novali. Novali…"

A playful twitter answered me somewhere to my left. I crept more slowly around the far side of the next stack of stone blocks, snatching up the red youngling from behind. "Gotcha!" I exclaimed, kissing her belly as she squirmed and squeaked. She planted her tiny talons on my lips, and I kissed them too.

Ari's daughter was just out of hatchling age, in the range when she'd be forced to Link to a hopeful gryphon rider before the wild ones demanded we raise the age of first Link to one year. She was of the first generation to spend more time with her family and grow before she selected a rider for life, and I was intensely glad of it as I transitioned to snuggling her. I'd barely gotten a month with her—I couldn't imagine handing her to someone else yet.

"How many times do we have to remind you not to play

around here?" I asked in a babying voice as I carried her away from the stacks of loose materials. She slow-blinked up at me innocently, knowing her human auntie practically melted into a puddle when she gave me that look.

It didn't help that I felt every bit of her effervescent happiness as her little heart pounded from her quick bolt into the veritable maze the building materials made for one as small as her.

I took her afield, where the workmen had hurriedly built a stable and placed a set of prefabricated buildings for themselves, as well as temporary housing for staff and cadets, until the roost was completed. I had a small room to myself that was starting to feel more like home than the staff quarters I shared with Ellie back at the fortress, as we were still unmarried women and Father saw it best to place us together again.

The grassy space between buildings and further down the slope toward the river was covered in gryphons. Wild Flight panted in the limited shadowy space to be found at high noon or with their front paws dipped in the water while the unforgiving summer sun scorched down.

Sunset sat up from where she basked amid a patch of yellowing plants. *"There's my little troublemaker,"* she said, crowing quietly aloud.

Once I placed Novali on her paws, the youngling scampered up to her mother and snuggled into the nook between her front talons and belly. I followed her at a more sedate pace, accepting a friendly bunt from the maroon and red gryphon and scratching behind her ears and into her neck where she had an itch.

Instead of feeling like I lost my gryphon to his mate, it more seemed like I had two gryphons now. They were rarely apart. She wore the saddle today, as Ari's wing was hurting him again. She'd flown me from the fortress to do a final inspection of the "grounds" and the people under my command, but I rarely finished a round without being distracted by something. Ari napped next to her with his weaker wing spread to bake in the sun. He snorted in surprise and came straight out of his rest when Novali leapt onto his face and took a good nip of his tufted ear.

"Still glad of your bouncing red chick?" I teased.

"She's lucky she's so cute," he replied. He was ever so gentle as he scooped her up and off his beak. She twittered a giggle and bit at his talons, eager to play. At her size, she was little more than a talon-full for him, but he was always exceptionally careful when it came to Novali.

From the moment Sunset's belly rounded with her egg, she became extra clingy, following me around as I helped around the fortress or Wild Flight's grounds and laying in my lap when I sat or by my side as the sun went down. She made purr-like sounds with the vibrations of her beak from the relief of a good belly rub. All of this was not the usual pregnant gryphon instinct when it came to a human, but she'd defied her nature to include me in Novali's life, and I was grateful for it.

When it came time to sit on the egg for a month, though, Sunset reluctantly shared her nest with Valtora and occasionally Roshawk. The older pairing had tried for an egg of their own to no success, but that didn't stop Valtora's motherly instincts or her mate's endless desire to please her, so Novali came into this world with four adult gryphons and one human all eager to meet her.

It was Ari that wanted me there for each of Novali's special moments, to share in them but also to help him experience them better. Through my eyes, he saw her hatching, the first time she blinked open her eyes, and each day as she grew bigger, redder, and more energetic. He always had that little twinge of fear that he'd accidentally hurt the brightly colored, fast-moving chick who liked to get underfoot with full childish curiosity. We worked on building up his confidence again until he felt it safe to frolic with her and acknowledge he was the closest thing to retired.

It was unlikely he or I would return to active service with how important my role was in communicating with the gryphons. I'd been able to put into words a problem that my fellow gryphon riders were contributing to for quite some time. Human tamers had broken many of the wild families in half, unwittingly separating pairs bonded with a mating Link that couldn't be severed except by death.

The human side of Wild Flight was attached to the Second Gryphon Flight, the biggest flight that employed riders, tamers, and trainers for the preparation of new riders and the *recruitment* of new gryphons. I was on the recruitment side, which I'd gotten renamed from "taming" as part of the wild ones' agreement with us was that we'd stop poaching babies and brooding mothers from the wild to force them to be combat mounts.

As part of this new initiative, I'd written to High Command to give leave to pairs reunited after the war, as several had celebrated and strengthened their old Link by having children. The leadership had agreed, grudgingly giving the minimum amount of time: up until a month after the egg hatched and the baby was deemed a youngling. It was a miracle to get even that much time, forced by necessity; fighting eldrafn had decimated several combat flights, and High Command was willing to compromise if it meant more gryphon riders.

I sat in the grass next to Sunset and nibbled on my bottom lip, anxious as always when my thoughts took me to where this path was leading. Once Novali and the rest of our fifty-one new younglings became adolescents at the end of one short year, they would have the opportunity to choose cadets to Link with...*or not*. While High Command absolutely salivated at the number of younglings born this year between the wild ones, the reunited couples, and a few established pairings who both had riders, not all of them were destined to become war mounts.

It was my will as Lord Orion's Chosen that they be given the chance to say no to any Link, but I still had several superior officers who would demand an explanation once it happened. Especially if the gryphons agreed to an idea I was only just starting to toy with.

"I can feel you worrying. Stop it," Ari put in.

"Tomorrow's a big day," I reminded him. I'd come out here to make sure everyone was fed, groomed, and ready, because tomorrow, the Gryphon Rider Academy would be opening its gates to a new set of cadet hopefuls.

Beside them would be kids of a different caliber to join Ellie's newest idea come to life, the Military School of Engineering, where students with academic scholarships would come in for a free advanced education in exchange for a five-year tour of service upon graduating. Fortress Aerie had space for students and cadet hopefuls alike, but it was a lot of new all at once, and there was no telling if it would be successful.

"It's going to work," Ari said in reply to my thoughts. *"Ellie thought of it, after all."*

"And our babies will find their proper riders when the time comes. The human leaders agreed to no Link thievery," Sunset added, apparently also reading through the waves and crests in my head. She was becoming increasingly good at it.

"It will take some time," I said. And I'd asked for a lot of time and faith to bend an already rigid system.

As I sat there, a pair of fuzzy younglings crawled in my lap. A few years ago, I would've been instantly delighted, but now, I looked up first to see which mother gryphons were staring at me in warning before I snuggled their babies close and cooed over how cute and precious they were.

The most distrusting members of Wild Flight were the mature females with young to protect. They hadn't been amongst the gryphons who'd flown to save us in the battle over Manarfell, instead staying behind with the yearlings and cloudlings to defend their territory. To ask them to relocate their nests to the relatively flat area Roshawk and Valtora had picked for the flock was a leap of faith they'd made warily at best.

We hadn't made as much progress with that particular set of wild ones as I was expecting, and tomorrow, the rider hopefuls would still want to see them. Father had me teaching a special class to this up-and-coming group of cadets on *safely* interacting with our gryphon friends, and as long as there were younglings around, some simply couldn't be approached.

Ari said, *"The whole flock knows Valtora wants them to play nice with the young humans when they to visit."*

"She's been coaching us on the stupid mistakes they'll make," Sunset agreed.

"Are any of those mistakes involving thinking a youngling is adorable and snuggling it?" I ventured.

"Of course." A shadow fell over me as a third adult stopped there, her golden feathers gleaming molten in the sun. Her pupils narrowed. *"Shouldn't you be working?"*

"Just taking a break, Skymother," I said cheerfully, placing my two young friends aside before I stood and brushed dried grass from my leathers. My gryphon and his mate remained where they were sitting, sending along feelings of amusement and farewell.

"You're starting to pick up wild gryphon habits. Only working when you have to," Valtora teased. She walked alongside me as I went toward the stables, where many more of the beasts were enduring the manmade structure in exchange for its shade. Sitting on a mound of hay just inside the first stall was Noah Sharde, a full grooming kit laid out next to him. Puzzlebox sat pressed against an unfamiliar wild one, who

shifted uncomfortably while Sharde pried something from his feline back paw.

"Hey, Lieutenant Walker," he called over to me.

"Yes, Lieutenant Sharde?" I called back. For two people who were at the bottom of the Academy's rankings for ages, it never got old to be called by our knighted rank.

He lifted the tool he'd been using, a set of tweezers with a long neck, rotating them to let me see the wicked thorn he'd just removed from the wild one's paw. "Where in the three hells did this come from?" he asked.

The wild gryphon showed me a patch of straggly trees and the bramble bushes that wound around their trunks like choking vines. I closed my eyes, picturing it with him for a moment. "A few miles north of here. The river bends," I said slowly. "He was sheltering from the heat and trod in the wrong place."

"Huh. You've gotta teach me how you do that…Lieutenant Walker."

"Of course, Lieutenant Sharde. We can try at least."

Valtora projected the impression that she was rolling her eyes at both of us.

He snapped his fingers and pointed at her. "Now that, I understood."

She clicked her beak back playfully. *"He will get it in time, I think,"* she said.

Sharde turned his attention back to the wild one as the scent of antiseptic hit the air. "Now listen here. This is going to sting, but that's a good thing, and you're *not* going to bite me," he said.

Puzzlebox followed his sternness with her higher pitched voice, *"It's okay. After this, we'll go play!"*

"Where?" he replied, watching warily as Sharde cleaned his wound.

"In the river?" she asked, nuzzling him with sympathy as he hissed through his beak. Soon she was leading him out of

the stall and stopping in front of me, her beak parted with a sparkle of happiness. *"Hi, Sivvy! Do you want to play too?"*

"She has to work right now, sweetling," Valtora put in.

"Aww." She wilted for half a second before leading her new wild friend back toward the water.

Few of the flock said no to frolicking with her, as they knew she was a cloudling and cherished her for it. Sharde, who struggled his way through the Academy on purpose to get the attention off his extra fluffy, small gryphon, was suddenly elevated in trust level by being her Linked rider. If a cloudling loved a human like Puzzlebox adored Sharde, then they were willing to come to him with their random injuries and pains.

"Need a break?" I asked with a chuckle, motioning for him to walk with me.

We toured the rest of the stables, in the process saying hello to Credell, who was mucking a stall alongside one of our two assigned caretakers from Fortress Aerie. The broad-shouldered southerner didn't mind the dirty jobs, which was a relief when two caretakers wasn't enough to keep every gryphon fed and groomed and their areas clean. Those of us the wild ones chose to trust all had to do what was otherwise seen as lesser work for the younger employees.

When Sharde and I stepped into the sunlight, he glanced down at me and raised a brow. "All right, what is it?" he asked.

"What do you mean?" I shaded my brow to look at his face.

Gods, Sharde had become a big man. We'd been concerned he was too heavy for Puzzlebox a couple years ago, but since then, he'd filled out from tall and fit into a well-muscled form. When someone pictured the ideal gryphon rider, they saw Credell or Sharde in their mind's eye, men who were towering and buff. They didn't realize Credell was too soft-spoken for the part, and Sharde was...well, Sharde.

He was out of regulation again with too-long hair and the kind of sad, wispy mustache a sergeant would force him to shave off with an ever-increasing pile of demerits back at the Academy.

He had the usual twinkle of mischief in his baby blue eyes, though. Sharde had figured out that he was irreplaceable because of his Link to Puzzlebox and that being ranked last still meant he'd be a gryphon rider.

"Hey, Biggs," he said, dragging over another former member of our training flight. He lined up the young man across from me with a friendly nudge. "She's got that face, doesn't she?"

Biggs cupped his sienna-toned cheek with one hand and squinted at me.

"*What* face?" I asked with a laugh.

"The one where you're considering every possibility of impending doom all at once," Biggs said, nodding to Sharde. "To be fair, the baby cadets are arriving tomorrow."

"Everything's fine," Sharde said, deadpan. "By the gods, everything's *fine*. You and Ellie are both going to go gray before you even meet one of the new cadets or students!"

"*He's right. We're well,*" agreed a gently voiced gryphon curled up in the stable's shadow alongside several tumbling younglings.

Valtora had gone over to sit with her and groom her long fur. Getting this particular wild one to talk to me or begin to trust us had been so important. That she sat so close to a human-made structure was a good sign as well, because at first, Alaula had wanted little to do with us.

And if the beating heart of Roshawk's flight turned her beak up at human help, so too would the mothers, yearlings, and some of the younger gryphons who'd flown to our rescue. Alaula was what Puzzlebox could be in six decades, an elderly cloudling who helped raise most of the flock. She had fawn-colored feathers and a cream underside of thick fur, plus beautiful blue eyes so rare in gryphons that I had to wonder if she was Reyos's great-aunt or other distant family.

She'd regarded me and my element's worth of friends with great suspicion at first, as she'd spent years keeping together whichever flock she was in without a drop of human assistance.

It didn't help that the flock's second cloudling had apparently refused to come along to this new location, leaving Alaula the single nanny gryphon to the record-breaking number of hatchlings born this year. Puzzlebox had been key to swaying her trust, spending many hours under the other fluffy gryphon's wing and squeaking about how kind we were.

The day Alaula had agreed to let Sharde massage the pain from her hips was the one where we all noticed a visible shift in how the wild flock viewed human help. There wasn't a gryphon who wouldn't sit with the old nanny in a puddle of sunshine and groom her spotless. Her approval radiated out with as much weight as Valtora's as Matriarch or Roshawk's as Skylord.

"Well, if you say so," I said, letting some of the tension loose from my shoulders. Aloud, I said to the men, "All right, I'm going to sit with Alaula for a bit. You two should head back to the fortress for a break and to cool off."

"I'll tell Weslecker where to find you." Sharde winked and sauntered away.

"You want me to get the princeling to pitch in somewhere?" Biggs asked with a growing smile.

We all got a little joy out of pulling the Crown Prince of Altare out of the fortress to do some Wild Flight duties. It was rare for him to be here anyway, rather than attending to his father in the capital. I thought he needed the physical aspect of working with the gryphons, as he was often "busy" reviewing paperwork or studying up on one thing or another until he emerged from his room for food, bleary-eyed, in the dark hours of morning.

Mireille would also go stir crazy if we didn't have her rider take her into the sky sometimes. "Yeah, see if he can come. There's always something he could be doing," I said with a nod.

Biggs whooped and cupped his hands, calling, "Echooooo, where are you girl? We have a prince to find!"

Oh, gods. Prince Mateo was going to come here out of sorts, again, from me sending Biggs.

With them gone, I sat in the grass close to Alaula and helped her move her head and shoulders into my lap. Her pointed ears were still folded backward from Biggs's shouting. Without needing her to ask, I started massaging one of her wing joints, and she released a grateful huff.

"Any new adventures to share?" Alaula asked. She'd developed a way of speaking unique to her, wrapping up each image and emotion in a safety blanket of kindness. It made her a warm presence in my mind. She asked this same question often of the adults around her, inviting conversation when she wasn't keen on a nap.

I dramatized my earlier chase with Novali for her, knowing she loved hearing stories, especially if there was a mischievous youngster involved. Any fun story with a happy ending brought her great happiness, and I noticed if I carried any kind of negativity or sadness around her, *she* would tell *me* a story of adventures long past to try and help me feel better. I saw why the wild ones returned to get a bit of affection from her. Sometimes, I needed it too.

"Oh, the storm children came bickering by earlier," she said. *"I think they may have been looking for you."*

I tried to contain my feeling of concern before she picked up on it. For her, "storm children" wasn't an exact translation, but an impression of two particular birds and the constant bickering between them, figurative storms from literal child-aged beasts. *"Did they say why?"*

"It wasn't important. Just one of their many arguments," she grumbled. She didn't like strife, so she sent Revna and Hvitorden away every time they came around. I'd originally been hopeful that the gryphons would take them under their wings, so to speak, but with Alaula's disapproval, they were only tolerated amongst Wild Flight.

"I'll go find them and sort it out," I promised.

CHAPTER 4

STORM CHILDREN

I WENT BACK to my temporary room, nearly tripping over several gryphons who'd made themselves quite at home inside the hall. It was probably my fault for sharing a set of Tulari-enchanted stones that remained chill to the touch, since they knew where to find them now. I took one to press to the side of my neck as I searched the room for my special leather gloves. Originally designed for falconry, they were now scored by the grip of bird talons much larger than what they built for. And this was my second pair.

Finding the storm children was sometimes tricky, as I'd made a project of creating simple wooden roosts for them in a few prominent places across Wild Flight's territory. When they weren't out soaring or spending time with their Linked, they seemed to pick a roost at random to have their semi-incomprehensible arguments.

Today, I heard them by the roost's construction area, twittering away in Rathi. Revna spotted me first with a happy bird cry and took wing, diving in for a quick landing on my right glove.

"Sivana!" she twittered musically. Both of them seemed to

sing my name, caressing the three syllables like the opening to a song.

Hvit, as Hvitorden preferred to be called, huffed as I tugged off my other glove and rubbed the soft feathers behind Revna's head. She closed her yellow eyes and leaned back. I'd worked with gryphons enough to know a happy beaked expression when I saw one.

"Hello, baby storms. Which verse is it today?" I asked, resigned to at least give my opinion on the Rathi sagas and stories they were so passionate about.

"Did Marus the Undefeated *stride* to battle or *stomp*?" Revna didn't hop off the glove when I reached the roost. Instead, she gave Hvit a stink-eyed look as I transferred my fingers to smoothing his chest feathers as he liked. She wasn't heavy for her nearly two-foot height, maybe a couple pounds, so she stayed proudly on one of her favorite places, me.

"The question doesn't make sense in Altarian." He, too, had a melodic voice, but both of them were noticeably young and squeaky. Judging by their oversized talons, they'd be grand and impressive blessed beasts...in a couple years, maybe. Until then, they were falcon-shaped with soft juvenile plumage.

One could tell at a glance that they weren't ordinary birds, though. Hvit was a cloud on legs with a white breast crossed with buff-colored banding and darker cream feathers along his back and blunt tail. The occasional mote of white electricity fell off him, as natural as shedding a feather. Revna was a shaded version of him, with dove gray under her chin and wings and a darker gray that looked suspiciously purplish for her banding and back. The fact that she had no electricity in her, unlike Hvit, was a sore subject.

I alternated petting them as they sang the offending line to me in the Rathi tongue, looking on earnestly as they waited for me to decide which one was superior. This was what

happened when their Linked riders were of different generations and learned the sagas in separate remote villages.

What was incredible to me was that they'd practically
come out of the egg knowing the sagas exactly as Solfrid or
Signe did. After a few months of making the more typical
noises associated with birds, like screams and chirps and twittery songs, they'd first displayed fluency in Rathi and then in
Altarian. While listening to Altarian in a Rathi's accent from a
small bird would've been adorable, they'd transitioned to
speaking without even a hint of one.

Very smart birds. I was so excited to see what they grew
into once they stopped using me to settle debates over the
sagas, as if they invited Solfrid and Signe into the conversation, the humans always agreed with their bird.

I ended up siding with Hvit today, and Revna abandoned
my glove in betrayal. Hvit took her place to bask in his
victory. "Where are your riders?" I asked.

I treated Revna like she was the Linked partner of Signe
even if the truth was a lot more complicated. Thanks to the
blessing of the goddess Idunn, Signe had been given time to
raise Revna and see her Linked to a new rider. They had a
deep bond of love and must have some kind of temporary
Link at the very least, as Revna could always find her.

Unfortunately, even with divine magic to sustain her,
Signe was not spry, so Revna's drive to soar across the sky for
hours on end meant she was doing it only with Hvit, or sometimes under Solfrid's watchful eye. The other eight eggs that
held the rest of their kind hadn't hatched yet.

"Getting her room ready. New cadets tomorrow!" Revna
sing-songed, flapping her wings a couple times in excitement.

Hvit cocked his head at a painful-looking angle. "And
she's harrying my rider to move the furniture for her," he
shared.

"Sounds about right," I commented.

"Oh, I can't wait to meet all the new people," Revna twittered. "And…test them, of course! My rider has to be strong in their convictions if they want to earn a Link with me."

"Uh huh," Hvit sighed.

"If only Signe were a little younger," she said in a smaller voice.

I donned my other glove and offered it to her. "C'mon, you two, let's get you fed," I said to distract Revna. She knew exactly what kind of rider she wanted, but the idea of Linking to a new person was a push-pull of emotion for her.

As I carried them both toward the stable, I lifted the glove to kiss the top of her head, and she twittered back sweetly. I'd carried her egg into dangerous situations for months, and it was like we'd developed a kinship while she was still in the shell. She'd saved my life several times by rerouting the electricity of eldrafn lightning and absorbing it.

Signe had given me her egg in one last desperate bid to have it hatch…and it had, with a little divine intervention. Revna was the first of her new kind, an ambassador for the rebirth of the eldrafn race made of hollow bones and feathers rather than clouds and lightning. She was well aware that any Link she forged would make her new rider the Chosen of Idunn, tasked with helping a surly goddess. It was a lot of pressure to put on a child who wasn't even one year old, blessed beast or no.

Plus, the moment she Linked, Signe's health would resume its decline. We still weren't sure if she would pass immediately or over a short period of time, but it was a weight around Revna's talons to know that claiming one Linked would mean losing the other. So, she'd decided to be exceptionally picky.

Hvit opened and shut his beak like a human would mouth words as Revna said, "My Linked will be as pure of heart as possible and full of life. He or she will be young enough to keep up with me—"

"But old enough to be a leader when the rest of our kind hatches," Hvit interrupted.

"Exactly! They'll need a strong personality to deal with Solfrid, too."

The feathers on his neck lifted. "What's that supposed to mean?"

"You know exactly what I mean," she said in the same snippy tone.

I watched the sky for any sign of gryphons from the fortress and spoke up before this could turn into another full-fledged argument. "Lunch should be arriving at any moment."

When it came in the form of a grumpy Prince Mateo hauling several buckets of fish, with Mireille holding more in her talons, I had to grin. When he was here, he was a part of Wild Flight's human element, and that meant I got to see the crown prince perform some less desirable jobs.

I SPENT my evening sitting at a circular staff table, toasting our last day of peace. Ellie was looking practically frazzled, but Sharde kept a grounding arm around her shoulders and encouraged her to eat between her last-minute planning and revision of a checklist on the clipboard she'd taken to carrying everywhere.

"We have all the schedules written out?" she asked.

I paused for a second. Did we?

"Yes," Acton said on my other side. "Lord Gadric saw to balancing class sizes personally."

"And we have second-year cadets available for tours," Sharde added, circling his fork toward a small group of young men and their gryphons sitting on the other side of the mess hall.

Ellie adjusted her glasses higher on the bridge of her nose. "I suppose it's fortunate we're changing how the Academy is run with a whole year group gone." With how we'd been promoted early to squires to reinforce the Storm Front, there was now a gaping hole in attendance where there should be third years.

"Their whole year is going to be the Trial by Fire," agreed another man from my training flight, Pereyra. The remainder of Kite Flight sat with me this evening: Sharde, Weslecker, Credell, Biggs, and Pereyra. When I'd first proposed the idea of Wild Flight, I'd wanted to keep as many of my friends close as possible, and someone in command had honored my wish.

We were a mostly intact training flight but had lost two men on the Storm Front, Feyring and Korvic. I missed their back-and-forth more than ever. Feyring would've been great with the new cadets, and Korvic would've loved earning the wild ones' trust.

In their places were our original honorary flight member, Ellie, and Prince Mateo in the other seat. He sipped his soup while reviewing his father's latest correspondence, always in two places at once. Mireille had left his side for the evening to squeeze in between Ari and Ironfeather where they sat behind our table on specialized cushions. She'd made a line with her body stretched out, exuding glum feelings that had Ironfeather whining and nuzzling her.

Acton was the first one to spot the Commandant approaching, saying quietly, "Look alive."

Father had a chorus of "good evening, sir" from all of us that he acknowledged with a nod. He was practicing his stern face, taking to heart the last Commandant's advice to never let a cadet see him smile.

"I'm just here to steal my daughter," he said but held his hand out for Ellie's clipboard.

Father was breaking his old uniform in with his new

Marshall rank. The front clicked with the hanging metal of a skilled and decorated rider, including the rare white and gold medal that signified he'd served in the First Gryphon Flight, positioned next to the pin of a rearing golden gryphon for graduating Ace of his year group.

Ari grumbled in my head the moment I admired it. *"We should've been Aces, too,"* he said.

"I'll pluck it off Mateo's uniform for you if it's that important," Mireille said with a sudden flash of anger.

He nuzzled her wing. *"I don't mean that you don't deserve to be an Ace. It's just that—"*

"I'm tired of the stupid Ace award," she continued, sitting up with a snap of her beak. *"Every time it comes up, I hear how Mateo and I didn't deserve it. He's a prince. He's busy! We were doing important things too!"* Her mental voice broke with a streak of upset emotions.

My gaze flicked to Mateo, who got up a few moments after his gryphon did and followed her as she left the mess hall in a rush.

I looked inwardly to my Link with Ari, finding him doing the same, the mental equivalent of us exchanging a glance. *"I just..."* He drifted off with an unhappy warble as Ironfeather pulled up to his paws and trotted after his sister too.

"It's not really about the award," I said.

"I think you're right," he said.

Yet I had the feeling we had a different idea of what was really wrong in that uncanny way our connection was a little wavering when we weren't in perfect sync.

He hesitated for a few moments. *"I'll stop bringing it up."*

My father tapped my shoulder, and I startled back into what he was saying. "Looks like we're set with the engineering students tomorrow. Walk with me?" he asked.

Ari, still feeling guilty, stayed to finish his dinner as we went into the hall and toured the stone corridors of Fortress

Aerie. Father deflated with a sigh as soon as we were away from prying eyes. "The Academy is going to run like a clock. I just…want to talk," he sighed.

I bit into my lower lip. "Oh?"

"Have you seen the new additions to the Hall of Graduates?"

"N-no," I said, swallowing to try to suppress my old stutter.

He flashed me a knowing look. "The first time is the hardest." He led the way there and it wasn't far, a room at the end of the third floor.

I'd avoided it for a reason, knowing there'd been new plaques installed since I'd been there last. They lined two of the walls, one side immortalizing the names of graduates and the ranks they'd achieved in their time at the Academy.

The other side listed when those graduates had passed, their final rank, and the way they'd died. It was hard enough to know that Alamid Maros, Ari's first rider and my father's old best friend, was immortalized here. Now I would look up and see dozens of names I recognized, posthumously promoted to the rank of Knight-Lieutenant.

"My predecessor told me that the most important thing to do before a class of cadets arrives is to visit with these names," he said, leading the way to the end to view the words I'd lived.

"To what purpose?" I asked quietly.

"Every one of the boys…the cadets whose names are on these lists, *and* their gryphons"—he gestured to the graduate lists—"will eventually make it to the other side. It is our burden as trainers to make sure they are prepared for what is to come, but we are inevitably sending them to an uncertain future."

I had the feeling the last Commandant shouldered this burden on his own and intended for Father to do the same.

But right now, just before his first year in the job, the weight was too heavy for him to carry alone. I'd take my share of it. I'd…finally look at the series of plaques that'd been needed to chronicle the deaths of my year group, and the one before it. The descriptions were shortened and the dates listed as the range that Altare had been at war with the Rathi.

Knight-Lieutenant Benton Korvic

Died honorably defending Daramaine from eldrafn "the Advisor."

And several lines down:

Knight-Lieutenant Oliver Feyring

Died honorably protecting a vessel of reinforcements from an assault of Lithosian rozash riders.

"That's all?" I asked, simmering with heated emotions to push out how it felt to see their names here.

But how much detail would've satisfied me? Did I want Feyring's memory to be colored by his gryphon's screams as a rozash smashed her wing bones or the way he'd saluted in farewell? He'd died right in front of me, a scene my mind relived even when I wished for it to stop, especially deep in the night when I was haunted by how quick and brutal it'd been.

I couldn't seem to stop fixating on the *way* it'd happened, the brutal details as crisp as if it'd still just happened. If I stilled my mind now, I could still hear the echoing *snap* of bones breaking, the crackle of fire, the screams…

No, get it together. As always, I pushed those memories in as deep as I could and prayed they wouldn't come tumbling out again tonight when I closed my eyes.

I hadn't been there when Korvic was struck by lightning, but I was told it was instant. Just like it'd been for the handful of riders who I'd witnessed meeting the same fate. Perhaps it was a mercy to remember them briefly, to acknowledge the victories their sacrifices had led to.

"It's not just the people," he said, patting my shoulder.

"But their gryphons, too. There's going to be a day when you see one of your most beloved beasts on one of these lists. Can you get your mind right about that before it happens?"

I wet my lips, knowing he was right. "Yes, Father," I promised. We'd only know if I was lying when it happened.

CHAPTER 5
BRAGGING RIGHTS

As I hadn't started at the Gryphon Rider Academy under ordinary circumstances, the first time I saw the welcoming ceremony was when I was on the other end of it. All the trainers and instructors made a gauntlet from the formal front gates of the school to the raised portcullis of the fortress's entryway, welcoming young cadets one or two at a time as they were flown in by Final Flight for their official first day.

Ari and Sunset flanked me, along with a few of the more curious members of Wild Flight, all keen to see the teens that would be competing to Link with their younglings. The only small gryphon here was Novali, who I cradled like a baby in the crook of my arm once she got tired of standing around.

She was content just batting the end of my braid between her paws, paying little mind to the occasional new cadet staring over at us. I was midway down the gauntlet and knew my presence would bring attention, even though Novali threatened to steal my thunder just by being herself.

We were out here as a sort of meet and greet, and I ended up saying hello to many of the incoming sixty cadets, and also to the eight or so engineering students who'd gotten noticeably intimidated by the military presence and the gryphons when they arrived.

Father had decided that sixty cadets for fifty-one potential Links was probably enough. There'd been a flood of applications, from the perfumed desks of well-connected young ladies to the untidy scrawl of hopefuls inspired from our victory parade months ago. He'd decided to put names in a jar and selected thirty boys and thirty girls purely by luck but developed a backup list of several more kids if the gryphons dismissed too many.

Throughout the welcome, I heard the gryphons whispering in my mind. *"Feel how scared that one's mind is."*

"He's quite confident for no particular reason."

"Can you believe she asked to pet me? What nerve!"

That last comment came in the wake of a girl with icy-toned skin, whose hair was extra-bright ivory reflecting the summer sun. I recognized her as Rathi even before she stopped before me and extended a hand to shake mine with a big, bright grin. "Hello! I am Geisel. Very happy to meet you, Hero of Altare," she said, her northern accent faint.

Her fingers were lined with calluses, and she had the makings of the stocky build her people were known for. Her midriff was also showing, as her shirt ended just over her belly button and her light skirt didn't make up the difference. The casual Rathi style showed off a couple black bands of tattoos up her right arm and a pair of inch-long crossed axes inked above her hip.

I replied, "Welcome to the Gryphon Rider Academy, Cadet...?"

"Cadet Geisel," she repeated, an etch of confusion over her features briefly. "Of the Iron Axe Clan. Oh! My people didn't fight yours—no need to worry. We wanted to come join Altare. I'm Altarian!"

I shifted my weight uncertainly. She was the third Rathi we'd welcomed so far but the first I'd talked to. I hadn't fully processed that we were letting Rathi into the Academy, but what she'd said was true. We'd conquered the islands, and any clan, peaceful or not, too proud to kneel to King Cortes was driven further north.

But in my limited experience, instead of family names, Rathi carried the name of their clan. We couldn't just call her Cadet Iron Axe.

"Well, we could," Ari put in.

"What do we do if another person from her clan was picked by the lottery?" I pointed out.

"Cadet Iron Axe Two?"

Geisel was taking my growing silence poorly, judging by her falling expression. "I know you're Altarian. There's no question of that," I said, putting on a smile for her benefit.

She perked back up. "Could I, if it wouldn't be a bother, hold that baby?" She pointed at Novali, who had my braid in both of her taloned front paws. Sensing the shift of attention, she lifted her head while in mid-attack pose, releasing a questioning squeak.

I reached out to Sunset for permission, who said, *"Well, go on. She looks beside herself to meet a youngling."*

As I passed Novali over, Sunset stepped forward, making her presence known to the girl who cuddled the youngling just as I had and tickled her belly. "Look how beautiful and fuzzy you are. Is this your mother? Wow! You're going to be bigger than *my* mother someday, and she's built like a wall!" Geisel laughed and came up to Sunset without fear.

"First rule of safety, cadet. Don't touch a wild mother before asking permission," I said, seeing that the Rathi girl was about to lift her hand toward Sunset's red-feathered neck.

"Oh, of course." Geisel lifted her head instead to meet the gryphon's bright gaze. "May I please pet you?"

Sunset released an approving murr and bobbed her head

in a clear yes. *"This one is going to be a gryphon rider someday,"* she said to the rest of the flock.

"She's Sivvy in miniature," Ari agreed.

Geisel was just beginning to giggle as Sunset nuzzled her cheek when Solfrid stepped out of line and hailed her in the Rathi tongue. Her spine straightened, and she turned toward the tall woman striding over, responding in kind.

Solfrid had arranged her multicolored scarfs carefully today, covering the white tattoos of fangs crossing her cheeks. Her style hadn't changed much in her time at the Academy, her mane of white hair still tamed in many small braids and her heavy fur-lined leathers exchanged for lighter summer clothes. She wore a scuffed leather shoulder pad where Hvit stood, putting on his best stately bird glare.

"Oh, I know of you," Geisel said, transitioning back to Altarian with a sheepish glance my way. "The honored Solfrid of the Icefang Clan, rider of sacred Hvitorden."

"Yes, that's—" Hvit started to say.

"That's right," Solfrid interjected. "But no longer of any clan."

"Just Lady Solfrid, then," she said, her cheer not to be dimmed. "And what a pretty bird you have. Did it speak just now?"

Hvit's feathers puffed with pride. For a moment, the older Rathi didn't seem to know what to say in reply to that. She'd been expecting scorn, I think. The first two Rathi who'd arrived were boys who'd barely avoided spitting at her feet. One had the same distinctive tattoos as she did, of the Icefang Clan.

Solfrid had tried to explain to me that her name was "Solfrid the Failed," as she'd failed to die with her eldrafn when we were on opposite sides of the Storm Front war. Her own father, her chieftain, had disowned her even though she'd shown him Hvit's new egg, and she was too proud to try speaking to him again, even though Hvit was old enough to display signs of being a former eldrafn.

"Come, I will tell you a secret," she said to Geisel, motioning for her to return Novali to me.

Once I held her again, the youngling and I watched them walk toward the fortress before she turned and looked up at me. Her emotions projected one big question mark. It was like she'd picked up on the complicated feelings that had to be hiding under Solfrid's stoic mask but didn't know what they all meant.

"Best leave it be, baby girl," I said, kissing the top of her beak. Both Solfrid and the elderly Signe lived with the kind of societal shame I'd never understand as an Altarian.

I shared with Ari that I was more concerned the other cadets would be unkind to our three Rathi, as Geisel was the last of the distinctive northerners to arrive. *"Anyone that stands out is a target,"* I said.

"That will always be true," he said. *"I think you're just more aware of it because we were targets."*

"Sure, I guess." But that wasn't necessarily a bad thing. Even if I was only teaching one class a day, I could keep an eye out for the signs of the same kind of bullying Ari and I went through.

I ended up letting four more cadets hold Novali and found that I liked them a little more for being so bold as to introduce themselves and take a moment to treat her like a kitten. She eventually got tired of being handled and took a nap snuggled up to Ari's side, sheltering from the worst of the sun in the shade of his wing. We went inside in the afternoon to enjoy some chilled water and watch the organized chaos of second years and sergeants wrangling the new cadets into tour groups.

I found Ellie giving a tour to the scholars. One of the three new engineering instructors accompanied her, so I was mostly tagging along to offer an encouraging smile when she needed one.

Ari and Sunset followed me, with Novali balanced in the saddle on Ari's back. Their presence might've been a little unwelcome, as the engineering students kept stealing glances over at them. But the students would need to get used to having gryphons around if they were going to stay at Fortress Aerie.

Well, I supposed that was less true than it used to be. The Academy used to limit admission to cadets who had already Linked with a gryphon and required the beasts attend classes with their riders. When I'd gone through, there were upward of ninety gryphons coming and going. Now there was one group with gryphons, about thirty total, with the majority of cadets being rider candidates that aspired to Link and take their beasts to class next year.

Once the new apprentice engineers were getting settled in their rooms, I turned to Ellie. "That went better than expected," I said.

She adjusted her glasses up and down, dangerously close to fidgeting them off her face. "It's just the first couple hours when everyone's happy to see each other. The real work begins once classes do."

"And then it'll be less of your problem," I pointed out. Ellie was finishing up her education too and entering the same deal as the other scholars. She'd attend classes and learn from the new instructors the military had sent, along with continuing her work helping Lord Gadric experiment with trying to recreate magic-made items with mundane materials.

"Whether it succeeds or fails still matters a lot. It was my idea," she said, sighing.

I steered her back toward the faculty room we shared. If I was ready to sit down, I knew she had to be downright eager to. "Name one idea of yours that hasn't been a success."

"Do all my failed magelights count?" she asked. Creating a working magicless magelight had eluded her for ages.

"Those were *prototypes*. That's different… Besides, one of them ended up being quite useful."

"For a prank!" Still, she giggled.

"Like I said, useful."

Both Acton and Sharde were waiting for us outside our room. We let them in and got settled together in our usual places. Ellie sat in a straight-backed chair, with Sharde standing behind her, rubbing her shoulders after he got a good look at her. I cuddled up to Acton's side on the couch. "Don't harm the messenger, but your father had an idea," Acton said to me.

Ellie's eyes widened. "What is it now?"

"Just the corps making everything a competition. Sivana *loves* that," he said with an edge of sarcasm.

"Oh, gods. Well? The suspense is killing me," I said.

"He had the idea while the cadets were coming in. What if they had someone of our age as a sponsor, as well as having a Cadet-Commander? Four of the five spots were jumped on right away. Do you want the last one?" he asked me.

I narrowed my eyes suspiciously. "Is this just for bragging rights if my sponsored flight ends up in first place?"

"Naturally," Sharde put in. "But I've already volunteered to be a sponsor, so you're guaranteed at least fourth place."

"And the other sponsors are…Biggs," I said. That man was far too fixated on winning.

"Yup," Sharde said.

"Pereyra," I continued, because I couldn't see Credell wanting to take on more responsibility or Mateo agreeing to anything when his father liked to recall him to Kaiamear at short notice. "And…you." I turned back to Acton.

He flashed his perfect teeth. "That's right. So, how about it?"

I scoffed. "My cadets will beat your cadets any day."

STARGAZING

I ate dinner with the flight I was sponsoring. They were still in their civilian clothes, as they'd spent the day getting their things settled and acquiring their uniforms. They'd be up and in their PT clothes bright and early tomorrow morning for their first day of classes, but until then, they had time to socialize and start to bond with their new flight mates.

Father didn't play many games with the assigning of cadets to their flights. Each was made up of twelve kids, six male and six female. I'd argued earlier that it made more sense to have six training flights rather than five, to split each flight into two perfect elements of five members, but precedent was taken into consideration over neat numbers.

Back when the Academy had significantly more cadets, there had always been five training flights. It was only during my generation that it'd been scaled back to four, with an additional reduction to three being considered before our recent youngling population boom. So, I met and tried to remember the names and personalities of thirteen people that evening.

I made sure Cadet-Commander Hanover knew he was truly in charge, with me there to offer advice and support when I could. He sat to my right, and Cadet Geisel had rushed to take the seat on my left.

"Eat your dinner, cadet. You're going to need the energy tomorrow," I warned when I caught her trying to sneak bites of her meal to Ari, Sunset, and Hanover's gryphon, Blink, apparently a reference to his speed in flight.

The most memorable person that evening was Cadet Runar, the young Rathi from the Icefang Clan with the distinctive white tattoos on his cheeks. His voice had already broken and deepened, and combined with his broad-shouldered stature, he already seemed like a natural leader. I was suspicious that he was older than fifteen, the maximum age we'd permitted for incoming cadets.

During introductions, he was one of the first to talk about himself. "I come from an Icefang Clan family that chose to move south upon our defeat at the hands of Altare."

I couldn't help but notice Cadet-Commander Hanover tightening his grip on his fork, holding it with white knuckles.

"For months, we've helped rebuild along the coast in exchange for a place to settle and a chance at the opportunities that come with being Altarian citizens—such as being chosen to enroll here," he continued.

"Your whole clan didn't move south?" I asked out of curiosity.

He turned to regard me with narrowed indigo eyes. "That's right," he answered curtly.

I put my palm up, not meaning to get his hackles up. "We're too remote to get much news from the outside," I said. He stared for another moment before finally nodding. "Mail is a big deal around here. The post leaves with a member of Final Flight every Sunday, and we get a mail drop on Wednesday. I still look forward to both days!"

I was content that the rest of Mistral Flight was listening to what I said intently, even if Runar wanted to remain at a distance. If we were lucky, the gryphons would eliminate him as a choice for their young.

"Hmm. Doubtful," Ari said in response to my thoughts.

"What makes you say that?" I asked.

"He has potential."

I didn't question the statement. Gryphons often *knew* when a human was meant to be a rider. The Academy had to reject even the wealthiest noble boys in the past when every single youngling would turn their beaks up at them. Even with a long history of forcing gryphons into Links, the beasts still had some agency. And they never made mistakes in picking someone they could be compatible with.

"But he is not a candidate for my darling," Sunset put in while introductions continued around the table.

"Definitely not. Sivvy has to love her rider too," Ari said.

"I can learn to love someone if she really adores them," I said.

Both of them projected a knowing feeling, like they were sure that wouldn't be a problem for me. Then, as they'd finished dinner, they started grooming one another and shielded me from the sappiest of their emotions. Novali was with her cloudling nanny right now, giving them a chance to connect without her underpaw.

My gaze wandered until I spotted Acton seated with the flight he was sponsoring, laughing at something a cadet said. He slapped his thigh in mirth, a habit he'd returned from the Storm Front with that I found oddly adorable.

I shook my head and shielded my side of my Link with Ari before I felt compelled to act on my feelings and walk up to my potential "mate" to plant a kiss on his mouth in front of everyone. A sense of loss accompanied the quiet over my Link, but the desire to kiss Acton didn't fade much. That was all me.

With him training under Commander Falirin daily in anticipation of the cadets' arrival, and my work with Wild Flight, I hadn't seen much of Acton lately.

I hummed along to Cadet Angevin introducing herself while I reached out to Ironfeather. *"Hi, Sivvy,"* he said happily.

"Hi, baby. Would you ask Acton to come stargaze with me tonight?"

He bumped his rider's elbow and met Acton's eyes. Acton turned in his seat and smiled my way, unleashing a flutter of butterflies in my belly.

"He says yes. I can't wait," Ironfeather said, completely oblivious. *"I invited Mireille too, and she also wants to come."*

I clutched my forehead. This sweet gryphon being unaware I was trying to get Acton alone for once was going to be the death of me.

It wasn't long until I could say my goodbyes to Mistral Flight and wish them luck at their first PT session tomorrow. Knowing our sergeants, they'd need it.

Ari was the one to carry me back to Wild Flight's new territory. *"I hear we're stargazing tonight,"* he said in amusement, sitting down in the field between Ironfeather and Sunset after I removed his saddle. Acton followed me to hang Ironfeather's saddle in the stables, and I finally had the moment of privacy I was waiting for to grab his shoulders and angle him toward me.

He got the idea fast, kissing me breathless before he released a chuckle. "I'm going to explain to Ironfeather what stargazing really means," he promised.

"I hope it doesn't mean I have to be scarce," said an unexpected voice from further inside the stables. Lira Rudrick peered around a stall door, waving sheepishly. She was our second caretaker, and I could've kicked myself when I saw her discreetly wiping her cheeks.

Commander Rudrick's eldest daughter had wanted to be a gryphon rider so badly, but she was seventeen. Father had decided that it was too risky to slip her into the cadet pool with how this year group would be scrutinized from every angle by High Command. But that didn't save her from mourning the missed opportunity while…definitely snuggling a pile of younglings, as she had one in the crook of her other arm.

"Evening, Lira. Want to come stargaze?" I invited since it wouldn't be all that private anyway.

"After what I just overheard, I'm not sure," she joked but came to join us after placing her fuzzy friend on its paws. She was a slim woman even without the caretaker apron pinning down her edges, her brunette hair still up in a messy bun outside of her duty hours. We'd long agreed to forego formalities, as she felt more like a friend than an underling to boss around.

"C'mon, it's just for fun," I said.

We stepped out of the shadows of the stables to see that Ironfeather had apparently invited several more gryphons, as a good twenty furry forms waited for us as evening shaded to night.

"Oh, this does look like my kind of fun," Lira said.

Acton shook his head. "That gryphon," he said mostly to himself.

He, Lira, and I laid out on the grass, with Ironfeather nudging Mireille between us. She laid on her back slowly, projecting uncertainty while he nuzzled her lovingly. *"It's fun, I promise. Sivvy knows all the shapes in the sky,"* he was saying.

Puzzlebox's speckled white fluff snuggled up in between Lira and me. She twittered happily as the other woman scratched her cheeks. "Busy day of fun, Box?" Lira cooed.

"Yeah!" she squeaked.

"Is Noah here?" I asked her.

"No, he wanted alone time with Ellie," she answered. Oh, of course he did.

Before I could ask, Mireille reached out to me. *"Mateo stayed at the fortress as well,"* she sighed. *"He's packing for a trip to Kaiamear."*

"Again?" I asked, picking up on the same glum tone to her feelings she'd carried yesterday.

The silvery gryphon loosed a growl in reply. I rubbed a hand through her soft belly fluff in sympathy. *"Let's forget about that for one night,"* I encouraged. *"Look at the sky, baby girl. Isn't it a nice, clear night?"*

She shifted her gaze upward, yawning like many of the beasts around us. The falling of darkness meant sleep for them, as instinctive as rising with the new dawn. *"I guess so,"* she said doubtfully.

"I'll show you my favorite constellation first." I traced the outline of a grand tower in the night, with the brightest star marking its sharp peak. *"Nilara's Castle. They say before she and Lord Orion descended to the earth, they lived in separate homes amongst the stars. Her old one remains in the night sky, in the shadow of the mother moon."*

"Who is 'they'?" she asked a little skeptically, though her beak traced the outline of the tower.

I gave a little shrug. *"The first people to write the deeds of the gods. Most are far-fetched, but they explain the unexplainable. How did the gods meet? Where did they come from? Some say Lord Orion is of the sun, his true form too powerful for a mere mortal to behold. They would burn to cinders before realizing what they were seeing."*

While the Mother…well, I'd seen her true form, and I shared the memory of it with Mireille. She'd seemed woven of dark matter and star dust while simultaneously being a towering silver-skinned woman with wings carved of moonstone and hair spun from rays of starlight. Her features were already blurring in my mind's eye, her incomprehensible power something I was not meant to witness.

She twittered in awe. *"I believe she would live amongst the stars,"* she said.

"Me too. Perhaps there is a grain of truth in every myth," I replied.

I continued rubbing her belly as I pointed out a few constellations aloud, guiding Acton and the gryphons that were still awake through a tour of the night sky. Lira helped name a few I didn't know or didn't realize were around at this time of year.

It was a shame Orion's Chariot only made an appearance as the weather turned. Mireille wanted to see the other scrap of evidence that suggested he'd abandoned a place in the vast beyond to come to earth by his wife's side. She was, at least, distracted from her worries as she rolled half on top of me and dozed off.

ROUTINE CLOSED BACK IN IMMEDIATELY. While it was nice to know the Academy was full of cadets, there were still stalls to maintain, messy wild beasts to groom, and many, many beaks to feed. The only significant change was that I reported to the aeries atop the fortress once a day with a small group of gryphons to teach Gryphon Handling.

It replaced the section where first-year cadets used to take Basic Gryphon Care, with the five flights rotating one day with me and the other four with Commander Falirin and Acton on the Green taking an extra-long session of Ground Combat.

In those first days, I convinced Roshawk to accompany me to meet the new cadets. The lightning-scarred male fit the stereotypes of a wild beast, both in his looks and his surly temper. But that was a good thing, as he did his part well, showing that not all gryphons were sweet and cuddly like Novali and Puzzlebox, who both came along as well.

I started getting a feel for the general personality of each flight, while Roshawk used this opportunity to mark certain cadets for elimination.

"We're trying to give them a couple weeks," I'd warned.

"They'll be out in exactly two weeks, then," he said with surety. I had the feeling he was irritated with me for wanting to wait to dismiss *eighteen* cadets.

And he, in turn, acknowledged my unspoken worries. *"They were selected at random, yes? Two-thirds being good enough to stand in my presence is a victory."*

He moved into a patch of sunlight, letting it catch on the crisscrossed red scars he wore along one flank. This level of pride from him was new, but his ego was growing with Valtora as his flight's Matriarch and a small group of humans answering at his beck and call. He'd had to work back up to his old levels of aggression to show the new cadets why they had to maintain a healthy respect when it came to our feathery companions.

The impending dismissals notwithstanding, I thought the class was a success, even if it did open up an opportunity for me to get waylaid after the hour was over by various fortress personnel and my own mother.

Mother stood out in Fortress Aerie like I did in her old place of work, Kaiamear's Temple of Nilara. She was immaculate as ever even amongst the hay and concentrated smell of gryphons, her hair in a perfect bun and her robes tied tight to lift the white hem over her sandals. "I spoke with the bailiff again," she said at the end of the first week, adding to the saga of her personality clash with the man. "He still doesn't want me establishing shrines to the gods."

"Perhaps his town isn't very religious?" I suggested.

"If the option isn't there, they have never had a chance to start a relationship with the gods," she scoffed.

I shrugged helplessly. The town that'd sprung up in Fortress Aerie's shadow was never a significant landmark in my life. I'd only learned from her that it was called Fenway when the lord's steward and the bailiff had separately and bluntly refused her services as a priestess. It was torture for her, as she'd never been one to lie around, not even at the beginning of my oldest memories when she was pregnant with Rissa. My little sister had been delivered at the temple, as Mother was on duty that day.

I didn't want to remind her that worshiping the gods wasn't such a significant part of many Altarians' lives. A small town like Fenway didn't need a lifelong devotee of Nilara in residence, not like in the capital.

"Perhaps you should return to Kaiamear's temple for a while?" I suggested instead. "See how Rissa is doing?"

"No, I'm not giving up. I know Fenway needs something —many of the residents want something to bring them together. So many of their friends and neighbors have moved away."

"That just makes sense. There's nothing around except for the fortress," I said with a shrug. Fenway served as a reward spot for cadets that won Academy games and a place to settle for civilian family members of the enlisted and corps men who'd been assigned to Fortress Aerie, but there wasn't much there. "Plus, military families are coming and going every three to five years anyway."

"They deserve amenities, too," Mother said, lifting her chin stubbornly. "I'll make Bailiff Sharde see reason."

"Bailiff...Sharde," I echoed.

"Sour-faced arse that he is." She continued on with her frustrations, gesticulating wildly while I half-listened. The blood was rushing in my ears at all the possible implications of that name and what little I knew about where my friend came from.

She did stop and glance down after a bit. "Oh, hello there," she said, stooping to pick up and hold Novali like she'd never cuddled a kitten before. Novali inched closer to her chest, her emotions projecting *stop talking so loud and snuggle me* so clearly I had to smother a laugh.

CHAPTER 7
PETTINESS

I didn't bring up the conversation with Sharde, not sure if I even wanted to crack the spine of the ancient history Fenway must've been for him. So my mother was having trouble with a man with his last name; that didn't mean that I had to make it his problem.

Besides, with the next mail drop came another headache. I'd recognized my brother's terrible handwriting halfway down my stack of correspondence and torn into his letter first, just to be disappointed by his lack of news.

"The instructors know who you're asking about. It looks like your friend didn't return to the Tulari Academy after the Storm Front war. It shouldn't be this hard to find a fellow student, but I'll keep asking around."

Five months had passed, and I hadn't heard a single word from the pyrojack Ari and I had flown to war with, Zuri Zaveri, or as she liked her friends to call her, Zizi.

After I told King Cortes about her plight with the staff Starfall and how her corerune had been stolen from her, I had waited on pins and needles for weeks to hear from Zizi. Had the king truly followed through on his promise to look into the matter? Had he forced the thief, Irene Merriweather, to return Starfall to her?

She didn't write, so I had no idea.

After two months of my letters going unanswered, I'd reached out to my brother, Nate, to see if he could find her at the Tulari Academy and make sure she was okay. That he was still trying was true Walker stubbornness in action, as he must've felt the worry emanating from my letters to him on the subject.

In the meantime, I'd received a polite note from Irene herself with a congratulations on becoming a fellow Hero of Altare. Even Acton, the master of reading the intentions back and forth of any otherwise cordial words, couldn't find a hidden message or motive to what she'd written.

She wasn't the only Hero of Altare to reach out either, and I'd struck up a few correspondences with people that were living legends to me a mere year ago. But that wasn't the point. Zizi was missing, and Irene was still out there, likely returning to the southern front to continue trying to break our stalemate with Lithos.

I should've turned up at the Tulari Academy personally, wearing my Hero of Altare medal, to inquire about my friend's whereabouts. But a niggling part of me wondered if she was still following Irene, waiting for the right moment to take Starfall when the other woman wasn't looking. I didn't want to come in the way of her plans... I just wanted to know she was all right.

I also added to Father's worries when I slid a list of names to him once Roshawk had gotten a look at every flight. He scanned it and exclaimed, "Eighteen cadets!"

"According to our least forgiving gryphon," I said.

He sat back in the Commandant's chair, blowing out a tense sigh. I didn't feel him reaching out to Valtora mentally, but I heard her response. *"I will be a second opinion."*

"We can't dismiss eighteen cadets all at once," he said after several long moments.

"I completely agree."

"However, this list can be narrowed. You and Valtora will pick two from each flight who are unsuitable, and I will send them home. Seems you'll have your wish of ten-person flights after all." He passed the list back to me, folded neatly. His practiced, strict expression moved from me to the gryphon who came to stand behind me. "Choose wisely."

FOR THE NEXT five training days, Valtora accompanied me to meet each flight as they took my class. She stood in Roshawk's place, helping me teach gryphon displays of aggression and warning and fluffed her fur proudly when I told the cadets stories of how unapproachable she made herself for most caretakers.

"Just because she's beautiful and 'tame' doesn't mean she accepts most humans," I said. Mistral Flight was gathered around me that afternoon, and I looked at their twelve faces with a sense of guilt. We'd be selecting two of them to leave next week.

"It is not so difficult," Valtora said privately. *"I sense that four of them are unsuitable. How many did Roshawk identify?"*

"Four in this group," I replied, a little grudging.

"We shall select the weakest two."

I had her stand back to bring up Sunset, who had admitted she still liked being touched and groomed, so I could demonstrate some grooming basics to the watching cadets before they came up one by one to try it for themselves.

"Yet you feel guilty," Valtora prodded when I didn't respond to her.

"It's not that I want to avoid dismissing cadets. I trust that you and Roshawk are simply sensing out the cadets who don't have a chance of Linking with a gryphon at all," I hedged.

She clicked her beak in realization. *"You feel guilty that you are the one that must select which cadets leave first?"*

"Well, yes. Plus, I'm the sponsor of this flight. Of the four that are unsuitable, I'll pick the two that don't get along with the group. But the other four flights, I could point out two that may otherwise have made their groups stronger, even though they aren't destined to be gryphon riders."

"You're concerned that you will use the power Nathanial gave you in such a petty way."

I nodded, watching Cadet Runar take his turn with Sunset. He was, unfortunately, quite perfect so far. Good grades, one of the best and most eager fighters in the Ground Combat class, and the first to earn an approving coo from Sunset as he smoothed the feathers along her neck and spoke to her warmly in Rathi.

I wished I could eliminate him, if only because his downside was a huge one. He refused to be in the same room as Solfrid when it was her turn to teach World Cultures, and he socialized with the rest of Mistral Flight as little as possible. The young man was rude, but he had the gryphons' approval.

"I worry I'm becoming quite petty indeed," I said.

Valtora's mental presence interrupted my thoughts. *"Here's how you avoid that. You take the list to the other sponsors and ask who they want gone by next week. They should know their cadets better than you do by now."*

"You're brilliant."

She projected a level of smugness that wouldn't be out of place coming from the demigod Glorium's glittering self. *"I know."*

Biggs, Acton, and Pereyra welcomed the question and list, helping me finalize who was leaving much faster than I otherwise would have on my own. I caught up with Sharde last, when we tended to Wild Flight right at dawn when the beasts woke hungry. We were both on fish duty with Lira, distributing breakfast evenly amongst the gryphons that didn't want to go hunt it down themselves.

"Can I ask you ladies a question?" Sharde said before I could bring up the approaching elimination.

Lira chuckled. "Uh oh. What is it?"

Alaula, Puzzlebox, and a couple more female gryphons also lingered, looking at Sharde expectantly.

He glanced around at his audience with a sheepish smile. "All right. Say you're madly in love with someone. He's handsome, and strong, and capable, and great with gryphons, and—"

"Is this person, in theory, you?" I interrupted.

He smacked his lips. "Sivvy, I'm taken."

"*It is him,*" Puzzlebox shared.

"So, imagine I'm Ellie?" Lira prompted.

"I was trying to be vague, but…yes," he grumbled. "I just wanted some advice. If you were in her shoes, what would you like if…how do I propose to her?"

I gasped in delight. "Oh, *finally*. I've been wondering when you were going to ask!"

The female gryphons didn't waste time. *"You've got to bring her fresh prey. Give her a feast she'll love."*

"Groom her fur for her. If you make sure she shines every day, she'll notice you."

"Compliment her and give her her favorite things," Alaula added in her kindly voice. *"Make sure she enjoys your company and wants to be your mate before you ask."*

Lira smothered a laugh. I couldn't be sure how much she was understanding from the gryphons, but she must've realized they were giving him a wave of advice.

Puzzlebox dutifully repeated everything they said before adding, *"I think you should just ask! She loves you!"*

"Well, you have to make it special somehow. Maybe you could take her to Fenway, buy her a nice meal?" Lira suggested.

His expression tightened. "I'd never...Fenway's out of the question."

"The capital's only a day's flight away," I pointed out quickly. "And knowing Ellie, she'll realize what's going on by the time you're halfway there unless you give her a reason why you're taking her from the fortress."

"You could just feed her by hand," the first female interjected, seeming confused by us overlooking her feast idea.

"Food will be involved for sure," Sharde said once Puzzlebox shared what she'd said.

I channeled my inner Ellie and held up a single finger. "Actually, I have an idea. I've been corresponding with Galak Nilessen on and off since I became a Hero of Altare."

"Who?" Lira asked.

"The man who invented the machine that can mass produce spiral-bound press books. Back in the day, Queen Cortes herself nominated him and awarded his Hero of Altare medal," I said, still a little starry-eyed that he was willing to exchange letters with me. "Anyway, Ellie's a big fan. She's let me send him some of her research because she wants his advice, but I've been trying to arrange a meeting between them.

"He seems interested, and lives in Kaiamear, too. Once he confirms the meeting, why don't you take her to it and use the trip as an excuse to take her on a couple dates too? You could propose at the end of the trip," I suggested.

"Hmm. I think she'd love that," he said, breathing out with relief. "Thanks, Lieutenant Walker."

"Of course, Lieutenant Sharde. By the way, I wanted to ask you about a couple cadets in your flight..."

FATHER SENT HOME ten cadets the moment the shortened list hit his desk. Morale amongst the remaining kids was low that night. I sat with Mistral Flight and reassured them that there would be no more eliminations until we took a break for Yule. "I know it's unusual to see cadets go home, but rest assured, your place here is safe for now," I added, meeting Geisel's worried lavender gaze across the table. "We are listening to the gryphons and what they want for their hatchlings' riders."

"Hmph." The contempt seemed to come from Runar.

"Have something to say, cadet?" I asked sharply.

His lip curled, threatening a sneer, but he leaned back to reveal Cadet-Commander Hanover and the blatant skepticism on his face. "If I may be frank, ma'am," he said. I nodded and gestured for him to speak. "The gryphons are still beasts, and the corps has run for many years without needing their input. When I first arrived as a cadet and Linked with Blink, the hatchlings didn't seem *this* picky."

I bit back on a surge of fire as a couple cadets at our table nodded in agreement. "That's because they were newborns, cadet. Have you ever heard of Link theft?" I asked.

"No, ma'am."

"The wild gryphons consider us thieves if we Link to their babies at the age we used to consider acceptable. Think about it a moment... Linking is a lifelong choice for both man and beast with soul-level consequences. Hatchlings don't realize how permanent a choice they're making or have a great feel for *who* they were making it with." I pictured Roshawk as I spoke and how biting his accusation of *Link thief* was before we got to know one another.

"Well, I think it's perfectly clear that that was wrong," Geisel burst out.

"Agreed," said the boy to her left, Cadet Canmore. He was nearly her shadow, always by her side if he could manage it and agreeing with everything she said. I made a note to warn him of the fraternization policy later, in private. Father was sure we'd have troubles with cadets trying to date, but I hadn't realized it'd start so soon.

The Cadet-Commander didn't seem so moved by my explanation, but he let the subject drop with a shrug. We went our separate ways, and I continued about my duties like nothing was amiss.

The other instructors seemed pleased that the number of cadets underfoot was more manageable. When I wasn't supping with Mistral Flight, I sat at the staff tables with a few of the men and women who'd taught me in the past. I learned that Commander Falirin occasionally put on a shirt and came inside for food and that Lord Gadric had an endless repertoire of stories from his many years here that put the minor hijinks of the current cadet class to shame.

I was feeling secure at last. So of course that was when the latest copy of *The Kaiamear Gazette* arrived with this printed big and bold on the first page:

"LADY GRYPHON RIDER'S NEW INITIATIVES THREATEN TO RUIN GRYPHON RIDER ACADEMY"

CHAPTER 8

FIT TO PRINT

I READ the whole article to my friends that evening in a fit of rage. Miles Glimmerwick's familiar sensational writing style felt extra venomous when it was turned on us. He'd spoken with more than one of the cadets we'd dismissed and printed their stories like they'd been wronged.

As I read, I heard shades of Cadet-Commander Hanover's confusion over deferring to the beasts and his contentment over "how things had been." I imagined the other, more experienced gryphon riders who would agree with him. More than anything, the first section of this article was telling all of Altare about how the school had changed and why it shouldn't have.

I'd learned that *The Kalamear Gazette* and its rival, *Voice of the People*, were published to reinforce what people already believed in. I used to believe the former was on my side when Prince Isaac owned it, but it seemed that with his passing, so too went any pretense of support from whoever purchased the *Gazette*'s publishing rights.

As I kept mocking the article, I realized it was covering more criticism than I expected, because he was equally scornful of the new Military School of Engineering being squeezed into the lesser-used middle floors of Fortress Aerie. I skipped some lines, hurt by Ellie's crestfallen face and not wanting to bring air to the way he'd asked the general public, "Was there no other place to put these poor scholars? We had to force them into the most remote reaches of Altare?"

But what made my blood chill was the last paragraph printed on this page. Glimmerwick had decided not to lead with a secret I'd wanted to keep, but included it all the same.

"A-and," I said, that biting edge leaving my voice as I scanned the words once, twice, even a third time. "There are two mysterious and large birds that are testing the remaining cadets at the Gryphon Rider Academy."

Sharde breathed a low curse, and I paused, nodding in agreement.

"The two Rathi women who instruct at the Academy have told a select few that the birds are eldrafn in a new form. You heard it here first, folks! At least two blessed beasts of our old enemy are now trying to steal Links with Altarian cadets to be their riders."

The rest of the article continued on a separate page. I folded the thin sheets of paper with shaking hands and placed it aside, burying my face in my fingers instead. The general public *did not* need to know yet that Mother Nilara had given the eldrafn race a new start, but if they were going to learn about Revna and Hvit, announcing it to the population in *The Kaiamear Gazette* was the worst possible way to go about it.

Acton scooted his chair closer to mine, putting an arm around my shoulders. "They threw everything they could in there," I mumbled.

"We knew there would be those who'd disagree with how we're changing things," he said quietly. "He's a small man, and his only weapon is his words. He just did everything in his power to hurt us."

I groaned into my palms and pulled my hands down my

face. "No, public opinion is his weapon," I said, feeling the grim set my expression fell into.

Paper rustled. I looked up to see Ellie scanning the innards of the newspaper. She made a sound like "hmm" low in her throat. And then she closed the paper and folded it, taking in the first page section. Her lips smacked in offense at the part I'd skipped before she made another "hmm" in a higher register.

"Mmhmm?" Sharde encouraged.

She fidgeted, tapping her fingertips together. "I posit that he only spoke to the three cadets whose names are printed in this article. He sought a negative view of what we're doing and got it. Which means the information here is flawed because it is an incomplete view. You see how he uses phrases to bait out anger?" She slid the newspaper over to Sharde and pointed in a couple places. "Wrongfully dismissed, remote reaches of Altare, old enemy, steal Links. Put that aside for a moment, what did he actually tell the public?"

"Well, we dismissed a few cadets, and they're angry about it," Pereyra said.

"We should have sympathy for the engineering students because Fortress Aerie is an odd place for them. A point that's reasonable," Ellie sighed.

"That Revna and Hvit are here," Acton said.

"And that they're reborn eldrafn. Something we did *not* want getting out," I interjected.

There were a couple exchanged glances around the table. "Uh, Lieutenant Walker," Sharde said. "They're singing for the cadets in World Cultures. The word is going to get out about our smart and huge bird friends."

My first reaction was, *they are?* plus a twinge of jealousy. I'd loved World Cultures class when it was just Signe instructing. But add in two singing blessed beasts, and despite Solfrid's prickly company, I was considering sitting in on a class just to experience the sagas anew.

I cleared my throat. "Okay, okay. So the cadets all know about Revna and Hvit. What that just did"—I stabbed a finger at the newspaper—"was introduce the common man to the most negative fact about them."

"Sivvy," Ellie said, drawing out the silly nickname. "I have an idea."

"I'm not going to like this idea, am I?" I asked.

"Probably not."

MIRA GALAV CAME AS SOON as possible, but that still looked like five days passing before she arrived by air courier. I *really* didn't like Ellie's idea, but at the same time, I made myself available instantly when word reached Wild Flight that an unfamiliar woman had arrived at the front gates and was asking for me.

Ari flew me back to the fortress. *"We can't be sure Voice of the People is going to be kind with the information we give them,"* I fretted.

"I have a good feeling," he answered.

"Why's that?"

"You're going to be handing her a youngling eventually. How could she write poorly of the experience?" He made a fatherly croon over his shoulder, and Novali, who was snuggled to my front, twittered back sweetly.

"I don't know!"

"Miss 'I've been to war, nothing's quite as scary anymore' afraid of talking to a reporter," he teased. When we landed, I was smiling and shaking my head at myself.

I knew there would be consequences for letting Mira see the inside of the Gryphon Rider Academy. Father had had to be convinced too, as the military in general liked to push reporters out of its business by a hand over their face. "Why does it matter what the public thinks of what we're doing?" he'd asked.

"The only reason I want to talk to a reporter is to bring some positivity in for Revna and Hvit," I'd replied.

And I still believed that as I approached the bespectacled woman waiting for me now. Three uniformed soldiers stood around laughing at something in their conversation while they waited, but those men turned and saluted when they spotted Ari and me approaching.

"At ease. I can take it from here," I said, sending them back to their posts before approaching Mira with my hand extended.

She was older than I expected, with bold stripes of silvery hair through her dark, tightly bound locks. Her clothes were wrinkled from air travel but fine enough for the long walk that was in her future. For coming straight off a gryphon, she looked composed and unflappable as she shook my hand.

"Lieutenant Walker, an honor to meet you in person," she said. She pulled a notepad and charcoal pencil from a satchel at her side. She flipped to a clean page and started writing rapidly, a habit that reminded me unpleasantly of the one and only time I'd met Miles Glimmerwick in person. He'd been able to jot down everything I said, word for word, to use later. "And who is this small creature with you?"

Novali watched her pencil bob and scribble, ears perked forward with interest. "My gryphon had his first hatchling this past season." As I told her of Novali, I walked her to the fortress. It wasn't hard to get me talking, as the small gryphon was one of my favorite subjects. Ari rumbled in amusement and followed the sound of my voice without a stumble.

"Well, she is a charming little thing," she said. We'd reached the stairwell during a class change, and the sound of many voices mixed in with a number of second-years heading outside with their gryphons by their side. Novali had found her way into Mira's arms and was in the process of taking a single chew of her charcoal pencil before shooting it back out of her beak with a hiss of disgust.

I dove to grab it and return it to the reporter. "Not everything is food," I teased the red youngling, mussing the soft feathers between her ears.

When the cadets resettled, I took her on a brief tour of the Academy, aware that her pencil was never stationary even as she kept up with our conversation. We stopped at a random table in the mess hall for the bulk of her interview. "When you wrote and asked for an article in the *Voice*, you mentioned the last copy of the *Gazette*," she began.

She paused, and I filled in the details just like she'd wanted. "Yes, I felt that their view of what we're doing here was narrow and incomplete."

"How so?"

"Well, it seemed like the article about us was written after speaking to three cadets we'd recently dismissed, the most junior people to discuss Academy matters, and with a reason to be disgruntled."

Her pencil scribbled away. "I see. Well, wanting a more complete story out there is understandable. I'm sure we will publish everything that is fit to print about my time here today, perhaps over a course of several editions. News about you has always sold." At my shiver, she looked up from her notepad. "Ah, the Crown usually dictates the tone we take with our articles. I've already been told to be purely factual. We don't want to get into another word war with the *Gazette*."

"Glimmerwick wouldn't be able to handle it," I muttered. My mother had been the one to guest write for the *Gazette* with as much skill as Mira and a couple other reporters on the *Voice's* staff back when there was a rivalry.

With a smile, she took me through a few pre-prepared questions about the Academy and the new changes that'd come into place this year. I explained Link thievery again and the harsh fact that not everyone has the invisible "something" gryphons look for in their potential Linked riders. I carefully spoke around the military secrets Father hadn't wanted me to tell the reporter; he'd made me aware that we walked a fine line of acquiring High Command's attention by letting her in in the first place.

When we were finished with her questions, I gave her one of my falconry gloves of the pair I'd fastened to my belt, and we went to sit in on part of a World Cultures class. Signe was teaching today and was warned that she'd have an interruption. Every cadet's head turned our way as I led Mira to the back of the room.

Signe ignored us the same way she never acknowledged the various scribes that'd sit in on her class to write down what had been an oral history of the Rathi people and their tales and myths. She was on her customary stool, her bad leg wrapped around a spoke to keep it out of direct sight. Though she was at her most frail, she still sat straight with Rathi pride and told a tale of valor punctuated by Revna's squeaky singing.

The purplish bird perched on the edge of the desk behind Signe. She'd shifted close enough to rest her weight on the woman's arm and looked up at her as though the old instructor were her entire world. When the class was finished and the cadets shuffled off, some with glances over their shoulders at the scribbling reporter and me, Signe petted Revna's silky feathers and returned her fond look.

"It is time we shared the first verses of your new story," Signe said.

"Already?" Revna sounded much like a small child and hid her face in the side of Signe's blouse.

She coaxed her to sit back up. "How will your new rider know to come find you if they don't know you're looking?"

Revna made a low sound in reply. She slid sideways away

from Signe and braced herself to take off. I slipped my falconry glove on, and Mira hurried to put hers on too as the bird flew the length of the room and came to roost on my fist. I felt the points of her talons, stronger than ever, threaten to pierce straight through the thick leather.

"Hi, Sivana," she sing-songed, leaning forward in a clear request for pets.

"Hello, baby storm," I tried to sing back, but I was horribly off tune. She made a croak of dismay.

"And Ari, hi," she chirruped like that hadn't happened. My gryphon made a soft murr in reply from atop the three cushions he'd stacked to rest his head on for a nap. Novali peeked out from under the feathers of his wing, beak parting happily when she spotted Revna, who, in turn, sang the three syllables of her name much like she did mine.

"But who is this?" she asked, finally rotating her head around at an awkward-looking angle to take in Mira.

The reporter, for her part, was writing at a furious pace as she listened in. I made the introductions, explaining that Mira was here to distribute Revna's story across Altare, and the bird pulled a skeptical face with the tensing of the muscles around her bright yellow eyes. "Should we get Hvit in here?" she asked.

"I was thinking Mira could talk to you and Signe for now," I said.

"Well, where do we even start? Hello, story distributor," she said.

Mira breathed a little disbelieving laugh. "Reporter," she corrected.

"Do you perform your own songs, or do you compose them for others?" Revna asked in her most polite tone.

I jumped back into the conversation quickly. "Ah, that's not what a reporter does. You're used to oral story telling. Mira does similar things with the written word."

Revna shifted on my glove with discomfort.

Signe cleared her throat, drawing our attention and a relieved noise from the bird. "Sacred Revna was once the great lavender storm that protected the Bear River Clan. She died from a tragedy decades ago…back when I was young," she told Mira, pausing to give her a chance to catch up on writing down her words. "And since then, she lay dormant in her egg, no matter how much natural power she was fed."

Revna bobbed her whole body in agreement. "It felt like a nap. A really, really long nap."

I exchanged a glance with Signe, who gestured for me to speak next. "As it turns out, the gods wanted to restart the eldrafn race. The deaths of the last nine tamed eldrafn were their opportunity to do just that."

"I have so many questions," the reporter mumbled.

"Trust me, so do I. More question than answers." I wasn't about to tell her every secret I'd learned in that place between time, the crossroad of fate where Mother Nilara and Lady Idunn had taken the remains of Revna's old egg and all the energy it'd gathered to create a new race of blessed beasts with their magic.

I petted down Revna's soft back, and she barely had to stretch to nuzzle my jaw affectionately. Still looking at her, I continued, "While the gods work in mysterious ways, they did make it clear that the old eldrafn were too large and too unpredictable to be good companions to our new northern friends. We don't know *what* Revna is yet, but we do know the Mother's design is a kindness for both man and blessed beast. She's solid and intelligent, able to speak and comprehend two languages, and was practically born singing. And look at these feet." I extended my arm out toward Mira, pointing at Revna's talons. "No matter how large she grows, her feet keep outpacing her. She's going to be a big girl. I wouldn't be surprised if she grew large enough to carry a rider."

"Those are some large feet," Mira agreed. Unlike with the

gryphons, she eyed Revna uncertainly when presented with the bird so close to her. I took that as a sign to rest my forearm over the desk I sat at instead.

Mira turned to a fresh page and started asking the questions we could answer, about every aspect of Revna we could explain. We talked about her diet and habits, and she even performed a song for the reporter, complete with the squeaks and squawks that came about when she tried singing any lower than her juvenile voice allowed. The only question that had Revna puffing in offense was when Mira asked if she had lightning magic.

"*No,*" she answered forcefully, ever upset that Hvit was able to summon sparks and small jolts while she was left without that power.

"We think it might develop in time," Signe added in a calmer tone.

When the next class change arrived, Signe and Revna hurried their last response. I rubbed the bird's neck in farewell before she flew over to the desk behind Signe and landed with an audible scratch of her talons. Good gods, that thing was going to get destroyed by her big feet before the year was out.

I escorted Mira back out of the fortress with Ari carrying a sleepy Novali atop his saddle. We'd pulled out the larger tandem one to fly the reporter up to Wild Flight's roost together. She was looking a little tired by the time she had a tour of the area and watched the workmen who were starting to build on the foundation they'd laid for months.

I spoke throughout about Wild Flight and what we were accomplishing in this groundbreaking partnership between man and blessed beast. When we went inside and sat down in the small meeting area in the prefabricated building, sharing water cooled by the chill Tulari-enchanted stones, the first question out of her mouth was not a follow-up about Wild Flight when she turned to a new page in her notebook.

She asked, "Will you tell me about your experience on the Storm Front?"

I frowned at the unexpected shift to this interview, but we'd talked about my favorite subjects so far: the new and improved Academy experience, Novali, Revna, Wild Flight. Wetting my lips, I gave her a short and blunt answer.

CHAPTER 9

NIGHTMARES

AND LATER, when the paper arrived, I clutched my head in dismay. "THE STORM FRONT WAS A NIGHTMARE, SAYS LADY GRYPHON RIDER" blared the front-page article of *Voice of the People*.

It didn't indicate that it was part of a series, as Mira had suggested. It seemed her takeaway from her overnight stay at Fortress Aerie was my answer to her unexpected question. I'd told her the experience was a nightmare; I'd watched my friends die and felt the loss of every gryphon that'd fallen. Becoming a Hero of Altare wasn't worth the grief and pain that followed me afterward.

Like a key turning a lock, that short conversation had opened the mental box I'd tried to pack with months of nightmares and terrors. I relived the worst parts of the Storm Front again and again, tossing and turning to wake up in a cold sweat and stumble out of bed to my Link quiet and dormant as Ari slept peacefully with his small family.

I was sure dark circles haloed my eyes as I tried to focus on the page in front of me. Gatekeeper take me; someone from High Command was going to fly up here personally with a reprimand on their tongue. I was supposedly a prominent war hero, now speaking out against the events that made me.

I hid in the stables long after my class that Wednesday, with the cadets and most of the gryphons having gone back to their own business. Sitting on a lump of hay in a clean, unoccupied stall, I set the newspaper aside and scrubbed at my aching eyes.

"Okay, that's enough of that," said Sunset, her brightly colored feathers catching my attention as she peered over the stall door. She nudged it open and guided Ari inside, the two of them bracketing my legs.

"Enough of what?" I asked dully.

"Self-pity," Ari answered. He nudged the newspaper out from under where he'd accidentally sat on it. *"Let's hear what it says."*

Dutifully, I read it to them. Mira had framed the changes to the Academy and the inclusion of Wild Flight as a choice made by me and my friends to embrace peace after the war we'd experienced. There was no word of Link theft or Revna, two things I'd stressed I wanted included in any message out to the general public.

Sunset rested her head in my lap, crooning quietly when I placed a hand between her tufted ears. *"She asked you about a tender subject, and you were truthful. Is it so bad she saw how badly the war affected you and reported on it?"*

"The whole point of her coming here was for her to tell Altare about Wild Flight and Revna, and this is what she decided to publish," I muttered.

Something passed between the two of them before Sunset withdrew to stand and shake out her wings. Ari shifted to take her place, stretching to cover my thighs with his head and one leg. *"Let's take a nap,"* he suggested.

"I can't just—"

"You absolutely can, and should." And because he wasn't fighting fairly today, he projected the feeling of a yawn and

some remembered time where he was intensely sleepy. My eyelids drooped instantly, and I gave in to the dark tide of rest that rushed in to meet me.

I JERKED AWAKE NOT long after. The oily feeling of dread remained on my skin, even if the memory my brain had decided to dredge up was already fading back into the pits of my mind.

Acton made a tisking noise with his tongue. "Sorry. Didn't mean to wake you."

I cracked my eyes open to realize I was nearly nose to beak with Ironfeather, and a feeling of déjà vu gripped me as he asked, *"Are you okay?"*

"I'm just fine, sweet boy."

He whined and dropped his weight onto my legs and Ari's back. *"You don't have to lie. Acton knows you've been upset."*

Ari woke with a grumble. *"Don't question a female when she says she's fine,"* he warned.

I breathed a little laugh and turned to see Acton sitting cross-legged a couple feet away on the bare stable floor, wearing just an undershirt and a pair of shorts. I could ignore the smell of sweat for how the damp fabric clung to his muscles, revealing his extra athletic outline that came from constantly training others.

Sunset stretched out between him and me, watching him as his eyes scanned the battered newspaper. "It's bad, isn't it?" I asked in a small voice.

"I would've answered the same way," he said, shrugging inelegantly. "The Storm Front *was* a nightmare, and we are all striving for some semblance of peace after it. I've tried for months to scour Korvic's death from my head. I swear I see the details of it every other night."

For a few moments, I just stared at him. "I-I see Feyring's death just as often when I try to sleep."

"Do you want to tell me about it?"

A heavy silence hung between us in the wake of his question. I'd never thought to burden him or anyone else with the details of what I'd seen and experienced.

"They say it helps," he added more quietly. "Even if it's hard."

I glanced down, wetting my lips. With a few gentle nudges, I freed myself of Ari and Ironfeather's weights and went to Acton. We held each other on that stable floor, and he cupped the back of my head when I went to rest my cheek on his shoulder. I don't know how long we stayed like that, but I barely wanted to stir from the safety of his arms.

Finally, I whispered, "I'm not ready."

There was shame there, that even after the several months of peace we had carved out following the war, I still wasn't able to tell him what I'd seen and experienced. The guilt I carried from participating, helping a pyrojack into the sky to rain fire upon our enemies. *Flames. Screams.*

"That's okay. I'm still here," he murmured, cutting into the ghostly chorus of blame. "You're still a hero, Sivana."

"So are you," I said, pressing my fingertips to his chest and adjusting an invisible Gilded Combat Cross where it would sit if he were wearing his uniform.

I'd done my job, the thing the Gryphon Rider Academy had trained me to do from the moment I walked into Fortress Aerie with Ari. I had to keep telling myself that, or those memories of the past would eat me alive. Maybe I hadn't looked up and realized the same shadows were in Acton's eyes. And if he was burdened, then we all must be, silently shouldering alone the same burden we'd once shared when it was time to fight.

"The first monthly competition is coming up," I said, fishing for anything else to talk about. "As fun as it will be to watch the kids compete…why don't we play a game of hoops or talonball or something?"

"I think I'd like that," he said.

This was about the time I would usually go off to the next thing that needed my attention, but Wild Flight could take care of itself for a little while. I was very comfortable in Acton's arms and stayed there catching up with him instead. It felt like it'd been a while since we'd last talked so freely about everything and nothing… When I finally looked over at our gryphons, Sunset and Ari were both laying on top of Ironfeather, keeping him from pushing his way between Acton and me like he usually did.

"Thanks," I thought to Ari. He replied with a free flow of affection.

By the end of the week, I was glad for the distraction the monthly competition brought. Prince Mateo and Mireille had returned with a short note from the King, addressed to me:

"Stop talking to the press, Chosen. I will speak with Mira Galav soon."

"Learned that lesson," I'd muttered upon seeing the order.

I left the note behind in my temporary room out with Wild Flight and joined Mistral Flight's huddle and the tail end of Cadet-Commander Hanover's advice for the group of cadets. "And remember, the group that finishes first will have their choice of where they want to spend their leisure time," he said. "Whereas last place will serve a punishment duty together."

"Usually laundry or scrubbing pots. Try not to be last. It's never fun," I shared.

"Like a flight with Lieutenant Walker was ever *last!*" Geisel exclaimed. Oh, if she only knew…

"I'll be cheering you on, of course. Good luck," I said, clapping her on the shoulder.

I'd told several wild gryphons what the monthly competition was about, and a good portion of the flight showed up and lounged about the Green to watch the cadets. They were the fighters who'd come flying to our defense months ago, not the more standoffish mother gryphons. Once we made sure they knew where they could sit to have little fear of a ball smacking them in the side, they were mostly content to watch.

But then they made me, my friends, and our two assigned caretakers work hard chasing them around, as they quickly became bored. A couple balls were punctured in between a young male's eagerness to join in and another's attempts at stealing one to play with when he decided watching wasn't interesting enough.

We had wild gryphons barging into hoops games, the aerial sport the second-years were playing. They motivated one poor flight by running after them during the mile race. I turned around and saw Sunset about to chase away another wild one who'd squeezed in between two cadets and was attempting to do pushups with them.

Eventually, Valtora reached out mentally to let me know that Father was opening up another section of the Green for the cadets who were between events to spend time with the wild gryphons. Once we herded all of them to that corner of grass and sunshine, I stood back with Lira and Sharde and simply watched as a mix of cadets and gryphons played with balls and hoops, running or chasing each other along the outskirts of the field. It was marvelous, really, to watch them use up all that energy.

Sharde chuckled and shook his head. "Hard to believe this is part of the monthly competition now."

"What a time to be alive," Lira agreed playfully.

"You should be having fun too." Valtora prowled over toward us, pausing to scold a young male who was starting to walk toward the ongoing talonball match between Mistral and Bittern Flights. He was quickly distracted when a ring went flying by, and she was soon bunting my hip and accepting scratches into her feathery neck. *"Ari told me you wanted to play some hoops too."*

"Wait, don't tell me," Sharde said, holding up his palm. "She's saying we should go play hoops?"

I blinked in surprise. "Close."

"You should go do that, Lieutenant Walker."

"What about you, Lieutenant Sharde?"

Lira rolled her eyes. "You two ever going to stop with the rank thing?"

"When I get tired of hearing my rank, I'll stop," I said with a grin.

Sharde gestured to where Puzzlebox was play wrestling with a wild one. "Agreed. Also, I'll pass and keep watch here. She's having a good time already. Hoops was never our best game."

"Suit yourself." I shrugged and took Ari up once I'd coordinated who was playing and who wasn't. As the afternoon wore on, we plugged holes in more casual hoops games verses second-year elements after they'd gotten a chance to jockey for a higher rank amongst themselves. Ari's heart soared with adrenaline and joy. Hoops was still his favorite, I felt, which had me grinning and whooping even though we didn't win every game.

I was back in good spirits when evening approached and Father called an end to the monthly competition. Mistral Flight was third, respectably average, but I wasn't the only one giving Sharde a playful stink eye when his flight, Lark Flight, ended up being first place.

He put his palms up. "Hey, that's all on them. They came in first *despite* me."

"It's almost frightening how well you deflect," Acton commented.

"Feeling *Bittern*?" Sharde answered with a proud grin.

Acton's flight was the one that'd be serving a punishment duty for coming in last. He shrugged good-naturedly. "It's the first competition. I imagine the rest of you will feel"—his nose wrinkled up as he repeated the pun—"Bittern, soon."

"So, what did your flight pick for their leisure time?" I asked Sharde.

His smile only widened. "They want to do our job! They want to spend the day with Wild Flight, with everything that includes."

"Oh, great..." Those kids would be interested in playing with the younglings, not mucking out the stalls and learning how to feed the gryphons without losing their fingers.

On second thought, they *had* earned leisure time, and I could think of no better way to spend it than on a carefree day with Wild Flight.

CHAPTER 10
A VISITOR

The mountainous highlands don't stay scorching hot for long. I noticed a shift in the air and the refreshing breeze with relief as I did my part that weekend to make sure no member of Lark Flight accidentally crossed a wild mother.

The ten of them had taken to my class well enough that they didn't try to approach any beast without permission. Two of the female cadets sat in the shade of the stables for most of the time at a respectful distance from Alaula to chitchat and help babysit many of the energetic younglings. A trio of male cadets had come prepared with hoops equipment and tossed the balls and rings around.

Those gryphons interested in spending time playing with them came and went on their own. Though I'd been initially worried about this leisure day, it was fine. It resembled the kind of relaxing time I would take—I saw my younger self in the girl who kept kicking a ball forward and up in the air for a pair of gryphons to bounce it back off the dome of their beaks.

I was going toward the staff housing for a water break when I walked into something hanging in my way. I jumped back and rubbed my head, looking up in confusion. Fluttering midair with a twittery laugh was Revna, her oversized talons holding something leather, with multiple dangling straps.

"Sivana!" she sang. "This is for you. Put it on!"

She dropped what turned out to be a leather shoulder pad like Solfrid's into my hands, and after I fumbled and strapped it into place, she came in for a landing to put the first scuffs on it. "Signe says I'm getting too big for gloves," the bird said, her tone pout-worthy.

I smoothed her feathery chest with my knuckles. "Sorry, baby storm, but you are."

She snapped her wings with a *hmph.*

"Do I have Signe to thank for commissioning this shoulder pad?" I asked, carrying her along with me for my water break. I held a glass up once I filled it with chilled water, and she dunked her beak and tossed her head back to sip from it.

"Yup. She and Solfrid wanted you to have it since Hvit and I talk to you so much," she said.

I'd need to thank both of them later. "Now I can try to be as awe-inspiring as Solfrid with my shoulder bird," I teased, tickling her.

She squeaked her giggles and batted at my wrist with a wing. "You *are.* At least you don't have the sagas all wrong."

"I barely know the sagas," I pointed out.

"We can fix that," she said quickly.

I snorted a laugh as I carried her back outside to resume watching for any trouble. She flicked her head back and forth attentively from her new perch. I had to say, it was more comfortable than holding my arm up at the same angle for a long period of time. The pad was built thick enough that I felt a hint of pressure from her talons but not the full squeeze.

"Hey, Sivana," she said once I found a place to stand and watch the cadets. "I made a new requirement for my rider."

"Oh?"

She bobbed her whole body in a yes. "Whomever it is has to have a good singing voice."

"That's a little specific, don't you think?" I asked, biting down on another laugh. She sounded quite serious about this.

"I consider it completely necessary to keep up with me." She stuck her beak up in a haughty angle. I rubbed her soft chin, and she make a twitter of protest, her snooty effect ruined.

"I think when you find the person you were meant for, you will want to be by their side, flaws and all," I said.

She leaned into my touch and whistled a sigh through her beak. "But how will I *know*?"

"You will," I said with confidence. She may be from another species than the gryphons I knew and loved, but I had faith that she would know her rider on sight. The gryphons could sense when a human had what it took to Link with one of their own. Why would she be any different?

"Hvit didn't have this problem," she complained. "I don't think any of our kin will, either. Signe thinks they'll wake from their egg at the touch of their rider."

"Maybe. Lady Idunn has put a heavy weight in your talons, but it won't be more than what you can handle," I promised her.

She made birdsong as she thought, the two of us lapsing to our version of companionable quiet time for a while. "I always like talking to you," she finally said. "You make me feel better. Could you, um..."

I tilted my head to look up at her. Her feathers rose, and she shook herself. I was pretty sure this meant she was a little embarrassed.

"Could you hug me?" she asked more quietly.

"Of course, baby storm," I murmured. When she was smaller, with talons that weren't like curved daggers, she'd let me pick her up like a baby gryphon and cradle her in my arms. I didn't think there was a bird alive other than her and Hvit that would ever want to be held this way, but I snuggled her to my chest like old times, and she went boneless with a trusting look.

I held her for as long as she needed, rocking side to side lightly. I figured she was a lot like Prince Mateo in that she would only ask for a hug when she desperately wanted one and would cling for as long as she could. It took at least an hour and Hvit finding us and coming in for a landing on my shoulder, exclaiming, "Revna! Come soar with me!" for her to finally leave my arms.

"Thanks," she said shyly before they were both off in a flurry of feathers.

I KNEW it was a Tuesday because I was finishing up a lesson with Bittern Flight. The days threatened to blur together if it weren't for my one class a day to keep things straight. Being in charge of Wild Flight was an everyday kind of job and I could lose myself to the rhythm of work if it weren't for events that shook up the routine.

I heard the *swoosh* of a pair of mighty wings landing nearby and a few gryphons calling to one another. Ari's attention snapped toward the unexpected rider's arrival. The shutters were wide open on this fair weather day, but we weren't expecting second-years until this evening, nor a mail drop until tomorrow.

Ari's mood lifted, and his beak parted happily. *"Tempest!"* he exclaimed.

I turned to look over my shoulder, distracted mid-sentence. From our place deep in the stables, I could just barely hear the rumble of a man's voice. I quickly dismissed the class of first-years and guided Ari with a hand on his wing to see if it was really Tempest that he sensed coming in for a landing.

Standing there with a fortress caretaker was Tempest's rider, a tall Black man with his back turned toward me. Knight-Captain Zachary Cherin… Actually, on second glance, I noticed the new insignia on his shoulders and broke into a big smile. "Commander Cherin," I called, snapping into a salute when he turned his good eye toward us.

He returned the salute and nodded to me, saying, "Lieutenant Wild." I felt a little prickle of awareness. As my mentor, he'd given me my call sign upon seeing me with the untamed gryphons. Since I was a part of the Second Gryphon Flight, I hadn't heard it since my promotion.

Tempest came over to nuzzle Ari in greeting. He was still a handsome gray male with white fur on his belly and the underside of his wings. *"Nice to see you two again,"* he said, as steady a mental presence as ever.

"Congratulations on your promotion, sir," I said. When Tempest came over to bunt my shoulder, I rubbed his neck, keeping it brief and respectful. He was as much our former mentor as Cherin was.

"Thank you for putting in a good word," he answered.

"You earned it. You kept us alive, after all," I said, gesturing between Ari and me.

A hint of amusement broke his usual stern expression. Cherin could give Father a lesson or two in keeping a strict bearing, usually stone faced no matter what happened. "I'll only accept some credit for that. The gods must've smiled on you two for surviving all the stunts you pulled on the Storm Front."

He had no idea how right he was about that.

He turned to the caretaker, who was moving to take Tempest's reins. "He doesn't need his saddle removed quite yet," he said. "Wild, I was hoping for a couple hours of your time."

"Of course, sir. Would you like to see Wild Flight?" I asked.

He nodded and followed Ari and me into the air with Tempest. We led him to the site of the roost-in-progress, with workmen in the process of building up from the foundation when we landed a few yards away. I was proud to take my former mentor on a tour of what we'd accomplished in just half of a year while Ari took Tempest aside to meet his mate and daughter.

I could tell about halfway into a loop around the gryphon's territory that Cherin had something on his mind. We were at the edge of the river, away from any of my friends and our two caretakers when he stopped abruptly. "Wild, I came here to give you a warning," he said.

I stopped short with a jerk. "A warning, sir?" I echoed uncertainly.

His lips were pinched as he gazed over the rolling field where half of Wild Flight was roosting, the other half swooping through the air or off hunting for their own meals. Whatever it was, it had to be earth-shaking to make a Flight Commander go out of his way to Fortress Aerie to deliver it personally.

The last thing I was expecting him to say was, "Paragon Hughes's gryphon has passed away."

"Gatekeeper bless her soul," I replied. Part of my Academy training was learning of the current Paragon's gryphon and of the Paragons and their beasts that came before them. Hughes's was Gorriset, a brutal wild-born female who'd brought him to the title of Ace and given him a leg up on his career many, many years ago.

Cherin folded his arms, waiting for the news to sink in further. "Wait...that means he's about to retire," I said, remembering the old tradition. Though some men continued serving in the gryphon knight corps if their beasts died, they could not be promoted to High Command or take control of the organization as Paragon. Only a rider and his gryphon could make command decisions for the good of the corps.

My heart sank. I barely knew the man other than his warm presence as a leader and his approval of me, but I knew he had to be in a world of pain without his gryphon. I hoped he was all right in his own advanced age.

"That's right," Cherin said. "And word is circling that his replacement will be Brekwell."

I ran that name through my head a couple times. *Brekwell...Brekwell...* All I knew was that he was a member of High Command. I had vague memories of meeting the men of High Command the night Ari and I had Linked and saved Kaiamear from a rogue rozash, but they were a mixed bunch in my head. Some had wanted to give me a chance to prove myself at the Academy, but others had called out in agreement with King Cortes when he'd suggested my execution.

I figured Cherin was about to tell me that Brekwell was one of the Generals that rejected the idea of a female gryphon rider. Why come all this way otherwise? I swallowed nervously.

I recognized the concern in his eye before I looked out at what Wild Flight had accomplished. With the scrutiny of a new Paragon coming, things were about to change. "You'll receive an invitation to the upcoming ceremony, as a Hero of Altare. Get your head together about it, Wild. Brekwell has made no secret how much he hates you and what you're changing here at the Academy," Cherin said.

There was a ringing in my ears as I turned back to him, afraid my fear was reflecting out from my eyes. "He could shut down Wild Flight and order us to attempt to tame all these gryphons. H-he c-could destroy everything."

"He could," Cherin agreed, giving me a stern look that had my spine straightening even now. "But the venture of yours is tied up in Crown funding, signed away by the king himself. You will have some time to turn Brekwell's opinion on Wild Flight. I'd say until this first year is done and we see how many new gryphon riders your program produces. You said there were fifty-one gryphons born this year?"

"That's right," I said, working my jaw.

He was right, of course. The King had approved Wild Flight and funded the roost, which meant it would remain tamper-free for now. Brekwell—and the rest of the corps—likely saw the coming spring as the first time to poke holes in the idea that we should give the gryphons more trust and independence.

"Imagine him eating his own new rank when forty or more Link to cadets and pledge to the corps. The biggest cohort of young gryphon riders we've had in a decade." While he sounded reasonable, I bit the inside of my cheek.

Would forty or more want to Link to the cadets we'd brought in? I stared my naïveté in the face as my thoughts spun. Forty of fifty-one was doable...except Valtora and Roshawk had told me that only forty-two of our initial sixty candidates were good enough for a gryphon in the first place.

We needed to bring in more cadets.

We had to push the cadets and younglings together more.

We had to influence the babies to think that...

I shook my head, trying to loosen the panic that gripped my mind. I'd said I wouldn't force the gryphons to choose riders, and here I was entertaining the idea of going back on that at the first sign of a real challenge on the horizon.

Taking a deep breath, I said, "Thank you for coming all this way to warn me, sir."

"I'm not here without an ulterior motive," he said with a chuckle. I didn't feel him reach out to Tempest, but I felt the gryphon's response. He flew across the field to us and turned to let Cherin root through his saddlebags. "First, take these."

He handed me two newspapers rolled up together. I undid the bow of twine and scanned the main headlines, recognizing them as the two most recent copies of the *Voice*.

"GRYPHON RIDER ACADEMY HAS NEVER BEEN MORE EQUAL" shouted the first headline.

"THE ELDRAFN RACE RECEIVES A NEW START" read the second, more recent edition. The air left my lungs as I did a quick scan of the page, seeing quotes from Revna and Signe. The reporter Mira Galav appeared to have written their story in a positive light, which had me nearly slumping in relief. It was the victory I'd hoped for from the moment I invited Mira to the Academy.

Cherin's question startled me from my thoughts. "And will you sign these for my daughters?"

Cherin produced two dolls of me, complete with red yarn hair and a matching pair of wooden gryphons painted to resemble Ari.

CHAPTER II

PREPARATIONS

Cherin and Tempest remained outside with Ari and me to talk some more strategy after I signed the dolls for his young daughters. They'd spend the night in guest quarters at the Fortress before flying out to rejoin the Seventh at their new posting down south. I was sure to see them again when the new Paragon was promoted, along with all the other important gryphon riders in the chain of command.

Instead of flying back to dine in the mess hall, I sat on a pile of boards in the center of the skeleton structure that would become a massive roost for Wild Flight one day soon. I just needed some time to think before I shared the problem with Acton and the rest of our friends.

And before I said or did anything that I would live to regret.

"I could use your advice, Lord Orion," I murmured as night fell in earnest and a chill sank into the dark.

The glimmer of magic and sparkle of an otherworldly being didn't come from the god I represented, though. After a few minutes, Glorium, the demigod gryphon, slunk from the shadows. *"He is occupied this evening. But it is a gryphon matter you want some help with, yes?"*

His voice was deep and sure in my mind. He was twice the size of Ari, his head on level with mine even with the boost of the boards underneath me. Every single feather on his majestic form glittered with inner light.

"That's right," I said, getting back to my aching feet and kneeling beside him. I rubbed him head to wing as if he were Ari, knowing he loved every second of attention.

He flexed out one of his wings so I could pet the sensitive underside. *"Well, what's on your mind?"* he asked.

"I think I have been too ambitious," I began slowly.

"You? Never," he said in a teasing tone.

I pressed my lips together, and he bobbed his head with a twist of playful emotion. At least one of us was in a good mood. "What I mean is I think I've changed too much too fast," I said.

He held himself still with a quiver of effort and didn't say a word as I explained Cherin's visit and the upcoming change of command, where Hughes would pass the responsibilities of Paragon onto Brekwell. "The best thing for Wild Flight would be keeping this new Paragon happy. And I know High Command wants more gryphon riders badly. We lost too many at the Storm Front."

Glorium tilted his head back and forth. *"So?"* he asked.

I kept my eyes on him, hoping he wouldn't disappear like the last time he'd dismissed all my concerns with that simple question. "The gryphons here get to decide who their rider will be and if they want a rider at all."

"Roshawk insisted. I remember."

"So," I said heavily. "Chances are good that High Command will be disappointed by all these changes to the Academy not resulting in there being more gryphon riders. I don't know what to do next that will make everyone happy. The last thing we need is for the Paragon to come in and insist on going back to how things used to be."

"Hmm." Glorium didn't seem all that concerned, rolling

onto his side and pulling one of his paws aside to display the glimmering, soft fur of his belly. Without thinking, I ruffled his fur just like he was any other gryphon, and he made a happy croon and rolled further to give me better access. *"What did you need advice on?"* he asked like an afterthought.

"What I should do next," I prompted.

"To make everyone happy, right, I remember now. And if I told you that everyone will never be happy at the same time?"

"Of course. I've heard that a thousand times."

"I understand why you're worried. Younglings are unpredictable and humans even more so. Have you perhaps forgotten that you're the Chosen of Lord Orion with his awe-inspiring presence behind you?"

"Definitely not—"

"Or that you can invite me to show up any time you please?" he asked, then seemed to consider for half a second. *"Well, it would be nice to get some prior warning so I know if I have to come in 'regal and proud' style verses 'rage and blood' style."*

I was taken aback, my fingers stilling in his fur. "That is quite generous, Lord Glorium."

"So is naming this roost after me. Well, that was the plan, yes?"

"When it was closer to being done," I protested. I was hoping to make it a pleasant surprise for him. "I wanted to name it Glorium's Roost and establish it as one of your holy spaces."

He placed his talons flat on one of the slabs of stone beneath him. A flash of iridescent magic marked a ring around his foot, there and gone like a flare in the night. *"There. It has my blessing now. I think I will stay for a while and watch the roost as it is built."*

"If you could meet Brekwell..."

Maybe the new Paragon would be so dazzled by the presence of a demigod that he would bow to the will of Lord Orion's Chosen. Wild Flight could continue past this experimental year without challenge. Now *that* would be an answer to a prayer.

"I'm not supposed to meddle in mortal affairs that much," Glorium hedged. *"But perhaps I could meet his gryphon."*

"That could work as well," I said with more concern. I hoped Brekwell had a solid Link with his beast.

"And perhaps I could put your mind at ease with a secret," he added. *"Because what is more disappointing than calling on a god and not getting a secret?"*

I wet my lips and contained my first thought. Most of my meetings with the gods ended abruptly with unresolved questions and a sense of disappointment. I'd spent more time, by far, with Lord Orion's gryphon than the god himself, and I was his Chosen.

"You do want a secret, right?" he asked in that teasing tone.

"Oh, yes," I said. "If it would put my mind at ease, secrets are always welcome."

"I guess it's not going to be very secret soon," he said with a whistling laugh. *"Orion and Nilara made Links possible between man and blessed beasts on purpose. But before any human Linked, they tested the magic amongst themselves. Orion waited for a gryphon to be born that was meant for him. Me. Hi."* He clicked his beak playfully.

"Hi," I replied automatically.

"Meanwhile, Anrathor got his pack of battle beasts and Da—"

I coughed, interrupting him before he could say the name I thought was on the tip of his thoughts.

"Right, well, dragons were involved too. The test was a success, and they sent me out to talk to the humans and tell them about Links. There are many things in this world that are both good and bad, but true Links are the best thing the gods have ever made."

"I agree," I murmured.

"You would say that, because you have a true Link."

My brow creased.

"What I mean is, you and Arimus were meant to be partners

from the moment you were both born." He patted my hand with his front paw. *"He was forced to pick a Linked partner when he was very, very young and chose Alamid Maros, who was also destined to Link with a gryphon. But his true partner wasn't actually Ari. In essence, he stole his Link with Ari, even though they had a warm partnership."*

"Ari loved him. We both did," I said, immediately defensive of my gryphon's first rider.

"I know. And I'm not trying to diminish how nice that was." He rolled back to his paws, sitting up properly. I had the feeling this was him at his most serious. *"But it is not a Link as Orion und Nilara intended it to be. All humans are born waiting for their companion, big and small. And without a Link, the beasts can not only sense humans meant for one of their kind, but also the one human they were meant to complete."*

"Really?" I breathed. "Why are there wild gryphons at all, in that case?"

"Most wild gryphons never see *a human. But that's beside the point. You remember how, your first night as a rider, a rozash came barreling into Kaiamear?"*

My lips quirked. How could I forget?

"Imagine if it was following the pull to Link with a human in the city, rather than being driven mad by its Linked partner dying. Do you think many Altarians would greet a green rozash with open wings?"

"Probably not," I answered.

He bobbed his head, a sense of sorrow weaving into his words. *"There are so many degrees of separation between humans and all the beasts of the world. Reasons they will never meet, or that one side will Link to someone they're not meant to. But you, Sivana…you have the chance to help along all these younglings to Link to the* right *person, rather than just a person, and that's more beautiful than giving more gryphon riders to the war machine you answer to."*

I felt a tightness in my chest and a stinging at the corner of my eyes. If I could truly usher all fifty-one of our younglings to Links with the human they were meant to be with...

Gatekeeper himself damn me, because I was going to do it.

Glorium nudged my arm with his beak. *"I dare to say it is what Lord Orion hopes you achieve as his Chosen."*

"Then I will do it," I said. I rubbed his neck, scratching into his feathers and fur as he seemed to like. "Thank you, Lord Glorium. This is important information I was missing, and I *will* act on it." Something I was shocked didn't come from Lord Orion himself when he explained how gryphons were going extinct and why.

He turned and pressed his forehead to mine, filling my head with his affection and gratitude. *"I believe in you, Chosen. Remember what you're fighting for."*

As expected, I received an invitation to report to Kaiamear for the upcoming change of command ceremony, hand-delivered by a member of Final Flight. The invitation was written out by Hughes's secretary and began "Dear Esteemed Hero of Altare."

Father summoned me to his office, and we compared letters. While mine was more personalized, inviting me to attend the event as a guest of Paragon Hughes, his read more like a list. A minimum of ten percent of every flight was required to attend, including the Commander and a Captain, though the rest could be Lieutenants. There was a clause for sending fewer men when there were ongoing combat situations, which didn't affect us.

The letters were placed aside like an afterthought as we discussed the incoming Paragon Brekwell well into the afternoon. While I didn't know much about him, Father was well acquainted with the man from his time in the First and the many times he'd had to report to High Command directly.

"Don't worry, kiddo. I know how to handle him," he said. We both stilled when we heard the shuffling footsteps of the next class change. "We leave for Kaiamear at first light tomorrow. Once you go teach your class, find someone who can take over for you for a few days, and get packing."

"Yes, sir," I murmured.

I went through the motions of routine for the rest of the day, before finding Sharde helping feed the gryphons their evening meal. "Evening, Lieutenant Walker," he said cheerfully.

"Hello, Sharde."

His expression turned serious; I'd broken the cadence of our ongoing game.

I took up a bucket of iced fish and got to work next to him. As we fed hungry beasts, I said, "Tomorrow, I have to go to Kaiamear. The change of command is soon."

"Were the rumors wrong?" he asked hopefully. I'd since told him and the rest of our friends the reason for Cherin's visit.

"No, unfortunately. But in the short term, someone has to keep things running in Wild Flight and teach my class." I glanced over at him meaningfully. He raised a brow and pointed the tail of a fish at his chest before looking over his shoulder in an exaggerated motion. "Yes, I mean you."

He flashed his usual carefree smile. "Me? Don't you think that's a terrible idea?"

"No, I think it's a great idea." I pointed out Puzzlebox, who was helping Alaula herd a cluster of younglings toward us. "Name another tame gryphon that's earned Wild Flight's trust to that degree. They trust you, too."

Sharde didn't reply for a long while, a furrow appearing between his brows. I waited for the usual excuses and deflections, the reminders of his incompetence any time he was trusted with a command role. He'd never just accepted responsibility without a smart remark.

"Okay, Sivvy. I'll do it," he said.

Until today, apparently.

"But you can't be upset if you return and everyone's toesies are painted and out of regulation," he added.

I couldn't help a smirk. "Puzzlebox would love that."

I didn't tell him *not* to do it, because that would guarantee that he would. But I trusted him. We were out of the situations where Sharde had to distract our higher-ups from paying too much attention to his gryphon. If anything, he and Puzzlebox had found their perfect posting here, where Wild Flight was quickly learning to love and accept the younger cloudling as one of their own.

"Something tells me the grumpy Skylord would not," he commented.

"I can see Roshawk liking red talons. Maybe a darker shade, like blood," I said.

He nudged me and lifted his chin toward the back of the thinning crowd of gryphons still waiting to be fed. Roshawk waited next to Lira, their heads tilted toward one another in a way that suggested they were trying to speak mentally. "We'll ask her to paint his talons," he said.

"Jokes aside..." I continued to watch them, shocked to see Lira edge closer to Roshawk and pluck some bits of dried grass and loose feathers from his side. "Since when was she able to touch him?" I'd given up on trying; even though he acknowledged that it was nice to have some of the tension massaged out of his scarred side, he just couldn't bring himself to rely on humans for anything so personal.

"Since today, I think," Sharde commented. "Sure you don't want to put her in charge? That's mighty impressive."

I patted his shoulder. "You're the one who graduated from the Academy. You're in charge for now."

He snapped his fingers. "Darn it."

Chapter 12

NOT DEAD

I was glad of the flight to Kaiamear, as it gave me some quiet time with Ari. My spirits were higher just to share a flow of emotions and thoughts with him while we were in the sky.

Sunset had stayed behind to look after Novali. At first, Ari was of half a mind to turn around and curl up in their nest rather than attend a drawn-out ceremony celebrating someone who we knew would oppose us.

"Changes of command are to celebrate the outgoing man," I pointed out, remembering the modestly sized ceremony we'd attended when Marshall Jamison had passed the title of Commandant of Cadets onto my father. Jamison and Father had both given speeches to the soldiers and riders who worked in Fortress Aerie and to the small crowd of their civilian family members.

The party afterward was our farewell for Jamison and Night. Sure, Father had earned a few congratulations and welcomes from the old staff, but the night was more focused on the outgoing leader and his gryphon.

I wondered how they were doing, actually. They'd flown off into the sunrise and not returned, nor had Jamison left any hints as to where they were going.

"I do think Paragon Hughes deserves a farewell," Ari said, abandoning thoughts of turning around. *"And considering Night's age, I imagine they're dodging an invitation to join Final Flight to go somewhere warm and remote."*

"I hope so." I couldn't imagine the proud pair doing anything as mundane as delivering mail. They'd earned better than that. *"Can Marshalls be forced into Final Flight? I thought it was voluntary."*

He projected the equivalent of a mental shrug. *"It is. I've met a few high-ranking gryphons in Final Flight since many of us prefer to stay in motion even after we retire. It's not in our nature to stay on the ground, not unless we're very sick or very old."*

He projected a memory of Night for us both to see those signs of age again. I realized that she preferred to stay grounded or inside the fortress where it was warmest. No wonder I hadn't seen them since they'd retired.

Ari and I chatted aimlessly for the rest of the flight, occasionally with interjections from Valtora. I appreciated the moments of peace and the freedom of the open sky ahead of us.

Father had chosen to go with us and left Commander Rudrick in charge in his absence. Since Commander Falirin was attending, Acton had had to stay behind to continue the Ground Combat classes. Captain Gemon and a few lower-ranked former tamers were also in our formation.

It would be strange to be without our close friends for a few days, but there was a chance I'd see Prince Mateo if he could spare the time.

Father and Valtora led us to land in front of a spacious building which provided gryphon riders with apartments and a stable with caretakers for the gryphons. We were on the outskirts of Kaiamear, in a military-owned section leading to an immaculate field kept for big ceremonies like the upcoming change of command.

The apartment I slept in that night was adequate in a way

I'd only seen with the gryphon knight corps—my needs were met, but there was little in the way of extra comforts. We'd arrived with a day to spare, which put me at loose ends while Ari slept in.

It was a rare day to wake before him. Due to our extra-strong Link, usually we were in sync from when we fell asleep or woke and felt the same ebb and flow of emotion. Judging by the gnawing in my belly, he would wake hungry, so I donned civilian clothes and went out to gather up a surprise for him when he did stir.

I left my flight goggles on the vanity and fixed my distinctive red hair into a high bun, which I hid under a summer hat. It was slightly out of style, but I doubted it would bring more attention my way than if I went out without my hair covered.

I went out and found the market with little trouble, walking the stalls like I used to as an anonymous teen with a few copper clorets jingling in my coin purse. Though the color of my coin had changed since then, my buying tendencies hadn't. I bought a quick breakfast from a street vendor and then started picking out things I thought my friends back at Fortress Aerie might like.

We didn't get much in the way of fresh fruit, so I had a sack of it thrown over my shoulder by the time I was done and turning toward the sound of a boy crying out the day's headlines on a busy street corner. I almost scrubbed my ears when he repeated himself. "Prince Isaac isn't dead!" he exclaimed.

"Let me get one of those," I said, flicking him a cloret. He caught it and presented me with a copy of the day's newspaper with a flourish.

"Thank ye, mum," he said.

I barely steered myself out of the way of passersby as I walked toward the dock with this copy of the *Kaiamear Gazette* held open in my fist. Sure enough, the headline in big, bold print was "PRINCE ISSAC ISN'T DEAD AND OTHER

TALES OF THE KING'S INCOMPETENCE" by Miles Glimmerwick.

I felt a clammy chill over one shoulder, like the Gatekeeper himself read over my shoulder at this blasphemy. Isaac was quite dead and long buried. I'd seen the body.

I decided to fold the newspaper and pinned it under my elbow rather than walk off a pier in shock at what I'd already skimmed. I would soon return to Ari, and I wanted to read this article to him, maybe even while he enjoyed what I was about to buy for him.

Salmon.

The military didn't buy expensive fish for the beasts, which included Ari's favorite and the fish that we joked that I owed him a lifetime supply of. Today, the fishmongers sold me five pounds of the coveted protein, the weight of which I juggled with my other purchases on my way back to my temporary apartment.

When I was close enough, my Link with Ari vibrated, letting me know that he'd woken up and was wondering why I was so far away. *"I have something for you,"* I projected to him mentally.

"Is it salmon?" he asked.

"Wait, how—"

"Could I know my rider?" he teased. *"But why do I sense that you're holding something back?"*

"There's news from the Gazette, *I'll read it to you."*

"Thrilling," he said dryly.

The stables were busy by the time I got there. Riders stationed in the furthest reaches of Altare were starting to arrive for the event tomorrow, and I dodged a flurry of activity with the caretakers coordinating the care of the new gryphons. I made my way to Ari's stall with a clean feed bowl, knowing he would already have one in his space with his standard breakfast within.

I was unsurprised to see that he'd already eaten that

breakfast and was projecting eagerness to have the salmon he scented through its paper wrapping. *"It was a long flight,"* he said a little defensively.

"I wasn't judging," I promised.

He might've guessed I'd gone out of my way to get him fresh salmon, but I hoped to surprise him more when he learned I'd paid the fishmongers a kingly sum to pack up and transport today's catch of salmon here for us to return to Fortress Aerie with. With a bit of magic to preserve them, he'd be eating his favorite fish for weeks.

I sat on a bale of hay and spread out the newspaper while he dug into his second breakfast, politely averting my eyes and holding in a flinch or two at the sound of brittle snapping. He murred in satisfaction.

Considering the number of people coming and going from the stable, I read the whole *Gazette* article to Ari privately. *"The title itself is enough to get Glimmerwick beheaded,"* he commented.

"I have a feeling this was planned for a long time," I answered.

In my mother's short tenure as a writer for the *Kaiamear Gazette*, I'd come to realize that Prince Isaac had wanted civil war for his own purposes and was using his newspaper to sway common sensibilities down that path. He was willing to use me and even my family to achieve it. I was a propped up symbol of change and a sign that King Cortes had become inflexible in his advancing age.

Mother and Father were willing to go along with it if Isaac, as king, was willing to accept me for being a female gryphon rider. What none of us had realized was that there was a fine line of separation between a *symbol* and a *martyr*. One was alive, and the other was dead.

In death, it would seem Isaac had become the martyr and figurehead for the civil war he'd always wanted.

My face was numb as I kept reading, a shrill tone in my ears. Glimmerwick had written and managed to publish a tell-all about how King Cortes had wanted me dead and had made several attempts at it. He mentioned Victor Callan by name, with a detailed account of how he'd broken Ari's wing during a jousting tournament. Ignoring all nuance to that situation, he then mentioned Callan's murder and blamed King Cortes for it.

But that wasn't all. There were facts and figures of mishandled money and an eye-watering number of clorets left unpaid to the families of those who'd lost a loved one on the Storm Front, *"a war he started."*

The last paragraph on the front page read, *"To salvage his reputation, he made a deal with rider Sivana Walker, deciding she was a weed he couldn't seem to pull. He promised to make her a Hero of Altare and falsely declare her the Chosen of Lord Orion if she was willing to help him with a political masterstroke to rid him of Crown Prince Isaac once and for all. It is the greatest hoax of all time played on the Altarian people."*

Ari's paws twitched with the agitation I felt while I flipped to the next section, buried deeper in the newspaper's folds. *"This reads like something Isaac wrote and instructed his people to publish in case of his death. Something to drag all of his enemies down one last time,"* he growled.

"But why publish it now?" I worried my bottom lip between my teeth, sure my mother would have a politically savvy answer to that question were she here.

I found as much of an answer as I would get within the extended section of this article. Glimmerwick wrote that Isaac was assumed dead or banished due to the announcement of Mateo as Crown Prince. But *"he is not dead, only waiting to see his loyal followers again"* and *"any and all who think that what happened to him is wrong should keep their eyes and ears open."*

Shivering, I rubbed a chill off my arms. The Gatekeeper disapproved of using a dead man's reputation this way, and someone would be paying the price for it.

"It's a call to rebellion. Perhaps those in charge of it are just now

ready to challenge King Cortes," I said, folding the newspaper carefully and sneaking it into the saddlebags hanging on a hook in the stall. I had no doubt the distribution of similar copies would be shut down quickly.

Ari stood and stretched, leaning his weight backward like a cat would. *"Saddle me up. We have to find Mateo."*

CHAPTER 13

CHANGE OF COMMAND

WE FOUND MIREILLE INSTEAD, which was just as well, as Mateo was in a meeting with his father, according to her. She lay in the bronzing grass of the Gryphon Yard, standing out like a white-gray beacon as we came in for a landing. The stables for the First and gryphon riders visiting the palace surrounded us, quiet for now with most of the beasts out on patrol.

"I want to fly so badly," Mireille complained. *"I want to go and be free of all this waiting around for nothing."* Her tail thumped the ground, and her mental presence was nearly unbearable for the level of yearning she projected.

"We could fly together, if you like. As long as Mateo doesn't mind it," I offered her.

"It wouldn't be good enough... We would have to come back here. This is not where I am meant to be." That yearning was tied up in a feeling, a breath of cold air that only she seemed to notice.

My mouth dropped open, and I glanced toward Ari. *"She feels the call,"* I said to him privately. He shifted on his front talons. A sense of discomfort radiated from him... He already knew. *"And you didn't tell me?"*

"Her rider is the crown prince," he answered, his head lowering. *"And…well, no rider has been willing to fly the Path of Glorium other than you."*

"Ari!" I exclaimed in shock. That was his excuse for not even telling me?

Suddenly, her extra snappy, put-out behavior gained new context. She was feeling restless and trapped, tethered to a young man with too much responsibility. With his brothers dead and his sister pledged to the Gatekeeper, he was the sole heir to a country still plagued by elements that wanted to burn the whole kingdom down from within.

"It's not a good time. We all know that, especially Mireille." He edged closer to me, nudging my elbow with his beak once he found where I was standing.

"Stop talking like I'm not here," she said with a hiss.

"Sorry," I said, including her in our mental conversation again. *"Does Mateo know about the call?"*

"He's too busy to notice, and I don't want him to worry." She sighed heavily. *"And you two came here like a pair of storm clouds looking for him, so I'm assuming there's more bad news?"*

"There is," I said, reluctant now to be the one to bring the matter of the newspaper article to Mateo's attention, if he didn't already know. *"Mireille…you're such a sweetheart. I can't believe you've been suffering in silence this long."*

"I'd endure much worse for my rider," she answered. Her devotion to my friend was rock-solid, and for a moment, I could only be grateful that Mateo had such a loyal companion. Was this what a true Link looked like? The unwavering support of Mireille, suffering in silence to be there for her overwhelmed rider?

Well, *I* wasn't Linked to him. I would say something the next time I saw him. *"Can you tell Mateo to come here when he gets a chance?"* I asked her.

She tilted her head and, after a few minutes, said, *"He wants you to wait for him in Odalis's old parlor."*

"That works." I stood and helped Ari to his paws before encouraging Mireille up as well. She shook her whole body with a great rustle and took up her brother's usual spot up against Ari's flank as his seeing-eye gryphon.

I felt akin to a ghost as we walked through the palace, my eyes darting toward doorways that used to be familiar. I'd lived in the palace most of my life as the daughter of the First's Commander, before everything changed. Now, another man and his family occupied those old apartments. A different family was using the Rudrick's rooms, and since three other men had chosen to follow Father to the Storm Front, that meant more new faces living down these halls.

No one stopped me on my way through the corridors, and I even snuck a peek into Isaac's old solar to see its fine furnishings and flickering magelight covered in a layer of dust. Odalis's room wasn't much better, two doors down from the solar. It was like she'd never come back once she'd left for the Church of Mercy.

"Probably," Ari commented. Neither gryphon sat until I dusted off cushions for them.

"Wonder if she has her nightbloom by now," I mused. She'd told me months ago that she had the soul of her old horse in a vine she'd had wrapped around her wrist. Once it took the shape of a form she could ride, it would have the ability to carry her between the realms of life and death, but that's all I or most people knew about the Gatekeeper's blessed beasts.

"Know what's interesting?" He seemed thoughtful as he and Mireille got snuggled up together. *"In that article you read, there was no mention of Odalis."*

I reached into his saddlebag and removed it, skimming its contents with a raised brow. He was right. *"Perhaps it's coming in its own edition,"* I said.

"Doubtful. You really think the Kaiamear Gazette *will run its presses again?"*

"No," I admitted. *"I see what you're saying. If Isaac and Glim-*

merwick are putting everything out there, why not mention the fact that King Cortes kept Odalis from her god for most of her life?"

He pulsed the mental equivalent of a shrug. I kept it to myself until the door creaked open, and in walked Mateo wearing what I could only describe as a princely outfit. Dark brown trousers paired with a double-breasted coat that was stark white and trimmed with golden buttons and accents. My gaze zeroed in on the pin of a rearing gryphon he wore even out of uniform, the one that marked him as Ace of our year group.

A hint of resentment burned at the back of my Link with Ari, but I didn't give it air to spill over into my feelings.

"Have you seen this?" I asked, standing and offering the newspaper to him. I looked up at his face and felt a pang for him. Mateo looked years older with his hair coifed and dark half-moons under his eyes. And here I was, pushing another problem at him rather than saying hello.

"You see it now," Mireille said at the back of my head.

My hand dropped as he reached for the newspaper. "I mean, uh, hi," I said.

His lips twitched toward a teasing smile. "Hello, Walker. If it's today's *Gazette*, then yes, I've seen it. My father has already ranted about it, and our people are attempting to apprehend those involved in publishing it. It's being handled."

The air pulled from my sails, all I could say was a meager, "Oh."

He barely swiped his hand over one of the other chairs in the room before he sat with a heavy sigh. "If that is all you wanted to talk about, don't mind if I just hide out here for an hour," he murmured, his eyes already closing.

"No, it's not. Mireille needs you," I said with such intensity that his eyelids flew back up and his panicked gaze landed on his gryphon, who bristled in my direction immediately.

"Don't give him something else to worry about," she protested.

"What? What's wrong?" he asked.

"It's not healthy to keep secrets from your rider, no matter who he is," I replied before saying aloud, "Do you remember that one summer Ari and I disappeared for a couple months?"

He blew out a sigh and sat back again. "Despite how it seemed, I wasn't keeping tabs on you that closely."

"Between our first and second years at the Academy, when I suddenly appeared on the beach at Acton's estate," I prompted.

"Right. You showed up with that streak in your hair. What of it?" He circled his hand impatiently. At some point, he'd picked this up from his father, who made it seem twice as callous.

He did drop the uncaring act quickly as I explained the call and the Path of Glorium to him. Mireille's reactions helped validate me when I mentioned that her needs were falling to the side while he attended his duties as the new crown prince. There was a distinct mix of discomfort and fatigue coming from Mireille that echoed on Mateo's face.

He considered for a long while, gaze fixed on his gryphon in such a way that suggested they were speaking mentally. "If she feels called to visit the gods, then we must go," he said finally.

"But the timing," she murmured.

"When will there ever be a good time?" His chuckle held an edge of bitterness. "There will always be one crisis or another to attend to. You feel this calling *now,* so I will start making preparations for our departure. And Walker will help."

I choked on a swallow, before saying, "Y-yeah. I sure will."

"I'll have a plan for this by the time I see you tomorrow for the change of command. You'll have a spot in the front row next to me," he said.

He must've seen the flicker of uncertainty on my face. "You *did* get invited as a guest, right?" he asked.

"Well, yes."

"Then you're in the front row with me. We don't have to march in the pass in review—isn't that great?"

For a moment, he flashed a boyish smile like the carefree Mateo I once knew. I couldn't help but mirror his expression and nod.

We might've spent an hour in that room, maybe more, but I put the newspaper away, trusting what Mateo said about it, and steered the conversation toward more lighthearted topics. We spoke of Wild Flight instead of duty and avoided speaking of our worries, at least for now.

IT FELT strange to promise Mateo I would not do anything about the *Gazette* article, but I agreed with his reasoning. The Crown's people were investigating Glimmerwick's claims and the *Gazette* staff members who'd allowed the article to go to print in the first place while I showed up in my formal uniform bright and early the next day for the change of command. My Hero of Altare medal gleamed from where it rested against my collarbone.

The orderlies coordinating the event ushered Ari and me over to the tiered seating to the side of the field. We stood in the front row next to Mateo and Mireille, as he'd said we would. While civilians and gryphon riders alike trickled in, I was caught in a flurry of recognition and small talk with nobles and ranking officers of other military branches.

Well-dressed men and women wedged themselves between Mateo and me. If they weren't talking to him, they were trying to get a word in with me and vice versa. The last time I'd been surrounded so closely by this many people, it'd been at Temple Row with hands reaching out, plucking at Ari, a sickening whirl of sound and noise. I couldn't handle it then.

This time, no one was trying to get a feather as a memento. They stood at a respectable distance and mostly didn't speak over each other. One noblewoman wanted to tell me that she supported me, no matter what some "jumped-up rag" published about me. She also handed me a letter and hinted strongly that her teenaged daughter was fit and willing to travel.

Another man demanded I tell him why his son was dismissed from the Academy. My usual explanation only drew out a bigger scowl from him.

Meanwhile, the army officers wanted to make sure I knew their names. I'd served on the Storm Front with many of them, though our paths had barely crossed since we were in different military branches.

"Is every event like this?" I asked Mireille. I was tickling at her awareness, as she was trying to block me out. She was in a moody funk next to Ari, her emotional state too turbulent to hide.

"Where I'm ignored like furniture? Yes," she replied pretty promptly for a gryphon upset at me.

"Furniture?" I echoed, a little caught off guard by that response.

She put on the noble accent and lifted her beak skyward. *"What a lovely gryphon you have. So well behaved."* Her feathers fluffed out in irritation. *"I've heard them compliment tables and clothes more sincerely."*

"Mireille—"

"I know, I know. It's not personal."

"That's right—"

"But do they realize how insulting *it is to be talked about like I'm a prop?"*

"Baby girl, stop this," I said more firmly. I excused myself

aloud to the man I'd been speaking to, stepping around the small crowd Mateo and I had gathered to walk up to her and fluff her wing and neck feathers. Her raptor-like stink eye relaxed when I drew up to my toes and kissed the side of her beak.

I turned to the men and women within earshot, who were watching me with the same trepidation as if I were sticking my arm down a big cat's throat to prove it wouldn't bite. *"None of these people have the stones to do more than glance at you,"* I told her privately.

"This majestic beast is Mireille, the crown prince's gryphon. If we could put a pin on her saddle, she'd be wearing the same rearing gryphon Prince Mateo has on his coat." I turned from her intelligent gaze to the watching crowd.

Ari read the intentions from my mind and projected a sense of acceptance and approval.

"It represents the Ace award, meaning they were the top ranked graduates of our year group. They earned it because of her talent in the air and the crown prince's skill in the saddle," I announced. I regaled those listening with a story from our second year while prompting Mireille to take a good look at their faces. For a couple minutes, many set aside the polite veneer to show what was underneath.

"Impressed and a little afraid," I explained.

She sat straighter. *"As they should be."*

I noticed a few people stepping aside at the approach of an elderly man, but it took a second glance for me to realize it was Paragon Hughes. My story drifted off half-finished, and I snapped into a crisp salute along with Mateo.

As I'd feared, Hughes had lost some indescribable spark that'd elevated him from the ravages of age. With the passing of his gryphon, he'd transformed from a straight-backed senior military official into a man hunched over his cane. His free hand trembled by his side, yet after he dismissed the formality, he spoke with the same authority as ever. "What Lieutenant Walker is leaving out is that she served a step behind the crown prince during this military game. A supportive teammate." His steely gaze drifted from the two of us to the hand I still had resting on Mireille's neck. "Even now," he added as an afterthought.

"Good morning, sir," I said.

He nodded in acknowledgment. "I'm so pleased you could be here today." He hardly glanced away when a few orderlies started ushering everyone to their seats around us. "The ceremony will begin shortly, but I hope to catch up with you afterward?" Though it was framed as a question, I had no doubt that this was an order.

"Yes, sir."

"Good. We have much to discuss," he said.

He was beginning to turn away when I cleared my throat. "I'm sorry for your loss, sir."

His fingers flexed on the head of his cane, and for a moment, I thought he wouldn't respond. A sigh whistled from his lips. "Thank you, young lady. I take comfort in knowing the Gatekeeper took her eternal soul to the sun-washed lands away from the pain and heartache of age. More of our beasts should have the opportunity to pass peacefully, surrounded by their family and friends." There was stark pain in his voice, a weight I innately understood and respected.

"I agree," I said with sympathy. As I expected, he turned away and walked toward the stage set up in the center of the parade field, visibly refusing help from a few of the orderlies as he went.

I took my seat next to Mateo, waiting quietly for a few minutes. The event didn't start until Paragon Hughes was comfortably in place next to King Cortes. To the king's other side was another man in the formal gryphon knight corps uniform, a skinny gryphon next to him. His chest glinted with rows of medals, even at this distance. That had to be General Brekwell awaiting his promotion.

There were two more men on stage; one held a magical device to magnify his voice, and the other stood more to the side, holding up a flagpole with the Altarian flag. The announcer brought our attention to an approaching military band, a uniformed group marching in formation from the direction of the city. They began playing patriotic music and led the way for the gryphon riders who marched behind them.

I'd seen dozens of pass in reviews and marched in most of them. My foot tapped to the rhythm set by the band, and my heart thudded in time. As odd as it was to be here as a guest, I still appreciated that I could watch this special ceremony in which every flight was represented. The men and gryphons marched with slow formality in the numerical order of their flights behind the band, taking the long way around the parade field to first present arms to the king and leadership assembled on stage.

Behind me, the audience cheered and whooped as the announcer named each flight and its leader for their benefit. I clapped politely throughout, taking note of a few surprise promotions amongst the flights I'd served with on the Storm Front, people I wanted to congratulate at the celebration afterward.

Ari and Mireille yawned nearly in sync. He lay down over my feet, intending to nap like he always did when there was about to be speeches. Mireille rested her head on his side, looking like she wanted to rest too, but her flipping tail betrayed her inner agitation.

I settled in for the speeches with a sigh once the pass in review was complete and the stage was surrounded by the representatives from every flight standing at parade rest. King Cortes spoke first. Just as Ari had his coping mechanism —sleep—I sat looking attentive and let his words turn to white noise past the "thank yous" and the praise he heaped upon both Hughes and Brekwell.

When he passed the amplification device to Hughes, I shuffled the bend of my legs and leaned forward, more eager to hear what he had to say. By this point, Ari was whistling small snores through his beak, and Mireille was prodding him with a talon to get him to stop.

Hughes's list of "thank yous" was double the length of the king's, enough to glaze my eyes back over until he startled me by saying my name toward the back of the litany. "With the passing of my gryphon, Gorriset, my career, too, must come to a close. But what great strides the gryphon knight corps has made in the last few years. We fought and won against the Rathi, taking down creatures our best strategists thought we couldn't kill.

"The first gryphon rider Hero of Altare in an age was celebrated in my time, and with her comes a new wave of changes for the corps. We can only continue to grow and improve under the guiding hand of Paragon Brekwell."

There was a smattering of applause, and the named officer inclined his head in polite agreement. I heard murmuring behind me and the shuffling of clothes as someone stood and moved to a seat in the second row. I thought it was odd, then realized it was dangerous when he pulled the distinctive shape of a crossbow from the inside of his long coat.

Hughes was still speaking. "Paragon Brekwell has a history of excellence as one of the senior members of High Command. The king could not have made a better choice to lead us—"

I drew breath to scream when the assassin pulled the trigger on his weapon, shooting a prepared bolt toward the stage. Hughes reacted in an instant, throwing himself to the side like a man half his age so that when the feathered quarrel hit with an echoing *thunk* through the amplification device, it pierced his chest rather than King Cortes.

CHAPTER 14
THE MAGISTER

Though several people in the audience jumped to their feet and started for the assassin, he was laid flat in the next moment by a snarling Mireille. Chaos followed. Some fled; others grabbed unfamiliar men and women, trying to find a weapon on them too. I stepped in front of Mateo, which was laughable since I hadn't brought my sword. He was twice as proficient at unarmed combat as I was, but he was still the crown prince.

Despite the tears burning the corners of my eyes, I recognized my duty, just as Paragon Hughes understood his. What was left of the royal family had to be protected at all costs.

The sound of his body toppling from the stage was magnified by the device that'd fallen from his fingers, echoing around us. I tried to block it out, focusing on what was in front of me. Ari flanked Mateo, his ears pinned back and a hiss escaping his beak whenever he sensed someone nearing.

"Come with me, Your Highness," a desperate sergeant was saying, standing a leery distance from Ari's threatening pose. He was one of several orderlies trying to reestablish some sense of order. I remembered blinking at him in a daze before following him to an enclosed building nearby where the king and Brekwell were also escorted. They took Mateo but locked the door behind him and left Ari and me to wait outside alongside a few armed bodyguards.

At some point, Mireille came inside. I cleaned away a smear of crimson from the edge of her beak with a kerchief. *"They wanted to keep him alive,"* she said in frustration. She reminded me of Valtora in that moment, confused as to why we humans had spared a criminal.

"He has to pay for what he did," I replied.

An echo of that awful *thunk* rang in my head.

I balled the bloodied kerchief in my fist. *"Death is too easy."*

PARAGON BREKWELL WAS PROMOTED that evening in the royal hall in a rushed affair. There were no more grand speeches, just King Cortes assuring the gathered group of flight leaders, plus Mateo and me, that Hughes was with the healers.

"The gods were merciful. An inch to the left, and he would be with the Gatekeeper instead," he commented.

I leaned forward slightly, waiting for him to make a public thank you to Hughes for saving his life, but the king moved on to passing command to Brekwell like the Altarian flag he held was aflame. I sighed, weary to my bones. We'd emerged from hiding after a few hours to the news that the would-be assassin had acted alone and that Hughes was clinging to life by a few fragile threads.

Judging by the pallor of the king's usually rich skin tone, he was still grasping at his nerve after that unexpected attack, too. Which made me especially nervous when Mateo leaned over to whisper, "I'm coming back to the fortress with you."

I opened my mouth to reply but caught sight of Mireille's shifting expression. Her emotions brightened like a ray of sunshine, the warmth welcome in the sterile chill of the royal hall.

"You're answering the call," I whispered back.

"That's right. Father insisted I go when I mentioned returning to the fortress. Not for the call; he would be terrified of us flying into danger. But leaving the public eye for a few weeks? He liked the idea of it," he said, nearly casual. "With you and Acton covering for us, I think we can make the trip without it being a bother for him."

"Right," I mumbled.

When it was time, I left the royal hall with Father and a few other flight leaders and turned down a trip to one of the local pubs a split second after he did. After today, I just wanted to be in a quiet room with Ari and my thoughts, and that's exactly what I got, as no one moved into my path as I guided him into my temporary apartment.

I piled the bedding on the floor next to Ari and lay down, getting comfortable under the wing he stretched over me. I worked through my worries, and he listened, silently witnessing it all through my mind. It wasn't lost on me that Mateo had decided to accept the call as the weather would be turning for the worst up north. There was no real autumn in the mountaintops, only the start of the kind of brutal winter storms that made new, wild eldrafn.

Ari and I had just barely made the trip in the height of summertime. What if I'd made a terrible mistake bringing the call to Mateo's attention? What if they didn't return at all?

When Ari finally spoke, it was in response to those panicked thoughts. *"If left unanswered, the call doesn't last for long,"* he said. There was an echo of memory over our Link of the first time he'd ignored the phenomenon just outside of yearling age when his rider was still Alamid. *"It only returned when Lord Orion insisted we come to him."*

I closed my eyes, nodding briefly in acceptance. *"It's out of my control."*

In reply, he projected all the other things I'd worried about recently that were also out of my hands. Paragon Brekwell's promotion, the *Gazette's* last article, whether the gaggle of younglings would find their true Linked partners, and on from there.

"What can *you change? What deserves your time?"* he asked.

I thought on it for long enough that he settled in next to me, assuming by my stillness that I was about to drift off mid-thought into a deep slumber. My response was a sleepy mumble, but I had something to do before we left the capital tomorrow.

"YOU DON'T HAVE AN APPOINTMENT," the elderly secretary said the next morning. Multicolored light spanned her desk and cast the planes of her wrinkled face in aquamarine from the fancy mosaic window. The Tulari Tower overlooked the bulk of Kaiamear, gleaming like fractured gemstones from the outside due to its unique stained glass windows.

I'd left Ari back in his temporary stable, knowing the Tulari Tower was built with slanted walls and narrow rooms, sure to be a maze for a blind gryphon. I wore my Hero of Altare medal today and had placed my hands on my hips.

"I have a couple quick questions for Magister Scorvash," I repeated. "Is he in?"

"You don't have an appointment," she echoed back to me, unblinking.

We'd been going around in the same verbal circle for five minutes. I could hear the man bumping around in the room adjacent, probably listening to his secretary and me locked in a contest of who was the most stubborn between us.

"I'm afraid we don't have time to make an appointment," said Mateo from behind me. He strode in, wearing a coat of maroon fabric and black trousers. When I'd told him why I was going to fly back to the fortress separately, he'd insisted on coming with me, but it seemed he'd taken a detour to change out of his flight leathers first.

For a moment, she gaped, before standing to curtsey with practiced efficiency. "Good morning, Your Highness."

"Is Magister Scorvash available?" he asked.

I felt a twinge of resentment as she went to check, knocking on the Magister's door and returning to respectfully inform Mateo that he was awaiting us. He turned and motioned for me to go ahead of him, flashing a hint of his smile, and I breathed out that negativity. Mateo was just using his title to help me get my last-minute audience with the Tulari equivalent of the Paragon, the man who led the council that governed the affairs of Tulari mages.

Caladorn Scorvash had been the Magister since before I was a tot, and from the moment I was old enough to recognize him, I swore he matched his grooming and clothing to mimic the wizards of old. He wore a navy-blue robe today, decorated in silver trim and stitched with patterns of crescent moons and constellations. He'd always been bald, with an extra-large white beard hanging over the vee of his robe.

Despite his apparent age, he stood and bowed to Mateo without the assistance of the staff he had propped behind his desk. "What a pleasure it is to see the crown prince and the newest Hero of Altare so early in my day," he said, his voice deep and sure.

"Thank you for meeting with us. We won't take up too much of your time. We are merely hoping you can help us locate someone. Sivana can tell you more about her," Mateo answered.

I eyed the Magister's staff while Mateo spoke, taking note of the jagged lines that marked the angles of the shimmering blue-green crystal geode that was clutched by carved wooden fingers holding it to the staff. It was a tool of those blessed by

Lord Orion with crafter-level magic, and Scorvash was a shining example of it, as he was also dual-blessed. The circular rune on his cheek was both wizard blue and healer green, shimmering from one color to the other as he turned his face my way.

"Good morning, Magister Scorvash," I said politely. "Have you heard of Zuri Zaveri and her stolen corerune?"

Scorvash masked a surprised sputter behind his hand. "Why don't we have a seat? Shall I send for refreshments?"

"That won't be necessary." Mateo schooled his expression into a scowl as we took the chairs across from Scorvash at his desk. "My father heard Zuri's story from Sivana and promised to do something about it. Presumably, you were also informed."

"True," replied the Magister.

"I have not heard from her in months. What happened to her?" I asked, leaning in. I could see the recognition in the old Tulari's eyes, mixed with the hesitance to say more.

"Ah…" He scrubbed his face, his watery eyes seeming small and squinty with his skin pulled by his thick fingers. They darted to and fro, searching for an exit from his skull. My expression tightened, afraid of what he was going to say when he realized he wasn't escaping this conversation that easily.

It seemed he'd realized this quickly, as he answered with an air of resignation. "There was an investigation, of course. Zuri Zaveri leveled a serious accusation at one of the most well-decorated war heroes still breathing. The Tulari Council were present as witnesses to watch what happened when Irene Merriweather handed her staff, Starfall, to Miss Zaveri. The results were…deeply upsetting."

Mateo glanced my way when I took in a gasp of air. Had holding Starfall killed Zizi? Was that what he didn't want to tell us?

"So, you were there as well," Mateo interrupted.

"Of course, Your Highness. Though I was quite skeptical of the whole thing, I was the one to decide that this was the quickest way to resolve the matter. If Miss Zaveri was able to absorb the corerune on Starfall, then she was telling the truth," he answered.

"But that's not what happened?" I choked out past the knot of fear in my throat.

The magister made a sympathetic expression. "I have heard that Miss Zaveri was your assigned pyrojack. I'm sorry to be the one to tell you that she lied to you, Hero of Altare. She isn't the true owner of Starfall. She was simply an unstable pyrojack."

My hands tightened to fists in my lap at his pitying tone. We survived war together, Zizi and I, and she'd told me the story of Irene stealing her corerune and forging Starfall only when she thought our lives were forfeit. It was the kind of deep confession someone only made when they didn't want to die as the only one holding onto the knowledge.

Zizi was no liar. But I gritted my teeth and let him continue.

"When she attempted to take the corerune off Starfall, Miss Zaveri burst into flames head to toe. She nearly died on the spot," the magister said. "Such is the fate of the unstable when handed a tool of such great magical potential. But through some sheer willpower, she survived her brush with the Gatekeeper's shroud. With such an undeniable show of her nature, she was moved to a facility for the containment of the unstable. It is for the good of Altare that she remains there until she can get a hold of her magic."

I paled with horror. All that had happened without me? Poor Zizi. I glanced toward Mateo, who wore the same tight-lipped expression as I had. Nostrils flaring, I pinned the Magister with a serious look. "Where?" I demanded.

CHAPTER 15
MORPHOS

Ari and I set out in the opposite direction of the fortress, with Mateo going there instead and carrying news of where I was going and why. We'd parted ways with one of those long hugs that he seemed to need every so often.

"Good luck," we said at the same time.

Mateo and Mireille weren't likely to wait for us to return to Fortress Aerie before they set off for the Path of Glorium. I sent them off with a muttered prayer to Glorium himself to look after them as they sought the home of the gods.

Though the demigod didn't answer me directly, I could practically feel his amusement at the request. *That's been my job for centuries,* he would say.

In the meantime, Ari and I flew southwest toward the Tulari Academy and arrived as the sun was setting. Altare's young mages were educated in a castle that looked like a toy set from above, all of its ivy-laced stones appearing as smooth and shiny as painted pebbles. The nearby lake was akin to a mud puddle, especially in the darkening shadows of evening.

Magister Scorvash had given us directions to the reformatory where Zizi was being held. The House of the Unstable wasn't to the south, amongst the populated city that'd sprung up to serve the Tulari Academy, but hidden amongst the foot-paths that'd take us into the heavily forested north, where the failed experiments of junior Tulari were said to live and thrive. We had to approach by foot; otherwise, the magical wards would make sure we wouldn't spot it from above.

Luckily, I knew a magic user who could help us do this safely. Ari and I landed in the castle's courtyard and received immediate attention from a set of guards. They wore uniforms with the tri-colored symbol of the Academy stitched into the shoulder.

I lifted my goggles and waved. One of the men seemed to recognize me and gaped, elbowing his fellow and whispering behind his hand. I said, "Good evening, gentlemen. I'm looking for my brother, Nate Walker."

"Right this way, ma'am," said the first guard, the other still looking dumbfounded.

Ari made a low crowing sound. "And sir," he amended quickly.

I dismounted and grinned over at my gryphon. We took the walk into the castle slowly, as my legs were boneless from the long ride, and I could sense Ari ached. We shared the same mix of fatigue with a hefty dose of determination and pinch of mischief.

Ari wanted his favorite warm friend back safely. He'd liked Zizi before I had, teasing me that she was more comfort-able to sleep on, but it went deeper than that. He'd had this sense that she was a person he could trust and had been far more affectionate with her than with even some of our long-time Kite Flight friends.

Meanwhile, I was ready to free her from what seemed like wrongful imprisonment as soon as possible. But first, I had the rare opportunity to surprise my brother. I'd not seen the inside of his school before but found its drafty castle corridors familiar. It was like walking the halls of Fortress Aerie, except where we had sconces of fire to warm the air, the Tulari

Academy had magelights at regular intervals. It was both colder and better lit than what I was used to, and I was grateful for my fur-lined flight jacket.

The guards took us to a dining hall where I was likely to find Nate taking supper. We'd acquired another man in our wake, wringing his hands and eyeing Ari like he was a wild animal striding into their space. "Will the lady gryphon rider require a place to stay for the night?" he asked in a shaky voice when I noticed him.

"I would appreciate one," I replied.

"And the beast…"

"Will need to stay in the room with me. If that's a problem, I can find an inn in town." I hooked my thumb over my shoulder, and he shook his head rapidly.

"N-no, we can't…we wouldn't turn you away," he sputtered, hurrying off.

Ari huffed, lashing his tail. *"Let's find Nate. I can sense all the attention on us."*

The back of my neck was starting to burn with the same kind of awareness. The dining hall was half-full, mostly with Tulari students around my brother's age or older. There were several open books and casual displays of magic going on around them, including a floating spoon prodding at the lips of the nearest staring student.

I smiled and turned to pan the room for a familiar head of red hair. It was almost comically easy to spot my brother when he was one of the only people with his head still down. He was bent over one of his many experiments, completely oblivious to my gryphon and me in the same room.

I guided Ari over to the other side of Nate's table. "Hey, lil bro," I said.

He dropped his wand with a clatter and cry of surprise. The two young men seated nearby snickered. "Sivana?" Nate exclaimed. "What are you doing here?"

"I need your help," I said.

"Yeah, yeah," he snorted over at the two still laughing at his surprise. "I mean, why would you by here in person if you didn't need something?"

I blinked, taken aback by the grudging way he'd asked that question.

"Perhaps some dinner first for the lady gryphon rider?" The nervous man must not have gone far, as he was back with two bowls of chicken stew. He put one on the table in front of me before placing the other just outside of Ari's range of motion. "E-enjoy!"

I nudged the bowl closer to Ari, who sniffed it disdainfully. *"They don't have fish?"* he asked.

"I, for one, am grateful it's not fish soup."

"Our stay on the Iceberg was months ago."

"Still too soon," I commented. I sat and shook hands with the two young men, who turned out to be Nate's friends. The blond was Owain, and together with Nate, they made for a pair of disheveled wizards with the pasty skin tone that suggested they never went outside. He had a big grin that occupied much of his face.

Terrance had an emerald green healer's mark that complimented his coppery skin and dark, tightly curled hair. Just like many of the more experienced healers I'd met, he had a calm air that made him seem more mature next to Owain and Nate. He wore an unadorned robe of a matching green.

Now that I noticed it, Owain was also clothed in a colored robe, while Nate was wearing the drab brown of an apprentice still. I made a mental note to ask him about it later.

"Well, you might as well tell me what you want," Nate grumbled. He took up his wand and bent over the box that contained his experiment. From the other side of the table, all I could see was him drawing teeny blue runes with fixed precision.

I realized myself and the reason for his snippy tone a little too late. I could make things more awkward by stepping back in the conversation like I could manipulate time and begin with asking him how he'd been. Nate and I had barely seen each other in the past few years. While I'd been either at war or sequestered atop a mountain halfway across Altare, he'd been here. Trying to move up from the apprentice rank he'd been stuck at this whole time.

"How...I..." I stammered. "Uh. I found where Zizi is."

His gaze, reflecting the color of his magic with a rune hanging on the tip of his wand, flicked up at me in surprise. "Where?" he asked with full curiosity.

"Have you heard of a place called the House of the Unstable?" I asked.

Nate shook his head. So did Terrance and Owain, who leaned in to hear us too. I told them what Magister Scorvash shared with me and noticed how Owain whitened toward a shade reminiscent of a bedsheet.

"I'd say you shouldn't go out into the Morphos Woods, but I know you will anyway," Nate said, breathing out a sigh.

"Apprentices aren't supposed to, either," Owain pointed out. He spoke over Nate's immediate protest. "But I know you're also going anyway."

He lifted his shoulder. "True. Sivana's had me looking for this girl for months. I have to know why she's such a big deal."

Terrance shook his head slowly. "I'm more worried that such a place is hidden within the woods. We've lived here for how long, and we didn't know?"

I glanced between them and asked them to tell me more about the Morphos Woods. They obliged, letting me know that a morphos was the proper Tulari term for a spell of uncontrollable or improperly created magic. "Some spells never go away, so the Tulari Academy has a big section of woods marked off for all of the morphos spells created by mages in training," Nate explained. "And over the years, it's turned the Morphos Woods into a dangerous maze."

"I've been once. Nothing's as it seemed in there," Owain added. "The animals were all twisted up, the trees had weird nonsense runes written on them, and that's not even counting the spells darting around in some places."

I frowned, getting more troubled with every description. "Why would the House of the Unstable be placed there? Why would *anybody* be forced to live in the middle of all that?" I asked.

While Nate's friends nudged each other like one was daring the other to spill some kind of secret, my brother gestured for me to lean in. "Haven't you heard? There are no more unstable mages anymore," he whispered in my ear.

Before I met Zizi, I'd thought that too. "But—"

"Maybe we've discovered how the Tulari Council keeps it that way," he interrupted. "Meet us in the library tomorrow morning. I assume you're coming too?" Both of his friends nodded in agreement.

I DIDN'T SLEEP WELL, haunted by echoes of rozash fire and the dying screams of gryphons. I woke in full darkness and shambled to the library like a sleepwalker, vaguely aware of Ari's solid bulk pressed against me.

The nervous attendant had made sure to inform me apologetically that I wasn't allowed in most of the Tulari Academy, but the library wasn't included in the list of laboratories and classrooms that were off-limits. I sat in a well-used chair and waited for the fog to clear from my mind.

Zizi's laughter featured in some of my nightmares, her cackles those of an unstable pyrojack given leave to press her powers to their most destructive potential. In times of old, it was the unlimited power of unstable pyromancers that leveled battlefields and nullified ultra-hot dragon fire. My waking mind knew Zizi wasn't there yet and that she fought to hold back from letting her magic control her in such a way. But at night, well…not all fires in the Storm Front war were started by rozash, especially as my mind explored the *what ifs*.

I rubbed my forehead and eyelids, blinking the world back into focus. Ari and I were amongst the only living souls in this library, and I'd picked a table in the shadow of the stacks to hide from plain sight and get my head on straight.

Ari sent a pulse along our Link, reminding me that I was awake and needed to find Zizi. Now that she'd proven without a doubt that she was unstable, she'd been removed from these halls. But how could the Tulari Academy not have noticed this about her in the first place? She'd been sent to war and used where she was convenient, just to be discarded to a location within the Morphos Woods the moment she'd had a chance to hold Starfall. It wasn't fair.

"Hey, Sivana."

I startled, nearly falling out of my seat. Nate was right behind me, grinning ear to ear. "Ah, sweet payback. I knew you wouldn't sleep," he said.

I tisked, taking a breath to calm my racing heart. "Fine, you can have that one. What about you. You're up?" I asked.

"Maybe I haven't saved Altare, but I'm a Walker too," he replied, taking the seat across from mine.

I shifted awkwardly. "H-how have you been?"

"Well, I'm known across the school for having a Hero of Altare for a big sister when I can barely string a spell together. I'm one of the oldest apprentice mages here." His lips twisted bitterly, and he looked somewhere over my shoulder. "I've been thinking about going home, quite frankly. Wherever that is now."

"I'm sorry, Nate." From his letters, I'd assumed that he was on the cusp of a breakthrough. That he was closer to being a crafter-class wizard in need of a staff rather than what he'd just described.

He crossed his arms. "It's not like it's your fault. I know all you set out to do was save Arimus, not get mixed up in the gods and the royal family. But I want to be noticed by the gods and the king too."

"No, you don't," I blurted at the same time Ari made a squawk of alarm.

"Shh!" echoed a distant librarian on duty.

I lowered my voice. "Nate, c'mon. There's a space between chosen by a god and where you are now that's perfectly acceptable."

"You don't get it," he answered back, seeming a little frustrated. He pushed up from the table, saying he'd be right back. I watched him go, sure I hadn't scrubbed all of the concern out of my expression as he charged away.

"No comments?" I asked Ari, who was more quiet than normal.

He let me feel how sleepy he was over our Link. We yawned at the same time. *"He sounds like he's about to try something rash. I'm going to watch him more closely,"* he answered.

I lifted a finger, brow furrowing.

"Not literally," he added with another yawn.

Nate returned in only a few minutes, placing a few books on the table between us. He took a slim volume off the top and tucked it into his robe. *"See?"* Ari ventured, watching through my eyes.

"I see," I said.

Nate was in the middle of talking. "The Morphos Woods is mapped every year by journeymen mages about to graduate from the Academy. The most complete maps are kept and recorded with magic into books like these. Take a look." He gestured to the two books remaining, which appeared to be identical copies of *The Ever-Changing Wood*.

I flipped open the front cover, noting that the first map listed was created over a hundred years ago. The page was oddly flat, rather than bearing the marks of a quill or a press, and as soft as a piece of fabric. I paged through the maps, looking over how they changed over the years. Nate had opened his book to the very end and was flipping between the last few pages.

As far as I could tell, the Morphos Woods was a rectangular space, marked off with the straight lines that could only come from human-made wards. The frequency of dangerous occurrences increased dramatically as the years passed, while a few disappeared off the journeymen-created maps after being there for decades.

"Hasn't anyone mentioned how dangerous it is to have a dumping ground for spells like this?" I ventured.

"They're just mistakes. None have been strong enough to break the wards."

"Yet," I muttered.

He gestured for me to hurry up. "If we want to find the House of the Unstable and not wander lost after dark, we have to have an idea of where it might be. I was hoping there'd be an empty zone on last year's maps, but…"

I looked over the last six maps within the book, all recorded last year. They were wildly different. Two were inverses of each other, while the other four had similar locations, but placed at random. "Why did only these six maps make it into the book?" I asked.

"Well, they're the only ones that were finished," he answered.

"What about the rest of them?" I assumed plenty of Tulari graduated from the Academy each year.

He shrugged. "Destroyed, I guess."

I hummed, unconvinced, and flipped back in time to see the same kind of scramble on the maps two years ago. *The Ever-Changing Woods indeed,*" Ari commented. I could feel his presence inspecting the maps through my gaze with me, noting the differences.

Seven years ago, two of the maps looked similar. Eight

years ago, they were mostly the same. *"Perhaps a morphos spell began moving around the land itself,"* I suggested.

Ari didn't hide a severe twist of doubt. *"Ask him how often these maps are accessed."*

I did so dutifully, and Nate tipped his head. "Hard to say. I mean, everyone gets curious once, but I remember finding all this rather dull when I took a peek last year," he said.

"Something's hiding in plain sight," Ari stated, nudging my elbow with his beak.

"Ari wants to know how exactly we can access the Morphos Woods," I said.

"It's open to anyone of journeyman or higher rank."

Well, he was an apprentice and I wasn't a mage, so I had to ask. "Will you have to sneak us through a checkpoint of sorts?"

A little furrow appeared between his brows. "No. Owain can thin the wards in a place we agree on to sneak us into the woods. And out, too, presumably with Zizi."

"Oh, I didn't know that was possible," Ari mused. *"I have a thought, but he's not going to believe me."*

I chuckled under my breath as he shared it. I closed the book of maps with an air of finality. *"Sometimes, you're too smart for me,"* I said.

"Nate, what if we're not meant to find the House of the Unstable in the Morphos Woods?" I pitched to a whisper, causing my brother to squint to hear me.

He breathed a little laugh. "But Magister Scorvash himself told you where to find it."

"Yes, but…" I glanced over at Ari. "Humans lie."

CHAPTER 16

House of the Unstable

"So, let me get this straight," said Owain as he dragged his blue-toned robe out of the grasping branches of a shrub. "The *gryphon* thinks that Magister Scorvash tried to send you into a death trap."

"That's right," I said. I swiped a trickle of sweat from my forehead. We'd been hiking the invisible perimeter of the Morphos Woods for an hour with most of the air filled by Nate and me explaining what we were doing. The three Tulari had gotten last-minute approval to take a day off to "show me around the city."

Instead, I'd dragged them into the forest so they could probe at the invisible, straight-line barrier that kept us from the twisted morphos magic hidden just a few yards away. "He had to give an answer for where Zizi is because Crown Prince Mateo was right there, demanding one. So there probably *is* a House of the Unstable, and it's possibly somewhere close the Morphos Woods. But he sent me unprepared for what you've described as being inside of it. And he knew I was the one truly asking, not the prince," I reasoned.

"But…the gryphon figured this out," Owain pressed.

Ari clicked his beak in irritation. "He's just as smart as you and I are," I said.

"I resent—" Owain was cut off with an elbow to the ribs, courtesy of Terrance.

"I understand the urgency," Terrance interrupted. "But if the Magister was even remotely interested in sending you into danger on purpose, can we think about what we're about to find?"

In the silence that followed, I patted the sheath of the sword attached to my hip. "I think there's a possibility of a fight. But maybe we're completely wrong, and Zizi is in the Morphos Woods, having her instability treated."

I just thought too much didn't add up. My fingertips tingled with the certainty that my friend was in danger and that the Magister was hoping I'd either die in the Morphos Woods or get hopelessly lost long enough to move Zizi elsewhere.

"At the same time, she's been out of contact with her friends and family for six months. Preventing her from reaching out is a cruelty that can't be ignored. What if she was denied a chance to call out for help for a reason?" I finished.

They seemed to accept that answer, and none wanted to turn around at the idea of a possible fight. "I'd want someone to fight for me too, if it were me," Nate said.

It took over another hour of hiking to find an end to the barrier and the start of the longer edge that ran parallel to the school. We'd be out all night if we wanted to check the entire perimeter. At first, we were busy talking about strategy and laying down a plan for what we'd do in multiple scenarios if we did end up finding a hidden warded building.

I only started doubting that there was a hidden building at all when we stopped for a water break and to nibble on some of the food I'd squirreled away from the Tulari Academy's morning breakfast buffet.

"My feet," Owain complained.

I sighed to myself. While Ari and I were a little tired, we'd already visibly worn out our companions. There were stereotypes of out-of-shape Tulari for a reason. We'd be slowing as dinnertime approached, so it'd be smart to turn around soon and try again tomorrow.

The trio of mages had told me that the best location to hide an entire building would be up against powerful and near-permanent wards like the ones that held in the magic within the Morphos Woods. But that meant that what we were looking for could be attached to the outside of the wards, like we were checking…or we were wasting our time, and it was on the other side.

I chewed my lip as we returned to our hike, quieter than ever. Owain took over checking the wards with a quickly drawn rune from his wand. While I didn't see anything when the rune touched magic, apparently to them it showed a ripple of energy down the straight line of the wards. If there was something out of the ordinary, they'd spot it.

While they focused on the wards, I kept my eyes toward the surrounding forest. The leaves were changing, many already brown and carpeting the ground. It was a good day for a hike, if we weren't all tense like drawn bowstrings. I twitched at the rustle of underbrush, my senses evenly blended with Ari's and his superior hearing catching the fleeing of small woodland creatures and the occasional squeal and snap when we flushed a prey animal for a less skittish predator.

"There's a trap," Nate said, putting his arm out to stop us. He pointed his wand toward a tree and a big rune engraved into its bark. I snuck a closer look over their shoulders as they inspected it, seeing that it was oddly blocky compared to what I knew runes to look like.

"I think we can go around it," Owain said.

I carefully guided Ari in their footsteps, all of us taking the long way around the tree. "It's a sheet spell," Nate explained to me. "There was an invisible sheet of magic between the tree and the wards, and it had a paralysis spell for anyone who walked through it."

"That's suspicious," I pointed out. I was oddly heartened by the existence of a trap. That meant there might be something out here after all *and* that we were close to it.

Terrance tipped his hand side to side. "Depends on how many—"

"Another one," Nate interrupted. "Looks like a rooting trap."

We dodged the big, circular spell that Nate had only noticed because of a jut of rune-engraved rock that wasn't already coated in fallen leaves.

"Do they teach you all of this at the Tulari Academy?" I asked, impressed. I also loved the proud smile that crossed my brother's face, giving me a glimpse of the carefree young man I thought I'd be visiting.

"It's…" He looked ready to downplay it before smiling all the brighter. "I have full marks in all my rune classes. Even if I can't use them all, I know many of them on sight."

I praised him for that, glad to hear that something was going well with his magic. With his keen eye, we wove around a few more traps, all nonlethal but sure to stop the unwitting in their tracks.

I only noticed something else amiss when Ari lifted his beak. *"Do you smell that?"* he asked.

I drew in a deeper breath, picking up the same traces of smoke and cooked fat on the air that he projected through our Link. *"Perhaps a camp site nearby?"* I suggested.

"In the middle of the day?" he asked with the mental equivalent of a raised brow.

He had his answer when Terrance stopped abruptly and hissed for us to do the same. Following his line of sight, I froze up. A battle beast rested amidst the leaf litter to the side of the path we were on. It was the size of a wolf, with thick amber-brown fur contouring the swells of its muscular legs. Half-lidded crimson eyes began to fix on us and its canine ears cocked forward.

"Run!" Nate exclaimed, and I caught his shoulder before he could do more than jerk himself around.

"No," I snapped. He blinked at me uncertainly as the bark of my voice echoed around us. "If you don't want to be chased, don't run."

I released Nate when he nodded and turned my attention to the battle beast. It was fully awake now, regarding our group with its head tilted curiously. I looked into those eyes and saw the same glimmer of intelligence I'd come to recognize with my gryphon friends. Stepping forward, I steeled my nerve and the wild beating of my heart, addressing it directly. "Sorry for disturbing your rest. We are just passing through."

Ari stood at my side, crowing aloud. The battle beast barked.

"*What did it say?*" I asked.

"*He is telling us to keep walking,*" he murmured.

The dog-like beast got to his paws and shook out his thick pelt, scattering some lingering leaf litter. He jerked his head in a clear echo to what Ari had translated. With him standing, I could see that he was huge compared to the few battle beasts I'd met in my life.

I wasn't keen to meet many more of his kind, knowing what they were capable of. He was so large that he could press his nose to my shoulder without effort, and the relaxed spikes that lined his spine could be raised with his hackles to set his coat ablaze. He was one of Lord Anrathor's blessed beasts, bred for size, strength, and viciousness to compliment his fire.

But what was he doing *here*? I wasn't about to ask, choosing instead to nudge Nate along and hushing Owain when he opened his mouth. "Keep walking," I said in an undertone.

If we were lucky, the battle beast would curl up in the patch of sunlight where he'd been resting. But if we weren't lucky, well...he could call to his pack, undoubtedly close by, to hunt us down.

"Or follow us," Ari pitched in. *"Like he is now."*

"Uh...Sivana," Nate whispered.

I didn't have to look. I could feel the heat radiating from the battle beast as it fell into step next to Ari, growling and chuffing. *"He wants to know where we're going."*

With a hint of nerves, I spoke out loud for my other companions' benefit. "My friend has been missing for months. We think there might be a hidden building nearby where she's being held."

His growls lowered to a bass pitch, making me quaver on the inside. *"He knows what you're talking about,"* Ari said.

And he seemed quite angry, too. Smoke lifted from his spine and eddied in ominous curls from the corners of his mouth. It was only for Zizi that I gathered my nerve to ask, "Do you know *where* it is?"

He replied with a sharp *woof* and barks that Ari translated. *"He does, and he'll take us there for a price. His pack has been trying to go there for moons...months?"*

I shared this, taking a nervous swallow. "Would wards, in theory, block battle beasts from passing?" I asked the Tulari.

"Certain ones can," Owain answered.

We stopped in a clearing and took a water break for the painstaking process of translating the battle beast's demands. Four of his pack members had gone missing in this area, including his alpha's pregnant mate. They'd been in this area for "moons" trying to free her and the others.

"They hide behind a barrier we can't get around. We cannot get to our packmates, no matter what we try," Ari translated while the battle beast paced back and forth in frustration. At some point, we'd learned that he was Fleetclaw, second only to his alpha.

It was significant he was asking for our help at all. Battle beasts were remarkably reclusive creatures, and the secrets to their taming remained with Anrathor's clergy and his chosen berserkers. To think this pack had been here for so long went against their nature, as one pack needed many acres of wilderness and the game within to sustain itself.

"Do you think all those traps we've passed were for battle beasts?" Nate asked.

Fleetclaw snarled. I took it as a yes even before Ari translated. *"He says he will lead us around the rest of the traps if we agree to help his pack."*

"We need a moment to decide," I told Fleetclaw. He listened and glowered as I gathered up the three Tulari to share his demand: he'd lead us to a hidden building nearby if we allowed his pack passage to it. "Whomever is keeping these battle beasts captive is going to die a fiery death if we go this route," I warned.

"Well, *we* will probably die a fiery death if we turn him down," Nate said nervously.

Terrance twisted his lips and spoke with a healer's calm cadence. "Could we not talk about death so flippantly? Look, there might be innocent people there, including your friend, Sivana. We have to use some finesse rather than sic a pack of battle beasts into an unknown situation."

Fleetclaw barked. *"He does not mind being the only representative of his pack to come with us, as long as we leave the way open for the rest of his pack to follow. He's willing to try peace if it means his packmates are returned safely,"* Ari translated.

I repeated that back and added, "I think we can do this. We go in there and demand to see Zizi and the battle beasts. It's just an extra variable to our plan."

As we informed Fleetclaw of our plan, I noticed movement in the trees. Three more battle beasts crept closer, their glowing Anrathor-red eyes unmistakable. He left to share information with his pack before returning to tell us that he was ready to go with another tilt of his head. *"He says he agrees to our plan and will show us the way. The rest of the pack will wait out of sight to help if we need it,"* Ari told me.

I was grateful for Fleetclaw quickly, as he took the lead and showed us the safest path through the forest, avoiding all the traps. He and Ari kept up a quieter flow of conversation, with some amusement passing through Ari's side of the Link. He shared the occasional comment from Fleetclaw. *"He says the three male humans need him. He knew he could trust us from how not intimidating they are."*

"And I wasn't intimidating?" I huffed.

"You, at least, have a weapon that's not a twig."

Of course a battle beast would notice that. I shook my head, hoping we were close. The afternoon was burning its way toward evening, and it was looking unlikely we'd see the inside of the comfortable room I'd been lent inside the Tulari Academy to rest tonight. Nate, Owain, and Terrance were pushing their limits as well.

When Owain checked the wards and turned a wide-eyed look our way, I knew we'd found the mysterious House of the Unstable. "Remember, everyone. There's a chance this is all one big misunderstanding," I said. "But be prepared for it not to be."

Fleetclaw threw his head back to howl. He pitched it deeper than the battle beast cries I heard at war, making it more a signal for his pack rather than the sound of eminent death. While his pack howled back more distantly, Owain and Nate wove magic together to create a chain of blue runes. One side attached to Owain's wand, the other to Nate's, and they manipulated the spell like they had a sheet hanging between them, pressing it to the invisible wall of the ward at the same time.

A ripple passed through the air and a doorway-sized rectangle shimmered where their spell had been placed. "It worked," Nate whispered loudly. It was like they'd peeled back a layer of magic, showing a different angle to the world, very much like they'd opened a door. The five of us stepped through it, and my eyes adjusted quickly to seeing a whole different view of what'd been a grassy hill a minute ago.

The House of the Unstable was at the top of the hill, and we'd stepped onto a dirt path leading up to its front door. It was a massive structure of three stories, multiple chimneys sticking out of the roof and belching clouds of black soot into the sky.

The forest was neatly trimmed back, lined with terraces of labeled plants and a pair of Tulari attending to them. They turned our way, eyes widening in surprise as their gazes fixed on the gryphon and battle beast accompanying us.

"State your business," the woman of the two said, standing with the leverage of her staff. Real plant life cascaded down from the green bulb at the top of the weapon, each petal and leaf outlined with glowing magic.

For a moment, I hesitated. Back in the war, the couple crafter-class healers I'd met had worked wonders to keep us all alive. But she was a stranger, and the man with a matching green Tulari mark next to her was already starting to draw the runes for an unknown spell while my attention was on her.

"We're here for the pyrojack Zuri Zaveri, and the battle beast wants his packmates returned," I said.

"That's cute," she answered, raising her staff to the sky.

CHAPTER 17

PACK JUSTICE

THE OTHER HEALER Tulari finished his spell, which released a loud, shrill tone that sent a shiver through the plant life around us. Ari cringed, his ears pinning to his skull, while Fleetclaw took an aggressive stance next to him.

A shadow passed through the sky, coalescing into a buzzing cloud of insects that descended toward my friends and me. I grasped the hilt of my sword in a white-knuckled grip, watching the multi-bodied tide of bugs eddy around the crafter-class healer, touching her skin and hair without so much as a single sting or bite.

I swatted away the flies and wasps already starting to attack me, shocked that it seemed the healer had somehow summoned this endless stream of bugs. Nate yelped and cursed nearby, flailing his hands in panic.

Heat and flame bloomed with an angry bark from Fleetclaw. He barreled through the cloud of insects, scattering them in the wake of his fiery body. "We can still do this peacefully," I called, watching the battle beast prowl toward the crafter-class healer as insects became flying embers around him.

"You've found a secret you cannot walk away with," she

answered, pointing her staff my way in a clear challenge. I drew my sword, falling into a ready stance with the familiarity of muscle memory before charging uphill in her direction. Sparks of dying bugs and the stings of living ones peppered my face. My stance faltered as I swatted them away from my unprotected eyes.

"Stand down, and I won't hurt you," I said with effort. She was in the midst of casting another spell, runes appearing in a sheet around her.

I was momentarily distracted, watching more Tulari emerging from the House of the Unstable, many running full-on for the doorway Nate and Owain had opened in their wards. My gaze flickered from them and back to her, recognizing that they would try to close off the rest of Fleetclaw's pack.

"I don't take orders from the magicless," she spat. She pointed her staff at Fleetclaw, head turning and lips parted to bark an order to her companion as a stream of foul yellow liquid gushed from the bulb on her weapon.

The battle beast leapt aside, and the liquid continued pouring out, flung in an arc toward me as well. I jumped backward, nose wrinkling from the acrid, stinging smell coming from it. It steamed on the ground, killing any unfortunate plant life it touched.

"I've got the other one," Ari said. He shared a certainty in the back of my head that the other Tulari was struggling under his bulk right now. I caught a glimpse of Terrance casting a spell over him.

The insect cloud was either dead or dispersed, their bodies crunching under my boots as I advanced on the crafter-class healer again. Before she could cast another spell, I swung my sword and chopped off one of the vines extending from her staff. The steel caught in the wood and stuck there.

"Last chance. Stand down," I gritted out. I put my weight into my weapon, trying to snap her staff in half.

"Zuri has been here for some time," she replied, nearly conversational. "She's called your name, you know."

I bared my teeth in fury, shoving harder with my sword, forcing her a step back.

She laughed in my face, spraying the sensitive patches that'd been stung with spittle. "Every time we leave her burnt out and broken. First, she cried out to the gods. Then you, Sivana Walker. What took you so long?"

She was wearing out any mercy I felt fast, but in the midst of the red haze falling over my sight, I caught a glimpse of the runes starting to wrap around the head of her staff, even with the gouge I'd carved into it. My sword was stuck, wedged there with all my strength, and I realized this wasn't the stalemate I thought it was.

I released the hilt of my sword with the first rumbles of the earth below my feet. A massive vine uncurled from the dirt and whipped at me, glancing off the leather covering my shoulder. My fast reflexes had saved me from being impaled on the thorns lining its solid length, each dripping an acid-green substance.

It coiled around the healer Tulari's feet like an obedient snake, and she smirked, obviously thinking she had the upper hand. She didn't realize Fleetclaw was behind her, his hackles flattened, until he was close enough to tackle her out of the protection of her vine. He ignited into a fireball the moment his body struck her spine, and she tumbled to the ground face-first with a scream of pain and surprise.

The vine lifted and whipped wildly, its fine control lost as the staff jarred from her hand on impact. I seized it and leveraged the bottom half, breaking it into two pieces over the blade of my sword. "No," she gasped, reaching for the two halves with her mouth gaping. The moment the tool broke, the thrashing vine ceased its movements and darkened.

She burned beneath Fleetclaw, the smell of her clothes and skin melting singeing my nostrils next. "Call your pack *now*,"

I told him, seeing that we had no other choice. "I'll handle her."

He stepped off her back with a brief nod. I wasn't surprised when the healer rolled, desperate to put herself out. I flipped my sword around and struck her skull with the hilt, knocking her unconscious and smothering the smoldering ruin of her back with what remained of her robes.

She'd live, probably. But anyone who, in her own words, *left Zizi burnt out and broken*, didn't deserve much more of my care or attention.

Fleetclaw threw his head back and truly howled. The battle cry was more akin to an eerie wail, one that promised a painful death for crossing his pack. Answering barks and snarls sounded behind me, as well as the terrified shouts of strangers.

Terrance came up to my side, his eyes widening as he saw the Tulari on the ground by my feet. "Leave her," I said. "She's no friend of ours."

He must've seen the serious gleam in my eyes, as he said nothing, merely nodding. I gathered up Ari, who waited for one of us to help guide him.

"Did you see her magic? She was using spells that were the opposite of what a healer Tulari is," I commented, assuming he'd seen the fight through my eyes. I placed a hand on his shoulder and took a quick look at the devastation already unleashed from the battle beast pack.

They'd all ignited, leaving charred plants and unrecognizable corpses behind. Bile rose in my throat, and I swallowed the bitter taste down before I could retch. *"Gods, they killed those people without any hesitation,"* I added to Ari.

"Look at our wizards," he said.

Owain was supporting Nate, who had a bleeding gash somewhere on his leg. Ari could smell the blood and the lingering stench of ruinous magic from here, which he projected over our Link. While I'd been fighting her, they'd also been under attack. He gave me a wave of reassurance that we'd picked the right option by letting the battle beasts in. He empathized with the beasts. If he had to come to the rescue of his flockmates or, gods forbid, his chick, there would be the hells to pay.

I scratched into his neck, breathing a sigh. *"You're right. We picked this path."* And now I needed not to stray from it at the first sight of death. Nate said it best. Zizi deserved friends that would fight to save her, and I knew this was a momentary reprieve from an even bigger battle.

A few yards away, Fleetclaw's fiery self stood nose to nose with the one battle beast larger than him, the two squaring off in a chorus of growls. The alpha, I assumed, barked in our direction.

"He is asking for a human escort. The pack is ready to fight but needs to know who to spare," Ari translated.

"We should try to do this as cleanly as possible," I said.

The alpha snarled, his hackles raising further. A new wave of heat rolled off his body. *"He says the mages here have had many chances to make their mistakes right and not to stand in the way of pack justice."*

I put my palms up. "Who would I be to stand in the way of justice? Ari and I will go," I said, then turned to Terrance. "I think you should come with us once you heal my brother. Nate, Owain, stay here."

Terrance nodded, going to kneel next to Nate. He inspected the gash in my brother's leg and began to write a spell over his wound with the tip of his wand.

"No way." Owain puffed out his chest. "I can fight too."

My nostrils flared with frustration. "We need someone to keep the doorway open. You and Nate are the best options for that."

"I'm going," he said with a stubborn lift to his chin.

"I'll stay. I can do it on my own," Nate sighed.

"Fine," I groused, not wanting to waste time arguing

further. I started off at a jog following the alpha, who loped toward the doors at a dash. White-hot flames leapt off his form, transforming him into a canine comet seconds from cratering his way into the building.

Terrance, Owain, and Ari followed behind me, clustering close while several members of the pack outpaced us, howling and snarling, eager for bloodshed. "Listen to me closely," I huffed. "The battle beasts are going to kill anyone we don't identify as a friend. We're going to help them out of the building immediately, because this whole place is about to go up in flame."

My words were punctuated by the harsh impact of the alpha splintering the doors in a fiery rush. The threshold was already on fire as the rest of the pack raced in behind him. *"Maybe you should stay outside too. Your feathers,"* I said to Ari.

"And who will translate for you?" he asked, sounding offended. I nodded in acknowledgment and helped him through what remained of the doorway, carefully flecking burning shards away from him. Battle beasts barked impatiently behind us, but I did notice a few loping around the building, cutting off the back end.

"It's not like they're waiting around for us," I remarked.

Spells and flames flew in the hallway as more Tulari fought the beasts. While there seemed to be several wizard and healer Tulari here, I noticed no pyromancers around trying to take advantage of the fire spreading from the wake of the battle beasts. Thank the gods. A fire mage worth their Tulari mark could redirect the battle beast's natural elemental weapon to consume one of us in an instant.

Several doors were left open, and it was within the first one that I found Owain and Terrance trying to wake up someone strapped to a padded chair.

I assumed they had the situation under control and checked the next room. Empty, save for the pungent scent of herbs and smoke. It was an unusually small room from the inside, until I realized the walls were reinforced and lined with runes. The ceiling was sloped upward, toward an empty hole.

As I did a quick scan, a wave of pus-colored smoke billowed from that hole. It reminded me of the putrid acid the healer outside had summoned, and I dragged Ari out of the room quickly and shut the door. A series of locks rattled on the outside from the force I used.

My gaze narrowed on those locks, but I didn't linger for long. A sharp series of barks had drawn Ari's attention. The alpha had reached the end of the hall, and the pack bristled behind him, all their attention focused on a man hunched in a corner while Owain shouted and waved his arms.

"Wait, wait! Master Dalvin?" Owain blurted.

"Tell them to spare me!" wailed the cowering man.

I raised a brow at Owain, who nodded. "We need a moment to talk to him," I said to the pack, and Ari echoed what I said with a series of clicks and twitters. The alpha nodded and sat on his haunches, his fire flickering around him like an impatient halo.

"How many people are you experimenting on here?" I demanded, coming forward to stand over Dalvin. He'd barely uncurled from his cower, his fine sapphire robes smudged around him. Blood was smeared around where he must've fallen and dragged himself to the corner.

"T-three," he answered in a quavering voice. "And…five beasts."

I asked a few more questions to get an idea of where these innocents were, aware of the flames picking up speed in burning down our surroundings. I'd seen a series of large windows along the third floor, and at this rate, Ari would have to escape through one of them.

"I'll let you take care of getting him out," I said to Owain, already turning toward the stairs before he could argue. Ari followed me, stepping gingerly until his paws met stone. The pack took this as a cue to start up the staircase around us to continue their rampage.

I heard the howls before we cleared the landing for the second floor. *"The pack found their packmates,"* Ari reported.

According to the man Owain had known, there was one unstable person per level, and all of the battle beasts were penned in the same section of the second floor. I left Ari in the stone stairwell and braved the smoke-filled hall, finding the pack pacing around the area as Dalvin described it.

Half of the second floor was one long room lined in stone. There were five battle beasts chained to the wall, though one was barely the size of a housecat. That must be the alpha's pup, its eyes still baby blue and too big for its face as it whimpered and pulled at the slack of the chains fastened to its collar.

There was no fire here. All of the battle beasts were extinguished and unable to summon up a flame, even with their hackles fully lifted. A few chewed on the chains that kept their packmates secured, to no avail. Several of the beasts turned my way when I walked in, clear emotion in their canine expressions. They'd also already killed the Tulari who'd been in this room when they'd arrived. There were the remnants of charred wands and a single blackened staff amongst them.

That was pack justice at work, all right. Even if I'd arrived in time to try advocating for them, I didn't think the pack would spare anyone who was directly experimenting on their packmates. "Let me see if they have a key," I suggested, starting to bend toward the closest corpse with a poorly hidden cringe.

A snout nudged my hand away. It was the alpha, growling at me. His hot mouth fastened to my wrist, and I held my breath, sure I was about to lose that limb. Yet with all the gentleness of a guide dog, he tugged me toward a series of cabinets that lined the back of the room and pressed my fingers to the knob of one.

He released me and woofed, and one of the chained beasts barked in reply. I held very still as the alpha took my wrist in his mouth again and lifted up, bracing his front paws on the wall and guiding me toward opening the top cabinet. "Okay, in here," I murmured, pushing around several jars of unidentifiable herbs and carefully placing aside the sharp points of syringes carelessly discarded amongst the jars.

I found the edge of something small and irregularly shaped. It was a tarnished key, and I took it toward the chained beasts, kneeling before the first one and looking for a lock on its collar.

"Just to let you know," Ari interjected into my thoughts. *"Terrance and I are taking away the unstable Tulari on this floor. He's not Zizi, and I'm not going to be able to come back inside."*

"Okay," I replied, distracted.

So, Zizi was on the third floor. I should've expected that. What I didn't anticipate was that there would be no lock on this poor battle beast's collar at all. It was a smooth circle of metal, save for where it looped into the chains securing it in place. The beast bore a chafed ring of raw flesh around the metal and several furless scars in its neck and chest. It opened a wound in its neck straining toward me, brushing the key I held against its collar.

The metal sprang open, and the beast whined, licking my cheek in thanks. "You're all right," I murmured, pulling my hands away from it as it paced around me to barrel into its packmates, tail wagging frantically. I had no idea how the touch of the key had freed it, but it was obviously magical of its own right. I unlocked the remaining collars and watched as the alpha knocked over his pup with an enthusiastic nuzzle.

The largest of the freed battle beasts licked the pup and brushed against the alpha. She was also heavily scarred and growled toward her pack before she howled hard, the screeching wail echoing in the room. They all joined in like a chorus of ghosts, including the little pup.

"There's one more person we have to rescue," I said, drawing a pack's worth of crimson eyes to turn my way. The alpha woofed and trotted for the door.

It was Fleetclaw that approached me as the pack followed the alpha, rushing out of the containment room in a crush of bodies. Most of them ignited the moment they were outside the threshold.

Fleetclaw met my eyes and turned, lowering himself to the ground. He looked at me expectantly, and I'd seen that over-the-shoulder expression enough times to guess what he wanted. "Are you sure?" I asked.

He dipped his head and waited as I slung my leg over his back. He stood and let me adjust, my fingers digging into his thick pelt to hang on. "Just don't set me on fire," I said nervously. The spikes along his spine were flat as he trotted, testing my hold, before dashing out the door behind his pack and into what could only be one of the hells from the all-encompassing heat and smoke.

The building was still burning while we took our interlude freeing his packmates. Fleetclaw kept the flames off me somehow as we dashed for the stairwell. It seemed the fire curved away from him, or he was lifted far enough off the ground to keep me from the worst of it. Either way, I ducked over his neck as he climbed the stairs with speed, skidding on his long claws around every sharp turn.

The third floor was the most lavish by far, though the soft rugs and expensive-looking art on the walls were quickly catching fire in the wake of the full might of Fleetclaw's pack. He barely slowed, nose to the ground, before stopping before one of the few doorways still closed on this level. Giving his body a little shake, he barked over his shoulder at me.

"Thank you," I said sincerely, half-falling off his back. I

tried the door, and as it opened, my nose was filled with the scent of burned flesh and hair. *Yuck.* There was no fire in this room yet, but this particular smell lingered anyway.

Zizi was seated in a throne-like chair in the center of the room, right underneath a squared vent in the ceiling. It appeared that she was living here, with a cot and chamber pot to one side of the room, and shelves of bottled herbs, tonics, and healer's tools closest to the door. Two large windows overlooked the woods.

"Zizi?" I breathed, taking her in head to toe. Her head was lolled back, but she opened her eyelids to regard me with dulled eyes and a hesitant tilt of her mouth. There was no fire magic in her, judging by the darkening of her mark.

Her golden-toned skin was stained with soot, and her forehead with the sheen of sweat that had some coal-black ringlets sticking to her. Her brush with fire had reduced her shoulder-length hair to a haphazard few inches in patches, with half-healed burn wounds showing on her scalp, cheek, neck, and arms where they weren't covered by a charcoal-colored tunic.

"Five wonders." Her voice was a dry croak. "It's Sivana. Or another dream."

"It's really me," I said. "I'm here to save you." I didn't dare touch her, not with those burns, undoubtedly the source of the smell in this room.

She coughed out what could've been a laugh. "I prayed to all the gods that you would come. One of them listened," she whispered. "Probably the shiny gryphon."

"Glorium answers every time, if you remember him," I agreed.

Fleetclaw woofed impatiently from where he stood guard by the door.

I muttered a curse. We had to get Zizi out of here, no matter how many burns she had. I knew they were fresh from experience—she healed even the worst self-inflicted burn wounds in less than a day, and judging by the way the bubbled skin was closing over, somehow, she'd been induced to hurt herself recently.

A tiny smile lifted the corners of her lips. "Can we leave? Just...don't take off the restraints." She struggled to lift her wrists. A pair of metal shackles circled them both but were not connected by any chain or strand. Still, they reminded me of the collars that'd been used to restrain the battle beasts, and I patted my pockets, realizing I'd set the key I'd used on the collars aside in our haste to come up here.

"If you value your friend's life, you'd leave them on." I whipped around at the unfamiliar woman's voice sounding behind me. Fleetclaw growled at her sudden appearance while I reached for my sword.

She was a Tulari, her mark an unusually bright green. I took in the wrinkles marking her pale skin as middle-aged and the impression of her dark hair before my gaze was snared in hers. It was like she'd frozen me in place the moment our eyes met. Hers glowed a color similar to her mark, pupils thinned like a serpent's. "Sivana the Wild, Hero of Altare," she breathed, walking forward and reaching for my face. Her sharped fingernails ghosted over my cheek with a wave of tingles.

Zizi struggled to lift herself in the chair. "Leave my friend alone," she rasped.

"Oh, it's a little late for that. I'll hold her here until her body goes up in flames with the rest of my organization," the Tulari said with a sniff.

I tried to work my jaw, which was numb. Fear tickled its way through my insides, gripping my heart from within with a wave of anxiety. Could she do that? Would anyone be able to save me if she'd somehow locked up my muscles—

"Sivana? What's going on?" Ari asked. His concern pushed its way through the morass of fear threatening to overwhelm me.

"Make no mistake. You may have killed a few of my people, but you will pay for each one in blood even after your passing," the woman continued. "Beginning with your brother. He attends *my* school, after all."

Igniting fire sizzled nearby before it was spat toward the ceiling. I was aware of a sound like glass cracking, and then the magic holding me faded abruptly. My arms went limp like jelly, and I swayed on my feet, blinking away afterimages of the green-eyed woman, who'd disappeared like she'd never been there.

"It was just a projection. She never comes in person," Zizi murmured, gesturing to the remnants of what looked like a small magelight melting in a swathe of flame. Fleetclaw growled again in a deep roll like thunder.

"*Sivana?*" Ari demanded again.

I shook myself off. Now wasn't the time to linger, not even for the threatening projection of that woman. The temperature in the room was rising, and the hallway was likely impassable. The battle beasts were no longer howling anywhere nearby, suggesting they'd already left. "We need to get out of here now," I said, going to one of the windows. When it was obvious they didn't open, I broke the wide bottom pane of one with the hilt of my sword and signaled to Ari mentally.

While he made the flight around the building, I turned to Fleetclaw. "Can you get yourself out of here alone?" I asked. He bobbed his head, then looked at Zizi. "I'm taking her with me."

He barked uncertainly, shifting on his paws as he watched me try to heft her limp weight. She was always a small person, and that'd only gotten worse under the "care" of these mages. Fleetclaw helped me support her as I dragged her toward the jagged exit I made. I spotted Ari flying uncertainly several yards below us, his wingtip scraping the edge of the building.

The moment I found him, the Link between us solidified until he was seeing through my eyes. He sent a familiar pulse of disorientation toward me, as he rarely flew without me, and it was even stranger for him to see himself from above like this. I muffled a cough in my shoulder, sweating even by this open threshold to the cool air outside as smoke streamed out of the broken window.

It took Ari several agonizing minutes to circle up and around until he was slowly flying past the window. I nodded to Fleetclaw and jumped out of the window, dragging Zizi along with me. Glass scraped wounds down my back, but it was worth it when my feet found the stirrups on Ari's saddle out of old muscle memory. I held on to Zizi tightly with both arms and Ari's solid body with my legs, and we hurtled through the sky together.

Ari wheeled around to land on some of the only untouched grass left. The building was burning inside and out and starting to collapse judging by the heavy crashes I could hear. "Sivana! Have you seen Owain?" Nate shouted as soon as Ari's talons skidded and found purchase in the ground, nearly unseating Zizi and I with the abrupt landing.

"No? Last I saw him, he was with a man he recognized. We'd spared him from the pack. and Owain was going to walk him out," I said, wracking my brain for the man's name. "He called him Master…something."

Nate paled. He'd come up as close to Ari's side as he dared, looking up at me. "Master Dalvin?" he suggested.

"Yes! That was it," I said, frowning when his face fell. "Why?"

"There were a few Tulari who escaped out of the windows and back exit. They ran into the Morphos Woods to get away from the battle beasts," he said slowly, drawing a hand down the side of his face. "Master Dalvin was one of them. He's one of our teachers."

There was a sinking feeling in my gut. I dismounted from

Ari and had Nate help me tie Zizi to his saddle, bracing her weight on his shoulders. "And you haven't seen Owain since?" I asked.

"No," he sighed.

I took a deep breath and turned back toward the burning building. The battle beasts were mostly gone at this point, shaking off the flames in their fur and paws and leaving through the hole in the wards. Fleetclaw was amongst the last to leave, but he slowed as he saw us standing there. "Can you do me one more favor?" I asked him, earning a snort accompanied by a curl of smoke.

He listened as I described Owain and where I'd seen him last. He barked to one of the other battle beasts, who turned. They beckoned for us to follow, and it was the second battle beast who led us to the body. *"She says they watched him take a wounded man out of the back door,"* Ari translated grimly as Nate and I gaped.

Owain had landed on his back, empty eyes staring up at the sky while he held a wound in his middle. Blood marked his fingers and the grass around him.

I approached his body with a sick lurch in my stomach. *"He's...he died."*

"The limping man turned on him, along with several of the other fleeing Tulari," Ari translated.

With shaking fingertips, I lowered Owain's eyelids. His weight shifted...it was Nate straightening his limbs. He took Owain's wand and tucked it away. "Meet the Gatekeeper with pride," he murmured. His eyes were glassy with shock, and I knew I wasn't in much better shape.

I took in a dry swallow, my throat clicking. "Gods, Nate. I'm so sorry...I...he..." I stammered. "I thought he'd be okay..."

Nate shook his head, getting to his feet. "We can't stay here. There might still be more like our...teacher, waiting to kill us."

Fleetclaw barked, drawing our attention. *"They're offering to give him a warrior's funeral,"* Ari translated.

I knew what that was, but I doubted Nate did. It was an old honor, to have one's body incinerated by a battle beast on the field of war. Better that than have it exposed for the carrion birds.

"Nate, we can't take him with us...so, the beasts want to cremate him." It felt terrible to tell him this and see the whitening along his face as the necessity of it sank in.

"It's better than just leaving him here," he muttered.

Ari translated the sentiment back to the battle beasts. Fleetclaw lifted his paw and made a gesture for us to step away. I helped guide Ari back as Fleetclaw ignited and opened his mouth, drawing in air to fuel the inferno at the back of his throat. We didn't look away as the fire began to consume Owain's body.

Nate turned away first. "C'mon," he muttered. We raced to leave this place behind through the same doorway we'd entered. He pulled his wand out and was touching the spell he'd woven with Owain, making it disintegrate until the flaming ruin of the House of the Unstable was hidden away.

"Nate..." I was trying to say, finding the words hard to utter past a tongue that felt too swollen.

He held up his hand. "Don't. Just...save it for now," he murmured, head bowed. "We have to figure out what to do next. And we can talk about it later. Or never. Maybe...maybe never."

CHAPTER 18

WEST WINDS

The battle beasts insisted on carrying us to their pack grounds as the sun set and visibility grew poor in the deepest reaches of the forest. I rode on Ari's back, keeping Zizi's unconscious form upright in front of me. He was not as nimble as the beasts in their natural territory, but Fleetclaw and a couple others helped guide him around and over obstructions.

"They want to celebrate," Ari told me.

The mood amongst the battle beasts did seem merry. Those pack members unburdened by a mage were yipping and jumping around, the very youngest flaring up along their backs, only to extinguish from a stern bark from their elders. I watched them take care of any fire they accidentally started, rolling over the embers or patting them out of existence with their broad paws.

Nate had said nothing during this time, struggling to stay seated on his appointed beast. Terrance was more of a natural. He was holding up the rear, working what spells he could on the other two unconscious unstable mages we'd spirited away with us. They were both men, one significantly older than the other, and also pyromancers with little sign of lingering magic within them. Like Zizi, we'd taken them away with shackles still secured on their wrists.

"With us?" I asked belatedly, realizing I'd drifted off into my own thoughts.

"Kind of?" he hedged. *"The alpha couple wants to take us to a safe place after we helped them. The female—her name is Ember-moon—has been talking about what their experience in captivity was like..."*

"Well?" I prompted when he drifted off.

I rarely had the feeling that Ari was trying to withhold his thoughts or emotions, but there was a barrier between us now, holding our minds separate over our Link.

"It's been a long day. I think Zizi should tell you when she wakes up," he said.

I worked my throat, taking a dry swallow. Fatigue had my shoulders slumping, like I'd only just remembered everything we'd been through. Ari might've been trying to delay some difficult information, but I could accept that he was trying to protect me for a little while longer.

"Okay, I'll wait," I said.

The great drum of Ari's chest heaved with relief. He carried me through the fall of full dark until the pack finally stopped in a clearing that smelled of wood smoke and cooked meat. Terrance and I expanded a pit the beasts had already dug and stacked wood for a fire. One of the beasts lit it, revealing an expanse of crisped grass and the remains of a few trees reduced to charred stumps.

We used Ari's saddlebags as pillows for the three uncon-scious Tulari, placing them as close to the fire as we could. Ari draped himself over Zizi's legs, her body seeming all the slighter when compared to his bulk.

"The battle beasts want us to remain here and relax. Some of them are hunting for the pack, and they intend to share the meat with us," I said, repeating Ari's translation after he shared a few quick words with the alpha male.

His mate, Embermoon, settled by the fire close to him and watched the remaining pack members fan out. Some rested, others continued their play, and I noticed a few of the larger beasts fanned out to keep watch at the tree line.

"Relax," Nate repeated in a mutter. The fire reflected the glassiness that sheened his eyes.

I nodded in understanding but sat cross-legged next to my friend and gryphon, watching him and waiting.

"How can I relax when I have to go back to the Tulari Academy tomorrow and tell them how…" Nate drifted off with a hitch of his breath.

A flare of protectiveness rose in me. "You're not going back," I said firmly.

He refocused his gaze on me with a look like I'd sprouted rozash scales. "It's my *home*. I've been there longer than you've lived with the gryphons. I have to tell someone that one of the teachers…that he…" He turned away, his shoulders curving with a sob.

My hand trembled as I reached out to rest it on his shoulder. I recognized the mix of adrenaline and fatigue within me that rattled me to the bone and kept me shaking well past the moment it was needed. It meant sleep would be impossible, even though it was sorely needed.

"You have to stay away from there. I'm sorry, Nate. I'm sorry that he's gone," I said.

He shrugged me off, turning away further. "Someone has to bring Master Dalvin to justice for what he did," he muttered.

"You don't understand. Hells, I don't think I fully understand," I sighed. "When I was rescuing Zizi, there was this woman. Projection?" I shivered with a glaze of chill bumps over my skin at the recollection of her.

In my mind's eye, the woman wasn't frightening. She'd been average in appearance, except for her bright green Tulari mark and bewitching eyes. As I told Nate, and soon Terrance as well, about the meeting with her, I saw his skepticism when I described how fearful she'd made me as she gazed into my eyes and froze me, even as a projection.

My lips were numb with remembered fear as I repeated her parting threat: that I would pay for what I'd done in blood, starting with my brother. "He attends *my* school, after all," I repeated with the same emphasis she'd used.

Nate exchanged a glance with his friend. "I've never seen someone who looks like that woman," he said, lifting his chin stubbornly.

"Yet she was powerful enough to work magic on Sivana, even from a projection," Terrance pointed out.

"Is that difficult to do?" I asked.

They made sounds of agreement. "It suggests she's crafter-class," Terrance said. "Most of the administrators and the headmistress are all crafter-class. When you've got a certain amount of power, you've got the choice to join the military, become a creator of magical items, or stay at the Academy to continue learning and growing your magic."

"The mages who stay have a certain personality," Nate added a little reluctantly.

"Most of them act like they are far superior to the less gifted Tulari like Nate and me," Terrance explained. "Like the woman you spoke to and..." He glanced toward my brother, who'd pressed his lips together tightly. "And our former teacher, Master Dalvin."

"We have to go back. We have to expose him," Nate muttered.

"This woman was clearly not acting alone. If you go back and try to raise the hells, you're going to be a target," I warned.

"But Owain—"

I shook my head. "No. Until you know who was working with Dalvin, we have to speak with people we know we can trust, which doesn't include anyone at that school."

Vulnerability shaded his face as he asked, "But where will we go?"

A bark preceded my answer, startling us. Embermoon was getting to her paws, nudging Ari, who'd fallen asleep while we spoke. He snorted and twittered sleepily, translating what she wanted to share. *"She says they can stay with the West Wind Pack."*

As I repeated this aloud, Nate's jaw dropped.

"She wants to take the unstable Tulari to see a trusted friend who might be able to remove the magical restraints on them. It sounds like she has a better idea of what they are than we do," he continued.

Terrance started to nod as I repeated this dutifully as well. "Where is this friend?" he asked.

"A run of two moons, atop a hill where only he dwells," I repeated, then shot Ari and Embermoon a confused look.

The battle beast tilted her head, like she didn't realize what she'd said was unusual. *"It's at the tip of their territory opposite of where we are now,"* Ari added after a moment.

"Two moons...two months?" Terrance guessed.

"Perhaps three since the pack has pups now," Ari said. *"She says her other packmates are wounded from their experience in the House of the Unstable as well. They will need extra help to survive the winter."*

"Surely the battle beasts will get tired of us before we travel with them for two months," Nate pointed out.

Terrance elbowed him. "You have a better idea? I got a look at those shackles and don't recognize half the runes on them. There's got to be a proper way to open them, but it'll take a talented Tulari to do it." Nate's face fell as Terrance emphasized, "A master wizard, if not a crafter-class one."

"I'm close to making my all-key. Maybe…" Nate shook his head. "Ah, who am I kidding? If I tried to open those shackles, I could really hurt the unstable. But if we are going with the battle beasts, we need to have a way to talk to them."

Embermoon woofed, clearly shaking her head *no*. "*She doesn't think there will be a problem with that,*" Ari said with a sleepy chuckle. He sat up slowly, turning his head to the side. His belly grumbled audibly. "*Smells like dinner.*"

A trio of battle beasts dragged the fresh carcass of a deer toward the fire. "Dinner," I echoed. Amusement roused in the recesses of my mind at the dismayed look Nate and Terrance shared. They'd have to get over that pampered mage squeamishness if they were going to stay with the West Wind Pack.

I'D TURNED in for the night in the closest spot to the fire, with my cloak serving as a makeshift blanket. Sleep didn't come easily and faded away in a greasy film when Ari prodded my consciousness. I opened my eyes and sat up, seeing him edging up the line of Zizi's body to lay his feathered cheek in her palm. Her fingers curled weakly.

"Zizi?" I whispered, aware of the whole pack of sleeping battle beasts around us.

"Is that you, Sivana? Or another dream?" she asked in a dry croak.

I went to retrieve a canteen and returned to her side. "It's really me. Here, drink," I said. Her eyelids were tightly shut, but she gulped down the water I tipped into her mouth. She drank down most of my water supply before finally stirring with a groan, stretching ever so slowly and taking a cautious peek from between her lashes.

"That was real," she murmured. "You burned down the House of the Unstable."

"Technically, the battle beasts did. We rested with the pack last night," I said.

"Smells like it." She breathed a laugh. "And this must be Ari." She curled her fingers further into his neck and pet the curve of his head, smiling when he murred at her. "Hey, buddy. I missed you too."

They cuddled while I eased the saddlebag out from under her enough to search within it. The beasts had efficiently gobbled down every scrap of meat we hadn't eaten, but I had a few pieces from yesterday's breakfast to feed her one nibble at a time. She regained her energy slowly, with no hint of fire in her Tulari mark or eyes. I suspected the shackles she wore were affecting her magic.

My encounter with her tormentor still haunted me. Zizi had asked to keep these shackles on, and the projection had echoed with, *"If you value your friend's life, you'd leave them on."*

We may have gotten her out of danger, but she was still carrying unknown magic on her person. She'd sat up and rested one of her hands on her knee. I inspected the loops of runes engraved in the metal around her wrist where it caught the light, unable to make sense of what I was seeing.

"They're protection," Zizi said quietly. My gaze flicked back to her face, where she'd followed where I was looking. "Suppressors, to keep my magic in check."

"We have to get them off of you," I said.

She shuddered, curling herself closer to Ari's solid body. "That's okay. I can live without my magic."

I bit my lip to keep from arguing with her. I'd seen the waves and crests of her magic firsthand, how she had a kind of manic energy at full strength, laughing and delighted by the destruction her fire could create. At her lowest, she was sluggish and dull, looking like she needed a week of solid rest to recover. That kind of fatigue was what I saw in her now.

"I *can*," she said defensively. "You…you probably don't know what happened after the end of the war."

"I heard you held Starfall," I said.

She nodded, her lips pressing together tightly. "Did someone tell you I lost control of my magic? I'm sure that's what it looked like."

"Why don't you tell me what really happened?" I invited.

Her gaze drifted somewhere off my shoulder, pain flickering over her expression. "No one else will believe this," she said, refocusing on Ari. He made a soft croak, nudging her hand encouragingly. "I was called in to hold Starfall and prove that I am the rightful owner of its corerune. The king and the Tulari Council were there to watch as *Irene* presented me with the weapon."

She spoke her old enemy's name with hatred between her gritted teeth, and for good reason. Irene Merriweather had used the intense fire magic within Starfall to masquerade as a dual-blessed battlemage and earned the title of Hero of Altare for her efforts. In the meantime, Zizi had spent her childhood trying to control her crafter-class fire magic without the proper tools, thus rendering her unstable.

"Then what happened?" I asked with the sinking feeling of dread.

"I held my corerune. For a moment, my magic was complete." Her teeth glimmered white as she grinned from the memory. It turned to a grimace as she fisted her free hand. "Then someone from the Tulari Council tainted the transfer somehow. I felt a gust of wind around me, and it fed my fire. What had been under control became an inferno instantly, and it consumed me."

"I'm sor—"

"And you want to know what Irene did?" she interrupted. "She laughed! The last thing I remember is the crackle of flames and that *laugh* hidden underneath."

Her face reddened, eyes bugging wide. "I spent an age in that place because of her. While she walked away with my magic, I went to the House of the Unstable to be experimented on like some…some rat!"

A soft growl drew my attention from her. "Zizi," I said in a warning tone, but she was finally, truly awake, roused to the reality of what'd happened to her.

"They tried to take my magic," she said loudly, shaking a shackled fist. "*Permanently*. It's not good enough that one of them stole my corerune. They wanted all of me. Every last ember and curl of ash!"

The battle beasts stirred, many growling their irritation at the sudden wakeup. The one that approached Zizi was Embermoon, and she didn't stop until she was nose to nose with Zizi. Her rant cut off with a startled yelp.

Then Embermoon licked her, bathing her face like any domestic dog. Zizi cringed in surprise until the battle beast's tongue laved over the Tulari mark on her cheek. The mark flared with orange light.

"*Are they Linking?*" I asked Ari, twitching with uncertainty.

"*No*," he answered. He watched the interaction through my eyes, feeling more confident about it than I did. Embermoon backed away a few steps, woofing quietly.

Ari translated, and I said, "She wants you to know that she heard your screams and understands your pain. Until you're free from your restraints, she will share her fire with you."

I expected her to repeat her desire to have the shackles stay in place, but with new energy, she glared down at them. "The sooner we get these things off me, the better," she spat. "It's coming back to me now…and I remember you, too. You're the battle beast with the puppies. Where…?"

Embermoon whined. She shifted to the side to reveal her child, who fastened itself back to her side.

"Oh," she murmured. Zizi reached out and petted Embermoon without fear, ruffling the thick fur up her neck and behind her ears. The battle beast settled close to her, displacing Ari, who stepped over Zizi's legs and rested next to me instead.

Nate and Terrance were also awake by this point, and my brother joined us while the healer checked the two still-unconscious unstable men. Terrance had a grim expression by the time he sat too. We had a round of introductions before Zizi painstakingly told us what she could, with Ari's help in translating what Embermoon wanted to add.

"As I said…I, err, we were part of an experiment," Zizi sighed. "There were several Tulari who came and went with different techniques, but they were all trying to do the same thing. Permanently remove fire magic from us to house it in someone else's body."

Terrance clucked his tongue. Nate paled significantly.

"Is that possible?" I asked, rubbing a chill from my arms.

"No," Nate answered first.

"I didn't think so, but maybe," Zizi added a breath later, quirking her lips with a glance in my brother's direction. "Apparently, it's possible with healer and wizard magic. But pyromancy is different…*fire* is different, harder to control and tame."

Embermoon barked, and I served as her mouthpiece. "This group of mages expanded their experiment to include battle beasts, thinking a different source of fire magic might be easier to steal. They…" I broke off, not wanting to say this last part, but she stared at me with those crimson eyes until I managed it. "They killed two of her pups by taking the fire from their bodies, thinking a younger, smaller flame might take to a mage."

The West Wind Pack rumbled dangerously around us. "*If they could kill the mages again, they would,*" Ari said, translating what I'd innately felt from their anger.

"But…why?" Nate asked. "Why twist Lord Orion's blessing in such a way?"

Zizi's laugh was distinctly sarcastic. "Why settle for anything less than everything he can offer, no matter the cost?" she countered. "Their leader thought no one would miss me or the other unstable pyromancers they were experimenting on. And no one knew they were trapping and doing the same to battle beasts. But…she was wrong. You all came for us." She smiled my way, but I could tell it was forced.

What shadows swirled behind her eyes? What insecurities had taken deeper root, considering how long it'd taken for me to realize she was missing?

"I'm sorry it couldn't have been sooner," I said. I cleared my throat, worried I'd get choked up. "I-I want you to come live with me at Fortress Aerie. No harm can come to you. You'll be protected by the might of Wild Flight."

Embermoon growled. *"The pack still wants to take her to their trusted mage,"* Ari reminded me.

With a sigh, I helped Embermoon translate her offer to Zizi since the other two mages present knew about it. "If they trust this person, so do I," she said. "I don't mind that it will take a while. These battle beasts…they feel like kin after what we've been through together. Maybe I can go to Fortress Aerie someday, but not yet. Not while the mage community has this power-grabbing illness festering within it.

"I'm afraid the leader of this group is much more powerful than she seems. This could be one of many operations of hers. Every time she would project herself in to watch us get experimented on, the mages…they'd call her *Madam Morashi.*"

Zizi paused, and the other two Tulari gasped in her silence. I glanced between them, eyebrow rising. There was some obvious significance I was missing.

"That's the name of a legend," Nate told me. "The kind of bedtime story to keep little Tulari in their beds after dark."

Terrance looked a little skeptical but added, "She has impossible abilities, so I wouldn't worry too much. This is probably an imposter wearing the name to scare her people to secrecy."

"It makes sense, though," Nate said in an arguing tone. "Morashi is known for two things, and isn't stealing life force the same thing as stealing magic from others?"

"Not even close," Terrance muttered. "Two fantastical ideas, anyway. Tulari are born only able to do certain things."

I looked to Zizi for some explanation instead. "I think it really was her," she said. "The legend goes like this… Morashi is ancient because she keeps herself young by stealing the life from others. Children are her favorite. Their youth tastes good. Most Tulari don't believe she exists since her rumored abilities are so far against what Lord Orion would accept. But…" She lifted a shoulder in a tired shrug. "Lord Orion clearly doesn't care about us."

"Zizi!" I exclaimed, shocked.

"If he cared, he would've never allowed my corerune to be stolen," she said woodenly. "If he cared…I would've never had my magic experimented on. So, she does exist, and we met her. She steals life and magic, and once I'm free from her shackles, I'm coming for her. And for *Irene*." Zizi bared her teeth angrily. "I'm done trying to do things the right way. It's time I had my revenge."

I recognized that a younger, more idealistic version of myself would've tried to lead my friend from declaring vengeance. But what could I say? She'd done everything right, and in return, it'd gotten her corerune taken and her magic experimented on. She had every right to be furious and to reduce her enemies to cinders.

"You're going with the battle beasts?" I asked for confirmation.

"Yeah."

"Us too," Nate said after a glance toward Terrance, who nodded.

"Once you're free of those shackles…write to me. You're

not alone," I said. Ari made a croak of agreement. "We'll get your revenge. We'll do it together, even."

Nate murmured agreement, watching with me as Zizi's more genuine smile split her face. It stretched a little too far, betraying her unstable nature alongside the eager flare of orange within her eyes. "I can't wait to watch them burn," she sing-songed.

CHAPTER 19

FENWAY

I RETURNED to the Gryphon Rider Academy with mixed emotions. Everyone, from the pack to the Tulari, wanted Ari and me to leave them to travel together rather than having an individual fly ahead with us. I felt like I was abandoning my brother and friend to the wolves…more literally than figuratively.

"I don't know of a place safer than the heart of a battle beast pack," Ari said. *"Besides, we have our own problems to contend with."*

Our own problems? All I could think of was our adventure and Zizi…then it hit me. *"The new Paragon!"* I exclaimed. *"Oh, gods. Do you think Hughes is still okay?"*

"Probably. Do you think the king has contained the Kaiamear Gazette*?"*

"I hope so," I sighed. The blasphemous rumors that Prince Isaac wasn't dead would only turn folk against each other. As I'd promised Mateo, I'd set aside my worries and assumed the Crown's men had it handled.

"I'm more concerned that the king will notice Mireille and her rider have disappeared," he said.

I projected the mental equivalent of a shrug. Sure, it was a concern, but it didn't even make my top ten worries as I watched the details of Fortress Aerie sharpen as we neared it. The king seemed to have eyes and ears everywhere, so he was bound to realize that Acton was impersonating Mateo's correspondence. I'd been on the receiving end of King Cortes's anger many times, so I was willing to take a dressing down if it meant my friend and his gryphon could make the incredibly important journey north without worry.

"Well, if you're not going to agonize about that, I'm taking you straight to my mate and chick," he said. He tilted his wings, taking us past the fortress and out into the wilderness where Wild Flight roosted. For once, he didn't need me to guide him at all. He drew on his mating Link to locate Sunset where she rested in a nest of dried grass.

We shaded our Link with the ease of practice to give him privacy to share a moment of affection with her. Novali made a complaining twitter and squeezed out from under her mother, bounding toward me.

I scooped her up, snuggling her happily. "Hi, baby. Oof. You're getting so heavy!" I pretended that she was three times her weight, sagging with her in my hold. She giggled, projecting childish affection for me and hooking her front talons over my shoulder.

"Sivvy," she said clearly. *"Sivvy!"*

I looked down at her fluffy red self with astonishment. When had her mind rearranged from a baby's babble into a word I could understand? "You're growing up too fast. Stop that," I said gently, and kissed the top of her head. She was about the size of a hunting dog, approaching too big to hold in the crook of my arm.

"Sivvy Sivvy Sivvy," she replied, joyful.

We weren't alone for too long, news of our arrival echoing from gryphon to gryphon. Puzzlebox reached us first, her beak parted happily. *"Hi! Where have you been?"* she asked.

"I had to help a friend," I answered. I adjusted my hold on

Novali and placed my free arm around Puzzlebox's neck in a loose hug.

She shuffled her front paws and looked over her shoulder. Her mental presence shrank in my mind, like she was whispering. *"You should help Noah too."*

My attention sharpened. *"Did something happen while I was gone?"*

"Nooo…I mean, kind of," she hedged. *"It's his sire."*

I recoiled from Puzzlebox, dropping my arm to my side. Ari and Sunset froze, growls rising from their throats, and Novali whined, her ears pinning down. Unlike with human speech, where inflection suggested what someone thought of what they were saying, the words I understood from her gryphon speech were colored by emotion, images, and memories.

When Novali said "Sivvy," I experienced a shred of the love and security she felt with her human auntie.

When Puzzlebox said "sire," she'd projected a muddy impression like she shared secondhand memories of Sharde's pain. An upraised voice, the sting of a blow across the face. "Bailiff Sharde," I said aloud, just to infuse the words with proper contempt.

Puzzlebox cocked her head to the side at a painful angle, and I changed to mind speech where she understood me better. *"Sharde's…father. He is the bailiff of Fenway, the town close to Fortress Aerie. My mother's been trying to establish shrines to the gods in Fenway, but he's been blocking her."*

I felt Puzzlebox's understanding; she already knew this. She took me to Sharde, leaving me to say goodbye to Ari and Sunset so they could have some time together. I cradled Novali upside down as I walked, petting her silky belly fur. The youngling was half asleep by the time we entered the stable and found Sharde painstakingly picking burrs out of a different youngling's coat. A pair of adults crowded the stall, watching him closely.

"Finally," he said, barely looking up as Puzzlebox and I paused right outside the stall door. "Take your job back, Lieutenant Walker. I don't want it ever."

"Anything to report, Lieutenant Sharde?" I asked.

"It's not like I can understand gryphon speech, but I have the impression that Valtora and her mate are less than impressed with me." He continued combing and picking with a steady hand. "Same with grandma gryphon and the rest. Which is a problem, because Paragon Brekwell did a walk-through while you were gone."

I sputtered, my heart leaping straight to my throat. "W-what?" I choked out.

"His first order of action." Finally, he put the comb down and looked my way, pulling a grimace. "The princeling handled him and explained your absence away as you taking an extra day off to visit with your sister in Kaiamear."

I felt a sudden knot of guilt. As busy as I'd been, I hadn't thought to venture down Temple Row to see Rissa. *Next time I'm in Kaiamear,* I vowed. I blew out a slow breath. "Okay, that could be worse. What did Brekwell do here? Just tour the grounds and the fortress?" I asked.

Sharde stood and popped his neck before picking up the youngling he'd been attending to. "Off you go, Sadry. Careful now," he said in a cooing voice.

He edged past Puzzlebox and placed the little creature outside, where it bounded straight to where Alaula sat in the stable's shade. She greeted the youngling with a soft croak and a nuzzle that nearly staggered it. The elderly cloudling was in a playful mood, tumbling onto her back next to him to encourage him to pounce into her plush fur.

We returned to one of the less used stalls and sat on piles of hay. Puzzlebox crowded close to Sharde with a whine, draping herself across his lap. I still held Novali, who'd since fallen asleep cuddled to my chest. "Brekwell had an aide behind him the whole time he took his tour. Any time he wanted to take notes, he'd do this." Sharde put his nose in the air and then turned to glance over his shoulder. "The wild gryphons are lazing about. Instate exercise regimens," he said in a stuffy tone.

"He didn't," I murmured. That comment alone showed that Brekwell knew nothing about wild gryphons.

"He ended his walk in your father's office. They were in there for hours," he continued. He slouched and fiddled with his thumbnails. "I'm not important enough to know everything they talked about, but I can tell you that your father called me in to discuss..." He drifted off, shifting with discomfort.

I'd rarely seen Sharde so out of his element. Part of me wanted to rush to fill the silence, but if he was going to begin sharing his past, I knew he needed time. Even though he was one of my closest friends, he'd only mentioned Fenway and his father once to me, in telling the story of how he came to the fortress in the first place. It was a footnote in his history, a set of facts better left forgotten.

Until now, as he sat in quiet consideration. "There's no easy way to tell you this, so I'll just...Fenway, the town close to here," he said, suddenly speaking quickly. "Apparently, your mother has been trying to move in and establish herself as a religious leader. My father's been in opposition to her and took the time to write Brekwell about it."

"He...what?" I asked in shock.

"She won't take no for an answer, so he reached out to Brekwell himself. I know, it's insane," he said, his voice rising. "But he told Commandant Walker to get his wife in line."

"In line with *what*?" I was getting heated too.

He took a deep breath, visibly forcing himself to relax. "I'm getting ahead of myself. Sorry." He glanced down at Puzzlebox with an apology in his gaze and ruffled the fur around her ears. She peered back at him like he'd hung the moon, her liquid dark eyes full of affection.

I snuck a look at Novali, who was peacefully snoozing. One of her front paws twitched, and she chattered quietly, undoubtedly chasing prey in her dreams.

"My father wrote to Brekwell and signed the letter *Lord Fenway*," Sharde continued in a calmer tone. "Commandant Walker called me in to look at it, and I recognized the handwriting immediately."

"Wait…" I tried to arrange this revelation to make proper sense in my head.

"My father, the longstanding bailiff of Fenway, impersonated the owner of Fenway in a letter to the most powerful person in the corps," he said.

"You're sure? I mean, you haven't seen his handwriting in—"

"I never told you." He barked a cynical laugh. "He wrote me for the first time when he received word that I was graduating as a knight. It wasn't much. A congratulations on surviving and not being so useless. I gave it to your father to show him the handwriting was the same." Though he waved it off, I had the distinct feeling that he knew every word by heart. Especially if he'd kept such a mean-spirited message.

"Why would he forge Lord Fenway's signature, though?" I asked.

"I don't know, but your father's asked me to find out once you returned. And, look, you're back now. Which means—"

"We," I interjected. "*We* are going to find out."

"Have you seen yourself, Lieutenant Walker? I don't know anyone more distinctive than a red-haired, female gryphon rider. And this is Fenway, where everyone knows everyone," he said.

I fiddled with the end of my windblown braid for a moment, lips quirked in consideration. "So?" I said, channeling my inner Glorium.

"Everyone in Fenway is already going to know who you are," he argued.

I started to smile. "So?" I repeated. "I won't be alone. Leave this to me, and you won't have to be involved much at all. You'll never even have to see him, Noah. You can leave him in the past where he belongs."

There was a battle within him, judging by the jump of his muscles and the dart of his eyes. But he breathed out what sounded like a relieved sigh and said, "Thanks, Sivvy."

I LEFT Novali to rest with her mother and gathered up Ari to fly into the fortress. After I freshened myself up a bit, we reported to my father. The conversation took hours, between me giving my father an extra coating of gray hairs after describing the House of the Unstable and the horrific treatment of the captive unstable Tulari and battle beasts. It took a nudge from Valtora for him to acknowledge that he, too, would stand aside and allow the battle beast pack their revenge.

"I'm proud of you," said my fierce Skymother. I knew if anyone would approve of my actions, it would be her. I sent her a pulse of gratitude, and she replied with a wave of motherly affection back for Ari and me both.

"This is troubling news." Father tapped his quill on the parchment where he'd been taking notes. "And you missed a visit from Paragon Brekwell. He has stated that he will be back in a fortnight to watch the next monthly competition. We had best impress him, because he was quite unhappy with what he saw here a few days ago. That's all I will say on that subject for now.

"He was also rather rude concerning a matter with your mother. I would like your assistance with a covert investigation." Father clenched his jaw, a spark of rage flaring to life in his expression. I knew it well. Though he was slow to anger, one of the only ways to stoke the embers of his temper was through messing with Mother.

I told him what Sharde had shared with me, and he filled in the gaps. As Commandant, he was supposed to have a working relationship with Lord Fenway, but he'd never met the man in person. "Until now, I figured it was a side effect of how busy I've been filling old Jamison's shoes." He rubbed his bottom lip with a thoughtful look. "Perhaps it's nothing but the bailiff trying to step around his lord's will to see less of Talase. We won't know until someone is able to speak with him in person."

"I agree, Father. Leave it to me," I said.

He raised a brow. "Just you?"

"Well, you might see a few extra requests on your desk for leisure time," I said casually. "Make sure you approve them all."

CHAPTER 20

LEISURE TIME

It was evening by the time I spotted Acton leaving the mess hall. While I'd been finishing up planning with my father, most of the fortress had been eating dinner. Acton looked up when Ironfeather crowed happily upon seeing me, his surprised face lighting up the moment our eyes met.

My worries faded for a moment, my heart and step light. We met halfway, Acton grabbing and spinning me while I squealed a laugh. Once he set me back on my feet, we kissed. I would've taken longer than a moment to greet him, but Ironfeather muscled between us. *'You're back! Where's my hug?'* he asked with a twittery giggle.

"Hello to you too, sweet boy," I said, hugging him around his stout neck. He lifted one of his front paws and curled his talons around my lower back, pressing me closer.

"Acton missed you. A lot." He released me, his pelt fluffed happily. He trotted over to Ari and brushed against him with a friendly murr, tapping out a happy dance with his front talons.

"I missed him, too," I said, smiling fondly up at my intended.

While Acton and I walked arm in arm through the mess

hall so I could grab whatever was left over to eat, Ironfeather fell back into his role as Ari's seeing-eye gryphon and guided him behind us.

"What new adventure did I miss?" Acton asked. While his tone was light enough, his eyes betrayed something more serious as he looked me over head to toe.

"It's not quite a mess hall kind of conversation," I hedged. "Want to come up to my room out with Wild Flight?"

Acton agreed so quickly I nearly laughed. I bundled up my meal to take with me and flew with Ari back to the remote area where we'd placed the temporary barracks. We stored the gryphons' saddles and reins, and my gryphon nipped Ironfeather on the ear when he moved to follow us in. *"Come here. I want to show you something,"* he said, drawing the young gryphon aside.

"What is it?" Ironfeather laughed.

By the time he realized it, Acton and I were inside and sitting in different places in my small, temporary room. I sat at the desk and swept a pile of letters aside to inhale my dinner, and Acton propped himself on my cot, his boots resting by the door. He spoke first while I ate. "Mateo left to follow the Path of Glorium. I've been mimicking his hand in any correspondence he receives. I hope he and Mireille return sooner rather than later."

"It took me a couple months, and that was when it was the summer. They could be gone that long or even longer," I pointed out.

"Great," he said dryly. "Well, we're in luck for now. The king wants Mateo lying low while they search for the man who's been impersonating Prince Isaac."

"There's...an actual person pretending to be him?" I asked, shocked. "Do they need our help finding him?"

Acton smirked. "The king also included not to tell you any of this in his letter. The last thing he wants is for any of us to blunder into a Crown matter."

I huffed reluctant acceptance and picked through my mail while he updated me on how things had been at the academy while I was gone. Sharde had taught my daily class and given advice to my first-year flight. "No tricks or pranks?" I asked, feigning shock.

"Not a one," he replied, mirroring me. We dissolved into laughter quickly.

Other than Paragon Brekwell's visit, it sounded like things had been normal here. I took a moment to read a couple letters—one was from the now retired Paragon Hughes. I smiled with relief as I read that he was back on his feet and had settled in an estate in the foothills. He'd listened an address. *Come visit me if you can.*

It still felt like he had something important to tell me, probably about Brekwell. I folded the letter and placed it under a paperweight, making it stick out to serve as a reminder to reply and find time to fly out and see him.

The other letter was from Galak Nilessen, the fellow Hero of Altare I'd struck up a friendship with through the mail. I felt a little guilty, looking at the date and knowing he'd been waiting for a reply for a while. "Looks like they're working on..." I said, mumbling the rest.

"What was that?" Acton asked, flashing his teeth in a big smile.

"My...my statue," I said a little louder. All Heroes of Altare had their likeness immortalized in the Hall of Heroes. Nilessen reported that it was shaping up well and extended an invitation to me and any friends I wanted to bring to see it in person. It was the invitation and opening I was waiting for to get Sharde and Ellie to Kaiamear and a situation where he could take her on a date and finally propose to her.

Acton stood and took the letter from me, reading it with his smile only widening. "Your statue! Sivana the Wild, the fiercest girl and gryphon to ever be immortalized in marble. We *have* to go see this!" he exclaimed.

"Soon," I sighed. He seemed to catch my mood and set the letter aside, laying out with me as I went to rest on the cot. I reached for him, and he reached for me, the two of us snuggling together tightly while I told him the short version of saving Zizi and the problem ahead with Sharde's father.

Our foreheads were brushing, and the gold flecks in his eyes gleamed in the low light of the single lamp I had lit on my desk. While he didn't interrupt, I could tell he was disappointed that he wasn't there for the House of the Unstable. I wish I'd been able to bring him for the change of command. I needed him for the way he grounded me; plus, he and Ironfeather would've been another competent fighter and gryphon there to help.

He had a lot more to say about Sharde and his father when I explained what I knew. "I know something of this as well," he'd said. "A town the size of Fenway can reliably be run by three men: the lord, his steward, and the bailiff. It is quite interesting that the lord has disappeared."

"Why's that?" I breathed. My eyelids were heavy, lulled by the deep vibration of his voice.

"Think about it," he said. I was definitely not thinking all that hard, not when I was so comfortable and warm in his arms. My eyes closed, just to open a crack as he explained. "Of those three positions, one is hereditary. The other two are appointed. If the lord was infirm or dead, who would have the most to gain from hiding it?"

I answered with a sleepy mumble, drifting off. The last thing I remembered was the feeling of Acton's callused fingertips smoothing my hair behind my ear.

⁂

THE NEXT MORNING, I parted with Acton reluctantly. There were morning duties to attend to, but I wasn't going to skip breakfast in the mess hall. It'd be the best time to talk to our friends and tell them the beginnings of the plan I had for Fenway.

I helped distribute breakfast to a cranky set of gryphons alongside a quiet Sharde and a tired Lira. She told me everything she'd been doing while I was gone, mostly taking over the more basic tasks like grooming and feeding. "We need at least five of you. Are any of your siblings looking to become caretakers?" I joked.

Lira's lips turned down. "Well, my brother will be of age next year," she muttered.

Gods, if only I could grab what I'd just said and shoved it back into my mouth unheard. As the eldest Rudrick, Lira was going to be the only one of her family that was "too old" to attend the academy as a prospective rider.

"How are you doing?" I asked in a gentler tone.

She worked her jaw before putting on her usual humor-filled expression. "You know who I've gotten to accept massages lately? Roshawk. His scarring is extensive, but he's letting me try to loosen him up," she said.

My eyebrows rose toward my hairline. I knew she'd gotten to brush him down occasionally, but massages? Valtora had practically had to threaten him to let me work on his scars. "Really? How is that going?" I asked with a nervous laugh.

"No need to worry for my limbs. He seems to like it," she said cheerfully. She spoke of the specific muscle groups she was targeting with old familiarity, like she'd been a ghost seated in the back of my Anatomy and Physiology classes with Lord Gadric. On second thought, perhaps she had picked up a textbook in the years she'd been here, present but apart from the training of gryphon riders.

On a whim, I invited her to breakfast once we made sure Wild Flight had theirs. She accepted, and once we washed the smell of fish from our hands, she rode with me on

Sunset to the fortress since Ari was still resting off the last few days.

By the time we settled in the mess hall with our allotted breakfasts, the cadets had already rushed off to their classes. I preferred it that way, even if it meant that we had to lower our voices so we didn't fill the giant room with the echoes of our plotting.

It felt like old times, seated at a full table with my Kite Flight friends. Acton, Sharde, Biggs, Pereyra, Credell, and Ellie. Plus, we had Lira and my mother today. It was a little startling to have Mother draw the empty seat and slide in like she, too, was an honorary member, but she knew me well. She must've been waiting for this meeting of the minds.

"I've never taken leisure time to Fenway," I began once she told the story of Bailiff Sharde and his message to Brekwell to catch everyone up. All the while, Sharde kept silent, moving the food around his plate without a single crumb making it to his mouth.

"I have," Biggs said, waving his fork. He glanced toward Sharde, his tone turning critical. "Place was a slum. I thought, *this* is the sought-after spot for cadets to fly off to?"

"It's a shame more folk don't live there," Credell said in his thoughtful way. "With all the fertile land around Fenway, it should be a bustling farm town."

I sat back, glancing between them. "How often do you two visit?" I asked.

Biggs flashed a toothy smile, one I recognized as his nervous grimace when he was trying to hide something behind his back. "Look, the tavern there is still pretty good," he said.

So, often. That wasn't a bad thing. If the locals were used to his presence, all the better. He could ask a few questions for us without raising suspicion.

I shook my head to clear it. "Our goal is to find out how Lord Fenway is doing."

"It is quite suspicious that he has not spoken to me. Plus, the matter of his forged signature," Mother said, reminding me of Acton's suspicions last night. "It appears that the lord's steward, Martin Orra, is in charge of maintaining the estate. Meanwhile, Bailiff Sharde—"

Sharde muttered something. I bit my lip, nervous of an outburst when he lifted his head.

"What was that?" Mother asked gently.

"I said he's in charge of chasing people away," he practically growled.

Her lips tilted. "Quite right, though I was going to say that he maintains the law and the taxes in Fenway. Knowing their personalities, I can tell you the bailiff is the one in charge. Impersonating a lord, if that is what we're dealing with here, is a serious crime." She met Sharde's gaze, holding it for an uncomfortably long series of moments.

He squared his shoulders. "What, are you looking to me for permission? If this is what gets him, then gods be praised. Just because he's my father doesn't mean he's kin to me. Do as you wish." It was unlike him to be so bitter, but then again, he avoided speaking of family ties for a reason. As far as it always seemed, Sharde had no family except us.

That meant it was past time we helped him seek out whatever justice he wanted to mete. "It's time we took some leisure time," I said, cracking my knuckles.

CHAPTER 21

OPERATION FRACTURE

The first evening, Acton and I joined Biggs and Credell in Fenway. I wanted to see the town and shake out whatever surface-level secrets I could get. Unlike with operations past, Operation Fracture needed more than a direction and a quick meeting to pull off.

If the bailiff and lord's steward were impersonating their lord, then they would spend the rest of their lives imprisoned. Hells, if Father had acted quicker and had proof then and there that Bailiff Sharde had forged Lord Fenway's signature, we wouldn't have to tiptoe around Fenway hoping to find breadcrumbs.

Instead, we launched Operation Fracture—thus named by Sharde for how it matched up with his name—expecting it to take weeks of quiet off-and-on work. There were no peace-keepers to call upon in a small town, only the men employed by Bailiff Sharde himself.

What we really needed was a shred of evidence to give Father so he could involve the corps directly. We were his investigators, his eyes and ears searching for that one scrap that would help bring down Bailiff Sharde.

Unfortunately, as I sat in a corner of the tavern with

Sunset and an untouched mug of beer, I realized that would be harder than I thought. *"You're worrying again,"* she commented.

Around us, unfamiliar men and a few of their wives sang and danced to a fiddler's tune. The group performance grew worse as everyone involved got progressively more drunk, making my still, scowling self stand out all the more.

"I should be with Acton," I muttered. My man was trying to call upon Lord Fenway himself, extending an invitation at his estate for them to meet. As I understood it, it was bad manners, like Acton inviting himself into the man's home, but in terms of money, Acton was still a duke's son, while Lord Fenway was a minor noble who owned a stamp of land in the middle of nowhere. If the lord was well, Acton could see him tonight.

"If the lord is fine," I added, sharing my actual worry, *"then we won't have an Operation Fracture at all."*

Sunset's ears pinned back to her skull as a burst of boisterous laughter came from the tavern. *"Would that be such a bad thing right now?"* she grumbled.

I looked for my friends, finding Biggs in the midst of a group of men, telling a story that had the group carrying on. Credell was with them, listening and participating in his own way with a raised mug. They looked like they were having fun.

"We're in the wrong place," I said thoughtfully. I eased up from my chair, leaving my drink there for someone else to have. Raising a hand, I caught Credell's gaze for a moment and signaled that I was leaving. We'd learned sign language phrases to help us in combat if our gryphons couldn't communicate, so what I was really signing was that I was *disengaging from the enemy.* And what he signed back was *I'll follow off your wing?*

I shook my head no, and he flashed a thumbs-up. Sunset followed me out of the tavern gratefully. She had to hunch and fold her wings in tightly to make it through the doorway, which was low and warped, poorly shaped for a Skymother-sized gryphon.

It was dark out, and Sunset stretched out her body and yawned before turning her sleepy orange eyes my way. *"Where shall we go instead?"* she asked.

"We're getting a meal at a quieter place," I answered. Because of my friends, I knew the town's basic layout. There wouldn't be many shops open at this time of night, so I guided her past the darkened storefronts to the next biggest building around.

Our surroundings had the air of age, not because everything was ancient and crumbling, but because any sagging wood or warped glass we passed wasn't in the process of being replaced. Just like how I assumed the tavern door didn't close right, the fundamental school probably had a draft, and the apothecary *definitely* did, judging by the whiff of pungent herbs I sniffed on our way past.

I rarely ventured into the impoverished sections of Kaiamear, but I was reminded of them all the same. When money was sparse, drafty windows and ugly siding were a small concern that could be ignored for a season or more.

"I'm also worried that I see evidence of wrongdoing where there is none," I mused to Sunset privately.

Her attention tickled my awareness, and I relaxed, letting her peer into my mind. *"If there is wrongdoing, I know you will find it,"* she said, her voice warm.

I rubbed her silky neck feathers, happy to have her vote of confidence. We strode into the town's inn together, with me holding the door for her as she squeezed in. I hadn't bothered trying to hide my face or hair with a hood, not when I was traveling with such a gorgeous beast. She caught the eye of the whole inn, murmurs following us as I sought a plate of the day's meal from the proprietress. She stood at a counter with sets of keys pinned to the wall and the heat of a lit hearth nearby.

There were maybe ten people here in total, scattered between six of the small tables that dotted the inn's open foyer. If they all clumped together, they would take up a third of the space, but they'd spread out instead, leaving no corner private.

"Spendin' the night?" the proprietress asked, eyeing Sunset, who shadowed me closely.

"No, ma'am. My friends speak well of your cooking. I thought it was about time I tried it," I said with some forced levity.

It wasn't a lie, either. The cadets who spent their leisure time in Fenway always ended up at this inn, tucking into a homemade meal made by the scoffing middle-aged woman before me. She wasn't a stranger to gryphon riders, either. She was clearly unafraid of the large beast standing with me.

"Last time I saw this one, she was with a boy. Tall, mean lookin'. Told me he was the next biggest thing." She laughed to herself. "'Lest the gods made more pretty gryphons like her.'"

I sputtered for a moment. It wasn't a stretch that someone would recognize Sunset, but to remember Victor too? "He has since passed away," I said.

She tisked her tongue. "So now she's yours, eh?"

"I don't believe she's anyone's," I commented, though she had caught my attention with her memory. I nodded to her politely for now and sat down to eat the stew she'd served me, full of roasted meat and potatoes. As I ate, my eyes rounded with wonder at the flavor. *"Now this is what everyone comes to Fenway for."*

"Let me have some too," Sunset whined, even though I'd already made sure she was fed before we went on this trip. Still, I finished the bowl and went back for two more, one for the gryphon and the other for me. It was only with this second serving that I started looking around at the other people here. Two of the women had the look of military

wives, with the harried appearance that was unique to young mothers trying to corral their kids into dinnertime without the help of their husbands.

One more intrepid toddler was pointing at Sunset and staring. I didn't blame her. Even in the low lamplight, her maroon and red feathers were vibrant. Still, as she ate her extra dinner, she shared her content feelings with me. *"Shall I play with the small human?"* she said, still sounding tired.

"If you'd like," I answered. I warned the toddler's mom and watched closely as Sunset went boneless like a cat, lowering herself as close to the ground as possible and chirping invitingly to the little kid. Her little hands ruffled Sunset's fur, squealing with delight when the gryphon nosed her every so delicately with the blunt dome of her beak.

My mind lit up with Ironfeather's presence, so sudden I startled. *"Sivvy! Where are you?"* he asked in a panic.

I took a breath. *"I had to get some air and ended up at the inn. We're eating dinner. How'd it go?"*

"We met with a few servants who told Acton that Lord Fenway wasn't available to be called upon. They politely told him that he was being rude, too, and not to come back."

"Hmm," I replied noncommittally.

"Yeah. Exactly! Very suspicious. We're going to fly home as soon as we know you're safe. Biggs and Credell are leaving too," he reported.

I promised him that Sunset and I were safe, urging them to go on without us. Sunset was having a great time, actually, fawning under the attention of the kids brave enough to come pet her. I sensed that she simply loved young creatures, seeing chubby features and playful attitudes as the human versions of the daughter she cherished and made her want to have another.

I cleaned up my table slowly to give her more time, returning the used bowls and utensils to the proprietress. We watched playtime together for a few moments before she said quietly, "Why are you really here, lady gryphon rider?"

"I wanted to see Fenway," I answered in an undertone.

She lifted a brow at me. "Did that weak excuse come from the tail end of your beast?" She asked archly. "You came here lookin' for something, a question on your tongue."

I coughed, not expecting her to be so forward. "I...I did, yes," I whispered.

"Normally folk show me the color of their coin and ask. No need to be shy."

Ah, so she wanted my clorets. "Sorry. Um..." I dug out a silver coin and slipped it to her.

"Ever ask for information a'fore?" she asked, her eyes twinkling with amusement at my expense. "Normally you *show* the coin, ask, and then pay when you have the answer." I opened my mouth to apologize, and she waved it away, suggesting in an undertone that I spit out my question.

"Is Lord Fenway alive?" I asked, going for the inquiry as blunt as she was.

"Ah," she said, accompanied by her feigning a spit to the side. "Hells if I know. All I see of him are his brutes. Not like he ever came around here to begin with."

"His brutes?" I echoed.

She pocketed my silver cloret and made a circling gesture. Annoyed, I pulled out a gold piece, which represented a hundred clorets, but only flashed her the shining color. Sunset was getting too tired to play, I felt, so I needed this woman more eager to tell me what she knew. And judging by her expression, she would be. "Bailiff Marus and his boys. They rough up anyone behind on their payments."

"When's the last time you saw Lord Fenway, then?" I asked.

"Five, maybe six years ago. He's getting old, girl. So are we all," she grumbled. "Word is he's using up all his clorets to cling to the edge of the gate as long as he can. Nobody's seen him, I reckon, 'cept the folk that work for him."

I felt a tingling in my fingertips. Operation Fracture was really onto something, and now I had a name to distinguish the bailiff from my friend, the young man he'd hurt and driven away. "One more question," I said.

"I don't have all night, girl," she answered impatiently.

"What of Lord Fenway's family? His wife and children, have they been around?"

She chuckled. "No family to speak of. He became lord late, with the wrinkles already set on his face."

"That's very interesting. Thank you." I slid her the gold coin, my mind already elsewhere as I considered what to do next with this information.

I RETURNED Sunset to her nest, waking Ari and Novali briefly before the three of them snuggled up together to sleep away the chill evening together. Novali asked, *"Sivvy?"* like she expected me to join them, and for a long moment, I was tempted.

"Sweet dreams," I said, turning to head to my own bed. I hadn't been out this late in a long time, my sleep schedule usually determined by the gryphons, especially Ari. The stars sparkled brilliantly in the sky around a full moon. Its icy radiance matched the autumn cold that had me bundling my cloak closer as I walked.

A single peal rang out, and the stars seemed to shiver in its wake. My hurried steps faltered, and I tilted my head, wondering what could make such a noise. Then a second, similar sound followed, plus a *whoosh* of wind.

Two bell-like peals sounded next. I turned my feet toward where I thought it was coming from, rewarded when the noise was echoed, closer. It led me to the half-built roost, and I peeked around a pile of timber to see what it was.

I blinked away a sudden blast of silvery radiance. Amidst the dazzled spots in my gaze was my mother limned in the moon's radiance, sitting on a different pile of building materials. She turned eyes of silver power my way, her mouth still open and singing out single, bell-like noises.

Across from her and atop one of my makeshift perches, Revna echoed back the peals with uncanny similarity. Silver-tinged fluff fell from her feathers. She turned when Lady Nilara did, nearly startling herself into flight. "Sivana! Guess what!" she exclaimed with all the enthusiasm of a child.

I emerged slowly, my voice came out a rusty croak, breath caught for a new reason. "What is it, baby storm?"

Revna bobbed her whole body as I approached. The Mother spoke first, "A pleasure to see you again so soon, Sivana."

"You honor us with your presence, my lady," I answered.

"I am a *vaersanger*," Revna burst out like the knowledge could no longer be contained within her. "The silver lady told me!"

I turned a curious look toward Nilara, who said, "In Altarian, she is a *stormsinger*. The first and strongest of her kind."

"Did you hear her say strongest? Wait until I tell Hvit!" Revna puffed up excitedly.

The goddess smiled fondly over at her. "I'm sure he will be quite jealous. We can sing more in a minute. Be a darling and give me a moment to speak with Sivana?"

Revna bobbed an affirmative and took off with a smooth flap of her wings, barely making a sound as she disappeared into the night. "She is developing well," Nilara said.

More fluff fell to the ground around the perch. I caught it and tilted my hand, shocked to realize it was moon dust, the silvery residue I'd come to associate with Mother Nilara. Had

Revna created it, or had the goddess showered her in it for some reason?

She patted the space next to her, and I sat without hesitation. I had a familiar lump in my throat, wanting so badly to spend time with this woman but not quite knowing what to say. Our time together was always brief. "Is it time we knew more about what she is to become?" I asked, deciding I was too excited to learn about Revna to dwell on my own emotions.

She tilted her hand back and forth, scattering more dust from her palm. "It may disappoint you to learn that creation isn't a straightforward process. I did my best to put all of Lady Idunn's wishes into the stormsinger eggs, but until now, I wasn't sure what had taken and what hadn't."

I leaned forward, hanging on her every word as she smiled into the dark where Revna had flown. "She possesses the magic Idunn desired. A choir of her kind will be as powerful as one eldrafn but able to weave weather and magic of all kinds, not just storms. She will be taller than the tallest man and glow with the magic of her companion…" Her gaze swung to me at last, and I had the feeling she wanted me to take note as she continued, "For stormsingers were uniquely created to seek out and Link with those already god-touched."

"*Any* god-touched?" I asked in quiet awe.

"From the healers in my temples to the berserkers who have not yet gained the loyalty of a battle beast, to Tulari and volta alike. I can't wait to see what happens when the vaersangers find their destined." She had a kindly smile for me, glowing with the moon's radiance. "Now you know who should be visiting the eggs when it is time. Lady Idunn believes strongly that they should only hatch when their riders are near. But we have sealed the eggs from hatching for now as we await Revna's Linking."

"Their true partner, their *destined*," I mused, trying the

new label on my tongue. "They are truly Rathi beasts, aren't they?"

"Quite so," she agreed mildly.

"My lady, who is Revna's destined? Who could possibly shoulder her burden with her?" I knew she wouldn't answer, not with that knowing look settling into place on her features. She looked most like my own mother in that moment, possessing a kernel of wisdom she wanted me to figure out on my own.

"I am shocked you would ask me something you will find out in time rather than inquire to your friend's location on the Path of Glorium. No, don't worry, I will tell you what I can." My expression had her laughing, which caused the stars themselves to shiver. "Mateo and Mireille are fine. Cold, but fine. They left well-prepared because of your example, so there is little chance of failure. I await their arrival to my home eagerly."

The cadence of her speech slowed just enough that Revna arrived right as she finished speaking. Her expression was nearly mischievous as I realized she'd somehow timed it so it interrupted my follow-up questions. Revna's enthusiasm had barely dimmed. "Was that enough time? Can we sing more now?"

"It was perfect," Nilara answered. "Say goodbye to Sivana."

"Bye, Sivana!"

I blinked, and both of them disappeared, leaving behind a scattering of moon dust. I lifted a hand to wave farewell as the silver specs fell to the ground and disappeared like they'd never been there.

If Mother Nilara could practice with her elsewhere, she'd chosen to have me stumble upon them to share all of this. I scrubbed the disappointment from my face, replacing it with optimism. As I turned to finish the walk to my bed, I thought, *that was the most informative meeting I've had with a god yet.*

CHAPTER 22

PARAGON'S VISIT

A FEW DAYS LATER, I ate breakfast with my little flight of cadets, trying to talk them up right before the next monthly competition. I pretended it was because they were just that nervous, but in reality, I needed to hear these words of encouragement too.

Paragon Brekwell was coming back to the fortress today. He'd given us less than a fortnight to institute the list of improvements he'd left on Father's desk. Many of them were impossible, like suggesting Wild Flight participate in midday PT so they weren't lazing around in the sunshine.

It was unfortunate that he was so out of touch about wild gryphon habits, because now I was present and in the unenviable position of being the one to explain said behaviors to him.

"We're going to be first this time. I promise," said Cadet Geisel. Her strong form fit her uniform well. I couldn't help but wonder if I needed to take her aside and introduce her to some stormsinger eggs once Revna Linked.

Was she a volta? Would she ever tell me if she was? The academy clothing may cover her clan tattoo, but she was clearly Rathi in appearance and—reportedly—ferocity. She and Cadet Runar were two of our best fighters. Unfortunately, that had not won them many friends amongst the Altarian boys and girls around them.

"Don't go promising anything," Cadet-Commander Hanover muttered.

"Don't you want to win too?" she countered and cleared her throat when he raised a brow her way. "I mean, sir."

"There's nothing wrong with wanting to win," I said. The tension between the two of them was so thick it could be sliced with a bread knife.

The bell rang to summon them all outside. I slapped backs and wished them good luck. They'd be lining up for a pass in review shortly. In the meantime, I gathered up my gryphons and headed outside at a more leisurely pace. Novali had wanted to come along today, which meant I carried her while Ari and Sunset followed us.

I looked down at Novali, who was snuggled into the crook of my elbow. She released a happy peep, unaware of the nerves rising in my belly. We'd see Brekwell on stage for the pass in review, where all instructors, the Commandant, and important visitors like him amassed to watch the cadets.

"He's going to love you," I said, pressing the pad of my finger to the top of her beak. Her twittery giggle had me smiling as I walked the rest of the way to the Green to meet this important man face to face for the first time.

"You know, I've always wondered where the gryphons go while the humans stand on stage," Sunset commented to Ari.

"In the front, right?" he guessed.

It was a detail I'd often overlooked as well. The last Commandant would stand toward the front of the stage with his gryphon. He and Night had a kind of magnetism, a presence that was impossible to ignore. But as I drew near the stage now, I saw that Valtora was sitting with her wing brushing an unfamiliar elderly female in the grass set in front of the structure I was supposed to stand on.

"Are we really coddling the new generation of gryphons this much?" sneered a man from above me. My skin chilled, arms covering with tiny bumps. I knew that voice, that tone, even though it'd been years. Even though I'd barely heard him speak.

"*If the gryphon was meant to die tomorrow, then I say his execution stands,*" King Cortes had said on the eve I'd Linked with Ari.

And one of the generals of High Command had loudly chased this statement with a, "*Hear, hear!*"

The same man was standing next to Father now, glaring down at the sight of me cradling Novali. Our gazes met, and I set my lips, trapping my thoughts within the cage of my teeth before words could leap out and form in a way that I would regret. I already knew Brekwell hated me. A man I trusted had gone out of his way to warn me, but still, it felt like an attack to see him there, wearing the Paragon's insignia on his shoulders.

"You're going to have to go down now, Novali," I said, starting to bend down.

"*No!*" she squealed, trying to cling to me. Gods, I imagined how it looked to see her doing this, and the kiss I placed on her head to calm her before putting her in the grass next to her grandmother.

Brekwell's gryphon turned to regard me with dark eyes, reminiscent of Puzzlebox's, except she had the cool presence of a predator. She wasn't quite Skymother-sized anymore with the hunch that came from age, and while she was skinny, she was still leanly muscled. Her dove-gray fur was thin along her back, revealing the bumps of her spine and the shape of her hips. Unlike her rider, she ducked her head in a brief show of approval as Valtora said, "*This is Sivana, the one Chosen by the shining man.*"

"*I see why,*" answered Brekwell's gryphon, her mental presence a rusty purr, like it was infrequently used.

I wanted to stay there and talk to the gryphons but knew I needed to hustle my way on stage. Father was telling Brekwell about how Novali was Ari and Sunset's first child and how I'd ended up like a doting aunt to the youngling. The new Paragon seemed less than impressed, judging by the disapproving slant on his face.

"Just remember, we survived despite him and people like him," Ari said. I could tell he was with me, watching as I ascended the stairs and saluted Brekwell. Father made the introductions, not that they were necessary.

"And we will continue to," I answered.

"Nice to meet you in person," Brekwell stated, looking me over. "Where is your Hero of Altare medal?"

"In a box, sir. No wild gryphon can chew off the ribbon that way," I said.

"Any beast who would do that has no discipline," he scoffed.

I added another wild gryphon behavior to the mental list I had running of things I'd have to teach him about, if he cared to listen.

"The wild gryphons are free, sir. They do as they please," I answered.

"Yet we feed and shelter them, paid for with corps clorets," he said.

"We will be rewarded, sir."

He didn't deign to reply, his attention turned toward the edge of the Green. A group of wild gryphons was settling to watch as the pass in review began and the cadets marched. I took a polite step backward, joining the other instructors lined up at the back of the stage. With some shuffling, I fit between Acton and Lord Gadric.

Acton bent to murmur in my ear. "Isn't that Glorium?"

I knew the demigod had suggested that he'd stick around to oversee his roost's construction, but as I found him in the group of gryphons, this was the first time I'd seen him since our last conversation. He glittered as a cloud scuttled away from the sun, turning him into a beacon.

"Hard to miss," I whispered back with a rush of affection for the big male.

I also realized I hadn't communicated with Wild Flight about the monthly competition. Most of the beasts lining up to wait were expecting the silliness of the last competition, when they'd rushed in to play with our sports equipment and chase the cadets. A cold sweat formed on my spine as I imagined what Brekwell would say if he saw a repeat of that.

"Valtora has a plan," Ari informed me.

"Oh?" I asked.

"You'll see."

As soon as the pass in review was completed and the cadets divvied off to their various challenges, I flanked my father as he attended to the Paragon. My gaze followed Valtora, though. She split off with Ari, Sunset, and Novali, coaxing Brekwell's gryphon along too. *"I think you will love the community we're growing here,"* Valtora was saying with full matriarchal authority.

My lips curved when I looked over at the gryphons later to see Brekwell's gryphon basking next to Glorium. More than one cadet was staring, too, awed with the sparkling demigod.

"I'll give you this much, Walker. It still feels like a monthly competition," Brekwell said. We'd completed a tour and observed every event, duel, and hoops game. "I'm sure it will be legitimate once we have three years' worth of cadets participating again."

"Yes, sir," Father said.

"Now, how do we get the wild gryphons more active in this process?" Brekwell asked, his gaze swinging my way.

I was prepared for this question, at least. "If you would like them to participate in more PT, sir, they will require extra feed," I stated. "In some cases, up to fifty percent more. When they rest on the ground like this, they're preserving their energy and body heat. They eat much less than combat beasts."

"Is this true?" he asked Father.

"Yes, sir," he answered stiffly. "My daughter is an expert in such matters."

This had the effect he wanted: Brekwell started aiming all of his questions my way. We stopped, pretending to watch a relay race, while he grilled me on everything to do with Wild Flight. At one point, I managed to inform him, "The in-progress roost already has the blessing of Lord Glorium, the demigod mount of Lord Orion. He's been spending time with the gryphons today, even."

The three of us turned to the group of basking gryphons, which notably didn't include a giant, sparkling one.

"Oh, really?" Brekwell asked, his voice heavy with skepticism.

"Well, he w-was, sir," I stammered.

I watched Bittern Flight take first place in the relay, sighing to myself. They'd gotten much better. My own little flight was lagging behind by comparison.

We moved on, standing in the crowd watching the remaining duels. Brekwell continued asking me questions rapid-fire, and I answered as best as I could. I think he wanted to watch me sweat, as much of what he asked he could've either seen for himself or read in one of the many reports Father had sent to High Command weekly.

"Sivana!" sang Revna, before she swooped in for a landing close by. A few of the cadets turned and waved to the bird, who bobbed next to me. "You're not wearing your shoulder pad." She sounded incredibly disappointed in me.

"Sorry, baby storm. I didn't know you'd need to talk to me today," I said. I widened my eyes and twitched my head toward Brekwell, but of course she didn't know who he was or why I'd hoped today was one of those days she'd soar for hours without pause.

She was nearly two and a half feet tall now, so she still had to crane her head up to look at him. "Hi, are you new?" she asked.

"This is Revna, sir," I said.

As Brekwell looked down at her, brows furrowed, Hvit came for a landing too and bobbed his way over to us. "Sivana," he sing-songed. "Solfrid and Signe want to talk to you. If you're not busy." He gave Brekwell an uncertain look.

"*These* are the new eldrafn?" Brekwell asked.

"Vaersangers," Revna corrected in flawless Rathi.

"Stormsingers," I rushed to translate.

Brekwell's eyebrows rose toward his hairline. "Well, show me what you can do." He gestured toward them expectantly. They would usually burst into a random song at this invitation, and rarely the same one, but in this case, they froze and stared at him. He grew impatient quickly and barked, "Sing!"

Hvit startled and spread his wings, hopping away to get some space before fleeing into the sky. Gods, how I wished I could join him.

"They're still children, sir. Their powers aren't developed yet," I said, barely keeping the chastisement out of my tone.

Father cringed on the other side of Brekwell, since the Paragon's back was turned to him. It was clearly the wrong thing to say, but I hated seeing how uncomfortable Revna was. Brekwell's face reddened. "So are the fifty-one younglings that haven't Linked yet because of *you*," he said through gritted teeth. "Am I to feel like a villain because I want two oversized birds to sing?"

I straightened myself further, going into parade rest automatically. "N-no, sir. Of course not," I said.

"It has become obvious to me that you think you are some… some mother figure to them. Bird and gryphon alike." He was sputtering with fury, getting drops of spittle on my face. I wanted to shrink down to nothing to avoid this outburst, especially since more than a dozen cadets were in earshot and definitely listening. "I will remind you that they are *animals*, Lieutenant Walker. Maybe you think you can talk and reason with them, but they will never be human! They also can't be our equals, and they don't deserve all the leeway you've been giving them."

For a long, terrible moment, he waited for my response, for the *yes, sir* that should follow lectures like this from a senior officer. I didn't want to say it, to give voice to any kind of agreement.

He swung toward my father without pressing the issue. Instead, he demanded, "Who is Wild Flight's second-in-command?"

"That would be Lieutenant Noah Sharde, sir," Father replied in his low voice. The angry one I recognized, which came right before the explosion.

"Put him in charge. She can be his second if he likes, but let's see if he can improve things around here." He flicked his hand dismissively at me. "Get out of my sight."

I exchanged a glance with Father. For a split second, he looked as shocked as I was before putting his polite face back on for Brekwell when the Paragon turned away from me. I grinned and beckoned to Revna, whistling a merry tune on the walk back to the fortress. She echoed it back to me, picking up on my sudden shift in mood.

"It's nice to have less responsibility?" she asked.

I finally released the laughter I'd been holding and rubbed away the tears of mirth welling at the corners of my eyes. "Gods, it's not that. Sharde's going to make him regret everything."

She regarded me with a tilt of her head. "But he did such a good job while you were gone."

I smiled and shrugged. "We'll see, won't we?"

"I really wanted to sing for you," she burst out. "But just

you! The silver lady taught me a whole song, but I only remember bits of it. It's embarrassing, because it was so pretty."

"Did she say she would practice with you more?" I asked.

"Yes! And with the other gods, too. I'm special." Her feathers puffed out happily, and I missed a step and nearly planted my face into the flagstones leading up to the fortress's front entrance.

She hopped a lap around me, giggling like a little girl from my graceless moment. "Every god?" I asked, both amazed and terrified for her.

"Not *every single* one. She said the angry god doesn't have a song for me yet, and the dead don't sing, or at least..." She paused and shook herself. "They *shouldn't*. And the war god doesn't really want to sing."

"Wait, which is the war god, and which is the angry god?" I asked.

She considered while we entered the fortress and I tackled the stairs. She flew ahead of me, landing on the railing to keep talking while I climbed. "Uh, I forgot," she admitted.

I had noticed the beasts didn't seem to remember the names of the gods, but until now, I'd assumed that was a quirk of gryphon mind speech. It was easier to project *the shining man* rather than *Lord Orion*, after all. Something to wonder about later, perhaps.

She led me to Signe's classroom, where she sat on her stool in front of the instructor's desk. Solfrid paced the length of the room and back, Hvit now perched on her shoulder. With a happy chirp, Revna hopped onto the desk with barely a flap of her wings, crossing the scuffed wood to press herself into Signe's side. "I found her," she sing-songed.

"Who was the man who spoke rudely to my vaersanger?" Solfrid asked. She stopped pacing to scowl in my direction, her scarves slowly falling into place around her shoulders.

"Paragon Brekwell," I sighed.

Solfrid glanced over at Signe. "Is that title supposed to mean something to me?"

"*Tch*. The leader of the gryphon riders," Signe answered briskly.

She put her hands on her hips. "Don't look at me like that. Why do I care what the Altarians call themselves?"

Signe folded her arms, answering in the same sharp tone, "Yes, yes. Why bother learning anything while you're here? Hvit will soon grow large enough for you to fly together, and then you will be gone. But where will you go, hmm?"

"We agreed that you would stay here and train Revna's rider," I said, brow furrowing.

"After that." Solfrid circled her hand vaguely. "This isn't why we wanted to talk to you. Revna has new magic and says you were there with some silver woman who taught it to her. Care to explain?"

Both of them turned to me expectantly, and I swallowed. I'd assumed Revna would tell the story of Mother Nilara's visit to them, but in retrospect, it was silly of me to assume the young bird would be able to explain the event completely. "The other night, she was learning a song from Mother Nilara," I said and braced myself. "I caught only a couple minutes' glimpse of it happening."

At first, I thought they'd both skewer me with their glares as I recounted the conversation and what I'd seen. Nilara wasn't revered by their people, seen as too soft and weak compared to the Goddess of Thunder, Idunn.

But it'd been the Mother who was teaching Revna a song, and she parroted what she remembered of it for us. She chimed and tolled like a bell, creating a shower of moon dust she shook with a little irritation from her feathers once she was done singing.

"It's itchy," she whined, extending her wing to Signe. The elderly woman started brushing lingering crumbles of dust from between her feathers.

"What's the point of this?" Solfrid asked. She brushed a finger through some of the dust on the desk, rubbing it between her thumb and forefinger.

"Well…it sounds like she's going to learn a song from almost every god. If this is really moon dust…" I went over and swiped some of it up too. I patted it over a scrape on my knuckles, and all of us paused for a moment to watch the small wound shrink as the dust sank into it. "The Mother taught her a song of healing, because that's what her magic does," I explained.

"She didn't teach *me* a song of healing," Hvit complained. If he had lips to pout with, he would.

In response, Revna made a bell sound at him. He shifted his talons on Solfrid's shoulder pad before repeating it back at her. He shook himself, though no moon dust fell from his wings. "I'll teach you everything I remember if you give me your lunch," Revna said.

"Deal," Hvit said.

Solfrid tapped him on the head. "Don't let the girl bully you like that."

"Can we *please* focus on the implications," Signe interrupted irritably. "The gods have songs to teach my beloved Revna that have her doing their magic. The vaersanger have a name; if we were to translate it directly, it would be *weather singer*. Whatever this is." She swiped at some of the moon dust. "It is not weather. Their magic is something we've never seen before.

"And the goddess who created them states she intended for them to Link with those that already have magic. We have been looking in the wrong place for her rider. None of the Altarian pups at the Gryphon Rider Academy have magic."

"We have been training a couple volta," Solfrid said.

"Runar and Geisel? Revna did not want either of them," Signe grumbled. I blinked in surprise. Well, that was news to me, and they were in my little flight. "We need to take her to the Tulari Academy."

Both Revna and I uttered a "nooooo."

Signe narrowed her eyes at me. "You cannot keep me alive forever. She must Link to the next Chosen of Idunn as soon as possible."

"Surely take her up north, then, where she can Link to someone who *believes* in Lady Idunn," Solfrid argued.

"You cannot find a concentration of volta like you can Tulari."

"That doesn't matter. The Chosen must be Rathi, not Altarian."

"It is the *same thing,* Solfrid! There are no Rathi anymore. We are all Altarian. Our people lost the right to be anything different."

The younger woman leaned away. Though she hid her mouth behind her colorful scarfs, I could tell that had struck a nerve. "All I was going to say was the Tulari Academy cannot be trusted right now," I said to draw attention away from their argument. "It's a long story."

"Well, draw up a chair, girl," Signe said, brow rising in challenge. "You're talking to two former Rathi. We love stories."

CHAPTER 23

RETIREMENT

"You can't just *leave*," Sharde said that evening once most of the gryphons were fed, groomed, and slinking off to rest. Puzzlebox sat between us, giving me a mournful-eyed look at the news.

I had the paperwork in hand, signed by my father, allowing me time off over the weekend. The last thing to do was to report to him, as the new leader of the human element of Wild Flight.

"Wait, this isn't because of the demotion, is it? Because I don't want your job," he said in a panicked rush.

The only other gryphon still around was Roshawk, accepting Lira's presence and touch. She rubbed ointment into his scarred flank and they stood out of earshot, but his tufted ears were pinned toward us anyway. "*I thought we made it clear that you would be our human representative,*" he said crossly.

"I know it feels like bad timing, but it has nothing to do with the demotion," I said, putting my hands up. "I'm going to visit Paragon Hughes this weekend. Besides, your flight won the monthly competition again. There's going to be plenty of hands around here to get everything done."

He considered me for a few long moments while I reached out to Roshawk, letting him see how the demotion happened from my memories. *"This male's treatment doesn't make you furious?"* he asked in disbelief.

"I know it's temporary. Besides, I trust Sharde to take care of you all."

To my surprise, Roshawk pulsed agreement, even though it was reluctant. *"He is Linked to a cloudling. If I must accept someone else temporarily taking your place, he is a good choice."*

The hatchlings were mellowing the old Skylord. It was the only explanation for him saying something kind.

"At least tell me you're taking Acton," Sharde said, bringing me back to the conversation I'd left halfway.

"Taking? Oh, yes, I invited him," I said.

He smiled with approval. "Thanks. Last time you left him, he was as sad as a shipwreck. I shall ever so incompetently await your return in the meantime."

I couldn't help a small laugh. "How incompetent are we taking?"

"The Paragon requires I put twelve improvements into place by Yule. Best I can do is…none." He shrugged, clicking his tongue to Puzzlebox as he made to leave. "As far as I'm concerned, I'm keeping the spot warm for you. It's not like he can fire me."

"Don't jinx it," I said.

At about the same time, Puzzlebox squeaked, *"He wouldn't send us away, would he?"*

Roshawk's daggerlike talons hooked into the ground. *"I'd like to see him try,"* he growled.

DESPITE THE HEAVINESS of the last few days—few weeks, really —Ironfeather and Ari played midair for most of our northwestern flight, and the air was colored by Acton's and my laughter. Through our gryphons, we talked about Caershire as we flew over and past it. It was one small settlement of many that dotted the fertile land between the Church of Mercy and the distant Orelian Mountains.

"You're sure that's Caershire?" I asked through Ari. I'd never seen it, despite how important it'd been less than a year ago. It felt like an oversight not to visit it and see the royal bunkers for myself.

"Yep. And the explosion was over there." He pointed with his whole arm. *"Looked like a silver starburst for a minute, like Lady Nilara's wrath. The wind currents went crazy too!"* That last part sounded like it was all Ironfeather, enthusiasm and all.

"I'm still glad you two got away unscathed."

Acton's head turned my way, his expression hard to read with his tinted flight goggles in place. *"Same to you and Ari. But the gods know I would've had words with them if it were any other way."*

I put one of my gloved hands over my lips. *"Oh, not words! How would they survive if they knew you were most displeased?"* Ari helped me infuse my response with teasing energy.

"You mean a lot to me," he answered more seriously through Ironfeather. *"To both of us."*

I felt myself flush. *"You mean the world to Sivana,"* Ari answered for me. I was stuck fumbling for a response that didn't feel too much like a mirror, so he sensed my intentions and spoke without missing a beat. *"And I love you too, kid,"* he said for himself.

"Aww, you do?" Ironfeather practically squeaked.

My sweet boy, I thought.

"We both do," I had Ari say.

Ironfeather's happiness rolled over me like the warmth of sunshine. I basked in it even as I kept a lookout for the red-rocked butte that Hughes had written about. It was the main landmark for the town he'd settled in, a place simply called

Towering. While I stayed alert, my mind wandered, and I found myself wondering if Brekwell had ever had such a warm and loving relationship with a gryphon that wasn't his own.

Could my problems really stem from such a cold source? During my stay at the Academy, it'd felt like my love for the twins, Mireille especially, was discouraged. Neither Ironfeather nor Mireille were my gryphon, and yet I'd felt like an attachment to them all the same.

If I hadn't become a rider, time would've dulled their memory of me and how I'd stepped in to care for them when their mother, Snowpoint, grew tired of being both a mother and a war mount. In reality, we were the exceptions, not the reality. How many of my fellow riders realized they could learn the language of gryphons? How many *wanted* to?

"I will remind you that they are animals, *Lieutenant Walker."* Brekwell had said this with a full measure of scorn, and it still sat poorly with me. Sure, gryphons were beasts…he was right about that.

But if they could think like us, feel like us, and reason like us, surely that made them worthy of better treatment than a common animal. That was the thinking that inspired Wild Flight in the first place. *That* was what I needed Brekwell to understand, because sticking our heads in the sand and refusing to implement his orders, as Sharde planned to do, was going to get more of his hostile attention, not less.

"Cloret for your thoughts?" Ironfeather asked.

I must've seemed like I had my head in the clouds with how I'd let our conversation lapse. *"I do my best thinking on gryphon back,"* I answered.

He pulsed agreement. *"It's something about the cool air through your feathers, isn't it?"*

I chuckled. *"It sure is."*

It wasn't long after that that I spotted a butte made of layers of red and brown rock. Out of its squared shadow sprung a large town, our destination. As we circled our way downward, I spotted a single gryphon with its rider seated atop the flat top of the butte, keeping watch or simply spending the day as close to the sun as possible.

A flutter of silent communication passed between the other beast and Ari. *"He's a member of Final Flight,"* he told me.

I hummed. While Hughes had written of where to find this place, he hadn't said much else about it, but I had my suspicions from the name. Apparently, he would be easy to find. I started to see why when we came for a landing and walked the main street in search of directions. We spotted three more elder gryphons, with Acton pointing out a fourth on top of an inn's sloping roof, dozing.

"This a retirement community," I murmured to Acton.

"First I've heard of it," he whispered back.

I flagged an older woman and asked if she knew where I could find Hughes, fully expecting to be waved away. Instead, she gestured and said, "Usually he's at the graves this time of day. Bring him this, why don't you?" She had us wait as she bought a round of bread and wedge of cheese from a street vendor, passing it over with barely a glance at our two gryphons.

"Thank you, ma'am," I said, exchanging a glance with Acton.

She must've seen this, as she chuckled. "What? We look after the new widowers, be they gryphon rider or otherwise."

"Of course, ma'am." I stepped away, following the directions she'd given. Giggles preceded a group of kids that ran across our path, and I shook my head wryly. This town was full of life, not just the errant members of Final Flight and what must've been their families. I wondered if I'd just spoken to a gryphon rider's spouse.

"Maybe they don't want us young things living with them yet," Ari commented. I had the feeling most of the older gryphons we passed were making remarks quietly to him and Iron-

feather. Even though they weren't including me in the conversation, I felt the intention. The two males with us were far too young to retire. In fact, Ironfeather was due for a smothering from a few grandmotherly beasts if we stopped for too long.

"They seem nice about it, though," Ironfeather said back to him.

"That's because you're still young enough to be cute."

"No I'm not," he protested.

Their voices faded out to silence as we wove around the buildings on the outskirts of town and emerged on a grassy rise. Gravestones dotted the gently rolling ground, gray and uniform amidst a sea of well-tended grass. "Ah, I thought so," I said abruptly upon seeing how nice and peaceful this area was. "Towering Plains Cemetery."

"Wait, *this* is it? Where the senior gryphon riders are buried?" Acton asked, stopping by my side.

I nodded and looked over my shoulder. I hadn't been aware that civilization was being built around this place, especially amongst those waiting to be buried here. It seemed almost… morose. "My father's mentioned it a few times, to *bury him in the plains* should he leave us too soon. It's by invite only, but officers of any branch and their families can choose this as their final resting place rather than the Church of Mercy."

"I wouldn't be surprised if several Mercy lived here," he muttered. "It is close enough, is it not?"

"It is," I agreed and set off with Hughes's snack in hand to find him. There were a few men and women here, either sitting by a gravestone or tending to the land. And there was significant ongoing work that needed to be done to keep flower bushes trimmed, grass cropped, and gravestones polished, as the Towering Plains Cemetery just seemed to go on and on. I was considering hopping back onto Ari's back to fly to the end of it when I spotted Hughes.

He was gardening. Of all the things I expected, it wasn't to see the old Paragon kneeling, wearing knit gloves and delicately trimming a rosebush. "If it isn't Sivana Walker," he said, barely looking up. "I was wondering if you'd forgotten about me."

"Never, sir. I even have food for you."

"Ah, that must be from Nava. Or perhaps Betsy? They're always trying to feed me." He had a weak chuckle. "And who is this young man with you?"

Hurriedly, I made introductions between him and Acton. Ironfeather stepped forward to say hello too and blinked in surprise when he received a fond pat on the head from Hughes. "You remind me of my gryphon. Same storm cloud gray. She's right over there." He gestured, and I went to the last grave on this row. There, Gorriset was immortalized with a range of her years. A vase of freshly cut flowers rested against the stone.

Acton offered his arm as Hughes lifted to his feet with the aid of his cane. "I know how it must seem, to find me here. It...helps me feel close to her." He puffed with effort, both speaking and moving seeming to tax him.

"I understand, sir," I said. I could see myself doing the same thing if Ari left before me.

"*Must we dwell on such things?*" Ari put in, distinctly uncomfortable. We were both too aware in that moment that we were about the same age and that a gryphon's thread of life was snipped shorter than a human's.

I cleared my throat. "How are you doing now, sir?"

He turned to head back to the town of Towering, leaning on his cane. Still too proud to accept help, he waved Acton's offered arm away. "I have quite the scar, but I am fine. You are speaking of the attack, yes?"

"Sure," I said after a moment's hesitation. "Perhaps we could fly you to your home?"

Now he was waving me away. "It is a fine day for a walk.

Besides, you came all this way to hear what I had to say, even though I have been exceptionally vague."

"I feel like I could use your wisdom more than ever, sir," I said honestly.

"Well, then, I will make you some tea, and we can chat. I do have another pair of visitors who you might find most welcome, as well." I hated how much he now reminded me of my Gramma in her twilight year, when she'd been so lonely. As a kid, her tea and snacks had felt like traps, but as an adult, I recognized she'd just wanted to talk. I saw that she hadn't wanted to fade out before she was gone and wanted her voice and strong opinion heard.

Those visitors remained a mystery as we walked back to town and into a residential section. He had one of the newest, largest houses around and smiled as he let us in. "Go ahead and set your things down. Unsaddle your gryphons, too. There's plenty of space for everyone."

I was hit with a blast of heat as soon as I stepped inside, and Hughes closed the door behind us. Ari and Ironfeather padded into the next room happily while Acton and I strung up their saddles where there were hooks in the storage closet right off the entranceway.

I nearly stopped dead in the doorway when I went into Hughes's living room and spotted who his visitors were. "Marshall Jamison, sir," I said, shocked to see the retired Commandant lounging casually in civilian clothes.

"He's a person, too," Ari teased. He was seated by a massive hearth, grooming the wing feathers of Night, an elderly female beast. The hue of her yellow eyes had paled, especially in the iris. She probably didn't see very well, though her head still tilted in my direction.

"Hello, Walker and Weslecker," Jamison said, nodding curtly. He'd maintained his military-style haircut and apparently the stern façade he'd cultivated over several decades as the Commandant of Cadets. He may have taken off his uniform for the last time, but little else had changed.

"Of course the first cadets to find us would be you two," Night whispered, accompanied by a pulse of affection. My brows rose. She'd never been so friendly when we were at the Academy. But she'd also never accepted affection from the younger gryphons as she did now. I'd admired Night for her shiny black coat and feathers. She was like a swoop of shadows in the air, gorgeous and deadly, and even the signs of her own twilight didn't diminish her.

Hughes walked out of the room, murmuring about tea, and Acton followed him. I sat and twiddled my thumbs, feeling a little off center. "He's been hoping you would visit," Jamison said.

"Yes, sir," I answered automatically.

He glanced over at me, and his face softened by a fraction. "I've been *yes, sir'd* for a lifetime. I'd prefer you spoke your mind now."

I forced myself to loosen from the stiff way I'd perched on this chair. "Do you know what he wants to say?" I asked.

"He wants to be involved again. It's not that he wants to say anything in particular. He wants to be looked to for advice like he's still in the service."

"Like you," Night interjected.

"I suppose I am guilty of this as well, else we'd be leaving for our own home," Jamison added.

"This is basically our home. We do everything but sleep here." This time, I felt that Night was speaking to the other two gryphons in the room. Jamison had a small furrow appear between his brows.

"I'm glad you can keep each other company," I said.

"He needs it," he said in an undertone.

Hughes came back and sat in a padded chair closest to the fire. He ate the bread and cheese I'd given to him while Acton wheeled in a tea service, passing out cups and crispy cookies for the rest of us.

We worked through several rounds of both tea and cookies, talking. As I suspected, I'd been lured here as someone to talk to, but also to hear the opinion and wisdom of a pair of men who knew exactly how to help me. They worked all the current events out of Acton and me: how Wild Flight was doing, what Paragon Brekwell had done so far, and even the drama with Fenway and what we suspected was happening there.

"Terrible time to retire," Hughes remarked to Jamison.

The other man shrugged back. "There was never a good time. At some point, we just had to leave."

"Too true," he sighed. "Well, where to even start?"

"I've tried to buy Fenway in the past. It's a liability to have Fortress Aerie so beholden to civilian-owned land," Jamison said abruptly to me. "Lord Fenway was not willing to part with it at the price the military was willing to pay. If you want to sus out if he has truly passed away, it's time to make the offer again and see who shows up to negotiate."

He named the sum Father should seek out, and I nodded, committing it to memory.

"If it's Marus Sharde, then your father can call in the military police to investigate. It's about time someone took him down a peg." His face twisted like he tasted something sour.

"A military-owned Fenway could become a community like this one," Hughes said. "Not for Final Flight-aged riders, but for the civilian riders your methods are undoubtedly going to produce."

"Civilian riders, sir?" I echoed.

"Say we embrace the idea of true Links when the yearlings are ready to Link, like you intend, and a gryphon finds its true partner with a toddler. They will be civilians until the rider comes of age," he said.

"I can see dozens of other pairs who would end up civilians." Jamison rubbed his forehead. "Unless the rider is a teenager and in good health, they won't be ready to attend the Academy."

"*However, it is good for the overall health of my kind,*" Night said, and he repeated it aloud without a pause.

"If I'd known this was how you intended for the gryphons to Link, I'd have suggested the Academy change how they train first-years," he continued. "It used to be that the Academy only trained boys who were already Linked. What do we do now with the hopefuls who are trained for a whole year but overlooked? It's a waste of resources."

I frowned and said, "I hadn't thought of that. So, you're suggesting that, once this group of gryphons Links, we only train them?"

"That's why you ask for advice. Yes, that's what I'm saying. The Academy can be a two-year program for gryphon riders who want to join the corps. We just have to have faith that the patriotic spirit of our people will lead them to military service," Jamison said.

"It will. There's nothing else out there that pays as well. You get a pittance for delivering mail," Hughes interjected. "Plus, there is the feeding and quartering of the beasts to consider. Fenway will be a necessity for civilian riders."

"How will we get Paragon Brekwell on board with this?" Acton asked.

The two older men exchanged a glance. It was Hughes that broke eye contact first with a roll of his. "Over the course of my career, Brekwell was always the loudest person in the room. He has all the subtlety of a battle beast in a potions store, but he's gone quite far by telling the men ahead of him in the chain of command how great they are. Now that he's at the top of the corps, there's no one to praise except the king."

Acton nodded along and said, "He's expecting praise instead."

"That's not to say he doesn't have a track record of

outstanding leadership during the last war," Hughes continued. "One does not get promoted to High Command without surviving at least one war as a winning Commander or higher. You'll find that he is merely set in his ways."

So, he was loud, proud, and resistant to change. "I've seen that before," I muttered.

"Defiance is the worst possible option. As difficult as that can be for you and your friends," Jamison added, raising a brow toward me. "Your best option would be to have the king remind him that the Crown wanted to change how the Gryphon Rider Academy is run."

"Except the king is a little busy with his…" Hughes circled his hand vaguely. "Imposter son situation."

"*What* imposter son situation, sir?" Acton asked.

They mentioned the final run of the *Kaiamear Gazette*, with its blasphemous claim that Prince Isaac wasn't dead. I'd put it out of my mind for long enough that it was a slap in the face to be reminded that the king and his men had been handling this for a while now.

"I've seen the body. I know he's dead," Hughes said, shaking his head slowly. "But word is the imposter Isaac is the right shape, size, and disposition to mimic the old prince exactly. And he only emerges to stir the populace against the Crown. The king is working hard to be seen as actively helping the people and paying off his debts while his men hunt the fake Isaac. It's a bad time to be seeking his help unless you intend to deliver the fake Isaac to him trussed up like a turkey."

I glanced over at Acton, a plan half-formed in my mind. "No, Sivana. Mateo wanted you to stay out of it, remember?" he said firmly.

"It wouldn't hurt to pay him a visit," I sighed. Just like it'd been a fantastic idea to finally see how these two riders were doing in their retirement.

CHAPTER 24

TAXES

ACTON and I stayed in Towering for the better part of the weekend, arriving back at the fortress Sunday evening with our saddlebags laden with snacks and little gifts from the kind retirees around town. It wasn't until the next morning that I got Sharde and Ellie to sit down with me.

I'd picked the staff room Ellie and I were supposed to share, though at some point, my things had migrated out to the temporary quarters I had out with Wild Flight, and Sharde's things had migrated in. Puzzlebox sprawled on the bed that'd used to be mine, placing her head in my lap. She was the only gryphon here, as Ari and Sunset remained in the mess hall rather than making this room any more cramped.

I petted Puzzlebox's head and neck and shared the extent of Hughes's and Jamison's wisdom, starting with the new Paragon. Sharde had one arm around Ellie's waist, but his other hand tightened on his knee as I spoke.

"He wants bowing and scraping for his every decision," he said through gritted teeth.

"It's more that the worst thing we can do is show defiance, even with how he wants to change Wild Flight," I explained.

Ellie tapped her cheek with a thoughtful hum. Sharde and

I turned toward her expectantly. "How many improvements did the Paragon want? Twelve?" When he nodded, she continued, "The worst ones…or at least the ones you've told me about are those that seem impossible. Like getting Wild Flight to exercise."

Sharde nodded again. "Impossible," he echoed.

"Or having the cadets attempt to socialize with and form Links with the younglings on the weekends," she said. My eyes bugged wider. This must've been something Brekwell added to his list of requirements after he pushed me out of my job.

"I mean, if you want to see Roshawk maul a few cadets, sure," Sharde sighed.

"And then be put to the sword for it," I said.

They both turned to stare at me. "What if that is part of the plan? High Command has to know by now that Wild Flight is run by Valtora and a human-hating Skylord." Ellie fidgeted with her glasses, raising a single finger slowly. "I posit that this may also be a decision made to push the gryphon knight corps back to what it used to be. Why train cadets who don't have gryphons?"

"That brings me to something else, something for Operation Fracture," I said, hesitant to change the subject now. I'd get Sharde to show me all the things Brekwell wanted later.

He perked up. "I thought we would have to declare that operation a failure. It's not like we've gotten more than hearsay."

"Well, apparently, Lord Fenway has turned down the corps in the past when it tried to buy the land from him. That was during Marshall Jamison's time as Commandant," I explained. Ellie's mouth rounded as she realized where this was going immediately. "But if there is no Lord Fenway anymore, he will not be able to come to the negotiating table to say yes or no to the sale. It would merit an investigation."

"Let's do it!" Sharde exclaimed.

Ellie was frowning, though, shaking her head. "Wait, how do we even get the military to make another offer on the land? The Crown is struggling to pay its debts right now. I doubt they're going to care about buying a little town out in the remote reaches of Altare."

"I'm not exactly sure. But I know who needs to be writing the letter to the king," I said, grinning.

"Acton forging Prince Mateo's handwriting?" Sharde guessed.

"What? No! My mother. No one else dreams of Fenway tripling in size as much as she does. Picture it, Sharde. A town without your father, put under the control of a military-appointed governor—"

"You had me at 'without my father.'"

"—where we can bring in the friends and family of every civilian gryphon rider. It'd be perfect," I concluded.

"It would be a closed loop, which is what the king will really want to see," Ellie interjected. "Fenway, Fortress Aerie, and Glorium's Roost. Food, training, and population growth. Not to mention...*taxes*."

Sharde snickered. "What?" she asked, giggling along with him.

"Just the passion you put into *taxes*. I've never heard anyone so thrilled for them," he teased.

Her murmured response devolved into the two of them kissing, and in looking away, I caught Puzzlebox's gaze. *"Why do they do that so much?"* she sighed.

MY PARENTS AGREED to the whole logic of buying Fenway, and Mother spent days crafting the letter that would go on to grace King Cortes's desk. Then...silence.

Routine closed back in like nothing had happened. I still

taught a daily class and fulfilled my duties to Wild Flight. Only, a new gryphon was spending time with the flock, encouraging them to help the workers midday as they toiled to build the semi-circular structure that would become Glorium's Roost. It was starting to shape up with all this extra help.

Glorium himself was the new face, his very presence inspiring tireless work in the men and a helpful nature in even the most obstinate of our beasts. At first, the giant, glittering gryphon caused a stir every time he arrived in a blink, his bulk seeming too great for how silently he would appear.

But as soon as the shock wore off, no one said a word about it. The workers stepped over or around him, and the most adventurous amongst them rubbed his wing or back like he was a way overgrown cat. The demigod ate up every moment of attention.

I would sit with him more days than not. Sometimes he would start by saying, *"You know I can't tell you anything."*

And I would say, "Not even that they're still alive?"

Eventually, he whispered in my mind, *"Mireille and Mateo were…lost for a while. But since they don't need me now, I'm here in my new holy place. It's too bad there are so many humans here."*

"What do you mean, lost?" I asked, but his beak was apparently sealed on the matter.

Every time I saw him after that, it was an aggravation. If he was here, he wasn't helping my friends follow in his path on their way to the gods. And while we were experiencing the first falls of sleet and freezing rain here, up in the Orelian Mountains, it was full winter.

But according to Glorium, they were *mostly safe, alive,* and *cold.*

"Don't go chasing things you cannot change," he warned.

His advice came at the heels of a couple weeks feeling like I was running in place, mired in the same loop of events. But he had some godly foresight, as the next day, an air courier from Final Flight arrived with a message for Prince Mateo. Acton had to practically wrestle it out of the older man's hand when the promise to "deliver it the rest of the way" wasn't good enough.

I was just finishing up my class when he ducked into the back stables, skin pale and letter open in his fist. "It's happened," he said.

He handed over the letter, and my gaze skimmed it, jumping from the elegant script, to the signature of King Cortes at the bottom, and finally to the order we'd hoped wouldn't arrive before Mateo did.

"Return to Kaiamear posthaste. The public needs to see its crown prince."

"He's still gone. Is there any way we can stall?" I asked.

He took the letter back while I paced between the stalls. I had thought I'd be ready for the consequences when this moment came…but I hadn't expected to feel so badly about denying the king help. For him to call his only son out of hiding to see the people, he must desperately need help.

"The courier is still here, waiting to take a reply back to the king," Acton said, stepping into my path. I stopped inches from him, and he drew me the rest of the way with an arm around my middle. At a murmur, he shared his plan while we pressed in close to one another. He would write a letter as himself, stating that Mateo was out on a private mission but that everyone else at the fortress was at the king's disposal. It would be true and accurate, but it would withhold the fact that Mateo and his gryphon were somewhere on the Path of Glorium, possibly suffering.

"Maybe tell him that we were going to visit Galak Nilessen soon?" I suggested. I'd finally replied to my fellow Hero of Altare, trying to set a date to see the in-progress statue of Ari and me. We'd get Galak's reply with a mail drop, depending on whether he gave my letter the same forgetful treatment I'd given his.

"I can do that," he promised. With a quick kiss, he dashed off to take care of writing it.

KING CORTES'S next response came ahead of the mail drop. This time, the courier left it with Acton and didn't wait for a reply.

Galak's prompt reply *was* a part of the mail drop, but his invitation was superseded by the fact that the king had apparently called him in, extracted the details of our friendly off-and-on conversations, and set the date that I *will* be attending an unveiling of the statue.

"The finished statue," I said in disbelief. I sat at the staff table with my friends, as had become customary in the mornings and evenings. A tall, dark-haired janitor in a pair of old overalls mopped under the table next to us.

Acton looked up from the king's letter, which he was reading aloud.

"That's right. He's hired a team of wizards to complete it ahead of schedule. His tone doesn't seem particularly pleased, but he's willing to let Mateo stay away in favor of this event entertaining the people instead," he said.

"But our presence is non-negotiable?" Pereyra asked. "*All* of us?"

"That's right. All of Wild Flight's human element are required to be there with Sivana."

I chewed on my lip, tracing the grain of the table with my gaze. The king had declared that this event would happen in less than a fortnight. It was, unfortunately, on the same day as this month's competition and would keep us away on the weekend when the winning flight would undoubtedly want to spend time with the youngling gryphons.

"Lira's going to kill me," I muttered. The janitor glanced

our way and rang out his mop, moving further into the dining hall. Strange, I didn't recognize him, and I felt I knew most of the fortress staff on sight.

"Well," Sharde said loudly. "I say we put on our dress uniforms and go! It's not like we can tell the king no, and Paragon Brekwell will have to understand if things are a bit of a mess without us."

"I thought his next inspection was happening around Yuletide," I commented.

Ellie held up a finger. "I think it's going to be completely random."

Sharde's big grin had frozen on his face. "Neither of you is helping right now," he said from between his teeth.

"Well, you're completely right, we have to go," Acton put in. "And we have to look *very happy* because it's a morale event for the common folk. They have to see that things are going well under the king's rule so they don't start dreaming about some imposter coming in and sitting on the throne instead."

CHAPTER 25

MORALE EVENT

Preparations were set, and the hours flew away. Events marked my days, starting with Ellie tugging my sleeve before I could fly off with Sunset after the evening meal. "I want to show you something," she whispered.

From her mousy smile, I figured this was a good *something*, and any good news was welcome. First, she walked up to a different staff table, where Solfrid sat with Hvit and a circle of empty chairs. She set her lips in a displeased line and placed her scarves over her mouth as soon as she finished chewing. "Yes?" she grumbled.

"Is it experiment time?" Hvit crowed. He flapped off his perch, which was just the back of Solfrid's chair. He landed before Ellie with a scratch of his talons and craned his head up to look at her.

Solfrid's eyebrows relaxed from the slope of a scowl when she noticed Hvit's enthusiasm. "Return him before light's out," she said.

I had them wait for a couple minutes and retrieved the padded shoulder guard designed for stormsinger talons. As soon as it was in place, Hvit launched himself at me and scrabbled the last couple inches up onto the leather. Like Revna, he bobbed his entire body when he was excited.

"Oof, baby storm," I said, trying to quell him with a hand on his downy chest. "You're getting too heavy for this."

"Sorry," he twittered.

I still carried him toward Ellie's workroom. Instead of singing wordless birdsong, he dipped his beak to pick at the strands of my hair where they were pulled tight to my scalp with my braid. I took out the leather tie rather than complain about the pain, letting him groom me with insistent tugs.

He balanced his weight carefully, which I was thankful for. He and Revna weren't growing upward so quickly anymore, but he had to be a good ten pounds, filling out in the chest to resemble a chubby falcon along with his ever-present over-sized feet. I had no doubt the next growth spurt would have him looking like a sleek raptor once more.

"I've had a breakthrough," Ellie told me.

"I helped," Hvit said proudly.

She smiled over at the bird, muffling a laugh behind her hand. "He sure did. He was bored the other day and wanted to see what I was doing."

"Revna was performing for the cadets. But I had more fun." The white bird fluffed up. It seemed they still hadn't solved their rivalry, even with Revna's recent visit from Lady Nilara.

"There's no greater joy than inventing," Ellie agreed. She let us into the workshop, which was attached to Lord Gadric's classroom. It was a perpetual mess back here, the air stagnant and equipment both magical and otherwise haphazardly arranged into boxes alongside one wall.

Ellie perched on a stool before a painted black table. She sorted through a box of glass orbs and wires. "It turns out the missing link was electricity, and there's only one creature out there that can control it, even a little bit."

"Me!" exclaimed Hvit, before his feathers flattened. "Wait, *a little bit?*"

Ellie pressed her lips together hard to contain a giggle. "Come over here and show her," she invited, patting the table. I wandered closer, spotting the telltale scrapes along its painted top that suggested an overlarge bird had used it to come in for a landing before. Still twittering soft grumbles, he hopped down off my shoulder and looked at her expectantly.

She put on a set of goggles and had me lower mine over my eyes. After she put on a thick set of gloves, she had Hvit shed a few sparks. They were bright enough on their own, but once one of her wires caught a spark, a blinding flash erupted inside the glass bulb she'd stuffed with a pair of wires. It dimmed over time but still left me blinking away wire-shaped shadows from my eyes.

It glowed for a good minute, dimming down to nothing. I clapped politely, excited for her to finally have some resolution for this project. "Isn't that amazing?" Ellie enthused.

"You did it! You made a magelight with no magic," I said happily.

"Do you think Mr. Nilessen will be impressed? Even if I don't bring Hvit?" she asked.

"Definitely! If this works out, they might be inducting you into the Hall of Heroes next, holding your light ball." I flashed her two thumbs-up since I wasn't keen to get any closer to Hvit's sparks or the hot-looking wires attached to her experiment.

Ellie's eyes lit brighter than Hvit's electricity. "You think so?"

"Absolutely. I hope they put your statue next to mine."

Father was stressed in the face of the Wild Flight element all flying to the capital together. He barely spoke to me except to shove a list of names my way. Caretakers that could be spared from the fortress as long as the wild gryphons accepted them.

I spent the eve of my departure arranging for these ten individuals to come visit with the toughest critics amidst the flock: Valtora, Roshawk, and Alaula. They approved of three, two boys and a girl, sending the rest away with barely a sniff.

Lira was *definitely* going to be upset. I sat with Alaula afterward, massaging her aching shoulders while a crowd of younglings tussled around us. *"Why so picky?"* I asked, careful to keep any frustration from my thoughts.

"These babies are the future of our flock," she answered. As always, she spoke with a kindly presence, which eased some of the tension in my shoulders. *"I would be a poor keeper if I allowed any and every human close. Any potential Link thieves must stay away."*

"Oh, I see," I murmured. If we weren't always hurting for extra hands amongst the caretakers and other staff, maybe we wouldn't have this problem now.

"Any new adventures to share? You've been coming and going so often lately." She tilted her head to regard me with one blue eye, a questioning curiosity about her.

I considered telling her about my visit to Towering, but I wasn't sure she'd want to hear about the retirement community. *"I do,"* she said, surprising me. We didn't usually make such a strong temporary Link, where she could read the thoughts from my head. *"Death doesn't scare me. I know it is not far from your mind right now."*

Blowing out a breath, I let her in to see my memories of Towering for herself. Despite how kind the retirees were in general, a part of me was still shaken to see a great man like Hughes reduced after the passing of his gryphon. If you'd asked me a year ago if Paragon Hughes trimmed rosebushes in his spare time, I would've laughed. Yet it was a daily ritual for him now, cleaning and caring for the Towering Plains Cemetery. Alone except for the community who stepped in to make sure he was cared for and fed.

"*You are afraid,*" she said gently. Her presence in my mind pushed those memories around until we were both looking at the specter of Hughes kneeling in front of that rosebush.

"*It helps me feel close to her.*"

Tears pricked at the corners of my eyes. Alaula made a low sound and lifted from my lap, laying out in front of me and indicating she wanted me to lie down with her. When I stretched out, she rested her wing over me like a hug.

"*In the wild, we have the instinct to fly away from our flocks when it is our time to go. We find a glade or a hill full of flowers, a place of beauty,*" Alaula said. She flexed her wing, the feathers brushing down my arm in soothing strokes. "*Those that love us most follow and are present when our strength fades and we must, at last, rest. My past flocks have had many beloved members whose last flights were attended to by all, from the elderly to the younglings on a parent's back.*

"*We all strive to live a life that will lead to such an assembly, followed by a burial where we may nourish that place where we landed for the last time. I respect the human from your memory for maintaining that beauty for his gryphon. Their Link stays strong even through his grief.*" She was lost in thought for a few moments as I wiped my wet face. "*I am not...familiar...with humans and gryphons being so strongly connected, but I would like to think when he departs to the next life, he will follow his Link back to her.*"

"*Thank you,*" I said, sniffling.

Something small and furry worked its way between us, peering at me with concern. It was Novali, trilling like a cat and rolling to show her belly. "*I'm okay, baby,*" I promised, leaning in to kiss her soft fur until she grabbed my face with all four paws with a complaining twitter.

"Now, let me tell you a happier story before you go. This morning, Sadry was one of the first to the feeding buckets. He stole a round of ice and ran away with it like it was a prize," Alaula said, soon regaling me and a handful of younglings with the rest of the lighthearted tale until I was smiling again.

WE FLEW OUT to Kaiamear a day before the event and stayed at the palace in guest rooms that were a good jaunt from the gryphon stables. Sharde and Ellie left pretty quickly after dropping their things off, giving me a chance to whisper to my friends about Sharde's plan before I flew off with Ari into the city.

We landed on the steps of the Temple of Nilara, and I tuned out the whispers and pointed fingers with unexpected ease. The woman on duty at the front was a steel-haired friend of Mother's, who immediately grabbed me into a hug before saying, "Couldn't your beast stay outside?"

"He's clean," I said, figuring she was worried about Ari tracking dirt in the pristine silver depths of the temple. "Is Rissa in?"

She left to look for her, leaving Ari and me standing at the front instead. I waved awkwardly when a few women filed in. "Hello. Mother's blessings upon you," I said, trying to ignore how they gaped at my gryphon.

"Smooth," Ari commented. He sat proudly next to me, head upraised like he was in parade rest.

A familiar giggle distracted me from making a cross reply, and I perked up, opening my arms to catch a gray-clad young woman.

"You're *finally* coming to visit me, huh?" Rissa asked, beaming up at me.

My little sister had returned to mimicking Mother, her platinum hair up in a bun and cosmetics giving her a perfect blush and a highlighting rim around her pretty green eyes. She wore the dove-gray robe of an acolyte of Nilara, with the fabric pinned in place at her hip with a silver pendant of a crescent moon.

"That's right. With an invitation," I said, catching her mood and grinning back. "Are you busy tonight and tomorrow night?"

"I mean, *someone* has a statue being unveiled at the Hall of Heroes tomorrow." She squinted playfully. "But what's tonight?"

When she heard, she squealed and promised to be there. We parted ways for the moment for her to finish her shift at the temple, while Ari and I rushed off to the city library, where we'd agreed to meet Galak in person for the first time. Sharde and Ellie were walking and taking in the sights together, so I made it there with time to spare.

Kaiamear's public library was a work in progress in that it was a big space, crafted with love with many nooks and two stories, but many of the shelves were still empty or half full. At this hour, it was empty of the big study groups that descended on the space after fundamental school and the couple universities in the city let out for the evening.

I'd seen Galak Nilessen in marble, of course. My fundamental school took regular trips to the Hall of Heroes to let our little hands touch the plaques and feet of the many great people who'd shaped Altare as it currently was. Though decades had passed since Queen Cortes had awarded him his Hero of Altare medal, Galak looked just like his statue, except he had more color to his skin than the pale stone suggested. His hair stuck out at the same random angles, like he'd rolled out of bed that way and finger-combed it into a tousle, and he wore a comfortable sweater and pants rather than the suit he was immortalized in.

He stood from the chair he'd claimed toward the front of the library, coming forward with his hand extended. "Miss Walker, a pleasure to finally meet you in person," he said. "And your gryphon, of course."

I shook his hand, beaming. "The same to you." I felt the stink eye of the worker on duty at the service desk. "He's clean!" I promised for the second time.

After we settled to talk, I realized Galak and I had the same problem. There was a level of starstruck wonder that came with speaking to a Hero of Altare—and we felt it for each other. He'd heard of the war tales and the extraordinary death of the Kingmaker eldrafn. And I'd been reading press books since I was a tot, made possible because of his invention.

Now that we were here in person, without the constraints of short letters, we had little in common to actually talk about. I was relieved to know that Sharde and Ellie would be arriving soon, because Ellie would talk his ears off about her inventions and work.

I made introductions when they arrived, with Puzzlebox happily laying on top of Ari while we talked. As I expected, Ellie and Galak had a lot to talk about as she told him about her success with Hvit's electricity.

Sharde and I sat closer together as that talk quickly became too smart for me. Galak spoke enthusiastically of the potential for a magicless magelight, distracting Ellie for us. "Is everything good?" he asked.

"Everyone knows the cue, and Acton's taking care of reservations," I said.

"What are you going to do in the meantime?"

"I dunno. Read a book?" I glanced around with a shrug. "Don't worry about me. I can mess around until nightfall."

I said my goodbyes after a while, thanking Galak for meeting with my friend on my way out. Ari projected boredom when our next trip was a short jaunt to the queen's gardens within the palace grounds. *"Why must human courtship be so complicated?"* he complained.

"Hush. I'd do this for you if Sunset wanted to be wooed," I said, ruffling his feathers.

He snipped his beak at me playfully. *"She did, but she was content with a whole goat for a mating gift."*

"Where'd you get one of those?"

I went over to Acton, where he was working with a uniformed mage in activating magelights around the garden and adjusting their placement. "Where would he be without us?" he asked, putting an arm around me. "I rented these for the evening."

"For the record, I can still hunt for myself," Ari said, staying close to my other side. *"Just not well."*

"I'm proud of you," I replied. Aloud, I said to Acton, "I didn't realize you could *rent* magelights."

"You can rent most anything, with the right amount of clorets," he replied. At my wry look, he shrugged. "What can I say? I was spoiled as a kid."

"As long as you recognize it," I said. In that moment, while he smiled so prettily, his strong arms around me, I wondered when he would finally go to these lengths for me. Was he planning to? Wasn't there still *some* time in our busy lives for that?

"Three," Ari said.

"Hmm?"

"That's how many chicks Sunset and I think you'll have with him."

I flushed suddenly, and Acton reached up to adjust my coat to open a small vee at the top, like I'd overheated. "It's a warmer day than I expected," I said lamely.

Meanwhile, I fumed to Ari, *"Why did you have to say that right then?"*

"You're doubting he wants to be your mate, but even a gryphon

without eyes can see that there's no reason to worry. Patience," he replied.

"Did Ironfeather say something about—"

"Sivvy," he tutted.

Frustrated, I went to sit on a nearby bench to wait for nightfall. Acton finished directing the magelight placement and sat with me while our gryphons found patches of flowers to lie in. Our friends trickled in, scouting out places to hide around where we thought Sharde might bring Ellie. Acton assured us that he'd made a clear path with the lights.

"I'm here. I'm ready to witness," Rissa announced as she came up the path. She'd bundled herself in a thick gray coat. As evening fell and the light waned, a little shiver passed up my form. Acton reached over and buttoned up my own coat again, an action my keen-eyed sister didn't miss. She clapped her hands briefly with an approving nod.

I also didn't miss the prim way she brushed off the other side of the bench before sitting next to me. "Someday, these robes are going to be white," she said in answer to my raised brow.

"So, what's new?" I asked, rather than tease.

"Well, this is probably the most exciting thing to happen to me lately. I've been doing acolyte things…cleaning, fetching kerchiefs, welcoming visitors to the temple, you know. I'm lucky we don't look alike. Folk come to the temple looking for your sister, and their eyes skim right over me."

She sounded positive enough, but I still slung an arm over her shoulders. "They'll forget about me soon enough," I said.

"Hardly," she huffed.

"In a few short months, there's going to be plenty of female gryphon riders. That's going to change things," I assured her.

She eyed me skeptically. "You're still going to be the *first* and the one with a *statue,* Sivana."

"That doesn't look like you," I teased, tickling her side.

She giggled lightly and batted me away, though she was protected by the padding of her coat.

"Have you ever wanted to be a gryphon rider?" Acton asked her.

Her lips twisted thoughtfully. "Hah, well, the thought crossed my mind. If my sister did it, so could I...but my place is serving Lady Nilara. I don't think I could do that along with caring for a gryphon. Besides, can you see *me* going to war?"

"It's hard to stay so pretty in the air anyway," I said, reaching up to muss her perfect hair. She leaned away from me with a whining "noooooo."

"Shhh shhh!" hissed Biggs, our lookout. Acton perked up and clapped his hands, making a series of magelights whir to light in the garden. We stood and retreated into the new shadows the gently glowing lights made, crouching down.

Rissa primly held the hem of her robe up around her ankles, but her grin was wide enough to split her face. "Remember when we dressed her up?" she whispered.

"That was for him," I whispered back.

It wasn't quite full dark, but the sun had set enough to make Sharde and Ellie's shadows proceed them, ambling toward this stretch of the garden arm in arm.

"Really?" she asked, lowering her voice further. "Has he grown some? He was so awkward."

"Shh, don't give us away," Acton breathed.

Rissa didn't say anything, but she looked like she was about to burst. She contained it behind a hand, muffling a few giggles before they could get any worse.

"I thought we could see something in the gardens before we got dinner," Sharde said, loud enough for all of us to hear the cue. I mimicked my sister, clamping down hard on making any noise as I leaned forward with a thrill of anticipation.

"It's very pretty here," Ellie was saying. "It's nice they

have the queen's gardens open to the public. Maybe we should come back when it's daytime, though?"

"I just want to show you something," he said, stopping under a halo of magelights that marked a split in the path. "Ellie, you're the smartest person I know. Every time I look at you, I can hardly believe how lucky I am to have you by my side."

She was in the process of fidgeting her glasses up the bridge of her nose, but her hand froze. I saw the moment she realized what was happening, her intelligent gaze darting from the magelights, to the flowers around them, and back to Sharde. He noticed it too, and the apple of his throat bobbed. He shifted and rubbed his palms on his pants. "I don't have any family but the friends we've made along the way, but I was hoping...I would like to start a new family with you. If you will have me as your husband."

Lowering to one knee, he presented her with a small box. I hadn't seen the contents, but he had told me it was a necklace. He'd known that fidgety Ellie wouldn't be able to wear a ring while she experimented, nor would she want to, so he went the old-fashioned route and bought her a token instead.

She gasped, framing her face with her hands in delight. "Yes...of course! I love you, Noah." They kissed, and I barely contained my applause until Sharde closed the clasp of the necklace behind her neck. He hugged her and laughed when she had a brief startle at the sudden appearance of all of us cheering and clapping for them.

The men clapped Sharde on the back, and I patted Ellie on the shoulder with a big smile. "Congratulations!" I exclaimed.

"Glad he's found his words," Rissa said right after me. I squinted and reached for her hair. She ducked to the side to avoid me. "I mean, congratulations. The Mother has seen and acknowledged your engagement."

Ellie seemed a little bemused by us. "Thanks," she said, giggling.

We were swept up in the group, heading down to the restaurant to eat dinner together, though we gave Sharde a seat at the head of the table, where he leaned toward Ellie just to his right and fed her morsels all evening.

CHAPTER 26

FIERCE AND WILD

I woke late the next day. We'd stayed out far past when I usually slept, and when I flipped over to see that I was in bed alone, I heaved a sigh and buried my face in the pillow. Acton and I had turned in for the night in separate rooms, but I missed him more than ever.

Your turn will come, I told myself. Still, I gave myself the luxury of lying there until my belly rumbled.

King Cortes had invited me to afternoon tea with him before the big event tonight. I took my time bathing and brushing out my hair, patiently picking out any hint of knots before upending a bag of cosmetics. Rissa could dress her face in ten minutes flat, but I took at least half a bell by the distant city chimes to apply ointment to my dry cheeks and touch up my face.

"I've got to do this more," I muttered, putting on my dress uniform and finishing it with the Hero of Altare medal. I tugged on the ribbon around my neck before deciding it would chafe if I had to wear it for the rest of the day. I put the golden disc in my pocket and ambled out of the room.

I checked in mentally with Ari, who was resting off the flight here, as I expected. He longed to return to Sunset, a feeling I retreated from lest it add to my weird mood. Alone, I followed the familiar path down to the palace kitchens, where even the meanest cook took one look at my formal gryphon rider uniform and my red hair up in a puffy bun before plying me with all the food I could hold.

I used the dining hall to wolf down my meal, and that's where they found me. Ironfeather was first, coming in low to sneak his beak into my lap and then up to sniff at the piece of seared fish I was avoiding on my plate. "Here, I don't want it," I said, scraping it into his waiting mouth.

"*Thanks,*" he said. He didn't retreat, just blinked up at me.

"What is it?" I chuckled.

"*Acton wants to talk to the king with you,*" he said. "*He wants to protect you. Are you two going to become mates?*"

I nearly choked on the food already in my mouth. Taking a sip of water, I switched to mind speech. "*Has he mentioned anything about it to you?*" I asked carefully.

Ironfeather's eyes widened, and he ducked away from me quickly. "*Uh, no! Why do you ask?*"

"I fed him this morning, I promise," Acton said. He didn't startle me, because I figured if his gryphon was here, he wasn't far behind. He'd also put on his formal uniform, filling its broad shoulders, with the Gilded Combat Cross shining with fresh polish over his other medals.

"You know him, he's just silly," I croaked, still recovering from how my food had gone down sideways. "So, you want to come to teatime with me?"

"Ironfeather told you, huh. Well, yes. Just in case the conversation gets uncomfortable when Mateo comes up," he said with a nod.

"I wasn't going to say anything more than what you wrote."

"Implying you won't fold immediately when the king asks what, exactly, Mateo's private mission is."

I scowled and put a hand to my chest, just being playful. I knew that was exactly what was about to happen.

"Uh-huh. That's why I'm here," he said, gesturing to encompass himself.

Something helpful, indeed, for by the time we went to the king's favorite solar with Ironfeather and Ari a couple hours later, the first thing he asked was, "Where is my son, exactly?" His jowls quivered, and his face set with a scowl as he glanced between us. I felt my blood ice, all too familiar with King Cortes's rage when it came to his children disappearing.

"Gathering support for the Crown in the outer reaches of Altare, Your Majesty," Acton answered smoothly, and I nodded in agreement.

"And he could not take time away from that to attend the event this evening?" the king asked without a shift in his expression. He drained his tea in two great sips before holding the cup out for a servant to hop forward and refill it in a hurry.

"He could not, but he sent us in his stead with his sincerest apologies, Your Majesty." Acton spoke without a flinch. I had to hand it to him. I still had a lot to learn about the affairs of nobles. I would've wilted fast if I were caught in the stare-off the two of them engaged in.

"Very well. I know you are his closest friend," King Cortes said, looking away first. "News doesn't reach Fortress Aerie with much haste, but surely you are aware of the situation here with the imposter."

"Do you need our help finding him, Your Majesty?" I asked.

He laughed without humor. "I have a network of spies working tirelessly at that task, Chosen. What I need from you is a miracle. One night where the people of Altare can see we are the closest of friends and that everything is fine. They need to see a solid reason not to back the imposter in flat-out rebellion."

"I can do that," I said, not even cringing when he called us friends.

"Good, because I have some prepared remarks for you." He regarded me over the rim of his teacup. "I do insist you read them over and deliver them, unless you already have a speech prepared."

I felt my cheeks pinken. "I will review the remarks you have," I said, kicking myself mentally. Instead of sitting around, I could've been writing out a speech. Of course I'd be required to deliver one right before my statue was installed in the Hall of Heroes.

I cleared my throat. "But in the meantime, Your Majesty, I was hoping we could discuss something else. My mother wrote to you recently of the town established close to Fortress Aerie, Fenway?"

"It sounds familiar," he said neutrally.

With Acton's help, I laid out our case for purchasing the land and how it would further change how the Gryphon Rider Academy was run. King Cortes listened but dismissed us shortly after we were done, saying he would think about it. He passed me a few sheets where someone had painstakingly written out a speech for me to memorize in the meantime.

"Do you think that was a promising 'I'll think about it' or a no in disguise?" I asked Acton. With nowhere else to go for now, I took him back toward my guest room.

"Hmm. He'll think about it," he answered thoughtfully.

"*I agree*," Ari said. He'd been quiet today, putting his energy into listening.

"*You would know better than me*," I said, breathing a sigh of relief. Maybe everything would work out just as we wanted.

In the meantime, I memorized the speech, having Acton quiz me on it until my recitation was perfect.

THE HALL OF HEROES was in the public wing of the palace. I was glad to see several peacekeepers when I arrived with my friends. The men and women checked every visitor for weapons and stood in strategic spots, preventing anyone from going further into the palace than they should.

I hadn't been to the Hall of Heroes since I graduated fundamental school. The massive hall was L-shaped yet seemed smaller now since I was bigger. The original gallery was full of aging statues all at least ten feet tall and placed a respectful distance away from one another's posing. Each Hero of Altare was immortalized in the moment the sculptors found them most heroic, which made me nervous to see what they'd devised for Ari and me.

Palace servants stood in the shadows of the statues or bustled between the growing knots of attendees. The path down the hall was twelve feet across and furnished by a freshly dyed, crimson rug. Acton and I walked arm in arm, and I slowed us down, pointing out what I remembered of each hero. The tradition of naming them and placing their likeness here went back to the very founding of Altare, with King Altare himself and his shield made of a single dragon's scale standing guard at the front of the hall.

"I would try to touch his shield for good luck every time we came here," I said. I easily ran my fingertips over the black marble that'd been used to form the scale. Gold painted the Altarian symbol of a gryphon rampant on its face. My fingers fell to the medal I'd finally put back on, adjusting it with a tug.

"You might be surprised to learn that my tutors brought me here on occasion, when the fundamental schools weren't touring," he said. He pointed out his favorite hero, Varrok the Vast, with his flowing mane of marble hair and teeth permanently bared. He held a pike in both hands, though the sculptors had tastefully made sure it didn't extend too far toward us. "I always thought he looked like Lord Anrathor. It's the chest."

"It's definitely the chest," I agreed. He had the barrel trunk of a berserker.

We turned left when the hall ended. This addition came when there'd been too many heroes and not enough space, which suggested that someday, the Hall of Heroes would more resemble a T-shape, as long as the palace could make room for it. I stopped at the feet of Galak's likeness, with his flustered hair and a big smile, his marble hand holding a press-bound book—the first one ever made, a copy of children's fables that'd been meant for his son.

Close by was Magnus the Grim, his statue granite. He posed with weapons in his hands and a battle beast at either hip, sitting obediently like oversized dogs. "I hope you've all found peace in the afterlife," I murmured. I'd witnessed a younger, fitter berserker defeat him in single combat, a moment colored in my mind by the pain and grief that'd cut through his battle rage the moment he'd lost his second beast.

There weren't many other statues here yet, over half the hall still waiting to be decorated. I'd met many of these still-living heroes, including the one second to the end on the left, a robed woman carrying an ornate staff that was almost as tall as she was. My gaze narrowed in hatred as I fixed on the orb of polished red glass that'd been placed in the marble talons of this rendition of Starfall.

It was Irene the Fair, and I wanted to topple her likeness and watch it shatter. But I knew I couldn't, so I clamped my jaw tight and thanked the gods that it looked like I'd be taking a place on the right side of the hall, where blankets shrouded a lumpy figure. Several servants and peacekeepers formed a protective semi-circle around its base, while a table and podium were set up nearby.

The king and several important members of his court were

already assembled, talking amongst each other with glasses and appetizer plates in hand. My friends were starting to spread out to find a place in the crowd to stand when the real Galak called out to Ellie. Acton stayed by my side while we stood by, listening to those two immediately speak in depth about Ellie's inventions.

"I see it was not imprudent to arrive early." I couldn't place the woman's voice who spoke, husky in a feminine way, but felt cold when I turned to see Irene looking toward me. She was standing with Magister Scorvash, an empty glass dangling from her elegant fingers. She lifted to the tips of her toes to kiss his cheek before sashaying over to Acton and me.

My grip tightened on Acton's arm. This was the one social encounter I'd wanted to avoid with my whole being.

"Hello, Sivana. Congratulations again. You must be very excited to see your statue so soon," she said. Her lips pulled back to flash perfect, white teeth. Zizi had expressed frustration, never able to get this woman alone for how often she spent her nights surrounded by male admirers. She *was* pretty, with a thick mane of straw-colored hair, soft features, and a unique Tulari mark on her face. It glittered from sapphire blue to an orange-red as her smile creased it, suggesting she was dual-blessed as both a wizard and a pyromancer.

"I just hope they didn't rush it too much," I said, trying for humor when I caught myself staring at her mark a second too long to be polite. I wondered how she faked the unique shimmer of a dual-blessed mage.

"Men can be rushed. Magic users cannot," she replied. "Ah, you must try the berry wine. It is sublime." She flagged a servant who was balancing a platter on his palm, exchanging her empty glass for a delicate flute of bubbling pink liquid. I took one too, with no intentions of drinking it, even when she clinked our flutes together. "To our newest Hero of Altare!"

I tipped the glass, letting the liquid touch my closed lips. The wine smelled of honey sweetness, without as much as a hint of alcoholic punch.

"I'm surprised to see you here without your famous staff," Acton remarked.

Irene hummed, a shrug lifting her shoulder. The many silvery beads along her cloak clicked, suggesting that should she turn her back, I would see a piece of art rather than a cover to keep her warm. The blue robe she wore had an embroidery of stars. "Is a woman not a mage without her staff in hand?" she asked, a more subdued kind of smirk playing at her lips. "Are you not a gryphon rider without your beast beside you?"

Ari's awareness prickled. He'd selected an alcove to rest in with a pile of the other gryphons rather than endure the touch of several humans walking past him and possibly pulling at his feathers for a souvenir.

"I'm still a gryphon rider, no matter where Ari might be. He has a life and a family separate from mine," I said.

She swept her hand toward me like I'd proven her point. "He does, doesn't he? A baby to raise, a lady gryphon to pamper. Oh, don't look at me like that. You've got all the details published in the *Voice of the People*." Something about her seemed entirely insincere, perhaps the smug look on her face. I had the feeling she was taunting me, which raised my hackles further. "And I've read every word. You could consider me a fan, even, of the beautiful...fragile alliance you're building."

Acton put his hand over where my nails threatened to rip into the sleeve of his dress uniform. *"Acton says to let her keep talking,"* Ironfeather whispered in the back of my mind.

"Are you now?" I asked her through my teeth, baring them in an approximation of a pleasant expression.

She put on an air of concern. "Well, I do hope those

gryphons will be all right without you. The king required all your rider friends attend, yes?"

"They can care for themselves," I said shortly.

"Mmh. Well, we can but hope. It's good to see you." She raised her glass toward me and then took another sip. "It's too bad your little unstable friend couldn't attend." She sailed off before I could reply, turning her back to Acton and me. As I suspected, her cloak was a work of art along the back, but I still could've seared it with my glare.

I tried to pull Acton aside further, a difficult task when several people were waiting to speak to us as soon as Irene left. We didn't have a chance until the ceremony started and the king was at the podium, welcoming a large group of citizens and promising them dinner and refreshments afterward. Acton had successfully stayed by my side for the hour or so I'd had to socialize, and by this point, I was starting to doubt if what I felt Irene implied matched up to what she actually said.

"Was it just me," I muttered behind my hand to him, "or did Irene sound like she was threatening Wild Flight?"

"I think she was too," he whispered back.

Our gazes met. That was genuine worry on Acton's face, not the insincere veneer that she'd put on like a mask. "We need to go back," I said.

"First, we need to be here," he replied firmly. "Don't let worry taint your moment. You've earned this."

He squeezed my hand reassuringly as the king stepped back and motioned for me to come forward. It was Acton I thought of as I recited the speech prepared for me so that I'd speak confidently rather than show this crowd how shaken I truly was when I thought of Irene's quick jabs.

It was probably nothing. What did Irene know of Wild Flight, after all?

I was the hero of this hour, Sivana the Wild, as proclaimed by the plaque at the foot of my new statue. King Cortes and I pulled the blankets off, and I stared along with a gasping, cheering crowd.

"I love it," Ari said, admiring it through my sight.

"Do we really look like that?" I asked, a tug pulling at my lips.

"Hmm…yes!"

"You're blind."

"And you're ungrateful. Look how fierce we are," he exclaimed.

Sure, we appeared to be plenty fierce. My marble hair was unbound behind me in streaming waves, with a pair of goggles fixed above my forehead. The sculptors had put me in plain riding leathers, all the easier to rush this statue out. The statue brandished a cavalry saber in front of her body, with a kite shield bearing Wild Flight's gryphon rampant held like an afterthought.

It looked like I was holding a royal shield, with the addition of my personal symbol of a gryphon's closed eye carved in one of the top corners. The rules of heraldry stated that only the royal family could have a shield with a white field and golden gryphon, and the swirls of pale marble sure made it close. That was certainly a choice, probably made by King Cortes.

I glanced over at him, finally smiling in truth. He was waiting to see my reaction to this honor and inclined his head. His lips moved, shaping the word "Chosen."

"Thank you," I replied.

Ari tapped on my mind, practically demanding I take another look. His statue was wrapped around mine, the two of us cut from the same block of stone. He was shown with a snarl, front leg raised and talons extended. Someone had lovingly crafted his feathers, obviously spending more time on realizing his details than mine. His eyelids were lowered over his marble eyes, a polite nod to his blindness.

"Truly the fiercest," Ari said. I had the feeling he was

tapping his front paws in a short, excited dance like a gryphon half his age.

He came to my side as we left with the rest of the group to eat dinner and celebrate. I did as Acton suggested. I didn't let worry taint the hour I stayed, but as soon as the first guests started to leave, I glanced out of a window to gauge the placement of the sun. *"Think we can make it?"* I asked Ari, who cared little about the sun setting during a journey compared to the ever-present ache in his wing.

"Without a problem," he sniffed.

We snuck ourselves out, and I turned to see Acton fussing with Ironfeather's saddle as the younger gryphon pranced after us. "You didn't think you'd be leaving without us, did you?" Acton asked.

I smiled to myself. "Wouldn't dream of it."

CHAPTER 27

THE UNTHINKABLE

We flew into the night. Acton had looked after me and told our friends where we were going and why, but I hoped they stayed in Kaiamear to rest. My eyes were feeling gritty and strained from finding all of our familiar landmarks in the dark.

I knew something was wrong the moment we nearly collided with a riderless gryphon, still far from coming in for a landing at Fortress Aerie. In the dark, I didn't know if I knew this beast or not, and the brush of its thoughts were panicked and angry before it swerved around Ari and continued flying.

Confused, Ari reached out to a few more gryphons who were still in the sky until he found one we knew who was willing to speak to us. Descending to coast alongside us was the blue-white gryphon Reyos, his feathers and fur glowing eerily in the faint light of the moon and stars.

"Thank Glorium you're back. The unthinkable has happened," Reyos said in a rush.

He blasted us with a memory. I vaguely heard a sound of distress from Ironfeather before closing my eyes, watching what he shared play out.

It was daytime, and many of the Wild Flight gryphons were having a fulfilling afternoon playing with the cadets at the monthly competition. Reyos was one of them, more open-minded than some in his flock due to our friendship.

A shrill sound pierced the air above a distant *clack-clack*, a sound pitched for a gryphon to hear. My heart sank, as I'd been the one to order and pass out these whistles to the care-takers and riders who worked with Wild Flight. The whistle, along with the ringing of the bell above the stable doors, signaled an emergency to every beast in earshot.

Nearly as one, the gryphons abandoned the Green and flew back to their territory. Reyos, as a fit young male, was one of the first to land and muscled his way to the front of the group amassing. His beak parted in a scream, a cry of distress amongst many.

"*No,*" he said, nosing the limp paw of a freshly slain gryphon. Her blue eyes, so much like his, stared sightlessly toward the ground.

Reyos recognized claw marks over Alaula's flank but smelled the distinct musk of human sweat. Horror hooked into his middle as the shock set in. *Had a human done this? But…why?*

"*Count the younglings.*" Roshawk's commanding presence stirred Reyos back into motion, but the Skylord was distracted.

For the first time, Reyos noticed that the caretaker Lira was present, her fist still holding a whistle. Her hands and apron were bloodstained, her face as white as his down feath-ers. A second caretaker lay face down nearby, but the scent of his blood was already tainting the air with its metallic stink.

Roshawk pressed his head to Lira's shoulder. "*Are you injured?*" he demanded. "*Is that blood yours?*"

To my shock, Lira wet her lips and replied with a shaky, "N-no. I tried to save them both, but they were already gone…"

I blinked, and the memory faded away. I came back to myself with a flex of my fingers and a yawning pit of dread opening where my stomach should be. *"We are searching for the murderer even now,"* Reyos said. *"We believe he is a male Link thief. He…he has stolen twenty-one of our younglings."*

"What of Novali? Is she safe?" Ari demanded.

Reyos didn't answer for a few long, terrible moments. *"She is amongst the missing,"* he murmured.

With a sudden burst of rage, Ari flew past him, arrowing toward Wild Flight's territory with new vigor. Ironfeather yelped and tried to keep up, while Reyos resumed his search. *"That mage you spoke with…she was taunting you. She knew,"* Ari seethed.

"She did," I said. We were one in this moment, a blazing comet of fury that was hours too late to stop what'd happened.

Ari homed in on his mating Link with Sunset, landing not far from her. She was down the river a ways, pacing back and forth, trilling and calling into the night. *"Arimus,"* she breathed in relief, brushing against him for comfort with me still tied in the saddle. *"Our baby, Arimus."*

"Reyos told me."

"Some of our younglings are lost in the brush. They bolted in every direction when Alaula—" She broke off and paced around him in distress. *"Novali is gone. I don't sense her anywhere."*

I freed myself from Ari's saddle, falling to my knees. *"We will find her,"* Ari vowed.

He edged in my direction, standing steady for me to heft myself back up. Fatigue and fear made for an unsteady mix within me, but we parted ways with a silent agreement. Ari went with Sunset to search for any more younglings still hiding in the tall grass while I walked the rest of the way to the main territory of Wild Flight.

I felt the pressure of dozens of gryphon minds before I saw them. Any beast not combing the skies must've been sitting in the dark in one place. The weight of their combined grief had tears springing to my eyes before I found them and endured several hostile stares turned my way.

Lira sat in the heart of a circle of wild gryphons, a dim lantern set out next to her. She turned glassy eyes in my direction as I picked a path over wings and limbs. Roshawk was next to her and shifted back for me to sit cross-legged with them.

At some point, the body of the fallen caretaker had been removed and Alaula's body was placed on a blanket. In the dark, with her limbs arranged and her head tucked, she looked like she was sleeping. *"Tonight, we hold vigil,"* Roshawk said to me. *"Tomorrow, we bury her and seek revenge in her name."*

"So it must be," I replied mentally, as it seemed wrong to utter words in the stillness of night. On the edge of my consciousness, I was aware of the gryphons around us quietly sharing stories. Alaula's name was mentioned...but I could barely perceive what was being said. It was like I was purposefully being excluded.

"In the meantime, many of us have spoken," he continued heavily. *"And we have decided that Wild Flight was a mistake. The loss of our beloved cloudling and so many younglings... Whoever did this, whatever their reason was, it doesn't matter. We should have never trusted humans as much as we have."*

I looked over at Lira. She stared off into the night, her expression one of numbness. *"But you have Linked with a human rider,"* I replied.

If he was surprised I'd figured it out, he didn't show it. *"She is much more to me than that,"* he replied. *"It took me a long time to realize it, but she completes me in a way I never expected I needed until I had her there."*

He shared a feeling, a more lighthearted twist of emotion that I clung to like a lifeline. *"More like a soul-bonded* companion," I said aloud, trying to put the feelings into words.

"That's right. A companion. She can come with us, as can you. My invitation remains open from before your war." He used the human word like it tasted bad on his tongue, all levity between us vanishing. *"It used to be that we had no concept of war, and I long for those days. We came to your rescue, killed your enemies, and suffered losses, all thinking the war would pass. And this is what I have to show for it! Now Alaula is dead, and my granddaughter is missing."*

Some of his old fury was returning, spitting sparks as he sat up, glaring at me. *"And you weren't there. You, who we decided would speak for us. You, who abdicated that role the moment an old man told you someone else could do it better."*

"You're right." A couple tears made new tracks down my cheeks. *"You're completely right. And if you truly want to leave…"*

Roshawk didn't reply, and I realized he *didn't* want to leave. His emotions were a tangled skein, and he shoved them at me with his usual lack of finesse. I always took what he dealt, and tonight was no exception.

"I don't know how to fix this," I said, weeping harder.

"Nor do I," he murmured. Then, louder, like he projected to the assembled gryphons. *"Let us say goodbye together. Sivana and Lira are proven friends to our flock, as is Ironfeather's human. Make way for him."*

The gryphons shifted, grumbling, as Acton approached and Ironfeather flopped down with a despondent caw. Roshawk stood long enough for Acton to sit before curling back up with his head in Lira's lap. The voices of Wild Flight were no longer muffled and distant. They shared their stories with me as they did everyone else, and we all shared in grief for the rest of the night.

WHEN MORNING CAME, the circle of mourning gryphons had become the whole flock. The gryphons that'd been combing the skies had returned one by one, and a diminished group of younglings huddled under Valtora's spread wings, wide-eyed and terrified. Ari and Sunset had returned with two babies they'd found, bringing the number of missing young gryphons down to nineteen.

One of them was still Novali. Even bleary with exhaustion and dry from a tearful night, I knew there would be no rest for myself and my gryphon family until she was returned safely.

First, we had to bury Alaula, and the gryphons intended to do this where we were, in the center of their territory. "We should find a better place for her than this," I said aloud. Several distrustful looks flashed my way, and I rubbed at my eye, trying to remember all that Alaula had told me. "She... she was not able to fly away in her last hours, as would be her instincts. Which means we should do it for her, and pick a..."

How did she phrase it? I sniffed, and my nostrils flared with pain.

"*A place in nature, far from manmade structures,*" Valtora said. She stood straight, cooing to the younglings who clung to her limbs. "*Yes. You and Ari will fly her, and the rest of us will follow. What better memory can we give a cloudling who died fighting for her charges than a proper last flight?*"

"*It is not proper if a human is involved,*" snapped one of the wild mothers.

Valtora snipped her beak back, puffing out her chest and wings in a show of dominance. "*My son and human daughter have done nothing but support us. Besides, they have tools for this task.*"

I turned to Lira, who was aware enough now to meet my gaze. "I'll get breakfast started," she said dully.

"We need some shovels instead. Will Roshawk allow you on his back?" I asked.

She bit into her lower lip, glancing over at the scarred gryphon. He bunted her shoulder encouragingly. "Only if I don't wear a saddle," she answered.

"I will fly low to the ground," he promised.

"Wait," Acton murmured, glancing between them. He didn't have the energy to be surprised either and heaved a shrug as he went toward Alaula's body. "Ironfeather says you're carrying her body? You get on Ari's back. I'll hand her up to you."

"Okay," I murmured. We went about the task with efficiency. I would almost describe it as passionless, except when he handed up the blanket bearing Alaula's body and I hefted her to rest in front of me…I found some salt within me to cry a little more. At rest, she was too light, too bony, awkward to balance even with a cloudling's smaller body.

We will find you the perfect glade to rest in, I promised her silently.

Meanwhile, dissonantly, Ari seethed. *"We will find the one responsible and destroy him. And rend the wings off the gryphon who aided him."*

We checked our Link at the same time. He reminded me of Novali's absence and the terror of the remaining younglings, while I reminded him that Alaula still deserved to have her spirit sent to the Gatekeeper in peace.

"You're right," we said at the same time.

Ari quieted his mind over the flight. We were the head of a slow procession. When I glanced over my shoulder, it seemed like the entirety of Wild Flight followed, down to the younglings clinging to the backs of their mothers, Valtora, or bundled into Lira's arms.

Acton was carrying the shovels. The three of us went to work at the edge of a field of grass where I remembered a spray of wildflowers sprang up several months ago. We thought Alaula would like it.

CHAPTER 28

COLLAPSE

Adrenaline only took me so far. I was truly dragging by the time we flew back and found an incredibly confused cluster of Biggs, Credell, Pereyra, and their gryphons. They were wondering where all of us were, and Biggs was unable to hide his recoil when he saw my exhausted, dirt-streaked self falling off Ari's back.

"It might be over," I said numbly. "We may have just buried Wild Flight."

Acton escorted me away from them, intending for me to go wash up and rest. But with Ari and Sunset pacing at the back of my head, there was no way that was happening.

"Perhaps the younglings will share what they remember soon," Sunset was saying. *"Valtora has been trying to calm them down all morning."*

"They just watched us bury Alaula. How could they be calm now?" Ari growled.

"We have to see the human's face."

"What good will that do us? It's obvious he and his gryphon are long gone by now."

"It will give us an idea of what a human needs with nineteen younglings if we know who he is," she replied grimly.

Ari sighed mentally and pulled on our Link, an unspoken demand that I come over to them. They were walking over to Valtora, who now had a dozen younglings dozing around her. The rest were, in theory, with their mothers. Not every youngling had their mother around since they were born of combat beasts across the flights who'd returned to duty. Valtora's nurturing presence was the most comforting place for them.

Something passed between her and Ari silently before she bobbed her head. She nudged a young male toward him and Sunset. *"Show them what you showed me, Sadry."* When he made a squall of complaint, she cooed and nosed him tenderly.

Sadry huffed and closed his eyes. Unlike with Reyos, who was able to push me straight into a strongly realized memory, the youngling shared a shaky, incomplete thread. Patches of his memory were smells: soil, grass, sweat.

He'd panicked the moment his favorite caretaker raised his voice. "Hey! Put the youngling down now!"

The sound of a sword being unsheathed.

Sadry hunkering down in the grass as Alaula stood and spread her wings in a threat display with a soft, unpracticed hiss. *"You will have to go through me,"* her kind voice said.

And an unfamiliar female gryphon replying, *"With pleasure."*

Some of Sadry's fellow younglings froze in place while Alaula and the other female battled briefly. The old cloudling barely stood a chance, but still, she tried, ending up pinned and struggling, her mental presence raised to a scream. She was trying to sound an alarm, but the other gryphon's mind muffled hers.

The memory wavered too badly to continue. I blinked and saw the youngling trembling in place, his head hunched down under the line of his small wings. *"Just a little more,"*

Valtora urged, a hint of frustration in her tone. Sadry just curled further with a whine.

"We need to know where to find your friends," Sunset said more gently, joining Valtora in grooming and soothing him.

He shuddered and tried. It was even more disjointed than before, but I furrowed my brow and focused, my heart beating like a fluttering bird in my chest from secondhand fear. Sadry ran and hid in a bank of tall grass. From there, he saw the caretaker fall, and heard the screeching of the younglings and a blast of cold.

There was a flap of blue cloth, a fold of a robe as seen from something small. The unfamiliar person was a wizard with a staff, who'd cast some kind of spell to freeze several young gryphons in place.

"Kill this one too," laughed the rider's gryphon, distracting Sadry's memory from the Tulari. Sadry saw the flash of the sword and flinched, feeling Alaula's death rather than seeing it. With her out of the way, the adult gryphon herded as many younglings to her rider as she could. He was dressed in dark riding leathers, grabbing them and shoving them into a canvas sack with the Tulari's help.

"Ah, the red one. Easy."

Sadry saw him in profile, holding a limp Novali by her scruff. A lance of pain split my heart, and I jerked from the memory, gasping for air. I held my chest, wondering if I was having a heart attack, or if it was just a visceral reaction to seeing a face I had, quite frankly, tried to confine to the depths of my worst nightmares.

For dangling Novali, smirking victoriously at how easily he'd caught her, was none other than Commander Davis.

A few short years ago, a crown prince once promised me I'd never see Commander Davis again. He'd sabotaged the flight training net, trying to kill me. When that hadn't worked, he'd tried to carve the mark of Lord Orion into my forehead to sacrifice me like a heretic or an oath breaker.

And his gryphon…she'd just acted with unspeakable cruelty to her own kind. She was named Bittergale. During Flight Training, she would laugh, crowing with delight, with Davis and the rest when Ari and I failed or faltered. I'd never assumed she would follow Davis into something as cruel as killing a cloudling and stealing gryphon young.

Their presence revealed just another lie told out of the corner of Isaac's mouth, however, crumpling the moment he died.

I sat down hard and stared at my dirt-encrusted fingers, waiting for the urge to scream to pass. For once, I had more control than Ari. He threw his head back and unleashed a vicious roar. Sadry bolted behind Valtora's bulk, and she stared at him in disapproval.

"Commander Davis! I thought we were done with him!" he raged.

"You and me both," I mumbled.

"He took my daughter!"

"He targeted her." Sunset nudged the side of his neck. *"Think about it. You said you returned early because a human mage hinted that something was amiss?"*

He growled like a rumbling thunderstorm. *"And one helped him do this."*

"It's revenge for us helping Zizi," I said with dawning horror. *"They couldn't go after her or my brother, so they got more creative. And who knows how things run around here better than a former instructor?"*

The thought of rogue mages experimenting on or trying to remove the magic from Novali and the other younglings had despair nearly crushing me. Where would Davis and the unidentified wizard take her, other than a warded facility like the House of the Unstable?

"We must find Irene *and make her sing,"* Ari growled. He used a bit of Zizi's memory to speak her name with proper scorn.

"First, we report to Father what's happened." I took a moment to glance over at Valtora.

"He is aware. We may have a bigger problem on our claws soon," she said.

"What could possibly—"

"The Paragon is here. He's been here since yesterday and hasn't inspected Wild Flight yet. Nathaniel has been stalling."

"Gatekeeper take me," I muttered.

"Where is the young man I put in charge of your element?" Brekwell asked the moment I crossed his path right outside my father's office and saluted, saying I was ready to report in for Wild Flight. My face and hands were freshly scrubbed, and if he noticed the dark hollows under my eyes, he made no comment.

"Celebrating his betrothal in the capital, sir. I'm here as his second," I replied.

He put his hands behind his back and raised a strict brow. "Hmph. Something doesn't smell quite right, Lieutenant Walker. The gryphons seem upset, and the cadets who won this month's competition are too, given that they weren't allowed to spend today with Wild Flight. Care to explain?"

I scoffed openly before I could restrain myself. "We have been dealing with more serious matters, sir."

Sunset, who'd flown me to the fortress, nudged my shoulder from behind with the flat of her beak. *"Diplomacy,"* she reminded me.

I was practically in a cold sweat already at having to tell the Paragon himself what'd happened, but I nodded. "What I mean to say, sir," I said to Brekwell's reddening face, "is that tragedy has struck Wild Flight, and the crime has come from a fellow corps member."

Father looked at me with undisguised disbelief. It was unlikely that Valtora was able to tell him what we'd recently learned, so this would be news to him as well. "If we may speak in private?" I asked, gesturing to his office.

"By all means," Father said, turning to unlock the door and hold it open for us. Sunset settled next to Brekwell's gryphon in Night's old nest while the rest of us sat. I nursed a glass of water Father poured for me from one of his decanters, trying to take measured sips. My head hurt from a lack of water and care, and taking a drink was an effective way to interrupt the urge to cry again as I upended the whole truth of what happened for both men.

"A crafter-class wizard and…Commander Marcus Davis?" Brekwell asked once I told him the identities of the murderers and youngling thieves.

"One in the same," I said.

"I served with him in the Third. Never heard a bad word about him," he commented.

My jaw dropped in shock. "Sir—" I began.

"No," Father said, speaking louder than was polite and slapping his desk. "I will tell you a few bad words *right now*. That man tried to murder my daughter in the Flight Training room with a sabotaged net and nearly succeeded!"

Brekwell observed Father's outburst with a cold gaze. "Calm yourself, Marshall Walker," he said.

"Calm myself?" Father echoed in disbelief. "Davis was *dishonorably discharged* for attacking a cadet, and now he's out here stealing our future!"

Brekwell hardly raised his voice. "If he was dishonorably discharged, that means he and his gryphon were executed. Your daughter is fabricating the whole thing and trying to pin it on a convenient scapegoat." His gaze swung my way. "Isn't that right?"

"I-I know what I saw," I said, shaken by how quickly he'd

flipped this around on me. "*Who* I saw. I would know Commander Davis even blinded and deafened."

"And your only piece of evidence is that a baby gryphon told you so?" he mocked. "Where did the nineteen younglings really go, Lieutenant Walker? Did their wild mothers get tired of being catered to hand and foot by humans and leave?"

Anger swelled in my chest, and I met his stare defiantly. "I will remind you that I am the Chosen of Lord Orion, and my actions reflect his will." I silently prayed that he would flash his power through my eyes in the same way that unsettled the king. Brekwell's expression didn't change. "Everything I do, everything I've *done*, has been for the betterment of his blessed beasts. If a group of wild mothers decided to leave, I would let them and would tell you of the decision without hesitation. But they didn't. Their children were kidnapped, and a cloudling and caretaker were murdered right here on corps land. By a Tulari and a man who was unmistakably *Commander Marcus Davis*."

At the last moment, I remembered myself and appended an angry "sir" to the end of my rant.

"*I believe her,*" whispered Brekwell's gryphon.

For the first time, Brekwell's expression softened. He turned to look at her. She and Sunset were grooming one another and conferring quietly. I had the feeling that, as we spoke, Sunset showed the elderly female memories of everything we'd seen, done, and witnessed.

"Dawnchaser," he murmured, a hint of shock carried in her name.

"*I don't remember us seeing anything about what the new Commandant said. A sabotaged net? An attempted murderer right here in the Academy? The man they speak of was never discharged.*"

"High Command never heard the case for Commander Davis's discharge?" I asked aloud. "Then how…"

Brekwell whispered what sounded like a curse under his breath. "Let me think," he said.

"It was around Yuletide," Father prompted. "He was removed from his role as instructor here and replaced by Commander Darion Rudrick."

"There was that young man who was court-martialed around Yuletide," he muttered.

I felt doubt twist my lips. Was he being intentionally dense? "The year before that," I said.

"Oh, yes, I remember," Dawnchaser said, sitting up straighter. *"Hughes was furious. This man was pardoned and replaced before we ever heard the case."*

"How is that possible?" I asked, with a sinking feeling.

"The crown prince wanted him for something…"

"It was a long time ago," Brekwell said.

The feathers lifted on the back of Dawnchaser's neck. *"I told you we should've retired. Your memory isn't getting any better."*

For a moment, Brekwell made an expression of pure chagrin and switched to speaking to her privately. Father looked over at me with a raised brow, so I summarized, "They can't remember what the former crown prince wanted with Commander Davis, but he was pardoned and replaced before High Command could motion to court-martial him. I never heard anything about him after he left… I assumed he was posted to a different flight."

Father's expression grew even stormier. "And I was told he was dishonorably discharged, and thus executed, for violating the corps code of conduct."

"I think it's safe to say Isaac lied and used him for his own purposes. And now that he's dead…Davis is working with a different group now," I said grimly. *The mages who'd captured and tortured Zizi.*

The Paragon shook his head, freeing himself from what looked like a daze. "I will return to my office and pull his file.

But…no matter where he's been all these years, it's unlikely to help us with the problem at hand." He shifted in his seat, facing me. I felt like he'd lowered a metaphorical shield and was speaking to me as a person and a gryphon rider for the first time. "It's going to take a miracle from the gods to find those gryphon babies. If they had just Linked, their riders would be able to trace their location. But they did not, and they've been gone for nearly twenty-four hours now. The chances of us finding them started out slim and grow slimmer with every moment that passes."

"You're right, sir. But that doesn't mean that I, or Wild Flight, will give up trying," I said with a tired sigh.

"We will put a bounty on his head and offer rewards for any information," he said. "*But* if we have truly lost nineteen valuable young beasts, then you understand that your new way of running the Gryphon Rider Academy is over, yes? This is why I've been opposed to it from the very start. It made a vulnerability that our enemies could exploit."

I lifted my chin a notch. "That means I will find them, sir. I will beg the gods for a miracle if I have to. And Wild Flight… I'll beg them too, once their grief has settled and their younglings returned, to stay and try to trust us again. It *can* work out." I thought of Novali dangling from Davis's hold, and the rage that kindled in me was enough to rival Ari's. I bared my teeth. "It has to. What you are seeing isn't the collapse of Wild Flight. It's a hurdle we will overcome."

Father looked at me with pride. "All the assets I can spare will be allocated to help you."

"Good luck, young woman." A soft, disbelieving laugh left Brekwell's lips. "I, too, will pray for a miracle on your behalf."

I LEFT them and coordinated search teams, both gryphon and human and a mix of both. Our only plan was to comb the entirety of Altare, straining for a Link with any of the younglings. Brekwell had given me that idea in saying that they should've already had riders who could do this instead. He must've not realized that Links formed both temporary and permanent within gryphon society.

I sat in the partially built courtyard of Glorium's Roost and prayed. Strained, really, when neither Lord Orion nor his gryphon appeared. It felt like a betrayal, for one of the conditions of me becoming Chosen was that I would have the god's guidance along the way.

Maybe Zizi was right. Maybe Lord Orion doesn't care about us after all.

At some point, I dozed off and startled awake still sitting in a pose of prayer. It was dark, but dawn light was rimming the peaks of the hills around me. On a surge of panic, I fell off my perch of wooden boards. I'd passed out for hours, yet no one had roused me. Did they think I was that deep in supplication?

I bumped my head on the back of the stack of boards and groaned. Through the film of my grogginess came a peal of bells and a childlike giggle that coalesced into a song as pure as unfiltered moonlight. Revna fluttered in for a graceful landing on top of the boards next to my head, her outline and the banding on her chest seeming to glow lavender for the space of a blink.

She then looked at me upside down. "Hi, Sivana! Did your hit your head? Maybe this will help?" She opened a wing and showered me with so much moon dust I felt its grit run down my riding leathers. It was like she'd turned over a bucket of sand over my head…but the bump on the back of my skull did stop throbbing.

"Thanks, baby storm," I said, sure I was never going to get all that glitter out of my hair or off my leathers.

She hopped to the ground and pressed to my side. "I love you," she sing-songed. My eyes burned, too dry to cry again, but a lump formed in my throat. I put my arm around her, finding that she was the perfect size to snuggle now. "Um, I had a weird dream last night. There was this man, and he tried to teach me a song, but it was too complicated. He said I wasn't ready but that he wanted me to bring back a message to tell you when I woke up."

I worried my bottom lip between my teeth. "Did he tell you his name?" I asked.

"Yes, but I forgot. The whole thing is fading," she admitted. "The message was something like…*help can come from the most unlikely sources.*"

I stiffened. "Was he…shiny?"

She bobbed. "Very!"

I had the sudden urge to get moving, to see what Lord Orion meant and why he'd chosen Revna to share this rather than speak to me directly. As I got to my feet, Revna fluttered after me, keeping up with my pace with short hops and flaps of her wings. "I heard what happened," she said sadly. "Does the message help any?"

I stepped into Wild Flight's main territory, where Lira and our three temporary caretakers were preparing the morning meal of fish and scraps. I braced myself for a godly coincidence and received none until after the gryphons were fed and Revna was perched on the edge of the stable's roof, eyeing me uncertainly.

I wasn't sure there would be any help at all, unlikely or otherwise, when I turned to see Puzzlebox coming in for a skidding landing. Her sides heaved from exertion, and Sharde was jumping from her back and rushing to me, extending a rumpled piece of parchment my way. "Sivvy!" he exclaimed. "You've got to see this!"

CHAPTER 29

UNLIKELY SOURCES

I LOOKED at what ended up being two notes, a furrow appearing between my brows. I glanced up at Sharde, who simply said, "I know."

I'd read the more rumpled one first:

Hi, Sivana, I'm a big fan.

My friends and I know where your baby gryphons are and want to help you get them back. Go visit the Little Wonders Pet Shop in Kaiamear. Tell them Five & Chance sent you.

Instead of a signature line, there was what appeared to be doodles of a few animals. If it were any other day, I'd assume this was just another weird piece of fan mail and feed it to the fire.

The second note was from my sister's familiar handwriting:

Dearest Sivana,

A stranger gave me a letter to pass to you and stressed that it was of the utmost importance that you receive it right away. Well, I read it before she left, and she stayed to answer a few questions. She said a rather shy animal lover wants to help you.

Did Wild Flight suffer an attack recently? She seemed convinced that several baby gryphons were catnapped, for lack of a better term, and that you needed immediate help. I figured it was better to pass the message along and have it be timely than to dismiss something you might need as nonsense. Noah agreed, so he's taking these messages to you.

She signed her name alongside "Mother's Blessings Upon You," and my hands trembled as I tried to weep with sheer relief.

"Are you okay?" Sharde asked uncertainly. "Did… Were we really attacked?"

"Yes…and I'm going to talk to the person who wrote this message," I said, folding both notes neatly.

I reached out to Ari mentally. He was far, flying with Sunset, and sent back a questioning feeling. I tugged on our Link insistently, signaling that he needed to return right away.

"Hey, Sivvy?" Puzzlebox asked. She was still panting from their flight, but padded over to me, her head tilted curiously. *"Why are you covered in sparklies?"*

I felt a flash of playfulness. *"C'mere and I'll show you."*

She narrowed her eyes at me and backed away a step. *"What do you mean?"* she squeaked.

"I just want to give you a hug!"

We walked a few loops, her moving away from me, before Ari flew back into range to for us to talk. My mood turned sober quickly as I shared the messages and where we needed to go. *"We'll be right there,"* he said.

WE LEFT Pereyra in charge and flew off as quickly as we could grab supplies. I'd learned my lesson and took a small group with me, the rest staying behind to keep watch for any threats to our remaining younglings. Sharde and Acton flew to

Kaiamear with me, as did Sunset, who followed off Ari's wing with the mental presence of a concerned cloud.

"Do we even know where Little Wonders Pet Shop is?" Iron-feather asked for Acton.

"Yes! It's a fun place," Puzzlebox squeaked. *"Ellie was thinking about adopting a puppy from there. He had spots like me."*

"Why didn't she adopt him?" I asked.

"Well, she wants a house first so she and Noah can fill it with hatchlings and *puppies,"* she said, seeming happy at the thought.

None of us had taken the time to explain to Puzzlebox what'd happened. The flight ahead was a good time, I reflected, but even Ari pushed back at the thought, suggesting quietly that Sharde should do it in private. We tiptoed around the subject for hours in the air, letting her fill the space with stories about where Sharde and Ellie went and were planning to go in the city while they took some leave.

Ari and Sunset conferred privately on occasion, but I felt most of their discussions were about him getting some rest. Exhaustion jarred his bones with each flap of his wings, especially the left, which ached from his old injury.

"How can I rest when our baby is in danger?" his emotions projected.

"I'll fly Sivana next time if you're going to be so stubborn," her emotions answered in a medley of frustration and worry.

Humor. *"Where do you think I learned it from?"*

Still, he was slowing the group down, and we arrived in the capital by early evening with Puzzlebox puffing along at the head of our formation. She and Sharde steered us toward the more impoverished side of Kaiamear, marked by the castle-like reform school that squatted in the heart of this section of the city.

I'd rarely ventured this far from the palace before I became a gryphon rider. It contained the ending alleyways of the main market street, the only ground-level area broad enough for us to land. Ari stumbled and groaned once we stopped.

"Let's walk it out," I suggested, disentangling myself from the saddle. I gripped his reins to guide him down the road and back, ignoring a thin stream of passersby who slowed to turn and stare.

Acton, Sharde, and I walked to the pet shop, trailing Ironfeather, Puzzlebox, Ari, and Sunset. Ari walked shoulder-to-hip with Ironfeather to navigate the treacherous cobblestone street. They had to practically press against a few buildings along the way to avoid horse-drawn carts.

"Well, this is hard to miss," I commented. At a street corner was a building that had the bones of an inn, two stories high with a raised roof and an aged wooden sign swinging in the wind. The faded paint read **Little Wonders Pet Shop**. The front entrance had a short set of stone stairs and a wooden access ramp.

We entered, and my nostrils were immediately assailed by the smell of animals and all their associated needs. A man in a wheeled chair raised a hand in greeting and smiled, just for his expression to turn dumbfounded as our four gryphons flanked us.

Unexpectedly, Puzzlebox darted out from behind me and raced into the main room, where the pets waited in cages and kennels. Sharde chased her, but she was only going to a particular kennel and sitting close enough to almost be touching a small, spotted dog nose-to-beak.

The shopkeeper gripped one of the wheels on his chair to turn it. "Thomas!" he called.

"Coming!" a boy answered from upstairs. The innards of the inn this building had once been meant that there was a staircase lining the left wall, while the main area that would have a bar and hearth for patrons instead had many cages and kennels.

There was a young couple here too, though they'd paused

in speaking to another employee, a Black girl dressed in an apron. She wore it over a warm jacket and pants with colorful patches of fabric over the knees. All three of them were staring between us and Puzzlebox.

"We, ah, weren't expecting you so soon," the man in the wheeled chair said. He approached and stuck out a hand. "I'm Fletcher, a veterinarian and the owner of this establishment. Do any of your gryphons require a checkup while you're here?"

It was only then that I noticed the Tulari mark on his face, a faded green. It wasn't a perfect circle, but instead wavering around the edges, like it was melting. How strange. "Have you worked with a gryphon before?" I asked.

"Don't you dare," Ari grumbled.

"Yes, actually. I specialize in veterinary magic for all manners of creatures big and small."

"My wing is fine."

"Your gryphon's wing is hurting him?" he asked without missing a beat.

"You understood me?" he asked in disbelief.

Fletcher smiled kindly and tapped the side of his temple. "Part of the magic is communication." A small animal on his shoulder made a squeak, like it agreed with what he'd said.

I squinted at it, recognizing the spined back of a hedgehog with a pointed little nose and button eyes. It sat on Fletcher's shoulder, perfectly calm. "I've never met a tamed hedgehog before," I commented.

His expression brightened. "Oh, yes. This is Edgimus, my good friend. I don't suggest you try to touch him. He is quite wary of strangers."

If any of us were taken aback by him referring to a small animal as a good friend, none of us spoke up. Fletcher soon rolled aside to reveal a boy who couldn't be more than thirteen, tall and stick-thin, with a pale face marked by inflamed patches of acne.

The boy's eyes widened to twice their normal size. "Oh… can I take them upstairs to talk, Father?" he asked.

"That would be most wise," Fletcher answered, giving him an unreadable look. "Shauna and I can cover the front."

We had a short round of introductions, and Ari agreed, with reluctance, to see Fletcher once we heard what the kid had to say. I figured this was the shy animal lover mentioned in Rissa's note, though there was little about Thomas that struck me as timid right off. The pet shop was a nice, cozy place, but I also wondered if coming here was chasing fluff after all.

Sharde waved us on and caught Fletcher's attention, lowering his voice and gesturing to the spotted puppy. He was already reaching for Puzzlebox's saddle, where he kept his coin purse.

The rest of us scaled the steps to the next floor. It had a long hall and several rooms, and Thomas led us into the first one. "Hey, Heather, look who's here," he said cheerfully.

I had the feeling I was walking into a cat room, set up with a scratching tree, a few round cushions, and plenty of colorful toys. There was a single bench set up at the back, where the flash of a gray tail was retreating behind the cloak of a girl already sitting there.

She had much the same reaction as Thomas, her mouth popping open at the sight of the five of us crowding into the space. A muscle flickered in her lower eyelid. "Um, hi," she said, flashing her palm in a shy wave.

Thomas took over the third round of introductions, including accurately naming each of our gryphons. The girl, Heather, straightened and looked over at them with interest. She was short and thin-limbed, with brown hair neatly cropped at her shoulders and skin tanned from time in the sun. She wore a uniform that took me a moment to recognize. It had a shield stitched into the shoulder with RSI in the center over a pair of crossed keys, standing out yellow on the black cloth.

I propped myself against the wall and folded my arms, immediately less than impressed. She was an RSI kid, an enrollee in the Radcliffe-Stone Institute for Troubled Youth. It told me she was a troublemaker in the past and possibly the present.

"Which of you sent the note?" I asked.

"I did," she said. "Um, did you ask for Five and Chance?"

If this moment couldn't be odder, a brown mouse popped its head out of the corner of her cloak and scampered up it to sit on her shoulder. I exchanged a glance with Acton, who seemed about as underwhelmed as me.

I lifted a brow. "I didn't need to."

"Well, we weren't expecting you so quickly." She glanced down at her uniform with a twist of her lips. "But I meant what I wrote. I've wanted to help you get your baby gryphons back from the moment we heard they were stolen. There's a lot we have to talk about, but first…"

Thomas left us briefly to retrieve chairs, and Heather waited for him to return, murmuring too quiet to hear. The mouse squeaked occasionally, almost like he was talking to her. I took the well-used chair placed next to Heather, beckoning to Noah and Puzzlebox before Thomas closed the door on our gathering.

The gryphons spread out more, with Ari closing his eyelids and releasing a long sigh. Sunset let him sprawl out and settled into the line of his body behind him, grooming him tenderly.

I took my eyes off Ironfeather for those moments and realized he'd come over to stand right in front of Heather. His beak was inches from her chest, his gaze fixed on her mouse. He made a low, curious noise and crowded her further.

"Ironfeather, manners," I scolded, pushing him by the beak away from her.

He whined and retreated a step. *"I just wanted to see him,"* he complained, edging closer to her again. This time, the mouse hopped onto his nose, and my sweet boy's eyes crossed trying to look at it.

"Do you know what a little wonder is?" Heather blurted out. She seemed quite nervous and watched the two of them interact with her hands upraised, like she was ready to snatch the mouse back.

"Can't say I do," I said.

"Chance." She held her hand out with a click of her tongue, and the mouse returned to her, to her visible relief. He stood upright on his two back paws, squeaking and tilting his head, displaying a flash of white between his rounded ears. With a cautious smile on her lips, she extended her palm and the mouse out to me. "Here, take a look at 'im. He's a carpenter mouse, one of the smallest little wonders. He's got thumbs!"

I held out my hand next to hers, not missing the sudden enthusiasm in her voice and the way she spoke with a trace of the lazy street tongue most commonly heard around this part of Kaiamear.

Chance scampered from her to me, standing and extending his paws for me to see that he did have an extra digit. Heather handed him a crinkly cat toy, and he gripped it in both paws, turning it over and manipulating it. He had little teeny hands. *Fascinating.* I held him closer to my face to see him better, much like Ironfeather had tried to do.

"Is this a mutation?" Acton asked.

"No, he's a different species. Little wonders are like him… similar to a kind of animal and usually able to blend in with them but still different and magical in their own way," she said.

I passed him to Acton, and he held the mouse away from himself. He probably still saw him as a pest animal.

"If you saw the hedgehog on my father's shoulder, he's a different kind of little wonder," Thomas said. I blinked at him owlishly for a moment. "There are dozens of different species, and they all have small magics. Like your gryphon is a blessed beast, with a big power, telepathy, each little wonder has a small power. Carpenter mice have thumbs, dreamhogs like the one my father owns can put anyone to sleep, and so on."

Acton put Chance back on top of Ironfeather's beak, earning an excited *craw* from the gryphon. The mouse chittered back. Ironfeather pranced off with him.

"Next thing you're going to tell me is that they can Link," I commented.

"Well…yeah. Chance and I are Linked," Heather said. "Which means I can understand him."

Acton's nose wrinkled, and I nudged his foot with mine. With what I'd recently learned of true Links, the knowledge of little wonders was like slotting a missing piece to my understanding of Links into place. Not anyone could, or would, Link to gryphons or another blessed beast. There just weren't that many of them…

"Focus," Ari growled.

I pinched my brow. *"Sorry,"* I murmured, refocusing on Heather and Thomas. "That is interesting and all, but what does that have to do with the stolen gryphon younglings?"

"Background information," Heather answered. Her gaze skimmed over me, and I had the feeling she was measuring something about what she saw. "Fletcher, Thomas, and Shauna run this operation, one of the only places a little wonder can come and be themselves."

"We provide medical attention and a safe space for births and elderly care," Thomas added.

Heather murmured to the cat hiding between her back and the wall. Its little face peered out by her hip, eyes dilated with fear. "That means any information about disappearances makes it here quickly," the girl said. "Smoky, c'mon, little lady. We can trust 'em."

Acton shifted impatiently, muttering, "Really?" when I made kissy noises and rubbed my fingers together, as if calling out any old frightened cat.

But the moment Smoky emerged, he was the first to gasp in surprise. The cat had *wings*, attached at the shoulders like a gryphon's. She crawled into Heather's lap and looked at us with distrust. She was an aristocrat's cat, with a coat of blue-gray fur that was short and velvet-like. The wings, folded tight to her sides, were feathered and full. I didn't doubt that she could fly if she wanted to.

"How?" I asked, dumbfounded. "How have there been winged cats like her, and I didn't know it?"

"Little wonders are great at hiding in plain sight. This is Smoky, a small feligryph. I know one that's twice 'er size." Heather soothed the winged cat with gentle strokes, petting down the spine and over the curves of her wings. "She came here for help after her litter was stolen."

"She's one of the most recent victims. Little wonders have been disappearing at random all across Kaiamear," Thomas said.

"And you think the stolen gryphon younglings are one more disappearance?" I asked.

"Well…" He reached into his pocket, withdrawing a slim roll of parchment. "You're going to find this hard to believe."

"We've come a long way hoping to believe," Acton commented.

He unrolled the paper and flattened it, showing us that it was blank on both sides. "There's a group of Tulari organizing a secret auction, and this is one of the invitations. If you don't know the password, it just looks blank. But it's actually an exact copy of the same piece of parchment and was recently altered. Here."

He gave me the invitation and the password. The paper

was soft and worn, feeling like a piece of fabric between my fingers. "Cabexios," I repeated. It was the name of the plant that was the main ingredient in truth serum. A poison, as I'd learned.

Ink flooded the page. Acton looked over my shoulder and had to say the password too to view what the page really said. "You are cordially invited to a one-of-a-kind event," I read aloud in a murmur, nausea rising in my belly all the while. "Are you a Tulari in need of unique reagents? Or perhaps you have dreamt of owning a living myth? Creatures big and small will be...sold at auction price."

I swallowed a mouthful of bile. This was also, apparently, the third annual auction of its kind. The main invitation was written with fine penmanship in black ink. Someone had listed to the side in a splash of red:

Over one hundred small creatures from your wildest imaginings!

An exceptionally rare triple-headed rozash!

Nineteen young gryphons just waiting to Link with you!

"Our younglings," Ari snarled. The sight stirred the embers of his fatherly rage.

"We're one big step closer to having them back," Sunset soothed.

"If you would keep the invitation kind of nice. It's the only one we have," Thomas said apologetically.

I'd drawn the parchment taut, my fingers indenting the sides. "Here, take it back," I muttered, making fists with my hands once it was safely in his care.

"It really is revenge," I said to Acton. I wished I could've said I had a definitive idea of what to do next rather than an animal panic that the Tulari who'd targeted Zizi and my younglings weren't done. They could also try to steal Rissa from her bed or Mother from another one of her fruitless trips to Fenway.

"We have a plan," Heather said, taking a deep, measured breath. "And we can find a place for you within it, if you all agree to a level of discretion. The auction is very soon, but it can still be canceled and relocated if, err, the Tulari in charge realizes they're going to have more guests than the folk they invited. Which means you shouldn't try to run to the peace-keepers and overrun the place they're set up at. They'll be gone like…" She snapped her fingers.

I swallowed thickly. "Fine. What do you suggest, then?" I asked. I wasn't in the habit of taking advice from a kid younger than Rissa, but the situation was dire. If any misstep meant we lost Novali, I would pick the path with measured care.

Heather smiled toothily. "We can do a lot with one invitation to the event." She sketched out the bones of her plan for us: that she and her friends, or "her crew" as she called them, would sneak several people into the auction using the same invitation. I would be disguised and smuggled into the event with their help.

"The biggest thing is, we need an auction-ending distraction, a huge disaster for those running the thing. That's where you come in. How many angry gryphons can you bring to Kaiamear in the next couple days?" she asked.

Sunset stirred from grooming Ari when I turned my attention toward her. *The entire might of Wild Flight would take wing for the chance to save our younglings and bring Alaula's murderer to justice.*

"Enough to make the most epic distraction you've ever seen," I answered.

CHAPTER 30

LADY

W_E left the Little Wonders Pet Shop that evening overwhelmed. We had exactly two days to intercept the auction where Novali and our other younglings would be sold to the highest bidder. On one hand, I felt like we could trust Thomas and Heather.

On the other hand, we needed to report to the king and ask for any help he could provide. Those two were still kids, and I was convinced we were dealing with the Tulari who'd made Zizi disappear. It was a mistake to underestimate what they were capable of and put the gryphon younglings' lives in the wrong hands.

"I need to go talk to my sister," I said.

Some reluctance passed over Acton's expression, there and gone in a fleeting moment. Rissa would be in her room at the Temple of Nilara. It was one place where he couldn't follow me, no matter how much he wanted to remain my protective shadow.

With a sigh, he said, "Ironfeather and I can see about getting lodging in the palace."

"Take Ari with you." My gryphon was groggy from the medicine Fletcher had just dosed him with. No magic was involved in directly healing him, partially because Ari was immune to the effects of healing magic after how often it was used on him. Instead, Fletcher had given him an injection of painkilling medicine in his wing where it hurt worst.

Ari shared that he thought one of Edgimus's spines were used in making the medicine. From what Thomas had mentioned of dreamhogs, I wasn't surprised that Ari was suddenly overcome with fatigue. After the ordeal we'd already been though, it was more of a miracle that he was still standing.

"Bring him back in three months for another dose," Fletcher had said cheerfully. He'd seemed flustered when I pushed a few silver clorets into his palm, double the fee he'd asked for. I'd felt the sudden numb relief as Ari had, a void of nothing where there'd been nagging pain.

We needed more veterinarians like him back at Fortress Aerie. Perhaps he would be willing to relocate to Fenway since the fortress itself would be an inaccessible nightmare to someone in a wheeled chair.

Ari grumbled but followed Ironfeather into the air, trusting the younger gryphon to guide him. The medicine had also mellowed out his anger, meaning he would pass out the moment he was given a clean stall and a bowl of fresh fish. It'd be good for him.

Sunset turned toward me, a soft whine in her throat. "I know. You'll see him again soon," I murmured, running a hand down her neck. She was saddled, a requirement in accordance to Altarian law, but I sensed her reluctance to take to the air.

The sun was setting, and unlike Ari, Sunset was still sensitive to the dark. She was remembering her old rider, Victor Callan, making clandestine trips under the cover of night. He wouldn't care that she was uncomfortable or hurting from a long day's training. "We could walk if you prefer. Or I could call them back to take you along to the palace stables," I suggested.

She shook herself, rustling the maroon feathers along her wings. Her sun-bright gaze met mine. "No, *let's fly*," she said, kneeling so I could climb into her saddle more easily. We took off smoothly, spiraling upward to gain a better vantage of the city.

I tugged the reins, turning her head toward the distant but distinct shape of Temple Row. *"What do you make of everything we've learned?"* I asked. She'd been so busy soothing Ari that I felt I'd barely heard from her.

"My daughter and my flight hang in the balance. What I am to think?" At first, she seemed cross that I would even ask, but her mind turned it over all the same, speaking for her in a stream of consciousness. *"You believe you were targeted specifically, but I feel it is more how Roshawk sees it. A gryphon is at its most valuable without a Link. It is full of potential. It could be a war mount as much as it can be a companion or a wild Skymother battling for her flock's territory. Whoever was behind hiring the murderer understands this. Before Wild Flight, there were poachers and Link thieves of all sorts. There still are. Your alliance with us has not fully solved the problem, but it has made us easy to steal from."*

I felt ashamed, really, that I'd been too preoccupied with other things to see what a target Wild Flight had become.

"It's a lesson we all needed to learn. I'll be the first to tell you that we took advantage of human care and became lazy for it. We so quickly forgot what it felt like to be hungry and wary in the pleasure of being comfortable and carefree." She filled the Link between us with love, overpowering everything else I felt for a few happy moments. *"We love you for what you've done for us. We will just have to save our younglings and adapt. I don't believe Roshawk or any other gryphon truly wishes to abandon Wild Flight completely, not if we can learn and grow from this tragedy."*

"But we have to save the younglings," I stated. It was a fact.

"We do. We will. Together."

"Together," I agreed. We both pictured the many gryphons of Wild Flight. Sunset was filled with surety that they would all fly to Kaiamear the moment they knew why the request was made. But the one downside, if it could be called that, was that there would be a race to deliver justice upon Commander Davis and his gryphon for what they'd done. The memory of their appearance had been passed from beast to beast.

Let it happen, I thought. It was time for pack justice. I just hoped the likes of Paragon Brekwell understood why it had to be done.

Once Sunset landed in front of the Temple of Nilara, I dismounted and came around to press my forehead to hers. We shared a pulse of affection and a feeling I had no words for. Something we'd tiptoed around for months. A spun thread of love and hope, mixed with a worldly understanding of why it should just remain an unanswered question.

A feeling that said, *Are you my gryphon too?*

And her answer like a dazzling spark in my mind. *I would have no other companion. Ari may have your one permanent Link, but I will still be here by your side for life.*

I would've never dreamed to claim two gryphons, yet here we were, my heart full to bursting in my chest. Ari and I both needed her optimism and care, especially in the bleakest of moments. "And I am yours as well as your second rider," I said aloud. She murred and leaned into my touch as I scratched into her neck and the space behind her ears.

Our moment ended with a woman clearing her throat. On the steps leading up to the temple stood an evening crowd of worshipers and white-robed Nilarites. It was not unusual to come here by moonlight to feel closer to the Mother, and so we had arrived at a busy time. I kissed Sunset on the beak and urged her to come with me, the two of us joining the line for entry.

I answered questions and supervised a few people who asked to touch Sunset. She allowed it, even inviting a little girl to cuddle while we waited. The gryphon wrapped a wing around that girl and *ached*, wishing it were her youngling instead but happier all the same to cluck and fuss over her head of curls. More than one woman stared and flinched, only seeing the sharp beak and not the tenderness that echoed my childhood with Valtora.

We were soon inside the temple, and I'd received hesitant approval to head up a hidden stair to seek out Rissa's room. She shared a space with other acolytes, I learned when someone else opened the door and screamed at the sight of Sunset behind me.

I winced, and she took another look at my face, covering her mouth and starting what felt like it could be a long string of apologies. "Is Rissa here?" I asked with a sigh.

"I should've known it was you!" my sister exclaimed from somewhere in the modest room behind the startled acolyte.

She took the other girl by the hands and murmured to her before joining Sunset and me out in the hall. "Hi, Sivana. There's a bench over here," she said. It was about the most private place she could offer, situated under a mosaic of clear glass that depicted the phases of the moon. "So, you got my message, huh?"

"I did and...there's something I need to tell you," I said heavily. We should've had this conversation already, before it became an oversight.

"Is it about Acton? Because it couldn't have been easy to watch Noah propose before him. I could give him a piece of my mind if you want." She propped a fist on her hip with a huff.

I blushed immediately. "What? No! It's...it's not about that. It's about safety, actually."

Her expression fell, but she listened as I told her in a hushed tone about the House of the Unstable. "You left Nate in the *woods*? With a pack of *battle beasts*?" she whisper-shrieked, most horrified by this so far, it would seem.

"That's what he wanted. And…judging by what's happened since, a decision that's kept him safe."

"Mother's grace, Sivana," she grumbled.

I put my palms up and told her of the connection I'd made between the younglings' capture and the upcoming auction. She paled further, a ghost in the shadows of early night by the time I was done and finished by saying, "If they are willing to go after Novali, they will do the same with you. I want you to come with me for a while. You can help Mother start a temple in Fenway or—"

Or *something*, I wanted to say, but I bit my tongue. Rissa looked a little lost, dazed by the idea that her life might be in danger because of me. Again.

"You should apologize," Sunset suggested.

"I'm sorry, Rissa. I know it's not ideal."

She fiddled with the crescent moon pendant on her robe, not looking me in the eye. "I will pray about it and see what Lady Nilara wills. The temple is a place of safety for all women, you know? No one gets abducted from here for revenge, not even by a group of Tulari as evil as the ones you're talking about."

I put my hand over hers. "Rissa, they stole young gryphons from Wild Flight in broad daylight. If anyone would be capable of snatching a Nilarite from the Mother's temple…"

"I know, but this is my home now," she murmured. "Not everyone can go off into the wilderness or out in the middle of nowhere. I'm needed here to help the women of Kaiamear until Lady Nilara deems that I can do more good in another place." Still, she clutched my hand with hers like a lifeline.

For a moment, I marveled at what a lady my sister had become. "Of course. I will honor whatever is decided between you," I said.

She shifted and leaned against me, a carefree look taking over her expression. "So, about Acton. Does the son of a duke need a reminder of the quality of woman he's seeing?"

Sunset and I didn't get to leave the temple until I had a fresh touchup of cosmetics and a bucketful of advice from Rissa and her acolyte friends, who'd seized on the idea of a reluctant lord waiting to propose.

I did feel awkward when I met him at the palace's Gryphon Yard, having maintained a pose with my hip cocked outside Ironfeather's stall for long enough that it was uncomfortable. "Hey," I said in my best husky voice.

"Are you quite all right? Not catching a cold, are you?" he asked primly.

Startled, I relaxed into my usual stance. "Uh, no, I don't think so."

"Well, I'm glad of it. I've secured us quarters for the foreseeable future and the king's attention on the morrow." He offered his elbow, and I took it. "We're going to get those baby gryphons back."

"You're going to get those baby gryphons back or else," said the king.

I had not been expecting a sympathetic audience, but King Cortes eyed me over his lavish breakfast feast like I was an insect come to gnaw on his morning pastries. He looked like he hadn't gotten a wink of rest in several nights. The bags under his eyes were more pronounced than ever, and he chewed with lethargy, as if the act of keeping himself fed required too much energy.

In truth, he knew almost everything I had to say, including that there would be an auction tomorrow evening. "It's in an abandoned warehouse off the pier, yes," he'd more specifically said with an impatient flick of his hand.

"What assistance will the Crown be offering us?" Acton asked.

"My people are working on it. You're staying in one of the guest rooms? I will have further instructions sent to you," the king promised. "Follow them, no matter how unusual."

He dismissed us soon after, joining a swarm of attendants who ushered him to his next meeting and carried platters of food and drink along with them. Acton and I waited a few tense hours in my room before there was a knock on the door.

I answered it, surprised to see a grown man holding out a letter for me, rather than a palace page. "Good afternoon, Miss Walker. I heard you're in need of some information. May I come in for a quick chat?" he asked.

I glanced over my shoulder at Acton, who eyed the stranger warily over the back of the chair he'd settled in. He nodded toward me, and I stepped aside for the man to come in. "And who might you be?" Acton asked.

The man drew up a spare chair with a shrug, sitting across from Acton and me once I settled. "A friend, here to give you a better understanding of what's about to happen at the upcoming illegal auction. I understand you've been invited to sow discord at the right moment."

I raised a brow, taking him in again. He was wearing the uniform of a lowly palace servant. Hundreds of men and women like him kept the day to day functions of the massive structure around us going. Yet he clearly was more enmeshed with the dealings of the Crown than any random servant.

"That's right," I answered.

"I know you are quite invested in having your baby gryphons back safe and sound. The Crown is as well. If no one acts rashly, you should be leaving here with nineteen young gryphons in a few short days." I could tell there was a catch he was about to share and waited. "But inviting you to come personally to help is a risk."

"You think I'm going to act rashly?" I asked, brows raising.

"There is always the potential when loved ones are involved. I have my doubts that the gryphons you are able to call upon will have the self-control to follow the plan we've already made." He sighed and pressed his fingertips to his temples. For a moment, it was such a familiar gesture that I took another look at him, but I didn't recognize him. He was a common middle-aged Altarian man, dark-haired, bronze-skinned, with a long face and a recently trimmed patch of facial hair framing his mouth and chin.

I glanced over at Acton. "He's not wrong. The wild mothers, especially, would kill anyone between them and their babies," he said.

I couldn't deny that was true. Once they flew over the city, Wild Flight would sense the presence of their younglings and go straight onto the offensive unless we could convince them otherwise.

"However, now you are here. And there is a place for you in the plan." The stranger gestured to the letter I held unopened. I tore into it and angled it so Acton could read it too.

There was just a short note inside:

Hi, Sivana. We will get you ready for tomorrow. Come alone, and don't take a gryphon. We want to make you anonymous.

It included an address, a point of contact named Margot Connery, and a time. I was expected tomorrow. Instead of a signature, again, this note was signed by a doodle of a smattering of animals.

I turned to Acton, who looked deep in thought. "I know that name. Good family," he murmured to himself.

"They signed it with little animals. That means this is from those kids we met yesterday," I said.

"Led by the most talented young thief we've seen in a long time," the stranger added, raising his index finger. "Reformed, of course."

"Heather?" I guessed, my mind's eye flashing back to the RSI uniform she'd been wearing.

He simply smiled for a moment. "Do you know what an inspiration you are for girls like her? To think, a Hero of Altare…one of our living legends, came in person to save those she cares most about. And you're used to taking the direct route to victory.

"If you choose to work with us, you have to understand that for every beacon of light like you, there are others who have to exist in the shadows. They will think and act differently than you, but they will still get the job done their way. The kids who sent that message are working with the Crown, and you can trust that their interests align with yours."

"Are you saying that if I, or my gryphons, cannot fall into the place made for us in your plan…?" I led, leaning on the last word expectantly.

"That you should take a step back and wait, yes. The choice is yours, Miss Walker. And with that, I bid you a good day." He stood and swept into a perfect courtly bow.

Acton and I saw him to the door, and once it was closed once more, we were deep in discussion about what to do from here.

CHAPTER 31

THE PLAN

Acton and I eventually brought our gryphons into the discussion. Sunset had already flown off on her own to gather the flock, since we all knew the wild mothers would arrive in force to save their babies, plan or no.

"From the moment they arrive, it will look like pack justice," Ari had said furiously. "There is no way around bloodshed, and why should there be in this case? They have stolen our children and intend to sell them."

"And this is exactly what the Crown's man was talking about," I'd pointed out.

Ironfeather was the one to suggest I go to the kids who served the Crown and ask for our new allies to either wear something identifying or for them to develop some kind of hand gesture the Tulari running the auction wouldn't know. If Wild Flight could tell friend from foe, then we could participate in liberating Novali and the other younglings. Even Ari agreed with this logic.

So the next day, I showed up at the address at the proper time, learning that it was a large boutique. A bell rattled against the filigreed door as I stepped inside, and an elegant blonde came forward to intercept me before I could wander the rows of prefabricated clothing looking for a Margot Connery.

It turned out she *was* Margot, a cheerful young woman with a highbrow accent that reminded me distinctly of Acton. "Come along now. No need to be shy. We're just giving you a makeover, darling, and a rundown if Heather is feeling talkative."

"That sounds fine to me. Who is 'we'?" I asked.

"You'll see. She's here, everyone!" Margot announced, steering me into a changing room large enough to fit two bedrooms. It had three vanities, tri-fold mirrors ringed by tiny magelights, and a few people who turned to stare like startled deer.

"She's actually here," whispered a girl toward the back of the room.

Margot closed the door behind us. "You remember Heather, then," she said, nodding to the girl nearest to the door. She wasn't wearing the RSI uniform anymore and was mid-pace, it seemed, her mouse, Chance, held in her palm close to her face.

Heather waved shyly. "Hi."

I nodded back to her, a little bemused. The Crown's man had warned me this was a group of kids. Other than Margot, who seemed to be a few years older than the rest, they could all be thirteen or fourteen.

"She's all yours," Margot said, nudging me toward Heather.

My Link with Ari stirred. I could feel him using my senses to get an idea of what was happening.

She put her free hand on her hip and took a deep breath, visibly grounding herself. "Hello, welcome. You got our message. Let me introduce you to the crew, then, and we can get to work," she said.

Crew. Now that I knew she was a "reformed" thief, I had a better idea of what was going on. She told me a bit about her friends as we were introduced. There was Margot, bright and outgoing, the first one to talk to me and the most comfortable doing so.

Heather herself, small and unassuming, who wore a belt that had multiple pouches and tools. I spotted a coil of rope and what appeared to be a flat-headed screwdriver close to one hip and wondered what other items she carried hidden on her person.

She guided me around to say hello to the rest of the group. "This is Fariq, our genius," Heather said.

"It's a pleasure to meet you in person," he said, shaking hands with me eagerly. His dark skin tone and accent reflected an obvious Lithosian heritage, and there was a brightness to his expression that was pure earnestness. He may not have been born Altarian, but I could tell he was one.

"Next is Vance, our Tulari," Heather said, gesturing him over even though he gave her a dirty look in passing.

He fixed a white smile on his face and came forward to shake my hand. Though he was surprisingly easy on the eyes, given his age, I didn't spot a Tulari mark on his face. "Really?" I asked.

"I suppose we're telling you all our secrets today," he replied.

My brow furrowed as I caught onto his put-out attitude. "If we're working together, I need to know what you can do."

"Yes, well, you'll find out," he grumbled.

Heather moved along quickly to introduce me to the last person in the room, Carmen, who jerked her chin when introduced. She had her hair cropped short and sharp features that shaped a vague scowl as her resting expression.

"She's a talented fighter," Heather supplied.

"Oh? Weapon of choice?" I asked.

Carmen brightened quickly. "My body is the only weapon I need."

Judging by her tall and lithe form, I could believe it. "My

best friend's father taught me the same thing when he drilled me in hand-to-hand combat," I said.

Something like eagerness burned in Carmen's eyes. Heather put her palms up, and Chance echoed her, shaking his little head. Ignoring them, Carmen said, "We should spar after all this."

This must be a common offer, I thought in amusement, deciding to laugh it off for now. "Perhaps later. One of us would walk away rather hurt from that encounter," I said before addressing everyone. "Well, it's a pleasure to meet you all. You must be the five of Five and Chance."

"How did you—" Heather began to ask.

"Five people and a mouse named Chance." I lifted a shoulder. "The crew I was told to trust because our interests align."

Margot invited me to sit in front of the middle vanity with a gesture, and I did. "That's right, darling. We're getting you into the Morashi's auction tonight."

Vance and Margot stood behind me, inspecting my reflection in the vanity. I noticed them exchange a glance, like something about what they saw would require a lot of work. It was a look I was accustomed to seeing on Mother and Rissa's faces but made me bristle when it came from two strangers.

Wait. "Morashi?" I repeated.

"Morashi Venom. Heard of them?" Vance asked.

A trill preceded a calico cat interrupting my answer by jumping on the vanity in front of me. She was…huge, fluffy, and winged, but purring the moment we made eye contact. "Another feligryph, wow," I murmured, daring to offer my hand to sniff. She nuzzled my fingers and rumbled like a thunderstorm when I started to pet her.

"That's Patches. Looks like she likes you," Heather said.

The feligryph meowed, transferring to my lap when Margot shooed her out of the way. "I can't say I know what

Morashi Venom is. I know of a woman who claims to be a Madam Morashi, though," I said to Vance as Patches settled into a crescent, leaning her bulk into my belly.

There was a tense pause as all five of them seemed to stare for a moment too long. "Shall we share gossip, then?" Margot invited. "We do have some work to do to make you look like someone else."

"I'd like to hear what you intend to do first," I said.

Heather was the one who answered. She paced back and forth as she spoke. "We're one piece of a larger plan, one crew amongst many tonight. But because of you, we're the most important," she said. Carmen seemed to get annoyed by her pacing before I did and stepped in her way, steering her to stand behind the mirror I faced.

She shifted with restless energy. "Our success dictates everyone else's, basically. We're going with a simple enough strategy. One hand distracts while the other steals."

"A smash and grab," Vance said.

"I thought we were just going straight for the chaos option," Carmen commented.

Margot rolled her eyes. "Can we keep it together in front of a guest?" she beseeched.

I gestured that it was all right, watching them with interest. "The first thing we're going to do is scope out the event," Heather added, shaking her head. "There's a viewing party that's happening throughout the day and ends right before the auction itself starts. Margot, Vance, and Carmen are going in, and if all goes well, Carmen will be staying and taking the place of a guard."

I lifted an eyebrow. "No offense, but isn't she noticeably younger than most guards?"

The tall girl seemed annoyed at the fact, or that I brought it up. "Vance's magic will fix that," she muttered.

Heather continued, "Once they return with their intel, we're sending you in dressed the same way as Margot. With a touch of Vance's magic, no one will look at you twice or realize two different people are using the same invitation. And then we wait for the right moment to unleash chaos." She met my gaze in the mirror, her eyelid flickering and her brown eyes betraying her nerves. "You…did bring the gryphons, right?"

"They're on their way," I promised.

She breathed a sigh of relief. "That's the short version of your part in the plan."

"What about the peacekeepers?" I asked.

And just as quickly, her expression fell to one of distaste. "What about them?"

My eyebrows rose. "The Crown approved this plan? Without supplying peacekeepers to arrest those attending this auction?" I pressed.

"They'll be waiting outside, darling. But since the Morashi are involved, we're not storming the event. There's too high a risk that someone, or something, innocent will be hurt," Margot interjected.

"Sometimes subtlety is the best option, and this is definitely one of those times," Vance said.

"There are other crews—" Heather began to say.

"About that," I interrupted, raising my hand to have her pause for a moment. "The gryphons would like our allies to either wear something identifying or have a sort of gesture ready so they're not mistaken as the ones standing in between them and their babies."

They exchanged glances behind me. "Palms up," Fariq suggested, flashing his. "It is universal for meaning no harm."

Heather nodded in agreement. "We'll get the word out. Like I was saying, other crews are also infiltrating the event and posing as extra servants or guests. They'll be wearing pins of the Altarian flag. Anything more noticeable is bound to be spotted by the Morashi and we can't have that."

I reached across my Link, checking with Ari. *"What do you think?"* I asked.

He gave me an impression of his emotions, which were grudgingly accepting. *"I agree with a subtle plan if it means Novali is safe. And I'll share with the others that there will be friends showing their palms."*

"If that's what it takes, let's do it," I said aloud. Patches meowed and bunted my chest. She was large enough that it took the wind from my lungs, yet I had the feeling she was trying to express happiness that I'd agreed.

Margot brightened and flexed her fingers. "Well, then! Time to get started. Pretend you've taken a day at the spa."

"Where we talk about gangs and misuse of magic?" Vance asked, raising a brow. It sounded like I was finally about to learn what *Morashi Venom* was.

She picked up a brush and sniffed. "What do you think ladies discuss in their free time?"

I eyed their reflections uncertainly. Margot sought my permission before letting down my hair from its tight braid. Heather and Fariq motioned Carmen over to another vanity, the three of them muttering together.

"All right, look. You're technically not supposed to know any of this, okay?" Vance began. "Heather's trusting you with a lot of secrets already, so you can just add this as one more."

"Seems reasonable to me," I said. Ari and I agreed in that moment to keep this group's secrets. If they helped us understand the group of mages we were up against, all the better.

"There's a gang of Tulari that's grown big and bold called Morashi Venom. They're led by Madam Morashi," Vance said. A shiver passed over him, drawing a fine layer of bumps over his exposed arms. He repeated some things I already knew, that this so-called madam was as old as a myth and capable of twisted magic outside of what Lord Orion permitted.

But I didn't realize she was stealing Tulari infants from their cradles and indoctrinating them in what he referred to as "the old ways." Mages were taught a controlled set of spells, but their magic was capable of more if properly trained from a young age. He demonstrated by pulling a wand from a pouch at his belt and drawing a few healer-green runes midair. He then pointed the rod of wood at my face.

A tingle overtook my nose, and its shape blurred in the mirror. I released a surprised shout as it realigned shorter and more upturned. "This is what I'm capable of," he explained. "It's called formshifting."

I turned in my chair to look at him more closely. There was still no Tulari mark on his face, not even a hint that he was touched by Lord Orion. "Are you in this gang as well?" I asked.

"I was. But I was shown the error of my ways." With a smirk, he tapped a bracelet he wore like it meant something. "I was taken from my parents when I was five, but my contract with the madam has been destroyed. As long as I'm careful, she'll never get her claws in me again."

"Claws," I repeated. Now I was the one shaking off a moment of remembered fear. Since he'd told me about the gang, I felt that I had to recount my experience with the House of the Unstable. He used his magic on me sporadically, only interrupting to tell me it was temporary.

He shocked my hair and eyebrows blonde and turned my eyes blue. It was strange to see an older and tanner Rissa looking back at me and explaining in my voice the projection of Madam Morashi and the claw-like nails I'd almost felt digging into my chin.

"Oh, yeah, that was definitely her," Vance sighed. He looked troubled, and the room was silent, the whole group of kids listening to my description. "The thing is, she can look like nearly anyone. She's a master of formshifting, but no matter what she looks or sounds like, she can't hide those sharp nails or bright green eyes. Everyone with formshifting has at least one limitation. For me, it's voices."

"Oh?" I asked. He adjusted the bone structure in my cheeks, and I patted them, feeling like they'd really changed to match what the mirror showed me.

"Yeah. I can make you look like most anyone, but you'll always sound like yourself."

"We'll have to work out a way to sound similar," Margot interjected.

"Well, whatever guards are in place won't notice much amiss past the accent, darling," I said, mimicking Acton based off of old experience. His accent was always a source of teasing, and I'd done my fair share of it.

She clapped in delight. "You're a natural! I knew I liked you."

"That's all it took?" I asked, still using the noble accent.

"Heather liked you first, and I find that she's an excellent judge of character," she answered. I could practically feel the other girl's blush from where I sat.

"One last thing." Vance had us both make expressions on demand, and only after I scowled and smiled and frowned for him did he change the slant of my mouth. I was passably Margot, except she was notably paler. Vance, however, expressed that it wouldn't be much of an issue and that changing skin tones was a moral line he didn't like to cross.

I accepted that, and also the dusting of cosmetics Margot applied to make my appearance more convincing. "Now, when you want to take the glamor off, all you have to do is close your eyes and will the spell to end," Vance said. "Don't do it right now—it's really easy to remove. You say to yourself *I really wish I looked like myself again*, and you will."

"Got it," I said.

"We'll be right back. You wouldn't mind staying here, would you?" Margot asked, an apologetic note in her voice. "We'll be back in two shakes of the bells."

I nodded, not seeing much of a choice. They were obviously trying to keep it secret that Sivana Walker had walked into this boutique and would soon exit as Margot Connery. She had us leave the dressing room briefly to change into a tunic and shiny, fine pants with heeled boots. It was a fashion choice that'd raise some eyebrows, but we were apparently going to the auction as an ultra-rich and quirky woman, Lady Angeline Norston.

I was grateful they'd thought to include pants. I figured I'd be back in the saddle by this evening and didn't want to ride one of my gryphons while wearing a flowing dress.

Vance, Margot, and Carmen set out, leaving me with the two quietest members of their little group. Heather and Fariq bandied possible scenarios back and forth and startled hard the first time I offered an opinion.

We exhausted what felt like an innumerable amount of increasingly unlikely situations for the auction before Heather finally asked, "What's it like to ride a gryphon?"

"I'll take you up in the air for a ride if this works out," I offered.

"It will," Heather responded, fidgeting her fingers nervously.

"It *will*," Fariq echoed, giving her a friendly nudge. Chance balanced on his hind paws from where he perched on one of the vanities, flashing a thumbs-up.

"See?" I couldn't help a chuckle. "Even the mouse agrees." The two of them exchanged a knowing glance.

CHAPTER 32

AUCTION'S GEMS

I wasn't completely idle as we waited for Margot to return. Ari and I had a steady stream of communication, and he helped me relayed information to Acton through Ironfeather, keeping him up to date with the plan.

Acton responded that he would burst into the auction the moment chaos broke out, but I doubted that would be as effective as he thought. I told him to prepare for another plan…helping evacuate the little wonders alongside the gryphon younglings. He said he'd bring Sharde and Ellie to help.

"What of the three-headed rozash they claim to have?" Ari asked.

I sensed his revulsion and echoed some of it. Nasty creatures, rozash. But I'd never seen a three-headed one and imagined it had to be young to be smuggled into Kaiamear in the first place. *"We will let the authorities handle it,"* I replied.

Ari and Ironfeather later flew out of range of my awareness, meeting Sunset and however many Wild Flight gryphons had made the journey to Kaiamear. If everything went according to plan, they would circle the city after night fell so the Morashi had no idea they'd arrived to reclaim their lost children. I was confident Ari could convince them to wait a little longer.

We were poised to strike a mighty blow to the group of Tulari that'd been torturing unstable pyromancers and battle beasts. Much as I hated them, it was good to finally put a name to the faces. I knew what to call this new enemy, which gave me a box to put in names like Irene Merriweather, Madam Morashi, and even Magister Scorvash. Tulari who threatened my friends and family.

I didn't know how yet, but Zizi and I would take them on more openly someday and win. We'd get her corerune and peace of mind besides.

Margot and Vance returned in a couple hours, as announced by the city bells. She changed back into her street clothes, and instead of handing over what she'd just been wearing, she went into the boutique and returned with a nearly identical tunic, pants, and heeled boots, along with the tiny clutch she'd used to match the outfit. "Here you are, darling."

I shut myself in the changing room and put on what she gave me, aware they were conferring with Heather and Fariq in hushed whispers in the meantime. On Margot, these clothes looked fashionable and hugged her feminine form. I looked in the mirror and saw my narrower hips, thinking I needed more padding for our body shapes to pass as the same.

And the shoes hurt my feet almost immediately. Gods, I hated heels. I was just glad they had more sturdiness as boots.

Margot wasn't the only one doing a head-to-toe inspection of me when I stepped out again. "Good enough," Heather said. She offered an unexpected gift, a dagger with a strap that I fastened toward the top of my calf. The loose pants hid it effectively.

They had me join their circle, where they were gathered around a sketch of the warehouse. It had a central tower of three stories, and it seemed the Morashi were using every inch of space. "First floor had most of the little wonders. They are keeping the more valuable creatures in the tower," Margot explained, pointing to the second story. "All the gryphons are here, plus a rather exotic-looking rozash and a handful of the rarest little wonders. They intend to have the actual auction here." Her fingertip slid to the third floor of the tower.

"That's perfect for an aerial attack," I said. "Did you see the roof?"

"We were barely allowed onto the second floor, darling. But I will tell you the whole place is run down. They've covered the flooring with carpets and sprayed plenty of perfume to mask the mold smell. It's still dreadfully musty in some places." She flapped her hand under her chin like she was flipping a fan.

"I've forgotten to ask. Where is Thomas in all this?" I asked, my gaze flicking back to Heather.

"He's at the rendezvous point to help with any medical emergencies," she answered.

She showed me an address hidden within the lining of the clutch. I recognized the area as a more upscale part of Kaiamear. "The locals won't notice the sudden influx of little wonders?" I questioned.

"Let's just say it's more private than you think," she said. "Also, Fariq should tell you about this." She pulled a short length of metal from the bottom of the little purse, hidden under a silky cushion. It was contributing most of the weight, as the purse contained ordinary-looking cosmetics and the auction invitation otherwise.

Fariq took it from her and nodded. Edging closer to me, he pointed to one end. "You have a crowbar hook here for opening cages with leverage. And a lock breaker on the other end."

He showed me how it also included a pointed triangle of metal that folded up and could be locked in place with a tiny metal dial. "But what really makes it special is this." He flipped it over and pointed to a small circle of rusty-colored metal. "There is interest right now in materials that weaken or remove magic, both in traps and enchantments. This is a prototype that should do just that. Press the metal to something you think has magic and it will do its job in ten seconds."

"Really?" I asked in surprise, trying to take it and hold it up to my face. He resisted, tapping his cheek, and I remembered that I was wearing Vance's formshifting magic. "I can't touch it with Vance's magic on me?"

"It can't touch your face, at least," he said.

"How will I know when it works on something enchanted?" I asked.

"I made this intending for it to be used on any magical locks you find. They'll have tiny runes engraved on them. They'll flare with light when touched by the prototype. After ten seconds, if there's still light but it is dimmer, the spell was weakened. If the light is gone, no more spell."

"And you made this yourself? What is this metal?" I asked, pointing to the reddish disk.

His smile was apologetic. "I'm afraid I cannot tell you much more."

"Except if you're friends with a Tulari, don't touch them with it. It'll leave behind a burn," Vance put in. He and the others milled around, waiting for us to finish this conversation.

"All right, then," I said, opening the clutch for Fariq to place the tool back in its hiding spot.

"Wait here," Fariq said, going back into the changing room. He emerged with a box and a ribbon, showing me that the inside held a larger disk of the same reddish metal, this one about the size of my fist. When he flipped it, I saw its back had a handle welded on for it to be held a lot like a knuckle weapon. "It would be my honor to let you borrow this. It's a prototype too. I made it from spare parts, so it is small, but it is a shield. More combat-focused."

He threaded his fingers through the handle and swiped it through the air. "It erases runes as a mage writes them, disrupting spells."

"Sure to hurt if you punched them with it, too," I remarked.

"Punch? No. Very thin metal. You would warp it all out of shape. I wanted to make it as big as possible so it can also intercept completed spells. It has a cone of effectiveness that's a little wider than it is." He placed the shield back in its box and laid it down on the table, demonstrating the size of the cone with two hands twisting over it.

It seemed to be about a foot in diameter, which was tiny for the kind of shields I was used to, but if it could stop a spell, any radius was a blessing. "In theory, if you catch a spell at the tip of the cone, it will reflect back at your enemy. If it hits the sides, it will reflect at an angle, which could be dangerous with others around you. And any spell that hits the metal will be lessened or nullified."

"In theory?" I asked.

"In theory," he echoed. "None of us have fought a mage, but it seems likely you will tonight."

"Well, thank you. This is an incredible gift, and I'll let you know how it worked," I said, already seeing many uses for it. He smiled happily and placed it back in the box, tying it up with the ribbon to make it seem like a present. It just barely fit in the clutch like that. "Also, I have a friend I think you should meet. She can get you into the Military School of Engineering when you're a little older. You seem like you would be a great fit."

A hint of color darkened his cheeks. "I'm happy to be of assistance," he answered with a duck of his head.

His friends waited a moment before they dove right back into finalizing details with me. It was almost time I left and joined the event, it seemed. Margot said, "We're also changing clothes and trying to infiltrate the event behind you. If you can't find any of us, Carmen will be the one to give the signal. The hired guards are wearing all black tonight."

"Otherwise, I will give you the signal," Heather said, demonstrating it. She opened both hands with her fingers spread, holding them at about shoulder height, fingertips facing one another across her chest.

"When you do that, you want me to call the gryphons in?" I confirmed. "When about in the proceedings will you give this signal?"

"Before anything is sold, hopefully," she answered.

"Hopefully," I echoed with an unsettled laugh. "A simple enough plan. Best of luck to us all, then."

I bid the group goodbye and made the trip toward the pier alone. It was unsettling at first, to have such a void of silence in my mind with both Ari and Sunset flying well out of range.

With the heeled boots, I was forced to take my time heading down the slanted road toward the warehouse in question lest I break an ankle. This helped the cover of night begin to fall, and soon Ari flew just within reach of me with our Link.

"We're ready. I will lead them toward your location when you give the word," he said.

"Nearly there," I answered. *"This ordeal is almost over."*

He shared a moment of affection before he must've tilted his wings out of range for our Link again. In silence, I turned toward a cluster of warehouses, the smell of brine hanging heavily in the air. The Morashi had picked one of the largest and oldest buildings in this area, a crumbling ruin of sorts that sat just off the edge of the river. As a kid, I'd thought it would topple into the water someday soon, as its stones leaned toward a watery grave.

I'd have never thought illegal auctions would take place inside of it. But now that I looked again, it was huge and abandoned, the perfect location for the Morashi to move in. Its middle boasted a three-story-tall tower with a flat roof, accessible by anything with wings. To either side extended additions to the tower sized like barns, with the steep wooden roofs that come along with them.

I noticed the guards pretty quickly. They stood around inconspicuously enough in the nooks of the warehouse and its shadows, but the all-black clothing tipped me off. Yet no one stopped me until I was at the great wooden doors that led into the eastern wing of the warehouse.

"Can I see your invitation?" asked a man standing in the shadows just on the inside.

I flipped my hair over my shoulder and pulled the paper from my borrowed clutch. "Here. You should find everything in order," I said, affecting a noble accent.

There was a spark of blue—a wand tip, I realized, pointed at the invitation I'd just handed him. "Indeed," he said, giving it back after a few moments. His hand extended out, motioning me into the warehouse. My ears popped, and I blinked, suddenly in a place of sound, color, and light rather than the stuffy, dark place I thought I was walking into.

The mage behind me smirked when he saw me looking around. "You just passed through a ward, my lady. Protection from prying eyes."

I channeled my inner noblewoman and sniffed, walking away from him without acknowledging his explanation. My palms grew slick as I imagined the ward interfering with the plan. Would Ari still be able to reach me?

I made my way forward, entering a long corridor marked by the smell of savory foods and overpowering perfumes. A setup of makeshift rooms built of timber sheets lined the wall on one side, with people coming and going, escorted by guards or Tulari who held cages.

More people than I would've hoped were here, all dressed in their best or otherwise in suits—even the women—serving fluted beverages or finger foods. Tables interspersed the space, and upon each sat a single cage. People filtered around each, giving me little choice but to follow the flow of the crowd and see the captive creatures while I waited for the auction to begin.

There was a cage nearly full to bursting with carpenter mice, of little interest to the mingling folk when the next table over held a cute silver fox kit. Its form seemed to stretch and distort around it in an optical illusion as it looked around in distress.

My eyes roamed, searching the lapels of the servants circulating amongst the guests. Most of them had a single pin, a dagger with a snake wrapped around its blade and hilt. "Excuse me. When will the auction begin?" I asked once I spotted a young man with an Altarian flag pinned on his opposite lapel.

He stopped and looked me over for a moment. "Here, my lady." He leaned in as he offered me a drink from the platter he carried, and I picked one out to be polite. "They're stalling so the guests fall deeper into their cups," he whispered in my ear.

We both straightened, and he motioned down the hall. "The viewing party is nearly at an end," he said more loudly. "If you would like to see any creature outside of its cage, we ask that you take them to a private room with one of the mages. They can tell you anything you'd like to know about the animals."

"Thank you," I said.

"M'name's Ram if you need any more assistance, my lady," he said warmly.

I nodded and filtered back into the crowd. Ram... What an odd name. I sipped from the drink he'd given me, careful when I realized it was sweet and seemed only mildly alcoholic. As much as I itched to go straight to the middle of the warehouse and up to see my gryphon babies, I tried to act like I was meant to be here.

While I cooed over the various little wonders and asked inane questions to a few guards and Tulari standing around the cages, I counted and estimated. Approximately eighty cages. Two hundred guests, most of whom seemed wealthy or at least well-to-do. The guests outnumbered the guards three-to-one, and the Tulari were even less frequent, maybe twenty-five in total amongst the first floor of the warehouse.

Servants evened out the numbers. A whole flock of them jumped to the crowd's whim, and of them, over a dozen wore the Altarian flag. I made brief contact with most of them, learning that the auction itself would be held under the watchful eye of five crafter-class Tulari.

"Get your mind right, my lady," said a curvy young woman who'd shifted close to offer me a tiny stack of sliced and roasted vegetables on a diminutive plate. "There are three cages holding the so-called 'gems of the auction' that will be on display above the stage. One of them will be announced as your gryphon's daughter."

I sucked a breath in, feeling the room start to spin. "T-thanks," I mumbled.

"The lady needs some air!" she announced, helping me cut through the crowd and sit down at a chair posted on the outskirts of the viewing party. She fanned me with a new serving tray, having placed hers with the vegetable plates off to the side. It didn't help much, but at least it gave us some cover to speak further.

"What do you mean, a gem of the auction?" I hissed.

"The most expensive creatures they're selling tonight," she whispered. "Someone knows exactly who the little red gryphon is and wants to display her as a prize."

"Is there a gryphon rider here?" I gave her a quick description of Commander Davis and Bittergale, earning a short nod from her. At first, my heart sank further, but then I realized it could be a great thing. He would be arrested along with all the others here.

"Take heart, though. A small number of the well-dressed folk here will be makin' arrests when the night is up," she said, offering me a hand up. She nodded a farewell and returned to her job.

I filtered back into the crowd, wondering how many of the people around me were actually peacekeepers or agents of the Crown. She'd given me a moment of hope that there weren't this many wealthy individuals turning up with an interest in forcing a Link on a little wonder or a blessed beast they purchased.

Or, as I worried when I passed a cluster of people speaking animatedly in Lithosian, buying gryphons to train up enemy riders.

A set of brassy horns played a short song. A man's voice boomed around us, magnified to an almost painful level with magic. "Ladies and gentlemen, this concludes our viewing party. If all interested buyers would head toward the central tower, we will begin seating and the auction shortly."

Finally, I thought to myself, having found all this milling around to be unbearable. I was toward the back of the crowd turning to shuffle toward the tower stairs. Men and women murmured excitedly to one another, talking about the animals they would try to purchase or coordinating their strategy to make their clorets stretch the furthest. I still felt ill and off balance, knowing Commander Davis was here and helping the Morashi target Novali.

The guards and Tulari made a funnel for us to pass through, and I sweated under the watchful eyes of the magic users, expecting one of them to see through my disguise. None of them said much, though, past a polite "This way, ma'am." Or a "Watch your step."

There was a wall of guards in the second-floor room, preventing us from stepping across a stretch of aged floorboards to look at the smaller collection of cages in here. I caught a flash of fur and a hint of beak, my heart wrenching when I felt the younglings' fear this close to them. They crouched silent and trembling in their confinement, too closed off for me to try to Link with them and share some reassuring emotions.

One of the guards nudged me along with a gruff murmur, and I looked away from the cages, surprised for a split second to see an older version of Carmen. "Move it along," she growled. She looked entirely too convincing as a scowling guard, and Vance had efficiently aged her face without ruining her unique features.

I nodded and walked away with effort, straining mentally for Ari or Sunset instead. They were close, I felt, but not close enough to talk to. Perhaps it was a small blessing, because they would both flood me with fury when I reached the third floor and beheld the stage. I'd burn to a cinder if they both tried to express their anger through me, as I had enough lava in my veins for myself upon seeing the three cages hanging suspended over the podium where a white-haired man waited with a gavel.

I forced myself to look away, take a breath, and walk. Someone handed me a length of wood with a paddle on the end painted with a scarlet **143**. The floor had been covered with several fine carpets, and clusters of velvet chairs lined up a little too close together to make use of every inch of space. I picked a seat toward the last row to be in the aisle, standing to let people in and taking a moment to look at the stage more closely.

Behind the podium stood three of the five crafter-class Tulari I'd been warned about. Even with a scattering of mage-lights, the area behind the stage was too dark to make out the color of their marks. The last two stood behind me, at the back of the room with a handful of guards. They wore fine clothes and held staves of pretty, polished wood.

"Sivana, sorry for the delay," came Sunset's voice in the back of my head. I felt a sudden surge of energy through me as she and Ari flew close enough for us to Link. *"We are ready when you are."*

"It will be very soon," I told her.

"We're flying across the city now."

I didn't tell her about Novali. The gryphon youngling sat in a special cage made of black-colored wood, its bars spread wider apart so we could see her but not wide enough so she could escape. She sat with her beak hanging out, her head wedged at the temples between two bars. Her eyes were rounded and sad, yet she was as cute and plump as a stuffed doll, like the Morashi had oiled her feathers and combed out her fur until her appearance was perfect.

I tried to reach out to her mentally, just to find her as closed off as the other younglings. She sat on her belly like a cat and jabbed her head at the opening in her cage again, as if she could escape if she could just get her skull to cooperate.

A couple yards away from her, another metal hook and short chain linked up with a similar cage, but the occupant was not stationary. The three-headed rozash slithered back and forth, rocking its prison with every movement. I felt Ari's senses meet up with mine, and he wanted to kill it immediately.

"It's deformed," he grunted.

"It does look painful to have three heads sticking out like that," I agreed. It was about the length of my arm, with tiny flapping wings along its back. I had the impression it had six, sure to tangle in the air if it ever reached full adult size.

I didn't show him Novali, sure he would be better off if he didn't know what'd become of her yet. Instead, we looked at the third cage, the smallest by far. A cushion supported the potato-like shapes of three tiny kittens, mewling and as gray as Smoky. They appeared to have stubby wings, but it was hard to tell from this far away.

The auctioneer began to speak, and I sat along with a few other stragglers. He introduced the three gems of the auction as the last creatures sold for the night and named Novali as "the daughter of the famous gryphon, Arimus!"

There was no sign of Heather or Carmen anymore to give the signal, but I anticipated it at any moment. I searched the shadows at the back of the stage for Commander Davis and was rewarded when a spotlight-bright magelight came to life, illuminating a table where the first cage was set. A pair of beautiful women gestured over the gray fox kit and paddles went up in the audience immediately.

Between two of the crafter-class Tulari, Commander Davis stood with Bittergale, the two of them leering at the crowd. He was nearly unchanged from how I remembered him, down to the well-maintained riding gear and the big golden pendant of Lord Orion he wore openly, dangling from a leather cord looped around his neck. They were close to a short stairwell leading up to the squared outline of a hatch that led to the tower's roof.

"*He's there. The murderer,*" I heard Sunset say.

"*And his gryphon,*" Ari growled.

Unexpectedly, more of the flock crowded into the conversation. Roshawk's gruff presence added, "*Hardly a gryphon, to willingly work with a Link thief.*"

Valtora hushed the murmuring I heard until she was the only one speaking. "*Sivana, give me a report. What of the younglings?*"

Meanwhile, the auctioneer spoke faster than I could comprehend, shouting out cloret amounts that were reaching staggering proportions.

"*They're frightened but alive. Any moment now, our allies will give the signal for you to help me make a distraction. We have people here who will grab cages and run, and others who will start arresting those who attended this auction. But...Commander Davis is here, and there are five powerful Tulari who will try to cast spells at me when I stand up and start yelling,"* I told her.

"Be safe. We are ready when you are," she replied.

I reached into my clutch and untied the ribbon around Fariq's prototype shield, fitting my fingers into its grip. I had the feeling I would need it from the moment the gryphons landed and hoped it worked just as Fariq had described it...in theory.

I bit my lip as the bids for the fox kit settled. The auctioneer counted down with eagerness, announcing between numbers, "Plenty more wonderful creatures after this one, ladies and gentlemen!"

Something tugged at the hem of my pants. I looked down, spotting Chance standing next to my foot. I wondered if something had gone terribly wrong for Heather to send her little wonder.

He flexed his little paws and turned them, flashing the signal in miniature.

CHAPTER 33
FREEFALL

I STOOD WITH A SUDDEN SHOVE, nearly knocking over my chair. There was a rippling murmur as a few people turned and glared. The auctioneer's mouth framed the number one and stopped, noticing me standing in the aisle.

"Do we have an early upset? A last-second offer?" he asked in a flurry of words.

I closed my eyes, wishing to be myself again and calling to Ari and Sunset that it was time. Gryphons screamed in the air above us as I took in a deep breath. I stood tall and knew the glamor over my features was gone by the commotion around me, especially up on stage. The crafter-class Tulari reached for their staves, and the auctioneer started to pound his gavel for order.

"This whole auction is an affront!" I shouted, drawing on years of military training to raise my voice to its highest volume.

Thump. Something solid landed on the roof above us.

Thump thump thump! The cut logs that made the ceiling over our heads groaned.

"No magical creature deserves to be sold like cattle. Least of all the gryphons from my flock!" I shouted further, soon drowned out by the landing of dozens of gryphons. They screamed and roared, shaking the warehouse from their sheer numbers and scattering loose drifts of dust from the ceiling.

Several people stood around me. One shouted, "In the name of the Crown, put down your weapons!" The peace-keepers in disguise pulled out badges, wands, cuffs, and batons from folds in their fine clothing.

I raised my shield when I noticed one of the Tulari on stage flicking his staff in my direction. The spell flung at me was like a sharp green needle, and I barely caught it in time. It bounced away from me, embedding into the ground next to a woman's shiny heels.

My attention narrowed to that Tulari, a crafter-class healer, and Commander Davis, who'd pushed off the wall to head in my direction. I was aware of panic around me, but the pitch turned feverish as part of the roof started to buckle under the weight and fury of the gryphons. Talons emerged from the small hole created between logs, and a wild mother tumbled into the auction and landed close to the stage.

She shook herself, furious pinprick eyes swerving over the crowd. Many of us, myself included, put our palms up, and I added in a mental scream, *"Behind you!"*

She roared and lunged at the nearest crafter-class Tulari, swiping her talons across the man's chest. He lost control of the spell he was trying to weave, falling with his staff as his only protection from her pointed claws.

The room transformed into a stampede behind her. The auction patrons shoved each other out of the way, heading for the stairwell and an exit before they could be arrested or mauled, as a second gryphon was shimmying through the hole the first one had made and more pushed to join them. A number of the Morashi mages were shoved out of the way or engaged in duels with the disguised Tulari.

I was pushed around as well, jostled on all sides by fleeing bodies. It was with relief that I recognized the white and blue gryphon that squeezed into the room next. *"Oh, so sorry,"* Reyos said, backing off of a woman in a ball gown who he'd accidentally knocked prone upon landing.

"Reyos, on stage! Novali is in one of those cages!" I called to him.

"Got it," he answered, swinging around and heading straight for her.

I pushed people aside, wading through the sea of bodies between me and the cages hanging over the stage. My gaze was fixed on the swinging cage that contained Novali, her head still wedged in the bars.

But someone else got there first, and with a sinking feeling in my chest, I watched Commander Davis unsheathe his cavalry saber. He saw Reyos coming and swiped, opening a line of red on his shoulder. The wild gryphon snarled and launched himself at Davis with a powerful leap.

"No!" I screamed, already seeing the opening it gave Davis and the triumph that flashed across his face as he brought his weapon up. Reyos impaled himself through the chest on it unwittingly. His beak snapped down hard on empty air, his reach shortened. One set of talons slipped, but the other scoured deep lines across Davis's chest.

I felt his presence darken across all my connections to the gryphons a split second later. The sword had pierced Reyos's heart, and his loss felt like an explosion of glass shards. My breath came heavier, and my sight blurred as I so desperately fought the crowd in a haze of pain.

Reyos was the first wild gryphon I'd truly connected with, back when he'd been known as Blue, held against his will at Fortress Aerie to be forced into the taming process. He'd given me a chance and trusted me to free him, just as he'd trusted me today to direct him. I couldn't help but feel sick with responsibility as I watched Davis free his weapon from Reyos's body.

He lifted Novali's cage and started away with it just as I

pushed my way to freedom. With one last smirk over his shoulder, he slung his leg over Bittergale's saddle and directed her toward the short stairwell to the roof.

I stumbled to the stage too late. The metal of the shield clanged against my knee when I hunched, giving me the jolt of physical pain I needed at the moment. I could pay my respects to Reyos later. While I was too late to save him, Novali was still alive.

Davis and Bittergale had charged into the night, leaving a square of darkness in the roof. I started that way and realized another projectile was headed in my direction. This time, I dodged it the old-fashioned way, letting the poisoned needle hit the wall behind me. The same crafter-class healer pointed at me, green runes writing around the head of his weapon. Another needle of acid green shot toward me, and I clipped it out of the way just in time with the shield, sending it spinning back toward him. He jumped back with a shout of surprise.

I charged onto the stairs leading up, holding the shield toward the stage to protect me as I took the steps two at a time. The moment I emerged into the night, I collided with a furry form.

"There you are," Ari exclaimed. *"I felt Reyos pass. What's happening?"*

"One moment," I murmured, leaning down and feeling out the edges of the hatch that connected the tower's third floor with the roof. I shut it and stood on it, sure it was the most secure place when I could see the illumination of the floor below between broken and claw-marked logs. They'd already been weakened by time and neglect, just to be cratered by the force of several furious gryphons.

My eyes adjusted to the darkness slowly as I filled Ari in mentally with what'd just happened. He pressed his bulk to my side. *"We will make him pay. I felt Davis pass by. Sunset is in pursuit with a few gryphons who could be spared. The rest are in the warehouse."* He knelt down as I fumbled into the saddle and slipped the shield into the saddlebag behind me. The boot heels felt strange where I wedged them into the stirrups, but there was no time to take them off.

We took off without me securing the riding harness. Ari flew in the direction of his Link with Sunset, passing over a massive hole that'd been made in the west wing of the warehouse. Wild Flight must've broken in everywhere.

"There is no chance they'll escape with Novali," I said, nudging him with my knee. Though I didn't have a pair of riding goggles, I felt confident enough in the saddle for him to speed us toward a knot of gryphons I spotted in the dark, their wings illuminated by starlight.

Davis hadn't gotten far. Bittergale lunged and snapped at one of the smaller wild gryphons, but a larger form intercepted her. *"They're mine to kill!"* Sunset snarled.

"And mine," Ari asserted. The formation made room for him to barrel in, pointing his beak toward the tusseling shadows falling out of the sky. There was a flash of metal, and they disengaged before Davis could shove his sword through Sunset. He gave a shout of surprise when Ari tackled them from behind, latching his talons into Bittergale's saddlebags and dragging her further downward.

The wild gryphons kept a respectful distance but still circled in case Ari and Sunset needed help. I felt Sunset's rage like the rays of a too-hot sun as she banked sharply and hit Bittergale in her front, chomping her beak down on the other female's wing and twisting. Pain flared over our Link as Sunset parted away again, agony flooding her shoulder where Bittergale bit her back, deep into a set of muscles important for flight.

We were all losing altitude fast. The enemy gryphon screamed shrilly over the familiar popping sound of fragile wing bones breaking. Davis turned in the saddle, his shadowed face creased with hatred. "Let's see who hits the ground first," he said. He hurled Novali's cage away from us.

"Watch her break open like an egg!" Bittergale's unfamiliar voice was an unpleasant screech in my mind. She laughed like she'd enjoy seeing the youngling's death, even as she plummeted from the sky without the use of one of her wings.

Ari pushed away from her and dove properly, stretching out the line of his body. I hunched over his shoulders to reduce our drag. *"Get your eyes on her,"* he said desperately.

I searched the gray shades of darkness urgently for the shape of a falling cage. A drift of clouds moved aside just in time to bathe the incoming ground with silvery shades of light.

Novali tumbled within the confines of the rotating cage, a red ball amongst black bars.

"Novali! I'm coming!" Ari cried, realigning his body. He pushed a feeling at me, too overcome for words. I pulsed my agreement and was the one who reached for the cage as the ground grew nearer and larger.

My hand closed around one of the bars. I tucked it between my chest and Ari's shoulders.

Ari pulled up at the last moment, but we still struck the ground with too much momentum. His paws slipped out from under him, and we flipped, tumbling several times until I was flung out of the saddle, landing on my back. Stars danced across my vision when my head slammed into solid ground.

Both of my arms were around Novali's cage, my fingers in a death grip on two separate bars. The body inside was too still. "Tell me you're all right, baby girl," I croaked, struggling to lift my aching head to look at her.

She didn't move. I pried my right hand loose one finger at a time. It was difficult to uncurl my stiff fingers and reach inside to touch her fuzzy side. "Novali?" I whispered.

The youngling jolted from the touch of my cold skin. I felt her take a startled breath and then reach out, whispering back, *"Sivvy?"*

My eyes flooded with relief. "Let's get you out of there."

I checked my Links with Ari and Sunset while I sat up slowly and reached for the clutch at my side...just to realize there was no clutch at my side. It and its cage-opening tool were lost somewhere between here and the warehouse.

Sunset was closer. She limped over from the shadows as I pulled uselessly at the lock separating her from her daughter. *"I'm sorry. We'll have to open it when we have the tools,"* I said. Displeased, she growled at me and settled lengthwise next to the cage, shoving her beak a few inches between the bars as she tried to comfort Novali with a motherly murr.

I stood to wobbly feet after withdrawing the dagger Heather had given me, still secured in its sheath on my calf. I followed my connection to Ari to find him struggling to stand. Pain radiated from his side where he'd struck the ground the hardest, encompassing his ribs and the joint where his right wing met his back.

And walking toward him was Bittergale's bulk, her feathers dulled by dirt in the moonlight, a squawking laugh escaping her beak. Her broken wing hung limp and dragged across the grass. It looked like she couldn't put weight on one of her front legs, yet she still bristled with menace. *"Well? Did she shatter into little pieces?"* she taunted.

"What happened to you to twist your mind?" Ari replied, as angry as he was taken aback. He spread his wings and puffed his feathers and fur in a threat display once I helped leverage him up onto his paws.

"Nothing twisted here," she cooed.

"To turn you against your own kind and commit atrocities against gryphon young? Why?" Ari demanded.

"Ask my rider. I'm just a good gryphon that does what she's told. Perhaps you could learn a thing or two...if you weren't about to die to his blade." She turned expectantly, and there he was, cavalry saber in hand. He hadn't escaped their crash unscathed, his approach hampered by a bleeding wound that

started at his left knee. Dark rivulets stained his riding leathers.

He pointed his sword at me. "Face me, heretic."

"Only two of us leave alive," Bittergale screeched.

I weighed our odds, stacking their wounds and advantages on a scale versus ours. My mind reached out, tugging a Link, begging a gryphon to go against her instincts by showing her the conversation with Bittergale.

Davis had leather armor compared to my civilian clothes and heeled boots. Plus a sword with better reach than my dagger. His clawed chest and wounded knee versus the concussion that made it hard for me to focus.

Bittergale's broken wing versus Ari's throbbing side.

A man and his female gryphon versus a woman and her male gryphon. We were smaller and outclassed on all fronts.

"I accept your challenge. But there's one thing you should know," I said.

"What's that?" Davis sneered.

"I'm not the same helpless girl stuck in a sabotaged net," I stated, hearing wings beating our way at a frenzied pace. "And *four* of us are leaving this fight alive."

Sunset tackled Bittergale, taking her by surprise. They tumbled into the night in a whirl of beaks and talons. *"You wanted to break my youngling!"* Sunset screamed. *"I'll break you instead!"*

Davis charged at me, holding the cavalry sword over his head. I stepped out of the way, feeling clumsy and slow as the world blurred around the edges. Ari reached out over our Link, trying to steady me. *We'll do this together?* he seemed to ask as our consciousnesses melded along one edge.

Ari didn't have a concussion. I didn't have a rib injury. We could do this.

Always, I willed.

Davis turned on his heel, leaning into his reach to keep me backing away from him. He jabbed at me with reckless fury, punctuated by the words he flung at me. "You've slandered my god's name!"

"You're wrong. I've met Lord Orion and act in his name." I didn't need to look over my shoulder to know that Novali's cage was nearby, now unguarded. If I stayed on the defensive for too long, I would give him an opening to harm her through the bars.

"Liar." His next jab was low and caught me off guard, sending a white-hot line of pain through the outside of my thigh. "Twisting his worship with your lies. You deserve death and the embrace of damnation for what you've done!"

Ari bowled into the back of his legs. As Davis dropped, his sword flung out of his grip, becoming another dark shape in the night.

"He's mad," Ari growled.

I disagreed. This was the Davis I knew, a sober zealot for the version of Lord Orion he believed in. Unfortunately, it was the wrong version of the god, one he'd built up to resemble him and his twisted ideals. Trying to chase that Lord Orion his whole life had bent Davis and made his morals unrecognizable. Perhaps he was the human version of the monster Bittergale had become.

I brought my dagger down, trying to strike his neck or head for a clean kill. My blade nicked him as he twisted out of the way. He kicked up from the ground, jabbing his boot into Ari's weakened side, and again, our Link flared. I took some of the pain and, in return, felt a little more clear-headed when Davis jerked back to his feet and tried to wrestle the dagger from my fist.

I didn't quite feel like myself, not with Ari's protective fury boiling over into my blood. He lent me his viciousness and strength in the punch I cocked back with my free hand, slamming it into Davis's nose with a satisfying *crunch*. Davis cringed, and then it was my turn to lend Ari my sight.

My gryphon didn't hesitate. He clamped his beak around

Davis's already damaged knee and tore, dealing him a grievous wound.

Davis lunged, catching my throat in his fist. I hit the ground first, pinned under his bulk, knocking my head a second time. Ari took some of the pain, our Link too strong for mere pain to stop either of us. Blood dripped on my face as I writhed on the ground. He'd caught my right wrist with his elbow, rendering the dagger useless as I struggled for air.

"You think you've won? Not even your gryphon can save you from this." His grip on my neck doubled in pressure, crushing in force. "I'll gather bones from you both and turn them into an effigy to the true Lord Orion."

The world grew hazy, darkness closing in with terrifying speed. It was like my strengths with Ari reverted. Blindness stole my vision away; pain flooded my skull and ribs and a phantom wing joint trapped under my shoulder. Blood roared in my ears.

I'd fought larger evils since Davis left the Academy. Matched wits with a too-ambitious crown prince. Slayed rozash, helped burn down Rathi islands, thrust a lance through the mutated heart of the Kingmaker.

I'd witnessed the rebirth of the eldrafn race. I'd held my gryphon's first, precious hatchling and let him see her every expression and growth spurt through my eyes. Rewritten the rules of the Gryphon Rider Academy and found myself at odds with a new Paragon.

Just to die at the hand of my first tormentor, Davis. But the pressure from his fingers vanished, and I drew the most excruciating breath of my life.

I traded pain for clarity, darkness for sight. And there Ari was next to me, blood staining his beak. He laid his body atop Davis, who was now the one struggling to move. *I broke his collarbones. The kill is yours,* he stated.

Ari existed in a halo of awe, a rainbow of color in my mind amidst the shadows of night. I took a moment to find my senses and stood, heading for the shape of a sword discarded not too far away. Davis's sword was longer and heavier than I was used to, yet I thought it was poetic to kill him with his own weapon.

By the time I motioned for Ari to shift out of the way, Davis had given up struggling, his lips forming his final word. "Whor—" His last breath escaped his lips in a rattle.

I placed the tip of his sword in the right place and pierced his heart. Even though he was dead, I drove the weapon deeper, embedding the blade as deep into him as he'd done to Reyos.

I'd killed so few people directly that I almost expected to feel sick at the sight of his still body, knowing I'd been the one to end him. But all I felt was relief. Straight, bone-melting liberation to know I no longer existed in a world that also had Davis in it.

"Or Bittergale," Ari commented.

Sunset approached, dragging along the bloodied corpse of the other gryphon by its scruff. She released the body next to Davis's and scuffed her back paw toward them as if she was burying droppings.

"What happened? I felt something strange between you," Sunset demanded.

At the same time, Ari said in a similar tone, *"Are you badly injured? What happened?"*

They shared a moment of amusement and pressed their foreheads together, passing back and forth the memory of their separate fights. Sunset had gotten scraped up, but she was a Skymother and had come into the fight with Bittergale less hurt. It'd ended with her ripping out the other female's throat.

Ari's memory was interesting, and I tried to get a closer glimpse at it. In the moments where I'd thought I was dead, Ari had felt whole. Uninjured, clear-minded, his senses doubled around the marbles in his eye sockets. He hadn't seen, but he'd known exactly where Davis and I were, spatially, and torn the man off me in the nick of time. Davis had stood no chance once he released my throat. Ari had hardly felt his punches and feeble kicks before disabling him and waiting to hand me the honor of taking the kill.

"Thank you, by the way," I said, wavering on my feet. We were fully separated again, and I had to sit down, else I'd fall from a nasty dizzy spell accompanied by a twist of nausea. *"During the fight, what do you think that was? The feeling that we'd merged."*

Ari answered without hesitation. *"Our true Link."* He didn't seem to know how he knew, but his emotions seemed to say, *what else would it be? Of course we'd Link together so strongly when we need it most.*

"Beautiful," was about all I had the energy to say.

I startled in shock when Chance emerged in a brush of warm fur from the collar of my tunic. He climbed down me, leaving a scratching feeling along my dirty arms on his journey to my palm. He squeaked and gestured toward Ari's face.

"Have you been there this whole time?" I asked, hearing the hoarseness in my voice.

Chance nodded his pointed head. *"The mouse is afraid for his Linked partner. He thinks something bad's happened to Heather and wants our help,"* Ari translated.

His little nose twitched as he turned pleading, button-like eyes my way. "Of course we'll help," I mumbled. "She can open Novali's cage for us."

Ari stirred with a hint of amusement. *"He says, quite literally, 'I lead you to Heather and she do for you, yes yes?'"*

"Yes yes?" I echoed.

"You won't last a minute walking. Climb on my back," Sunset said.

"But you're hurt—"

"And you are hurt worse." She knelt right next to me. *"No arguing, now. Go get Novali's cage, and climb on."*

"You sound like Valtora," I said, but I followed instructions and climbed into her saddle, holding the awkward bulk of the cage in front of me.

Novali hunched between the bars closest to my chest, accepting petting strokes from my fingertips. *"Sivvy,"* she whined, expressing a strong claustrophobic sensation.

"We'll get you free, baby girl," I promised her, my heart breaking for her discomfort.

Chance scampered onto Sunset's beak, where she'd have to cross her eyes to see him. He pointed and squeaked. *"The mouse will guide us,"* she said. With a chuckle, she waited for Ari to stand and led him with her tail on his shoulders. We made for a slow procession.

We couldn't fly, and it seemed we were in the middle of nowhere. Chance squeaked and pointed again in a slightly different direction. *"Yes, little one,"* Sunset replied.

The pointing mouse led us into a maze of streets in one of the residential districts of the city. The journey passed in a blur for me, leaving only a little room for worry that the rest of the plan to foil the Morashi's auction had gone off successfully.

We slowed, and Sunset poked at my mind, encouraging me to try and focus. I dismounted and placed Novali's cage on the ground gently. A small person wandered in our direction and passed under the nearest streetlamp, illuminating the brown of her hair. Heather wore a servant's suit with an Altarian flag pinned on her lapel. She froze at the sight of us.

I approached her and realized her eyes were fully dilated, blown out circles of black. "Hey. You okay?" I asked, resting a hand on her slim shoulder.

She jolted hard and took a step away. With a few rapid blinks, she seemed to focus on me and then our surroundings.

"Where…? I must've…" she muttered. "You're not Madam Morashi."

"Far from it. What happened?" I asked in concern.

"She looked into my eyes, and the next thing I know, I'm here…" Her pupils were shrinking back down to their proper size as she spoke, and she looked past me to the three waiting gryphons. "The plan! I think…it must've worked. I didn't quite get to the rendezvous spot, but you found me all the same."

"All I know is your plan helped save my gryphon's daughter. Do you have any tools to free her from this cage, though?" I asked.

Heather giggled briefly. "I always have tools."

She pulled out a similar cage-opening tool to the one I'd lost, getting to work on the lock first. After taking the magic from the lock, she pried it open with one side of the tool before opening the door. Novali bolted out immediately, winding around us to fit herself in the gap between Sunset's talons.

"Thank the gods for you," I said.

Heather gave a bashful shrug, blushing. "I just wanted to help."

We watched the reunion between the gryphon family. Novali spent equal time between her parents, and they showered her with love and relief. She had some aches from her tumble, but in true child fashion, she seemed to shrug them all off for now.

Ari left Sunset to groom their daughter and approached us first. He expressed a desire to me, and I guided him with a hand on his shoulder until he was right in front of Heather. "He wants to hug you," I said.

"Oh, um, okay," she murmured, looking up at the great beast in awe.

He wrapped his talons around her back, drawing her in to his furred chest. Tentatively, she looped her arms around his neck. I felt the blanket of gratitude he covered her with, the closest thing to a *thank you* a gryphon could express.

Sunset joined him, nuzzling the girl's cheek. I looked down to see Novali padding my way. When I scooped her up, she curled in my arms. *"Tired, Sivvy,"* she murmured, snuggling tight to me.

"Me too, baby," I sighed. I rocked her in my hold, more than relieved to have her back.

Once the gryphons were done sharing their gratitude, Heather cleared her throat and told us quietly that everyone had to be waiting for us at the rendezvous point.

"How far is it from here?" I asked.

"About a bell's walk away," she answered. The idea of moving my legs for another hour made my head throb worse.

I added, "Also, have you ever ridden a horse?"

She blinked owlishly. "No?"

"It would be faster if you rode one of the gryphons. Sunset is offering if you guide us," I explained. Soon, I was giving her a boost into the maroon gryphon's saddle, her smile brilliant even though all we were doing was walking. Ari felt well enough to let me on his back for this leg of our journey.

CHAPTER 34

HUMAN SUPERIORS

ACTON AND IRONFEATHER flew out to meet us halfway. Heather, the gryphons, and I all hung on his words as he gave us the rundown on what'd happened in the auction after we flew off. He rode on Ironfeather's back, and the gryphon happily fell into his role as Ari's seeing eyes.

Acton said, "A group of kids showed up out of nowhere once one of them disrupted the wards around the event. It was at the same time Wild Flight landed and started to carry on. They worked together to steal cages, passing them hand over hand to get them all removed quickly.

"We felt Reyos die, though, and the Wild Flight gryphons went into a frenzy. It was insane for a while there… Anyone who was not obviously a civilian or who didn't know to put their palms up is probably dead. I've never seen the beasts turn on people like that." He shuddered at the memory.

I muttered a curse under my breath. They'd gone straight for pack justice, all right. The Crown had to be displeased they allowed the flock into their carefully crafted plan.

Sorrow bit into me from two sides. *"I almost forgot Reyos died,"* Sunset admitted guiltily. *"I felt it…we all did. But all I cared about was saving Novali and getting our revenge."*

"We'll hold a vigil. Hopefully we can retrieve his body to honor him," Ari said. He felt guilt for the same reason, though he'd pitched his presence to reassure her.

"Not every gryphon went straight to violence," Ironfeather reminded Acton.

"Some of Wild Flight saw what we were doing and helped us move and relocate the cages. We retrieved them all, I believe. The same group of kids were the ones to break into the cages holding the younglings. Things calmed down quite a bit once the mothers were reunited with their babies," Acton shared.

"And everyone is at the rendezvous point now?" I asked.

"Everyone but us," he remarked. "What happened with you all, then?"

I fought a wave of dizziness to turn a woozy smile over at him. "Please tell me the place we're going has friendly healers."

Concern flashed across his features. "There are several."

"I'll tell you everything as soon as they take a look at us," I promised him while secretly hoping I'd be knocked unconscious for a magic-induced sleep to avoid doing so a little longer. Acton would *not* be happy to hear he'd missed my near-deadly fight with Davis.

We passed by several spacious family homes before stopping before one. It was dark on the inside like every other home we'd passed, considering the time. But Heather encouraged us that this was the place and dismounted last, with Acton's help.

I felt the presence of dozens of gryphon minds but didn't see them until Heather knocked on the front door and had us admitted. Dim magelights hung in the space around us, which was filled with bodies. Gryphons, kids, and little wonders, most of whom were asleep together. There were blackout curtains over every window and no furniture at all.

"What is this place?" I asked.

"A safe house," Heather answered with a shrug. "Until someone buys it, at least."

We were funneled by a few young adults toward the side of the house with a stripped kitchen. There, Fletcher was in the process of inspecting one of Smoky's kittens while the feligryph looked on anxiously, the other two already curled up asleep on her belly. A tired Thomas intercepted us. "Little wonders and gryphons need to be seen by my father. Any injured people have to continue into the next room," he said.

I turned to Sunset and Ari. "I can wait until they're seen," I said.

"We'll be fine," Ari said immediately.

"Leave Novali with us, and see yourself healed," Sunset agreed.

I was still holding their youngling, who'd fallen into an exhausted sleep against me on the journey here. I must've been in worse shape than I realized, as a dizzy spell had my knees crumpling below me. Acton caught me, and Novali jostled awake with a complaining cry. Her mother gathered her up and cooed over her while I leaned on Acton, who eyed me under the magelights.

"Is that bruise on your neck from someone's hand?" he asked, low and angry.

Well, there went saving the explanation for later. As we waited in a short line for a Tulari healer's attention, I shared what I could of the fight with Davis. His expression was stuck somewhere between furious and horrified. I knew he'd hate that he missed a chance to protect us.

"Gods, you did it. You killed him," he said. He patted my shoulder. "I'm proud of you. Perhaps...someone should do something about the bodies, though." By the time I was done, he was helping me sit in a rocking chair, which the healer used to lean me back for the inspection.

"I'll go ask someone," Acton promised.

The healer forced me to sleep soon after to heal off my concussion.

I woke in a pile of blankets on the ground, completely overheated. My consciousness returned slowly, as it did after every healing rest, but I was quite aware of how much I was sweating before I could do anything about it.

It took me the better part of an hour to peel my eyelids open and realize there were several gryphons resting around me. Ari, Sunset, and Novali were closest, but there was Ironfeather, Puzzlebox, Valtora, Roshawk, and several wild gryphons who knew me well enough to want to wait for me to convalesce. Other than the red youngling, who lay on my chest, fast asleep, the rest laid a paw, wing, or beak on me and pressed close.

The mood wasn't exactly happy amongst them, not with the death of such a beloved member of the flock happening so recently. I'd caught myself looking for Reyos amongst all these familiar faces and disappointing myself when I remembered all over again.

Davis killed him. But I killed Davis and avenged him.

I sought my temporary Link with Ironfeather first, earning an unexpected glare from him. He flashed with anger. *"You should've brought Acton and me with you. We could've saved you from all this,"* he growled.

"I'm sorry. There just wasn't time," I answered slowly.

"Ari and Sunset showed me the memory. But...you still could've tried, at least," he said.

I didn't know what else to say except, *"But I'm all right."*

"You just woke up," he muttered.

"C'mon, sweet boy. You know how this goes. I get hurt, and

when I wake up, you're always there to ask if I'm okay," I coaxed. I just couldn't handle Ironfeather, of all gryphons, being upset with me. Not when this ordeal was almost at an end.

He released a *craw* aloud and stood, waking most of the gryphons dozing around him. With careful steps, he picked around Sunset's spread wings and sat by my shoulder, leaning down until his beak was nearly touching my nose. *"You're really okay?"* he asked uncertainly.

"I am. Promise," I answered, petting his neck a few times. He moved to the side, and I repeated this greeting with Puzzlebox, who danced on her front paws happily to see that I was awake.

Valtora waited until I was aware enough to consider sitting up, if I didn't have Novali resting atop me, before saying that we were stuck in this house until sundown. *"The adults who herd all these human children think it is too risky for us all to fly out of here in broad daylight. I said it was reasonable. Now that you're awake, I'm going with one of them who promised to dig us a grave for Reyos in the forest outside of Kaiamear. We shall head there after dark and hold a vigil for him overnight before turning our wings towards home."*

"Okay," I answered simply. I couldn't think of any better plan.

Novali stirred eventually, allowing me some time to wander the house with her in my arms, the two of us in search of food and friendly faces. The blackout curtains remained, as did many of the little wonders. Thomas was in the kitchen with Fletcher. "Still working?" I asked.

"The body only needs four hours of rest to function," Fletcher answered. His wand hovered over the belly of a pink piglet. I couldn't tell right off what made it a little wonder, but it seemed uncomfortable as it shifted around on the counter.

"Bless you," I answered, glad he was working so hard to make sure every creature was all right.

I placed Novali on another section of the counter, the kitchen big enough for him to maneuver his wheeled chair comfortably and spread out several tools and tinctures. His dreamhog, Edgimus, was in the process of dragging over a small glass bottle.

I asked Thomas for some food, and he scrounged up some crackers, water, and a tin of tiny fish for Novali. She hid her face in my chest, whining, *"Sivvy."* She didn't want to be around any strangers. At this point, she was not willing to give any human another chance to hurt her, and I felt that pain resonate in me.

"It's okay. You can trust Fletcher and Thomas. They're good humans," I reassured her. *"Look, Thomas even found some fish your size!"*

She lifted her head reluctantly to peek at him, slowly turning and padding his way when he held one out by its tail. I devoured some crackers and watched her visibly start to trust him as he produced what had to be twenty little bites for her. It wasn't just the food, though. Her emotions had shifted, encompassed by a single statement, *"He is a good human."*

"We're going to do our best to reunite these little wonders with their families," Thomas told me. "There are a lot of them that were stolen from outside Kaiamear, so it will take some time."

I nodded, glad they had the means to accomplish such a task. "And our gryphons will be flying their younglings back to Fortress Aerie very soon," I told him.

"Oh, speaking of which," Fletcher said from behind me. "Your gryphon suffered from several fractures from the fall you two took last night. Most are in his ribs, but the most serious one is through his humerus—the first major bone in his wing. Unfortunately, I could not mend them through magic. Any further flying would be a bad idea until he has some time to heal naturally."

"He is immune to magical healing," I confirmed, having a

sinking feeling about where this was going. Ari must've been shielding his pain from me, as I hadn't noticed.

"It was worth it, for Novali," Ari said, joining in the conversation from the pile of gryphons where I'd left him.

The veterinarian advised that we wait three weeks minimum before he bore any weight in flight. *"You must return to Wild Flight without me,"* Ari said.

"We can stay here in the city—" I began to say.

"No. You have to go and argue the case for Wild Flight staying. With Reyos's death, there is talk already of the price of the alliance we struck. You...you have to do it. Talk to Brekwell, talk to Roshawk, talk to the wild mothers who just got their hutchlings back. And Novali needs to come with you too. She may seem fine now, but the reaction will come, and she will need her mother and her Sivvy," Ari concluded.

"You're sure?" I asked, feeling how he was about to insist.

"What are a few weeks away if it means my flock remains intact?" Ari reasoned. *"Besides, I like Fletcher. We have a kinship."*

The veterinarian smiled to himself. Had he heard that, even from across the house? "Ari wants to stay with you until his fractures heal. The rest of us have to go home soon," I said aloud. I waited for Fletcher to be done with his current patient before I started counting out clorets in silvers and golds, piling them into his hands.

"This is enough to keep my shop running for years," he murmured, eyes widening. "Sivana, you know I can't take this."

"Consider it payment for Ari's upkeep and a thank you," I said. "If it weren't for your son and his friend"—*or friends,* I thought—"there would be so many little wonders and gryphon younglings sold to the highest bidder."

"I did very little," he said. "But I will spend the money responsibly to help the often overlooked creatures of Kaiamear."

Gods, I wanted to stack a few more gold clorets into his palm with a mission like that. But I didn't need to overwhelm him, especially when Ari would be lounging around his shop for the foreseeable future.

"Hey," Ari said as soon as I thought that. *"It's not that he has to put up with me. I'm a delight."*

"Well, delight. Let's see if we can follow Valtora on foot," I suggested. I didn't think Ari wanted to miss the upcoming vigil.

Acton was also still in the house and insisted on coming with me when I told him I was taking a long walk with Ari. No one stopped us from leaving, so I took that as a sign that we didn't have to stay cooped up with the rest of Wild Flight.

I expected an explosion, but there was simply stony silence from both Acton and Ironfeather as we started our trek out of the city. We'd packed away provisions in our gryphon's saddlebags.

Consider my surprise when I opened one of Ari's saddlebags and found Fariq's shield prototype, but bent into a mushroom-like shape from the aftermath of the battle. I left it with Thomas, who promised to get it back to the boy who'd made it. He was still entertaining Novali while Sunset watched attentively when we left.

Since I didn't climb on Ari's back, not wanting to apply any more pressure to his fractures, I walked with his reins in hand, and Acton mirrored me with Ironfeather's. I only lasted a turn of the city bells before breaking the silence first. "I would have asked you to join us if there was time."

"There never seems to be time," he answered crossly.

"Commander Davis was flying away with Novali's cage. In this case, there was not a chance to call for you. I should've tried, but I panicked. I couldn't lose her, Acton. Not for anything." I turned a beseeching look his way, willing him to understand that it wasn't personal. Quite the opposite, in fact.

He pressed his lips together tightly and lapsed to his own thoughts. It took him a few minutes before he said, a little more like his usual calm self, "I found someone who said they would send a team to handle the bodies. Both of him and his gryphon."

"Thank the gods," I said.

"You could simply thank me," he said in full and prim Weslecker fashion. "We've shaped our roles for each other, it would seem. You run straight into danger, and I clean up after you."

I stopped walking and faced him. "Thank *you*," I said earnestly, holding my arms out for him.

He held me with a sigh, breathing in my ear, "I just wanted to punch him too, you know."

"And that's one of many reasons why I love you," I answered. We kissed for a few moments, but I was uncomfortably aware of the foot traffic around us. We garnered enough attention with two full-grown gryphons, but to add public affection to that...

Despite keeping it brief, we still were on the receiving end of a few whoops and catcalls. Acton rolled his eyes when a scruffy man called, "Better fly off with her before I do, gryphon rider! Ahaha!"

Acton offered his arm, and I took it, the two of us striding to our distant destination together. "One of many reasons?" he echoed, raising a curious brow.

"Maybe I'll tell you a few more along the way," I said.

"Mmm, maybe I'll share a few of my own about you if you do," he teased.

THE LEVITY of our walk faded to a distant, warm memory as we sat vigil with Wild Flight that evening. Acton felt the heaviness of the emotions around him, but I heard the stories about Reyos and added a few of my own.

Valtora had waited for Acton, Ironfeather, Ari, and me to find her, and we were amongst the inner circle of gryphons around the body as night had fallen soon after. Sharde and Ellie were here too, along with Puzzlebox.

As promised, a grave was already dug for Reyos nearby, with shovels waiting for us in the morning. I stayed up as long as I could and mourned my share, but many of the memories Reyos was immortalized with were happy and lighthearted. He'd been a goofy, unique gryphon and a solid friend many of the beasts trusted.

I'd miss him dearly. I stirred several hours later with that thought, having fallen asleep with many of the mourning gryphons when our stories became distant memories and the stillness of night lulled us away. We finished buried Reyos before the sunrise, and I prayed for his soul one last time before imagining new life springing up from the dirt here, as vibrant as he was.

A glimmer sparkled in the dirt between my palms before a delicate shoot pushed up, two fuzzy leaves uncurling from the growing stem. My eyes widened as I watched a tight bud form at the tip. It opened and shed a few grains of moon dust. I reached out to touch it in awe, to see if this little gift was real, but stopped when I saw the dirt clinging to my fingers. The flower was pristine, its five petals shading from white to blue at the tips, just like Reyos's unique coloring.

"Thank you," I said quietly, leaving the flower there to give it a chance to flourish.

After many of us had the chance to inspect the small miracle, I passed Ari's reins to Sharde, who agreed to get him back to the Little Wonders Pet Shop safely. He and Ellie weren't returning to the fortress yet, still content to spend time in the city together until things blew over.

IT WASN'T easy to return to Fortress Aerie without Ari. After a quick stop at the Temple of Nilara, where my sister told me she needed more time to pray and think, we left. Sunset, Novali, and I all felt the loss of Ari's presence as Kaiamear shrank in the distance. I had once found this kind of distance away from him unbearable, but Sunset and I ended up leaning on each other to endure for the necessary time he needed to heal.

Most of Wild Flight made the trip, and the air was heavy with fatigue from making this round trip so quickly. Sunset and I took the opportunity to fly alongside several gryphons, smoothing feathers and complimenting younglings along the way. We made our way up the formation until we joined Roshawk and Valtora flying at the front.

My father's gryphon had made this trip as if she were wild, abandoning him and her usual saddle to fly free and gleaming. *"Nathaniel will be upset when he learns what we did,"* she was saying.

"There is that Linked gryphon shame coming back. Is it not good enough that the murderer and his beast killed first?" Roshawk growled.

"Humans have a strange soft morality. They do not kill their enemies as readily as we do," she replied. *"Well…as we used to."*

"As we used to," he agreed in a thoughtful echo, his silence heavy afterward.

"You chose your human companion well, Skylord. The flock loves Lira," Sunset said.

He grunted, but it sounded like his way of agreeing.

Sunset and I conferred mentally. She wasn't sure this was a good time to push Roshawk to change his mind about leading Wild Flight away, considering how we were all still raw from the vigil, and I agreed.

"*I suppose you want to talk about where we go from here,*" he said like he'd read the intention straight from our thoughts anyway.

"*Not if it's too soon,*" I said.

"*It is too soon,*" he said frankly. "*I will be speaking with the gryphons I trust the most while Valtora waits to hear how your human superiors view us when they learn the truth of what we did. Then we can make an informed decision.*"

I'd already known we wouldn't have an answer decided on the flight back. I sought out what my "human superiors" thought once we arrived. To my utter shock, Paragon Brekwell was still at the fortress. Instead of taking the evening to rest, Acton and I were dragged into the Commandant's office to debrief him and Father on everything that'd happened. I took Novali and Sunset with us.

Acton let me talk, and I spared few details other than some white lies about the ages of Heather and her friends. Father gaped when he learned that I'd been the one to kill Davis. It felt like a risky admission with Brekwell listening, but I figured it was better to hear it from me rather than a report from one of the Crown's cleaners.

"And you're all right?" Father asked, looking me over anew.

"I was patched up afterward, yes," I said.

He smiled to himself, a candid reaction he tried to hide by looking down at his hands. "Well, Paragon. It seems Commander Davis received his dishonorable discharge after all."

Brekwell turned to stare at him in disbelief. So did I, shocked that he found the death something to joke about.

"You've never been a father whose chick was threatened," Sunset commented.

Father cleared his throat in the silence that followed. "Sorry, sir, but you know he deserved it."

A smile threatened Brekwell's face. "I know a few more who do, too."

Novali tilted her head, an echo to my astonishment. Had the new Paragon just told a joke back?

"Do the gryphons understand we can't have them flying off to exact this level of revenge at a whim, though? It sounds like their rage was excessive, and I'm sure I will have several civilian deaths to answer for once I return to Kaiamear," Brekwell said to me.

Valtora, who was resting primly in Night's old nest, stirred and cracked her golden eyes open. *"Tell him that I doubt we will have to attack another group of humans like this,"* she replied.

Dawnchaser, sharing the nest with Valtora, spoke up, *"There would have to be another catastrophe on the level of a murdered cloudling and an illegal auction of gryphon young for it to happen. Wouldn't it be better for the world to understand that our wild cousins have sharpened claws for any who would threaten their kin?"*

"I believe Dawnchaser speaks true, sir," I said.

Brekwell's lips turned down. "Hmm."

"She can understand me perfectly fine," Dawnchaser said a moment later, in reply to something he'd stated privately to her. *"I trust the Chosen of the shining man. You should too."*

With a bit of reluctance, he dipped his head. "Congratulations are in order, Lieutenant Walker. You did the impossible... You retrieved every youngling gryphon alive and safe." Brekwell gestured to Novali, who hunched a little and looked up at me for reassurance.

I kissed the top of her head, and the Paragon had nothing

snide to say about coddling her. "They want to know if they still have a safe place to roost here, sir," I said.

He watched Novali curl up in my lap and gaze up at me with full trust. "Well...of course. Let's see your movement for change to its end, Lieutenant Walker," he answered.

CHAPTER 35

STAY OR GO

BEFORE ANY DECISION could be made, we all had to rest. The wild mothers tucked their younglings away, and I snuggled into a bedroll out amidst the stars for the next few nights, watching the constellations form and the moon rise. The cold chill of winter seemed to make those celestial pinpricks crisper in the canvas of night.

Despite knowing that Wild Flight was debating its future around me—keeping those conversations private from my curious human ears—I was finally finding some peace. When I told Acton that I was going to sleep outside for a while with my gryphon family, he didn't question the decision. He simply unearthed his own bedroll to join us. We huddled outside together with Sunset resting on top of me and Iron-feather sprawled over our legs, our fingers intertwined in between.

Novali chose to tuck herself into the warm folds of cloth with me on the third night. She was akin to a wary animal by day, sticking close to her mother's side and avoiding any contact with the humans who cared for Wild Flight. It still hurt to see that she knew fear now, but she was back and safe, a small face peering out of my bedroll for the reassurance of a smile.

"It will be okay. We've got you," I promised her when I saw that look in her eyes. *"And remember, someday, you will grow big and fierce."*

She blinked and snuggled closer to me.

But not too soon, hopefully, I added to myself. As much as I wanted her to realize that she was an apex predator, I would miss being able to snuggle her close like this.

In a few short months, she would stretch into the awkward teenage phase of gryphon development and become a yearling. She'd fly, independent and free. If Wild Flight decided to stay, she would be amongst the first group of Linking age to choose whether she wanted a rider and pick the lucky person if so.

But if Wild Flight left, most of Novali's youngling friends would have to go too. It'd be a disaster for the corps and Altare, where new gryphon riders were needed more than ever. Worse, the shaky trust I'd earned from Brekwell wouldn't matter. There was no alliance with the gryphons if they flew away. Poaching and Link theft would resume out of necessity.

"I can feel you worrying, Sivvy. Go to sleep," Sunset murmured.

With a sleepy sigh, I did. Then I got up thinking it would be an ordinary day and waited to feed the flock in the morning with Lira and Credell, just to find the air still and silent.

"You know, I never got to tell you congratulations," I said to Lira. "You became the second female gryphon rider, and so quietly too."

She quirked her mouth. "Thanks. Roshawk didn't want it to be a big deal. He was embarrassed, really, and it hurt to feel that he was calling himself a hypocrite."

"Oh," I murmured in sympathy.

"But I think we're making progress. If Wild Flight leaves… he wants me to go too. He doesn't see a future without me, just like I don't want to do something else with my life. We're not just gryphon and rider, but companions for life. It's…" She smiled down at her hands. "It's the most special connection I've ever made."

"That's beautiful." I nodded my understanding, seeing a shade of myself in her words. "My life would be dull without Ari and Sunset. It feels like they own half my soul."

"And Sunset, hmm," she commented.

I coughed, making for an awkward transition. "Do you have any idea what the wild gryphons are deciding?"

She had a sparkle in her eyes. "Ask Roshawk yourself."

Instead of the whole flock coming for their morning meal, only Roshawk arrived, limping as he came to stand before us. *"Before we enjoy any more of your hospitality, the flock wishes to see the human candidates. All of them,"* he stated.

I exchanged a glance with Lira before informing Credell of what the Skylord had said. "That's a mighty tall order," Credell said with a low whistle.

"What does the flock want with them?" I asked carefully.

"We have spoken in circles of the good and bad in your kind. Humans prove to be complicated. Many of us, and I am guilty of this too…" He shifted and plucked at the fluff in his wings in discomfort. *"Have seen the matter of coexisting as a matter of either-or. Especially when staying has led to us losing two beloved members of our flock."*

Lira nodded. "Black and white," she said.

He pulsed a sense of agreement. *"We want to see the depth of character in the humans that would Link with our young. Only then can we make a decision on whether we should stay as Wild Flight or leave to become a separate flock once more."*

Gryphon communication was fully transparent. In the flow of his emotions, I felt a hidden request: *show us a reason to stay.*

"We have many great cadets for the flock to meet. But I'm not sure how this will work. None of them really know how to talk to gryphons…" I mused.

Roshawk explained how the flock wanted to conduct a test: instead of direct communication, the gryphons would make temporary connections. An honest exchange of thoughts to answer the questions that weighed heavily on the minds of many of the wild gryphons.

I warned him that a connection that deep would be uncomfortable for some of the cadets. *"If they refuse, then they are not likely to be our companions,"* Roshawk said.

I hummed. He wasn't wrong. All the cadets knew that we'd lost and then returned nineteen younglings. It was also impossible to hide how stirred up Wild Flight was. Perhaps it was time to have honest conversations with the cadets and to weed out those who wouldn't, or couldn't, form the empathy to bond with one of our young beasts.

"I'll speak with my father," I said finally.

AND FATHER MADE it happen that evening, calling all of the first-years out of the mess hall once they'd had dinner. He decided to phrase it as "the gryphons want to give you a test," and there were no serious complaints made.

They murmured in awe when three dozen wild gryphons circled in for a landing. My eyebrows rose; I recognized the majority of them to be the beasts least likely to interact with us. The old, the distrusting, and of course, the mothers. Every wild mother whose baby was stolen now attended this test, making up a third of the group.

"Remember, cadets. Manners save limbs," I said.

"Yes, ma'am," they chorused together, loud and a little nervous.

The gryphons came to the cadets, leaning down to look in their eyes. I was amongst several of the instructors circling to make sure there wasn't any trouble.

"Why do you want to be a gryphon's companion?" an elderly male asked Cadet Geisel. I couldn't hear her response, only noticing the beaming smile that creased her pale face.

As she'd learned when first meeting Novali and Sunset, she kept her hand by her side as she asked in return, "May I pet you, sir?"

"The young have a lot of audacity," he grumbled but allowed it after she complimented his plumage.

Many of the other beasts were prompting thoughts and ideals with more direct statements. *Tell me of the worst thing you've done. Show me why I should trust you with my youngling. I want to see the best and worst of you.*

I turned to Sunset, who'd peeled away from the cluster of gryphons to follow me. *"We should have started here,"* I said to her privately. It would've saved some of these hopefuls from wasting their time and energy.

"Next year, we adapt to what we've learned," she said.

"If Wild Flight stays," I sighed.

She draped a wing over my shoulder. We watched the gryphons circulate further, poking and probing for the answers they sought.

We had our first rejection, a wild mother snapping at a cadet and hissing, *"Where is your compassion?"*

Pereyra jumped forward to take him out of the lineup, the two of them conferring quietly. He shared what I'd told him to. Any sign of hostility meant it was time for the cadet to pack their things. By the low tones of argument, this partic- ular boy wasn't taking it well.

No one lost a limb today, but five more were dismissed by the flight before they were done. The sun was low on the hori- zon, and the gryphons seemed satisfied, starting to fly away to discuss what they'd learned and sleep.

All of them left but one, a dark-furred female who rubbed her head and neck against a boy's shoulder affectionately. Sunset cooed. *"A true Link!"*

Father called a dismissal for the rest of the cadets except for the lucky one, who remained. He tentatively patted her wing, looking stunned. "I think she wants me to Link with her," he said, looking up at Father with the wide-eyed fright of a cadet afraid of a surprise punishment from the Commandant.

"Then go fly with her," Father replied, clapping him on the shoulder. "We'll get her saddled up when she's ready."

She glanced to the sky. *"Now is fine. Why wait?"*

I couldn't help it. I beamed. This gryphon had recognized the person she was meant to Link with nearly on sight. Perhaps it was meant to be that easy before our ancestors over thought it and made it too complicated.

"Isn't that what humans always do?" Sunset teased.

"Hey, you. Hush." I reached over to push her shoulder, but she pranced away with a twittery giggle.

She took me back to Wild Flight's territory before long, both of us wanting to turn in for the night with Novali. The air was still, absent of any whispers from the gryphons. Any decision to be made would happen tomorrow and I did my best not to worry.

ALL OF WILD Flight's human element, plus Lira and our three temporary caretakers, stood waiting with the usual buckets of iced fish to serve breakfast the next morning. Lira was at ease, so I decided to try to be as well, even though there was no sign of the flock gathering to partake in our hospitality at dawn.

Feathers rustled through the territory, so they were awake.

Soon gathering as one massive group, they approached on foot. Roshawk and Valtora were the only two who came forward to speak to us, while the rest milled with the caw and call of so many beasts in one place.

The Skylord leaned on his Matriarch mate when they stood before us. She nibbled on his neck in obvious affection. *"We have come to a decision as a flock,"* she told us.

"A terrible tragedy was visited upon us while we roosted here, in these lands between human civilization and untamed wilderness," Roshawk began.

Out of habit, I translated what they said aloud for everyone else. "We sought a group to blame and fell back to old thinking. We feared that all humans were the same after all. It was a shock to see how little value members of your kind placed on our treasured young."

As long as my lips were moving to frame what they were saying, I couldn't speak up to argue how wrong that was. But they were just getting started, so I continued to be their mouthpiece. "Our hearts pulled away from our reason, and for that, we apologize. What we have seen since reflects a greater truth: that we have many strong human advocates, and the majority of them live and work with us every day. We have developed a kinship together, even shed blood together fighting for this alliance. So, together, we can come to a solution to make sure we are better protected than ever."

"So…they're staying?" Biggs whispered.

I whooped when both of the gryphons bobbed their heads. "They're staying!" I exclaimed. I grabbed the nearest person, Lira, into a crushing hug, and we hopped up and down like schoolchildren.

Wild Flight joined in with exclamations of their own, sure to wake the whole fortress with the cacophony they made. Then they approached us, bellies rumbling, for a bite to eat.

I STRUGGLED against the feeling that everything "went back to normal" after that. Paragon Brekwell left once he heard me report the news that the gryphons were staying, which, all in all, was a huge relief for the fortress leadership.

Classes with the gryphons resumed. After Yule, we planned on having a daily structured time for the younglings and remaining cadets to more seriously meet and form bonds. But until then, I taught my one class and counted the days until I got to see Ari again and feel his solid presence on the other side of our Link.

The next mail drop brought me a letter from Rissa, who'd dashed it off in a hurry. *Lady Nilara has given me my first task! I will wear her protection while I go off on this new adventure. I'll see you soon, probably in a few months. Then I'll explain everything.*

She'd penned a similar message to Mother, who seemed fit to burst with pride. "The holidays will be quiet, then," she said after setting the parchment aside.

Not with gryphons around, I thought.

"We'll invite your young man to our celebration instead," she added to me.

"He'd love that," I said, chuckling. Especially when she started politely enquiring as to why he hadn't proposed yet, like she did when she thought I was out of earshot. I would be tempted to edge closer the next time it happened, to see what his answer was.

I worried the problem was me. That I was too busy, or too dedicated to Wild Flight, or simply not as pleasant a companion as he originally thought I'd be when we'd been in the same cadet flight. Whatever the reason, I wasn't willing to ask and potentially lose his company every evening for dinner and a walk out in the gryphons' territory.

We'd established a route to take each night, making a loop

past the stables and through Glorium's Roost, which was shaping up in record time from the demigod's sporadic visits. It gave us a time to simply talk and enjoy one another's presence without the bustle of Academy life tugging us in one direction or the other.

One foggy dusk, where the dense breath in front of our faces could be mistaken for eddies of mist, we took a lantern and considered cutting the walk short with chill winds nipping our noses and ears.

Someone was already in Glorium's Roost, sitting on the deck where the first few gryphon families were starting to nest. There was a startled noise, and Acton lifted the lantern, revealing someone who I thought was a stranger.

Then Mireille screamed, *"SIVVY!"* and launched from where she sat next to this man, bowling me over in her enthusiasm. The air left me with an "ugh," the ground was hard underneath us, and stars circled the corners of my sight. But that was definitely Mireille lying on top of me, cooing and chirping as she rubbed her head and neck over me affectionately.

She seemed bigger, her feathers gleaming a metallic silver even in the fog. I ruffled her wings and gasped a breath when she lifted off my chest. She must've realized she was too heavy for me to support her weight like she was still a yearling.

"Mateo?" Acton asked, sounding about as shocked as I felt. He gave me a hand up, and I stood, one arm slung around Mireille's shoulders.

Mateo strode over to us like his old confident self, but he looked years older with an untamed beard and a leaner build that had his flight leathers loose on him. That being said, he needed a new set anyway, as the ones he wore were battered beyond rescue. His teeth were bared in a huge smile within the thicket of his facial hair. "We did it," he said. "We met a god."

We took turns hugging the crown prince while Ironfeather skidded around a corner. He leapt at his sister with a crow of delight, the two of them tussling like they used to until Mireille ended up sitting on him. Fierce sibling affection rose from them in waves.

"I'm so glad you're back," Acton said.

Mateo let out a rusty laugh. "Me too. So, what did I miss?"

Acton and I glanced at one another for a long moment. "Suffice to say, everything?" Acton snarked.

We escorted him to a spare room in the temporary quarters to rest off his ordeal first. He joined our table at breakfast as if he'd never left, showered, shaved, and changed into a princely double-breasted coat. He attacked his food with fervor as I explained what he'd missed in the last few months with the help of all our friends.

Of his trip to the gods, he had nothing of note that he could share. It was quite the one-sided conversation until I brought up Fenway and everything we suspected about it.

"And this is ongoing?" he asked.

"Your royal father doesn't seem all that interested in it right now," I said.

He made a dismissive gesture. "Of course not. With this imposter Isaac on the loose, why would he care? I will bring it up with him later, once I attend to his needs and do the things you told him I was doing."

"That's a long list at this point," Acton said.

The crown prince sighed. "Then I had better get started."

CHAPTER 36

FEATHER INSPECTION

3 MONTHS LATER

Mateo vanished again. It was almost like he was still on the Path of Glorium, except he popped by once a month to rest overnight in the fortress and give Mireille a chance to socialize with her kin. The imposter was still at large, stirring up ill sentiments, but we were too far removed to hear much of it unless Mateo himself shared the news.

It was a surprise that Mateo came by twice this month, a copy of a royal summons in hand the second time. "I told you I didn't forget about you," he said.

Father, Sharde, Acton, and I followed him back to the capital to wait for the results. Lord Fenway was given three days and a paid round trip with a member of Final Flight to appear before Mateo as crown prince. It was a first for him… to see his new title on an official summons and to sit at the head of a table decorated with several officials.

Paragon Brekwell sat at Mateo's left hand, and at his right was a wizened official who Mateo would stop and listen to no matter what he'd been doing. Since we were only here to observe, Sharde, Acton, and I stood against the wall amidst a significant presence of armed guards and city peacekeepers.

"Best case scenario, no one shows up," Acton was saying in a low voice, his hand resting on Sharde's shoulder.

"He's going to show up," Sharde sighed.

"Then you look him in the eye and stare to assert dominance," Ari interjected. He clearly thought Sharde's last-minute jitters were ridiculous.

I stroked my gryphon's wing, happy to have him and our other gryphons here. They formed a pile by our feet except for Ari, who leaned against me companionably. Once his wing had healed, we'd been more inseparable than ever.

Sharde glanced over at me, quirking a brow. "Did he say something about asserting dominance?" he whispered.

"What do you think?" Ari asked playfully.

"I...hmm. I think your advice is very gryphon-centric."

"It's what I know."

"You'd imagine, after spending so much time with Sivana, I'd be able to speak with other gryphons too," Acton said at about the same time.

"You've been a little distracted," Ironfeather pitched in. He was in a bubbly mood with Mireille, the two of them twittering away about what each other had missed in the time they'd been parted.

Her transition to Skymother had turned her into a sleek silver beast, a rival to Valtora or Night with the luster of her feathers and increased size. She lounged like a princess, her tufted tail resting over her brother's. The only gryphons I'd seen her defer to since her return were Valtora—grudgingly— and Dawnchaser, who gossiped like an eager grandmother with so many younger gryphons around.

Acton opened his mouth to reply to Ironfeather when the door to the audience chamber opened and in walked three men. Sharde stiffened with a gasp, while my breath caught for another reason. We were right... We had to be.

One of the men was a palace official and spoke first. "Your Highness, these two men have arrived to answer your summons and said they represent Lord Fenway. This is Martin Orra, his steward, and Frey Sharde, Bailiff of Fenway."

My gaze narrowed on the man that was clearly Sharde's father. He was large, both broad-shouldered and tall, with age only starting to lean out his muscles and leach away the color of his hair. He had a thick forehead and a natural frown tugging down the edges of a trimmed beard. It was apparent that he was sweating, as was the smaller man next to him, who hunched as if to hide in Frey's shadow.

"You may be seated," Mateo said, gesturing to a few empty chairs at the end of the table. I wasn't the only one staring daggers at the pair of men as they sat and the meeting was called to order.

"What'd I tell you? He always shows up," Sharde muttered.

"Mateo's going to destroy them. Watch," Acton whispered back.

The prince was conferring with the official to his right, nodding along as the man gestured to the newcomers.

Mateo straightened in his chair and cleared his throat. "I summoned Lord Fenway, not his steward and bailiff. Explain to us why you're here instead."

It was Frey who answered. "Your Highness, we mean no disrespect. Lord Fenway is in his twilight years and leaves the most important tasks of lordship to us, his two most trusted servants. We have his permission to speak on his behalf."

"I care not for his age when it was he who I summoned. Our concerns for Lord Fenway continue," Mateo sniffed.

"He has not been seen in person by the residents of Fortress Aerie, nor their spouses and children, who reside in his town," said Brekwell. He unfolded two pieces of paper and laid them flat, passing them around for the others at the table to see. "Apparently, he does not write his own letters, either."

"What a rude message to your son, Bailiff Sharde," Mateo said coolly. "It appears you have not learned many manners since, with the way you wrote about Marshall Walker's wife."

"Your Highness—" Frey began to say. Mateo held up his hand, and one of the officials bellowed that the crown prince was speaking.

"I have also requested a report with Fenway's tax revenue for the last ten years," he continued, gesturing to a woman wearing the symbol of the treasury on her tunic.

She nodded and consulted a few sheets of parchment as she spoke of a steady decrease in tax payments out of Fenway. It was the steward, Martin, who replied in a shaking voice, "We can attribute that to a declining population. Fenway is a remote location. Our youth, especially, seek to leave and learn trades elsewhere."

"And yet Lord Fenway has refused to sell the land to the gryphon knight corps?" Mateo interjected.

"It was his decision, Your Highness," the steward replied.

"Well, you've served him for many years, yes? Perhaps you can enlighten us on his choice," Mateo said.

Frey and Martin glanced at each other, having a muttered conversation as the room shifted impatiently. "The money offered was insultingly low, Your Highness," Frey ended up answering.

"For a remote location with a declining population," Mateo said skeptically.

"If the Crown is still interested in purchasing the land, we would be happy to carry an offer back to our lord."

Mateo scoffed. "I'm sure you would. I've heard enough. Guards, detain them."

They were removed by two guards apiece. The steward went without complaint, while Frey struggled as he was dragged toward the door. "Your Highness! We have done nothing to deserve this!" he shouted. In the midst of his flailing, he spotted Sharde across the room, and his lip curled. He pointed toward his son. "Has my ungrateful son poisoned your mind already? I demand a chance to explain!"

Sharde's hands shook. He folded his arms to hide it as Frey's voice grew quieter and the door closed behind him. I breathed a sigh of relief. "It's done," I said.

"It's done," he echoed in agreement. "I'll never have to see him again, or worry he'll find me at the fortress. It's...it's really over." I reached over and patted his broad shoulder in understanding.

Mateo was nodding toward Brekwell, saying, "Expect to house several inspectors in the near future. The Crown will be turning over Lord Fenway's estate for the truth."

Acton spent a couple extra days in Kaiamear with Mateo while the rest of us flew home. Mother was going to be elated by the news—she would soon have a lot more to do, if the results of the impending investigation turned out the way we thought they would.

The seasons were turning, too, fresh green shoots sprouting in Wild Flight's territory. I saw them from the air as texture of color on a cold white blanket. Still, most of the wild gryphons were resting in Glorium's Roost, which was completed enough to offer shelter to the flock. Ari came in for a landing in the courtyard, and Sunset emerged from the nest they'd built to greet us.

Glorium's Roost was built several stories high and shaped like a cylinder attached to the sheer mountain wall it'd been built next to. There were several tiers on the inside, with boxes deep and wide enough to hold a gryphon family's nest comfortably. Most of the nests were at least partially human-made now, blankets and plush bedding arranged by the beasts.

There was a canvas awning we drew in at night and when the weather was poor. The Roost didn't have gates yet, and the mountainside was awaiting some expensive Tulari work to form quarters for human staff members, but the flock still loved it.

I dismounted and waved up to the face peering over the edge of Ari and Sunset's box. "Hi, Novali! We're back!" I announced.

She blinked, shuttering her bright orange eyes, and reared back out of sight. *"I saw,"* she answered.

"You don't want to come down and say hi?" I teased.

"I see you all the time, Auntie!"

"But I miss my little Novali."

"I'm not little anymore," she huffed.

No, she wasn't, I reflected. She and the rest of the younglings around her were ready to start testing their wings any day now. We'd have yearlings and Links before we knew it.

"Sivana!" sang Hvit, flapping his way into the courtyard and skidding to a halt.

A few moments later, Revna landed too. He hopped around me so he was hiding behind my legs. "Sivana, tell her to stop raining on me," Hvit complained.

"It's just rain!"

"It makes my lightning act weird," he whined.

I sighed and stooped, picking up Revna with a grunt. She may be past my waist in height, but she was still a hollow-boned bird I could heft to eye level. "Hi, Sivana," she twittered sweetly, not even seeming to mind her talons dangling.

I put my best stern face on. "Hi, Revna. Remember when we were talking about boundaries?"

"When Hvit says no, I have to stop," she recited, sighing. "I guess. But it's not my fault he gets jealous of my songs."

"I remember a certain someone being jealous when Hvit developed lightning first," I pointed out.

"I still don't have lightning! See, he's special too. We can work together and make a proper storm," she said.

"A small one," Hvit agreed, peering around my thigh.

I couldn't help but smile again. "Remember, boundaries," I said, placing her back down. She bobbed in agreement, the two of them shadowing me as I returned to my duties.

"No Acton, huh?" Revna said.

"He might be—"

"Shh!"

"Sorry," Hvit sighed.

I had the feeling I should ask what they meant, but Revna was fluttering her wings and quickly saying, "Can we get your opinion on part of the sagas?"

They had more than one point they were quibbling about and sang each part for me with the same eagerness for a tiebreaker as always.

Once they flew off, though, I didn't see them again for a long while. Not until Acton returned late in the evening a couple days later and wandered off after planting a distracted kiss on my lips. I suspected something was wrong, as the next time I saw him was at breakfast, and he was eating very little.

Father came by with Valtora. "I'm told we have an update about Linking Day?" he asked.

I thought he was asking me, and my eyes widened. I didn't have anything new to tell him, but it was Sharde who nodded and said, "Yes, sir. If you would follow us back to Wild Flight's territory. The yearlings are ready for a flight feathers inspection."

"Very good. Let's move out," Father said.

I fell into step with Sharde. "What flight feathers inspection?" I demanded.

He gave me a toothy grin. "You'll see!" he hopped into Puzzlebox's saddle with more haste than usual, urging her into the air quickly.

Ari flew me back on their heels. *"Do you know what this is about?"* I asked him.

"They're done all the time to see when a yearling is ready to fly," he answered. *"I don't see why you're so worried."*

"I'm supposed to be in charge again, not Sharde."

Ari projected his humor with a twittery laugh. *"Trust me, no one thinks he took your job."*

As we circled in for a landing, I realized all of Wild Flight was milling around outside of the roost and stables. There was an air of anticipation that had me holding some of my breath and looking around for the cause.

Acton stepped forward, extending out his arm. "I wanted to show you something before we inspect any feathers," he said.

"What's happening?" I asked him in an undertone. He took me toward the grassy field up the river from Glorium's Roost, overlooking the rolling hills that transitioned to wild gryphon territory. The gryphons followed us, along with my friends and…Valtora must've brought both my parents here, as Mother clung to my father's side. It was her expression that tipped my understanding of what was going on.

Revna and Hvit landed in the grass nearby. Acton gave them a meaningful look, and they both cleared their throats in sync before starting to sing a tune of pretty, sparkling bell tones.

"I've wondered for a long time if anyone owns this patch of land. Mateo looked into it for me," he said, offering me a sealed scroll.

I broke the seal and read it; it was a property deed signed by Acton and King Cortes. "You bought this land?" I asked.

"And paid for the builders to stay a little longer to make a house here," he said. In a graceful motion, he sank to one knee and fished a small box from his pocket. "I knew you could not settle anywhere too far from the gryphons you've come to call kin, so I wanted to make sure you had that…with me. I love you and want to spend the rest of my life with you."

I gasped, bouncing on the balls of my feet as he opened the box, revealing a sparkling stone in the morning light. "Sivana Walker, will you do me the honor of marrying me?"

"Gods, yes. I would love to!" I exclaimed. My eyes prickled with happy tears as he walked the ring up my finger before we kissed and embraced in front of our audience.

The humans applauded, and the gryphons screamed and called. The two stormsingers huffed to have their song overpowered, both of them taking wing. Silver sparkles scattered in Revna's path as she circled us. Under the discordant noise, I heard some of the gryphons chatting to each other.

"Finally, they're becoming mates."

"A little early in the season for a mating Link, don't you think?"

"Shh. Sivana's wanted this forever," came Novali's voice, her young presence one of the most exuberant ones around us. *"She didn't think he'd ever give her a shiny."*

"Was this what you were waiting for?" I asked quietly, shaking the half-crumpled deed.

"Somewhere between the land and a split second of peace," he answered with a wink.

I nodded, thinking that made sense. We held hands as we chatted with the crowd. I made sure to keep my left free, as both Lira and Ellie wanted to see the ring up close, as did most of the gryphons. Many of them complimented my upcoming "mating Link" and admired my shiny, to the point where it felt like I was the last person to see it.

The band was shaped like a feather, with tiny and intricate details etched along its outside. It reminded me of a necklace I'd once been given, made of Lord Orion's power and Glorium's feathers, but this one would be much more permanent. The little tines that gripped the diamond were sharpened to look like tiny gryphon talons clutching the precious stone.

I adored it immediately. It was *my shiny* after all, and a precious gift from Acton. We were finally engaged!

And he knew me well enough to make sure we made a home with the gryphons. Any children we had—

"Are my uncle senses working? You're already thinking of having chicks?" Ari interjected gleefully. He'd caught me daydreaming of him and Sunset having babies enough before they actually did.

"Someday," I answered, laughing. *"I was just thinking that any children we have will grow up with gryphons, and what a blessing that will be. Are* you *thinking of having more chicks?"*

Sunset, who was pressed against Ari, nuzzled under his beak while he loosed a protesting squawk. *"I don't know about that,"* he hedged.

"Think about it, Ari. We could have another beautiful Novali," Sunset suggested.

"Isn't the first one enough of a talon-full?"

The real Novali hadn't gone far. She shot him a dirty look and flounced off.

"See what I mean?" he asked.

CHAPTER 37

LINKING DAY

THE YEARLINGS TESTED their wings not much later. There were a few days of them cluttering the sky, playing and tumbling and falling under the watchful eye of their elders, before we decided it was Linking Day at last. Brekwell and Dawnchaser showed up in a hurry, accompanied by several senior military officials, all wanting to see how this would go.

It was early morning, after the gryphons were fed and flying down to the Green to await the cadets, when I stepped into the courtyard of Glorium's Rest. I took in the tiered boxes and the signs of inhabitance within them. "Are you proud of what we've accomplished, Lord Orion?" I asked empty air.

Warmth crossed my back, like the sudden rising of the sun. My eyebrows lifted in surprise as I turned to behold the god who finally decided to answer my call, first blinded by the golden radiance that reflected off him.

Blinking away the spots, I saw that he was in his usual form. One of his clergymen, Duncan, had been kind to me and became the person I associated strongest with Lord Orion. Hot radiance filled his eyes, a telltale sign I wasn't looking at a mortal man.

"It is the eve of your greatest hour. Aren't you the one who is proud?" he answered.

"Don't lie," chased the voice of Glorium, who formed out of fractals of light next to the god.

I couldn't help a smile. "Okay, yes, I dare say I am."

"I am as well," Lord Orion said. He petted his gryphon's massive wing, the two of them leaning toward one another companionably. "Providing a home for the gryphons in Glorium's name is a nice touch. And look how much space there is for the flock to expand."

"I wanted to guarantee that there are more gryphons in our skies in the coming generations, not fewer," I replied.

He turned his regard my way, warm both literally and figuratively. "You have taken great strides to protect future generations of my blessed beasts. I don't think it's a stretch to say that this is the future of gryphon-kind. Well done, my Chosen."

I opened my mouth to speak, but he raised his fingers in a gesture for quiet. "And your efforts will bring the concept of true Links to all corners of Altare. For that, you have my personal gratitude." He folded his hand over his heart, his smile radiant. "The world takes a step toward perfection, as Nilara and I have seen it, thanks to you."

My heart soared from his praise. "It was an honor, my lord."

He nodded. I had the feeling he was about to disappear, as he never stayed long. "As a boon, I've arranged a coincidence for you. I hope you like it."

"Okay," I said, deciding not to cling to his robe. "Thank you again, my lord. I appreciate the visit."

He smiled and faded into golden motes that drifted on the breeze. "Until next we meet, Chosen." His voice, too, ebbed to nothing.

Glorium got to his paws, beak parted with excitement. *"Well, shall we see how it goes?"*

"You're staying, Lord Glorium?"

His glimmering feathers brushed out with pride to be referred to by his godly status. *"Of course!"* He followed me as I went looking for my gryphons.

We found Sunset and Ari waiting for me, two of the last gryphons still here. Her eyes dilated when she spotted Glorium by my side. *"How nice to be in your presence again, Lord Glorium,"* Ari said, hardly surprised.

"Ready for a victory lap before we see your yearlings Linked?" the demigod asked.

My two gryphons conferred quietly for a moment before Ari stepped forward, indicating with a toss of his head that I was riding him today. I climbed into his saddle and secured my legs slowly.

"A victory lap, my lord?" Sunset asked.

"You'll see," he said, pushing off after her and Ari. As we descended toward the Green, Glorium effortlessly pulled past them, spreading his wings wide to catch the light as he dove over the heads of cadets and yearlings alike. *"Fly with me, Wild Flight!"*

Boys and girls pointed, mouths falling open in awe. Most of the gryphons didn't hesitate, taking wing after their demigod in a multi-hued flurry of feathers and fur. Ari dove close to the Green, giving me a chance to wave to an astonished-looking Brekwell as Dawnchaser took flight behind us.

Glorium wove back and forth, laughing and carefree in the air. The wind itself seemed to bend to his wings, letting him barrel through the air with the grace of a beast a quarter of his size. By the time he was done showing off, there wasn't a grounded gryphon in sight. Hundreds of pairs of wings thundered behind him as he lifted higher to take the group away on a tour of their territory.

Parents flew with yearlings, and the eldest gryphons were pushed to the front of the group to ride along in Glorium's wake. I felt the touch of dozens of Links, formed strongest in the air with us flying together aimlessly.

Novali flew just off her parents' wings, puffing along with her beak parted in joy. She looked so much like Sunset, her eyes twin orange gems. She'd developed a brilliant scarlet coat of feathers, with a russet covering of fur along her belly and leonine flanks. Ari and Sunset heaped her beautiful self with praise, as many of the parents around us did with their yearlings.

It was like a heartfelt goodbye. Once Linked, the yearlings would have duties and trainings and riders to attend to. The gryphons needed this moment more than I realized.

Glorium eventually dipped his wings and took Wild Flight in for a landing. The panting yearlings flopped on the ground, while their elders sat and started to groom one another. We'd gained quite a crowd: most of the fortress staff and their family members were out on the Green, including Mother, all here to watch the culmination of all of our efforts with this year's group of cadets and yearlings.

Brekwell, the other senior officers, and my father stood in a separate cluster and wanted some kind of explanation for why a demigod had suddenly stolen away all the gryphons. I came over to answer a barrage of questions about Glorium. I ended by saying, "It was good for morale. The families all said goodbye to their yearlings."

When Brekwell smiled and accepted my answers, so did everyone else. We'd come far from him questioning my judgment at every turn.

It helped that the yearlings were already recovering from the exertion of their flight and now visiting with the cadets. All of the older officers held their breath as they awaited the first Links.

The easiest way to establish a permanent Link was to take a gryphon flying, and there were caretakers on standby with saddles once the beasts made their choices. I didn't expect it to take long or for it to appear spectacular for the watching crowd. The cadets had mingled with these gryphons since we returned from Yule, and many already knew who they wanted, starting to pair off two by two to the cheers and clapping of those watching.

I counted the new gryphon riders as they walked by… twenty-five, twenty-six, twenty-seven new pairings before the gryphons backed away from the remaining cadets. The rest milled about while the overlooked cadets started to console each other.

Of our fifty-one yearlings, only six had decided they didn't want to try to find a rider. They were, unsurprisingly, all from the group that'd been stolen away to Kaiamear. That left eighteen yearlings who wanted a rider and didn't select one from the cadets, and amongst that group was Novali.

I went to her first, petting her wing while she bunted my chest gently. *"My companion is elsewhere,"* she said, likely reading the question I was going to ask off me before I could pose it.

"Do you know where?"

She tilted her head thoughtfully. *"I think so. I could fly there…if that's okay?"*

I had her hold that thought and checked in with some of the other yearlings. Some knew what direction to fly in; others had no idea but wanted to stretch their wings anyway and see if they could sense something further inland. I took this information to Father, who nodded and proclaimed Linking Day complete, calling for everyone to head to the mess hall for a reception.

I walked at the back of the group with Father and Ari, the latter of which paused and tilted his head toward the sky. I halted mid-step and looked up and around, spotting the shapes of a few gryphons headed our way. "Father," I whispered, nudging him to look too. We hung back to see who was arriving.

The couriers came in for a landing nearby, all members of Final Flight with an extra person riding tandem behind them. The first person hopped free and primly brushed off her skirts. "Rissa?" I called, a huge smile breaking over my face. I hadn't heard from her in months! As she looked up and beamed too, a silvery streak that shot through her braided hair faded into its usual platinum.

I rushed over to grab her into a crushing hug. "Hey, is she the only one you're happy to see?" asked Nate as he dismounted next. Happy tears fogged my eyes as I held out an arm for him to join the family hug.

He looked thinner but well and hugged me back just as fiercely as I held him and Rissa. When we released each other, I saw the Final Flight members walking their gryphons over to the wild beasts, who greeted them warmly. Terrance, Nate's healer friend, waved and kept a polite distance next to an unfamiliar man, and the fifth person was already in motion.

Zizi launched herself at me, and we nearly fell. Her usual quick cadence of giggles sounded, and she carried the lingering smell of smoke. I took a step back to hold her at arm's length, inspecting her. "You look so much better," I said with relief.

All of the burns had healed. Her cheeks were rounded again, her skin an unbroken brown and her Tulari mark a simmering tangerine color, reflecting in the eye above it. Her black hair was still short and in frizzy ringlets, but she was still recovered and here, without the heavy manacles around her wrists.

She wore several bracelets instead, which clicked together with every motion as she spoke with her hands. "I feel so much better. Sivana, we made it! What an adventure we have to tell you about," she exclaimed.

"I can't wait to hear everything," I said.

Someone cleared their throat.

Later, I mouthed, turning and expecting a disapproving Brekwell. Instead, it was Father, who looked on with playful disbelief. "What, no hellos for your old man?" he asked. Since he was in uniform, his hugs with my siblings were brief, but he beamed all the while and encouraged them to head into the fortress and find Mother in the mess hall.

"We didn't come here with much," Rissa admitted.

"Don't you worry about that," he said. "Just go hug your mother. She's missed you both dearly."

While they headed inside, Terrance introduced me to Dorian, the younger of the two unstable pyromancers we'd taken from the House of the Unstable alongside Zizi. He seemed to be a man of few words, merely nodding and thanking me gruffly for helping him.

"What of the older pyromancer?" I whispered.

"He did not survive the trip through the wilds," Terrance said. "We did all we could to make him comfortable."

I nodded, saddened by the loss. I hadn't known him, but he'd had his life cut short by the Morashi all the same.

"Hello, Commander Walker," Zizi said with a short wave. I turned to watch this reunion.

"Good morning, Zizi. I've gotten a promotion since last we spoke," he said, smiling her way and motioning over his shoulder. "You all want to come inside and enjoy the reception?"

"It was Linking Day. Many of our yearlings just found their riders," I explained, as we headed into the fortresss as a group.

"Aww, I missed it?" Zizi asked, sounding disappointed.

I blinked in surprise. "There's still a small group that didn't Link. Did you want to meet them?"

"Well, you know I would be a gryphon rider if any gryphon out there was as good as Ari." She reached over and scratched behind his ears, earning a happy murr.

The reception was in full swing by the time we entered the

mess hall. Even the overlooked cadets enjoyed punch and a rare buffet of fresh foods flown in specifically for this event. I spotted Mother to one side, hugging Rissa and Nate together.

I noticed that Revna perched on a table, speaking with Runar and Geisel, two cadets I was surprised to see amongst the unclaimed. I drifted their way, nearly colliding with Signe, who stood close and watched.

"Sorry, ma'am," I said.

The elderly woman scoffed. "She must stop being picky and choose," Signe replied crossly, gesturing toward Revna. "My lady is impatiently waiting to teach her and her new rider the song of storms. She will not allow us to postpone indefinitely."

"If they're not meant to be her destined rider, then she won't choose them," I said.

Revna hopped to reposition herself, head lowered. She flew in our direction and spotted Zizi standing next to me. Her body glowed lavender for a moment before she put on a burst of speed and released a bird-like shriek of excitement. I wasn't the only one who jumped. "It's you! It's you, it's you, it's you!" Revna sing-songed, launching herself at Zizi.

My friend yelped and fell backward at the sight of the massive bird hurtling her way, but that didn't stop Revna from landing on her chest and mantling her wings around them. "*You're* my destined rider! I can sense it!"

"Thunder be praised," Signe said under her breath, her eyebrows raising in surprise.

"Your rider? But you're not a gryphon!" Zizi protested. She sat up, watching the purple-tinged stormsinger prance around her excitedly.

"No, I'm better! I remember you now. You were there with Sivana." She glanced my way and rustled her wings. "I felt two people touching my egg and making sure I was fed lightning. To think you've been there all along, and yet this is the first time we've met."

"Egg…?" she repeated before gasping. "The egg! You hatched from it? But you're not an eldrafn."

"No, I'm a stormsinger, or vaersanger, depending on your tongue. A flesh and blood eldrafn. I sing magic. Want to see?" Revna gave her an earnest look, all puppy dog eyes.

"I…of course! But you want to Link with me?" Zizi made an uncertain gesture toward her chest.

Revna bobbed her whole body in a yes. "I dreamed of a rider who is strong in their convictions."

"As pure as heart as possible, and full of life," I recited.

"Uh huh! Someone who can be a leader when the rest of my kind hatches, because as my rider, Lady Idunn has a task for you."

"A task from Lady Idunn?" Zizi echoed, paling at the idea.

"Oh! And someone with a good singing voice." Revna looked at her hopefully. "You *do* sing well, right?"

"Uh, I'm all right, I think."

"Then you're perfect!" the bird proclaimed.

Zizi stood, dusting off the back of her pants. "Perfect," she repeated more quietly, something like wonder in her expression.

"So, you'll be my rider, right?" Revna asked hopefully.

"Yes," Zizi answered.

I didn't know what to expect with a stormsinger Link. Gryphons had to either focus while staring into their new rider's eyes or fly with them for the first time. Surely something similar would happen between them.

I wasn't expecting Zizi to get struck by lightning.

CHAPTER 38

DUAL-BLESSED

As with most magical lightning, it didn't deafen, but it sure blinded. Sounds of surprise echoed around us, and a few plates and cups were dropped. I expected the sound of shattered glass, but it *was* magical. The strike had come out of nowhere without disturbing any of the windows.

I blinked spots away from my eyes to find Zizi still standing, but now her fingertips traced the circle of her Tulari mark. It shimmered from orange to purple.

"Dual-blessed," I gasped.

Revna flapped in place. "I bet Hvit's Linking wasn't as exciting as mine!" she exclaimed.

"Oh, hush. Silly bird. Always comparing," said Signe. While the rest of us gasped or screamed in surprise at the sudden flash of lightning in an enclosed space, she'd released a wheeze, deep and hoarse, that sounded like it'd been held for quite some time. Still, a smile threatened her stern face, as did a sheen of tears over her eyes. "Come, young lady. We have much to discuss, including a decision to make."

Zizi gestured for me to come with her, and I made the introductions between them. Signe gave me a stern look and a dismissing gesture as she limped her way to an unoccupied corner of the room. My friend followed, seemingly in awe of the other woman.

"Now that you have Linked, the seal that prevented the other eggs from hatching is gone…" I heard Signe say before she dropped her voice to a hush. She opened the pouch of eggs she had strapped to her person and showed her the other stormsinger eggs, which glimmered like gemstones in the sunlight.

As Revna's rider, in theory, it was Zizi's first decision to make: how to set up the process for them to find their riders and hatch.

The two of them spoke back and forth seriously, and I forced myself to wait with Ari, who angled his ears to listen. He maintained his favorite Tulari's privacy, though, not telling me a word of what they were discussing.

"Do you think they brought some salmon to snack on?" he asked.

I doubted it but promised we could check. He released a long-suffering sigh at me, sure it would all be gone since everyone was getting food while we idled around.

Zizi eventually came back to my side, Revna hopping after her. "I came here with several magic-wielding friends. We're going to show the eggs to them first."

"There are two volta here who could match with them as well," I said.

Zizi gave me a meaningful look. "Are they friends?"

I glanced up, looking for Runar and Geisel amongst the mingling clusters of people. "I would say so. I'm shocked they didn't get picked by a gryphon, but maybe it's destiny for them to be the fated riders of vaersangers instead?"

We headed toward them at Signe's pace, as she hadn't relinquished the satchel of eggs. I followed, watching her cradle the eggs in her wrinkled palms and murmur in Rathi over them.

"Let's let all the unbonded cadets try. Maybe we have

others marked by the gods here," I suggested quietly to Zizi, but first guided her to the table where most of my cadet flight sat.

"Should we just let them put their hand in there, or what?" Zizi asked.

"Maybe on top," I said, beckoning over Cadet Geisel, who waved with less enthusiasm than usual when she saw me.

She stood and approached us, and Signe released a long sigh of relief. "You are destined," she said solemnly, reaching into the satchel and producing an egg I recognized, though it shook violently and almost fell out of her hand. It was the Earl's, green with gray markings.

"Is there supposed to be some ceremony in this? Or a warning, maybe?" Zizi asked under her breath.

"I think it's clear the stormsingers are doing the choosing here," I murmured back.

"Um, congratulations," Zizi said a little awkwardly.

The downcast expression Geisel had been wearing vanished, replaced with slack-jawed wonder as the bird within the egg swiftly hatched, exploding into the world with a caw and an open beak.

"Fierce Lady Idunn...I can feel it. We are connected," she gasped.

I moved away from them, calling up the other cadets without a gryphon. One by one, they approached Signe, confused yet hopeful. Most didn't hatch an egg, and resentment flowed from them when Runar stepped forward and was handed one that wobbled actively. I recognized the slate gray and sunny yellow of the Chariot.

After him, a tall and bulky cadet from Lark Flight was last, and Signe gasped. "You are destined to a forceful one," she said, handing over an egg that was already split down the middle.

"The Knight," I said to myself.

Its crimson-and-black pattern reminded me of a place

between moments and a gruff goddess. *"Anrathor would like that one."*

"Young man, which god were you touched by?" I asked more loudly.

He flashed me a nervous look before his small eyes refocused on the hatching egg cradled in his large hands. "I bear Anrathor's mark, ma'am. But the temple turned me away when I couldn't summon a berserker's rage."

Well, Idunn would be happy one of her husband's followers was selected by the former Knight. "Come with us. You're about to be a part of something brand new," I said to him, Runar, and Geisel.

"Besides, we're not done testing," Zizi said, turning on her heel and hurrying toward the other side of the mess hall, where Nate, Rissa, and Terrance were also eating. She only paused and doubled back when Signe followed at less than half her speed.

Revna hopped up on their table. "Hey, come see my new rider! You might hatch an egg too," she said happily.

My sister wrinkled her fine little nose and tried to shoo Revna away from her meal, but the other two inspected her curiously. "She has a huge magical signature. You feel that?" Nate murmured to Terrance.

"What are you?" Terrance asked, nodding in agreement.

After Revna explained, Nate got up and came forward first. "Please. Please hatch," he murmured, reaching toward the satchel with flexing fingers.

"Hmm. Nothing, I think," Signe said, checking inside of it.

Nate's expression fell, and he slumped dramatically. "Really? They can tell that fast?"

"Perhaps. But this one just stirred. Congratulations, you are destined," she said, pulling out a sapphire-blue egg. It was the Advisor's, I think. I never faced a blue eldrafn, but my breath caught as I realized it was hatching for Nate.

"Congratulations," I said warmly, edging closer to watch the birth. It was taking its time, unlike the others, who had seemed desperate to be free of their shells at last.

What were the chances so many of the stormsinger riders were in one place at the right time? I just hoped they weren't settling for a second- or third-best match just to hatch and be free into the world. Then again...I couldn't imagine how terrible it must be for a young bird to be trapped within their eggshell, if these magical creatures were in fact aware of their situation.

"Enjoying the coincidence, Chosen?" whispered Lord Orion's voice behind my ear. I jumped and looked over my shoulder, but he was just a presence. Perhaps watching with the same curiosity I did.

"Yes, my lord," I said quietly.

"What are the chances one of them is for me, too?" Terrance was asking hopefully, getting up next.

Signe had him touch the satchel and peered into it afterward. She nodded and pulled out a small egg that was mostly a purple so dark it was almost black. It was the Soldier's egg, from the youngest eldrafn that'd died on the Storm Front.

"How many does that leave us?" I asked, astonished when she held up three fingers. We'd filled out Revna's flight in a few short minutes after she'd finally chosen to Link.

"There's at least one more person who has to try and hatch an egg," Zizi said cheerfully, beckoning to Rissa.

"What are you doing?" My sister leaned away from her. "I'm a Nilarite! I only serve my lady."

"That's okay. No one's asking you to change what you believe in," Revna said. She jumped down onto the bench next to Rissa in a clatter of talons. "I've learned songs from two of the gods so far. They've told me that every stormsinger rider will be capable of singing something unique."

"Why don't we listen to Revna perform some of the song

of healing Lady Nilara taught her?" I suggested, seeing that Rissa wasn't convinced.

"Oh, is that your goddess? She's very nice," Revna twittered. She leaned against Rissa's side and chimed like a bell, producing a shower of moon dust as she sang. My sister's reluctance faded to reverence as she started to sing too, matching a hymn to the tune.

Rissa rubbed a bit of moon dust between her fingers. "It is my lady's magic," she said finally. "I...I suppose I could try to hatch one of the eggs. But really, do you see *me* as a rider?" She laughed self-consciously. If it were any odd day at the Temple of Nilara, I would say no, but she wore traveling clothes and a more practical braid from her flight here. If she had goggles, she'd be ready to climb on a gryphon's back. What made this any different?

Instead of holding out the satchel, Signe took out the remaining three eggs one at a time. The silver and black egg remained dormant, as did the orange one, but the Duchess's soft pink shell wobbled the moment it got close to my sister. Her eyes became two saucers as a crack appeared in it from a tiny, determined beak.

"This bird sees you as a rider, and I think that's the most important part. It is destiny," Signe said, pushing the egg into my sister's hand.

"Wait, maybe Dorian will hatch one of the last two," Zizi said, going to fetch the quiet man.

I spoke quietly, hoping Lord Orion was still watching nearby. "Every one of the new stormsinger riders in one room, my lord?"

"*All but one,*" he answered. Once Dorian had the orange egg of the former Mage rocking in his palm, my gaze turned to the last, lonely egg. "*The one you knew as the King will have a more difficult path.*"

I looked on as the King's egg started to hatch on its own,

without the presence of its rider. It was the only one of its kind without one. "Why is that?" I breathed.

"The others will remember what he did."

"But his rider…"

There was no reply from Lord Orion to acknowledge that the King wasn't the only one at fault. To become the King-maker, the biggest living eldrafn, he'd consumed the pulsing heart of the Knight. An unfortunate act to bring into a new life alone. I felt for the tiny creature as he emerged and squeaked, shivering without the warmth of a person to hold him.

When we rounded up everyone holding a newborn storm-singer and presented them to Signe, I cupped the last baby bird in my hands, cleaning him off with a kerchief until he was a black puff in my palms. "Look at the variety," she said to herself. "One for every facet of the gods' magic, except for life and death itself." She patted Zizi on the hand. "We will raise them and train you all as best we can. Someone should go inform Solfrid."

"I'll do it!" Revna flapped off, no doubt excited to tell Hvit everything.

LINKING DAY WASN'T OVER, even after the miraculous hatching of all the stormsinger eggs. We decided to follow the remaining yearlings as they flew away from the fortress. First, it was one big clump, but the young gryphons peeled away from one another as they sought a specific person to Link with here and there.

I rode Ari again, who preferred my guiding touch for what proved to be a days-long journey. We followed Novali until she tired and was forced to land. Along the way, I watched a yearling pick a red-faced baker, startling him into dropping several loaves into a cooking fire. Sadry apologized and let the baker's kids try to climb his glossy sides, but it was the man who he wanted to climb into his saddle.

"Good thing we have Fenway," I thought to Ari. Commander Rudrick stopped at the shop with Snowpoint to convince the newly selected rider to move his family and business.

The investigation had turned up foul dirt immediately. It turned out that Lord Fenway had been deceased for some time and that his estate was nearly stripped of valuables by the steward, bailiff, and a couple servants posing as such to help with their ruse. The land was in the Crown's hands now, but it would soon gain a military governor and be transferred to the ownership of the corps itself. We would have the land and the space to support civilian riders.

Best of all, though, Sharde would never have to see his father again. The man was scheduled to sit in a prison for the rest of his days alongside his accomplices.

As more of the yearlings found their true Link, I grew happier that we had a place for those unfit for military service. The yearlings didn't care about young and old. They wanted the person they were born for. Novali was consumed by the same determination to be united with her perfect rider too, even though her muscles were sore by the time we spotted Kaiamear on the horizon.

She led us straight to Little Wonders Pet Shop, and I should've been less surprised than I was as she walked right up to Thomas and pressed her beak into his middle. The boy who'd been able to get her to eat after her ordeal was the same one rubbing her ears and neck and whispering, "Me?"

I was to act as the representative from the Gryphon Rider Academy for the person Novali picked, but Thomas wasn't the person I approached first. "Good evening, Fletcher," I said, extending out my hand to shake his. It was a slow night in the pet shop, no one around to listen except for the girl I'd learned was his adopted daughter, Shauna. "The corps could use a talented veterinarian like you. I wanted to make the offer before, but now I'm sure we have the space and resources to build you a comfortable home and office close to the gryphons. What do you say?"

Surprise danced in his eyes. His smile turned wistful. "Ah, if only I could, lady gryphon rider. It would be for the best for Thomas to find a place at the Gryphon Rider Academy while we stay here. I have some…unfinished business to attend to. And the little wonders come from far and wide to this location to see me."

How disappointing, if not entirely unsurprising. "I see. Well, if you change your mind…"

"I will write, of course. Let Thomas pack his things, and he can go with you at first light." He almost sounded eager for his son to go, but perhaps that was just mingled in the happiness of seeing him with Novali.

I approached them next, nodding to Thomas with a smile. "Congratulations, young man. On behalf of the corps, I invite you to enroll at the Gryphon Rider Academy to train for the next two years to become a knight and serve the great nation of Altare. It is optional, and if you refuse, we have a place for you and Novali in Fenway, a growing town close to where the gryphons live."

"I want to be a knight," he answered, beaming up at me. "A gryphon rider, just like you! It would be a dream come true."

"Excellent. I hope you get assigned to the flight I'm mentoring. But don't expect special treatment just because your gryphon is my favorite yearling."

Novali peeled away from him to rub against my side. *"Don't take it easy on us, Auntie Sivvy. We're going to be Aces together. Just you wait and see."*

I grinned immediately, seeing shades of Ari in her confidence and her goal. "I look forward to seeing it."

EPILOGUE

We had growing pains, but we made having three schools in one work. Gryphon riders, stormsinger riders, and engineers learned, sometimes alongside one another, and I received a short letter of praise from Paragon Brekwell on a job well done when thirty-four newly Linked riders reported in for training at the Academy.

Most of the hopefuls who didn't Link this year stayed in Fenway to await another chance. They saw the other eleven newly Linked riders arrive at Fenway too with their families. Sadry's baker set up shop, as did the carpenter whose ten-year-old daughter also Linked. In a few short years, we might have more teens attending the Academy and joining the corps. They just needed some extra time.

The halls of the Academy felt like they should again: filled with teens and beasts alike, all hurrying to avoid demerits. Girls just balanced out the classes now, forming a little under half of the first-year riders. All made possible, ultimately, because I'd loved a blind gryphon too much to let him go.

I'd taken to starting my days at the very top of Glorium's Roost, where a lip of metal connected to the roll where the canvas awning retracted during the daytime. There was just enough space for three gryphons, plus Acton and me to sit with our legs dangling, holding the reins of our gryphons just in case. Sunset groomed Ari. She felt extra lonely lately without a chick to mother, as Novali was exploring her independence as a cadet's gryphon.

"There it is," I said quietly. Ironfeather and Sunset glanced up, while Ari watched it through my eyes. The wild lands always had the most beautiful sunrises, dawning with shades of orange and sky blue intertwined.

"It's going to be a good day," Acton said.

His hold around my waist tightened as I leaned my head back against his shoulder, looking up at him. "That's what you say every day," I teased.

"I say that each day I get to see the sun rise with my soon-to-be wife," he teased, kissing the end of my nose. "That's not *every* day."

"So romantic. Ah, to be newly mated again," Sunset sighed.

"It hasn't even been a year," Ari protested.

"See what I mean? You used to agree with everything I said."

He complained further with a whine, folding his ears back. Ironfeather mirrored his expression before releasing a growl. I sat up, looking at him. *"What's wrong?"* I asked.

He lifted his beak toward the horizon. *"There are strangers heading this way."*

"Can you go get Valtora? I'll talk to them," I asked Acton. We saddled up and parted ways. Sunset followed off of Ari's wing as I guided him toward the rising sun, where I just started to make out the silhouettes of approaching gryphons.

Sunset, with her raptor vision, counted out a baker's dozen. I reined in Ari, circling and waiting for them to approach us.

The first hint of their mental voices hit with a dazzle of hope. *"Look, it's a human-gryphon pair! This must be the right place,"* one of them said.

"That sounds like a yearling to me," Sunset commented.

"Land and talk to us," Ari ordered. They did, all thirteen of them, some more clumsily than others. I stayed on his back when he placed his paws on the ground too, looking over the assembled group. All yearlings, perhaps the smallest one even a puffy cloudling.

The leader of their group stepped forward, a female with tanned plumage and speckles along her white belly. *"Hello, um, human. And tamed gryphons. We come from the wild."*

"Yes, we can see that," Ari said in amusement.

She puffed up her wings, trying to look bigger. *"We're from all over. Most of our flocks drove us out to find our own way, so we followed a rumor. Is there really a place here where humans look after gryphons? And there's even a human who..."* She lowered her voice with a little disbelieving laugh. *"...speaks like a gryphon?"*

"That's right," I said, startling her. She padded forward a couple steps, only stopping when Ari loosed a chuff of air in warning.

"Did you really just talk?" she asked in wonder.

"I did, and you've come to the right place. If you want to join us, our Matriarch is on her way right now," I said, feeling a little giddy at all these new faces. The wild gryphons knew about us. Maybe we would grow in time as more beasts like these chose to join us.

"They have a Matriarch," another yearling murmured. Not every flock was led by the eldest and most venerated Skymothers. It was an earned title that stacked respect Valtora's way before her golden wings batted at the air close by. Roshawk landed right behind her, inspecting each youngling while Valtora conferred with their leader.

"We heard it was a lot of fun here," squeaked the little cloudling.

Roshawk stopped in front of him and released a murr like I went "aww." He placed a wing around him. *"We try to have as much fun as possible,"* he promised. *"There's another young gryphon I would like you to meet, named Puzzlebox. I think you two will be best friends."*

The cloudling danced on his front talons, turning a hopeful look toward his leader. *"I think that's acceptable,"* she was saying, bowing her head to Valtora in a submissive gesture. The other yearlings quickly did the same while I watched in fascination. It was like they were all acknowledging her authority as their new Matriarch.

"You can see our territory and stay for a while as guests to see if you like our way of life," Valtora said to them all. *"The humans may care for us and feed us, but you will still be paired with an adult to learn how to hunt for yourself. They are our partners, not our servants."*

"If you choose to stay and wish to Link with a human companion, I can show you a few candidates," I said, thinking of the unbonded cadets who waited in Fenway for another chance.

The new gryphons made noises of agreement and understanding.

"Welcome to Wild Flight," Valtora said, spreading her wings grandly. *"Welcome to your new home."*

I HOPE **you enjoyed the ending of Sivana and Ari's story!**

DON'T MISS the next book in the Altare world, Royal Spy Institute 2: Five & Chance, featuring a crossover with this book!

STAY up to date with Gryphon Rider Academy and the Altare world by joining my Facebook group: People of Altare! In this community, we'll talk about fantasy book releases, share fun posts, and have the occasional giveaway.

PLEASE REMEMBER TO REVIEW! Reviews help other readers find stories they may love. Consider leaving a review for Gryphon Rider Academy 4: Wild Flight on Amazon and other websites.

ALSO IN THE ALTARE WORLD

ROYAL SPY INSTITUTE

Join an unlikely crew of five misfits and a mouse as they strive to become one of Altare's newest elite spy teams. Heists and adventures await!

The Gilded Wolves meets Six of Crows in this YA fantasy series in which a former thief uses her skills to become a spy. If you like clever heroines, strong friendships, and found family, then you'll love Royal Spy Institute!

- See Royal Spy Institute on Amazon -

ACKNOWLEDGMENTS

Gryphon Rider Academy is a story that took many years and several revisions to be told properly. It would still be in a lesser form rattling in a digital drawer on my computer if not for the support of the many people that have helped me shape it along the way.

I would like to thank my family first, for encouraging the seedling of creativity in me. They have helped me celebrate every success and dust myself off after every setback. I would not be here without their love and support.

Thank you to my editor, Victoria, for working with me through several projects that run a continuum of genre and tone. She has helped me through writer's block, creative brainstorms, and some of the tightest deadlines known to man. Here's to project number 20.

Thank you to Rebekah, who narrates the audio versions of *Gryphon Rider Academy*. She has really brought the story to life with her vocal talents and has been a joy to work with.

Thank you to my friend Justin, for helping me polish *Gryphon Rider Academy*. It would not be the same without his suggestions, but more importantly, without his enthusiasm, support, and encouragement.

Thank you to my friend Mike, for helping me develop the medieval setting of Altare through many Q&A and brainstorming sessions. I have enjoyed our deep dives into the characters and culture throughout the series.

Thank you to my beta readers for your willingness to dive

into an unfinished story and provide honest feedback to make *Gryphon Rider Academy* the best it can be.

And finally, a big thank you to my readers. Thank you for going on this journey with me and for cheering for Sivana and Ari despite the odds. It helps so much, every time you review and recommend this series for others to enjoy. Your love and enthusiasm for this series has been incredible and I hope you will join me for the next adventures in this world with Five & Chance and Zizi and Revna!

ABOUT THE AUTHOR

Elise Hennessy is an author of young adult fantasy full of adventure and found family. She holds a master's degree in journalism and enjoys crafting unique stories. When Elise is not busy writing, she's trying to reduce her prodigious TBR list. She lives in Texas with her family and is owned by two cats.

Find out more about her books at: www.elisehennessy.com